THE KILLING GAME

J.A. Kerley worked in advertising and teaching before becoming a full-time novelist. He lives in Newport, Kentucky, but also spends a good deal of time in Southern Alabama, the setting for his Carson Ryder series, starting with *The Hundredth Man*. He is married with two children.

Also by J.A. Kerley

J.A. Kerley

THE KILLING GAME

HARPER

Harper
An imprint of HarperCollins*Publishers*
77–85 Fulham Palace Road, London W6 8JB

www.harpercollins.co.uk

A paperback original

1

A catalogue record for this book
is available from the British Library

ISBN 978 0 00 732823 9

Set in Sabon LT Std by Palimpsest Book Production Ltd, Falkirk, Stirlingshire

Printed in Great Britain by
Clays Ltd, St Ives plc

MIX
Paper from
responsible sources
FSC™ C007454

FSC™ is a non-profit international organization established
to promote the responsible management of the world's forests.
Products carrying the FSC label are independently certified
to assure consumers that they come from forests that are managed
to meet the social, economic and ecological needs
of present and future generations.

Find out more about HarperCollins and the environment at
www.harpercollins.co.uk/green

To Alexa and John,
Have a spectacular voyage

I thank all the great folks at the Aaron M. Priest Literary Agency, as well as a fine team at HarperCollins, UK: Sarah Hodgson, Anne O'Brien, and the marketing staff behind the scenes. I also wish to acknowledge Dr Martha Stout and Ms Barbara Bentley, whose respective books *The Sociopath Next Door* and *A Dance with the Devil: A True Story of Marriage to a Psychopath* started a line of thought that became this book.

1

"*It sounds like a helluva movie,*" David Letterman was saying to the popular movie actor. "*Great cast. . .*"

Gregory leaned toward the foot-square mirror propped against the DVD player beside the television. The actor was performing the most complex series of faces Gregory had ever attempted. He reset the DVD to seconds before the faces began, when David Letterman asked his guest – who had a wife and three small children – about a rumored affair with his latest co-star.

"*I guess I'd be remiss in my hostly duties if I didn't ask about your relationship with your lovely co-star, Maria Glassier. You guys shared, uh, a love scene or two, right?*"

The audience gasped, tittered, awaited the reply. Gregory pressed Play on the machine. The actor's faces began. . .

Face one: the actor's eyes popped wide. Gregory replicated the face in the mirror set atop the player. But this was a simple face he called *Sudden Surprise #3* and employed dozens of times a week.

Face number two started, eyes moving side to side, rising at the corners as if swinging on pendulums, the mouth dropping open. Gregory tapped Pause. It was a difficult move, the eyes wanting to stutter instead of glide. And moving eyes couldn't be followed in the mirror. But he'd practiced into a video camera until satisfied, so he trusted the face.

The last face was the toughest: four separate actions, but Gregory had deconstructed the components and mastered each. Today was about flow. Gregory felt his intestines squirming and reached to the floor for the bottle of Pepto-Bismol. He drank and restarted the player. The actor's lips tightened, eyes rolling heavenward, eyebrows flicking, the head cocking to a thirty-degree angle.

Gregory's first attempts felt ragged; the head-cock started before the lip-tightening, or he forgot the eyebrow lift after the eye-roll. Gregory's jaw tightened in exasperation. The food in his guts turned into cramps and sour, flatulent gas. He smelled the ugly vapor from his bowels and began to shake in his chair, angered by failure. . .

Do Relaxed Face #1, he told himself. *Then do Quiet Face.*

Gregory took a deep breath and performed faces that

relaxed him. His guts settled down. After a minute of visualizing, Gregory re-performed face three, nailing it five times in a row. Satisfied, he pressed Play.

The difficult faces were over. The actor's smile widened until it eclipsed every other feature on his face.

"*I'm afraid we're just good friends, Dave,*" the actor said.

The audience laughed and applauded. Gregory put his hand over the actor's lower face. Without the distraction of the tooth-bright smile and uplifted cheeks, the actor's eyes were points of angry fire. Gregory knew the actor wanted to grab Letterman's throat and rip it from his body, holding the wet and dangling esophagus aloft like a prize. The actor had ached to do this since Letterman asked the moronic question, but instead projected a meticulous series of facial expressions ending in a glittering smile.

He fooled everyone.

And one day, Gregory thought, if the actor is a careful planner, he can track down and kill Letterman, and no one will ever know.

He turned off the DVD player. Gregory's cell phone rang in his pocket and he pulled it out with irritation, saw the name EMA on the screen, her third call today. He stuck the phone back in his pocket and practiced facial moves as he left the room, its walls plastered with faces from magazine ads. Beneath each was a descriptor: *Happy #4, Not Pleased With Someone's Answer, New Car, Hurray!, I Love You #3* and over two hundred others.

He rested his finger on the light switch and turned his eyes to his faces.

He showed them *I'm Glad You're Here* and flicked out the light.

2

The coins in the cash-register drawer jingled as I slammed it shut. The bleached-blond iron-pumper on the customer side of the counter started to turn away, but spun back to the lottery tickets beside the register, his guayabera shirt open to display a stunning collection of gold chains around a ham-thick neck. I'd just rung up his purchase of a pack of Marlboros, a half-case of Miller Lite and a three-pack of Trojan condoms. The beer was selling briskly tonight, thanks to a display of discounted twelve-packs fronting the nearest aisle. Condoms weren't doing too bad either, but then it was Saturday night.

Ham Neck tapped the ticket dispenser. "Gimme four Hot Odds scratch-offs and a dozen Super Lottos."

"You couldn't think of that before I rang you up?"

His lamp-tanned face twisted into a snarl. "Here's how

it works, moron: I'm the customer, you're the clerk. I want something, you shut up and get it for me."

"*Stay calm, Carson,*" said a voice in my head as I bit my tongue and peeled tickets from the dispenser. I glanced up and barely registered a skinny guy in a grubby denim jacket turning down the first aisle. Outside, a teen kid who'd just bought condoms and two Dr Peppers climbed into what had to be Daddy's white Yukon. The kid was grinning ear to ear, the girl looked uncertain.

Though it was forty minutes past midnight, outside the store it was as bright as high noon in the Sahara, a zillion watts lighting a dozen gasoline pumps on a half-acre of concrete. It was even brighter inside and on my first day I'd wondered if I needed sunscreen. There was an experienced manager on the shift – the three-hundred-sixty-pound Melvin Dobbs – but it was Mel's break and he'd booked to a nearby Waffle House to give his diabetes something to think about.

"C'mon, hurry up with those tickets," Ham Neck said. "I ain't got all night."

A shag-haired, net-hosed hooker by the coolers held up two forties of malt liquor.

"This all you got left of the Colt 45?"

"If that's what you see," I said, "that's what we got."

She shook her head. "How 'bout y'all stock this joint once inna while?"

I took Ham Neck's money for the lottery tickets. He expressed appreciation by telling me the floors were filthy and did I know how a mop worked?

"*Easy, Carson,*" the voice said in my head.

Monitors from the security cameras sat to the right of the clerk station, two cameras inside, two outside. One was panning past the coolers and I saw the hooker opening her outsized purse, ready to drop a forty into it.

"Don't even think about it, lady," I yelled. She scowled and set the bottle back in the cooler. A seventyish black man in a blue porkpie hat was at the grill station, nodding at wrinkled brown hot dogs spinning on heated rollers.

"How long these weenies been cookin'?" he said.

I feigned uncertainty. "What year was the Crimean War?"

"The hell's that mean?"

"*Carson,*" said the voice in my head. "*Be nice.*"

"About four hours," I said.

"Can I get a discount cuz they're so old?"

It was my second Saturday as a clerk working the midnight-to-morning shift. In the past six weeks there had been three Saturday-night convenience-store robberies, two ending in deaths. The third clerk was comatose, likely to remain that way. The C-stores had been just off I-10 on Mobile's southwest side. This was the only one in the quadrant that hadn't been robbed. My partner, Harry Nautilus, and I had judged it ripe for a hit.

"What about these weenies?" the porkpie-hat guy bayed. "They too old to be full price."

I checked the outside monitors, seeing a gray van slide into the rear of the lot and disappear until it was picked up on the second outside camera. It rolled into the shadows beside the dumpster.

"*Gray van*," said the voice in my head. "*Get cautious*." A gray van had been spotted near two of the three hold-ups. Whenever one pulled in, the voice in my head alerted me to be careful.

"You got ten seconds to get out the door," I told the old man. "But all the hot dogs you can grab in that time are free."

The guy gave me two beats of *are-you-for-real?* then started jamming hot dogs in his pockets.

"Hey," the hooker whined. "How 'bout me?"

"We're having a special on malt liquor, ma'am. Two for the price of none." I nodded toward the old guy. "But you gotta beat him out the door or the deal's off."

She grabbed the forties and booked, the old guy in her wake, two hot dogs in his mouth like pink cigars, four in each hand, a box of buns beneath his arm. Before the door closed it was caught in the hand of a petite brunette in her thirties: brown cargo pants, pink blouse, white running shoes. She saw me watching, waved and smiled and headed toward the snack aisle. She'd exited the gray van but my glance hadn't picked up any threat. There were a lot of gray vans on the road.

"*Check the customers*," the voice whispered. I did a head count. Exactly two people inside, me and the woman. The lot was empty. The woman came to the register with a bag of chips in one hand, flipping open a cheap cell with the other.

"Be a buck-eighty-seven," I said.

She pressed a button on her phone and opened a brown leather purse. Though the woman had looked fine from afar, up close I saw hair days from a washing. Half-moons of grit under chewed fingernails. Pupils so dilated I couldn't discern an eye color. I was moving my hand toward the weapon in the small of my back, beneath my uniform jacket, when I heard a shotgun rack behind me.

"Move and you're dead," a male voice said.

I froze as the woman across the counter pulled a black automatic from her purse. I knew the model: cheap Eastern-European manufacture with a trigger-pull so congenitally light it might fire if a mouse sneezed in the parking lot.

"Open the register," she said, pointing the weapon at my throat. "Now."

I nodded acquiescence and started tapping keys on the machine.

"Hold on," the voice behind me whispered. "Some asshole comin' in the door."

I looked up and saw Ham Neck returning, straight-arming the door open. "You gave me the wrong goddamn cigarettes," he snarled, waving the pack. "I told you menthol."

The woman slid her purse up to cover the pistol and stepped to the side. The guy at my back whispered, "Get the fucker gone or you're dead." The gunman slipped to the end of the counter and I grimaced. It was the guy in the dirty denim jacket I'd noticed not five minutes ago. He must have waited in the restroom until the woman's cell-phone signal told him the store was empty of customers.

My first job was getting the big buffoon out the door. I grabbed as many packs of smokes as I could hold, threw them Ham Neck's way, one bouncing off his chin.

"They're free," I said. "Compensation for my mistake. Sorry. Goodbye."

"You trying to be a wise-ass?"

"I'm sorry," I said quietly. "My mistake. Please, take your smokes and go."

But Ham Neck was one of those guys who look for slights. He strode toward me, one hand in a fist, the other thrust out and showing me the finger.

"Throw stuff at me? I oughta kick your goddamn—"

The man at the end of the counter whipped up a sawed-off twelve-gauge and fired. It sounded like a cannon. Ham Neck's finger and hand disappeared in a red mist. He fell to the floor screaming, arterial blood spurting from his stump. The woman pulled the Czech weapon for the kill-shot. I stepped between them.

"I can open the safe," I said, hands in the air. "There's maybe three hundred bucks in the register. There's at least six grand in the safe."

She looked to Shotgun Man and he must have assented. Her eyes were unhinged, one fixed on me, the other on some hellish inner vision.

"Do it," she said.

I nodded down at the moaning Ham Neck. "I gotta fix his arm."

"I'll kill you."

"It'll cost you over six thousand dollars."

Her knuckles whitened on the gun, the chemicals in her head about to reach full boil.

"I can cut the lights and close down," I reasoned. "We'll be alone."

Her eyes flicked to Shotgun Man. He thought about how many drugs six grand would buy and followed me to a panel behind the counter. I turned off every light outside and inside, leaving the glow from the coolers. Ham Neck was rolled in a ball and grunting as his stump painted the floor red. I could feel my gun against my back, but had two weapons trained on my head. No way to pull my piece.

I yanked a bungee cord from a display and snapped a tourniquet around Ham Neck's forearm. He was slipping into shock. *Move them to the front*, the voice in my head said. I spun and walked to the front door.

"Stop right there." The woman pointed the pistol at my forehead. It was shaking in her hand like a trapped bird.

"I have to lock the door," I said, pulling my car keys. "The safe won't open unless the front door is locked. You ever hear of an entry-securified safe before?"

The invention worked and she gestured me forward with the twitching muzzle of the nine.

"Wait," Shotgun Man said. "Someone's outside."

11

A big square black guy in a Hawaiian shirt had parked beside the air pump and was kneeling by the front tire of a dark sedan. He looked unsteady and kept dropping the air hose.

"Just some drunk putting air in his tires," I said, slipping my truck key into the lock and jiggling. I moved my hand back like I'd locked the door. Then pulled it open. "It's bent," I said, making a big deal of wiggling the door. "Some old lady banged her car into the door last week." I did the key-jiggle again. Opened the door.

"GET IT DONE!" the woman screamed.

I turned to Shotgun Man. "If we both pull from the inside I can slide the bolt."

He set the sawn-off on the counter and came to stand beside me. He smelled like an outhouse.

Shotgun Man looked to the woman. "He makes one wrong move, blow out his brains."

"On the count of three," I said. "Pull hard and I'll set the lock."

Shotgun Man gripped the door handle. I slid my key into the lock and shot a glance at the drunk at the pump. He was leaning against his vehicle and scratching his belly, apparently exhausted by his labors.

"One!" I said, loudly, taking a deep breath.

"Two!"

On three, I dove to the floor as glass exploded everywhere. Shotgun Man seemed to pirouette in slow motion, then hit the ground beside me. A half-beat later the woman's body slammed the floor as well, half her skull gone. There was nothing to be done for either of them, but if there had been, I probably wouldn't have done it.

Two cop cruisers skidded into the lot. The black guy was standing beside the car with a gun in his hand, smoke drifting from the muzzle. He spoke into a small transceiver in his palm. "*Looks like your clerking career is over, Carson,*" the voice in my head said. "*You OK?*"

I waved, pulled the tiny WiFi speaker from my ear, and ran to check on Ham Neck.

3

The waitress brought Ema her breakfast and Gregory stared at the plate of unspeakable monstrosities. He hid his revulsion behind *Happy #3* as the waitress smiled and backed away. Chewing food formed a bolus, a clot of spit and snot and food churned by the tongue and squeezed down the throat like a rat wriggling through a python. The bolus caused the stomach to squirm and convulse as chemicals reduced the lump to a suppurating goo. This reeking sludge was pumped past the pyloric valve and into the intestines, where it turned into unspeakable filth that decayed inside you for days.

"Are you all right, dear?" Ema asked as the server arrived with Gregory's toast and salad. Grains and green vegetables were easiest to digest.

"Why?" he said.

Ema cocked her head, teased-out blonde curls bouncing on the shoulder of her pale and frilly summer frock.

"You looked deep in thought."

Gregory pushed his plate of half-eaten toast aside. "Exactly, Ema, I was thinking. Until you interrupted."

"I'm sorry," Ema apologized. "Was it about work?"

"What else?" he lied. "I've put in forty hours already this week." Another lie.

Ema forked up a gooey lump of poultry ovum. "I'm glad to see you so absorbed in life, dear. Plus you're looking less thin and frail."

Gregory's eyes narrowed. *Frail? I've never looked frail.* Ema's constant sniping about his pallor and thinness had driven Gregory to a health club membership four months back, but the stink of bodies turned his stomach and the music hurt his head. That's when he'd invested in a top-of-the-line Bowflex home gym. He could run through a full workout in under a half hour and practice his faces at the same time.

He said, "I've been exercising."

"Wonderful!" Ema chirped. "How often do you work out? Do you have a specific regimen?"

"Not really."

"Do you exercise to a DVD or anything like that?"

"No."

"You should drop in on Dr Szekely. She'd love to see how you—"

"Your nattering is driving me mad, Ema."

15

Ema swallowed hard, looked away. "I'm sorry," she said, her voice breaking. "I only want for you to—"

"I'm teasing, dear," Gregory said. "Can't you tell by now when I'm teasing?"

"Sometimes you look, I don't know . . . serious, I guess. Even when you're teasing."

"If you can't tell whether I'm teasing, then I'm teasing."

"I love you so much," Ema said. "I want you to be healthy and strong."

"I *am* healthy, Ema," Gregory said. "I just said I've been working out. Didn't you listen?"

Ema's eyes fell to her lap, telling Gregory he'd failed to keep all the anger from his voice. He sighed internally and reached for his sister's plump fingertips, feeling microbes crawl from her flesh to his. But the gesture – *I Love You and I'm Sorry* – was important. Gregory found his most sincere face – *This is the Best Insurance You Can Buy* – and looked Ema in her green eyes.

"I'm so glad I have you," he said. "So very happy." He followed with three beats of *I Have a Powerful New Detergent*.

A newly buoyant Ema carried the conversation for twenty minutes, Gregory's contributions being murmurs of assent and smiling in all the right places. He averted his eyes when a fork moved toward Ema's mouth, looking instead at the ubiquitous pendant hanging from her neck, a shimmering pearlescent orb the size of a robin's egg, folk craft from Eastern Europe. She had other baubles on her wrists, jangly things. The woman spent her life watching shopping channels and soap operas and police shows. Gregory had started wishing she'd get a full-time job or some kind of hobby.

"How are the kitties?" Ema asked, returning to a recent topic, a population of stray cats in Gregory's neighborhood.

"Still howling all night. It's breeding season."

Ema paused in chewing, the fork poised beside her mouth. "A friend of mine had a problem with stray cats. She caught them in what's called a humane trap and—"

"What the hell is a humane trap?"

"It's like a box made of wire mesh. The cat goes in and a door springs shut. Then off to the shelter."

"I'll consider it," Gregory said, thinking a shotgun would be easier.

Ema's fat breasts wobbled below the pendant as she turned to wave for the check, the ritual over for another few days. Ema picked up her purse, a beaded concoction the size of a bowler's bag. Gregory watched her pudgy pink fingers scrabble for her wallet.

"It's my turn to pick up the check, right, dear?" she said, staring into the junkyard of her purse.

"I'll get it, Ema." *I don't have twenty minutes for you to find your wallet.* Though both had money from their inheritance, Gregory made additional money writing code for a company specializing in industrial controls. Ema had a part-time income doodling out chatty little women-directed newsletters for an HMO and insurance firm, and Gregory figured she did it while watching television.

The pair stood and Ema hugged Gregory so tight he smelled her body odor beneath the cloying perfume. After kissing his cheek – Gregory hiding the grimace – Ema waddled out to the parking lot.

Gregory went to the restroom and washed his hands for two minutes before opening the door with his elbow and striding toward the entrance. An elderly woman pushed the front door open and he jumped past her, drawing a sharp glance for the incivility, but he'd not had to touch anything.

On scene at the C-store until three a.m., I spent Sunday in busywork trying to push the attempted robbery from my mind. Sometimes it even worked for a couple minutes. When Monday arrived, I slept till nine, then walked the hundred paces from my stilt-standing home to the Dauphin Island beach, interrupting a flock of gulls and sending them into the cloudless sky.

I ran the sugar-white strand for three miles and returned, launching into the Gulf and swimming a leisurely down-and-back mile. Then I had breakfast on my deck – cheese grits and andouille sausage wrapped in a plate-sized flour tortilla, a grittito, in my parlance – and drank a pot of industrial-strength coffee with chicory. I felt steady again, Saturday night's memories fading away. I climbed into a beater truck painted gray with a roller, and headed thirty miles north to Mobile, Alabama.

Almost summer, the coastal heat was nearing typical

18

blast-furnace intensity, so walking into the chilled air of the Mobile Police Department felt delicious. Several colleagues called out as I walked the hall to the stairs.

"Hey, Carson, I need a bag of pretzels."

"Ryder . . . now that I know you moonlight at a C-store, how's about bringing in the Krispy Kremes?"

"Yo, CR . . . I need fifteen bucks on pump three."

They were congratulating me, but being cops wouldn't use those words. The accolades were in their grins. Or the thumbs up after the joke. I climbed the steps to the homicide department. Harry was on paid leave for three days, standard procedure for a cop involved in a killing.

"Carson!" a voice called. My supervisor, Lieutenant Tom Mason, stood at his office door, lean as a teenager though in his mid-fifties, wearing his cream Stetson and cowboy boots. Tom hailed from piney-woods Bama, but he always looked straight from a cattle drive across the plains. I banked in his direction.

"Chief Baggs wants to see you, Carson."

I winced. "Why?"

"Probably something to do with last night. Make nice, Carson," Tom said pointedly. "He's the chief, right?"

I went upstairs to a hushed and carpeted row of offices inhabited by the brass hats of the department, crossing the floor with the same thought I get in funeral parlors: *Where's the nearest exit?*

Chief Baggs's personal assistant sat at a desk outside the closed door of his corner office. Though Darlene Combs was only in her late thirties, she'd already buried two husbands, one a suicide, the other OD-ing at a Jimmy Buffett concert. Her green eyes always seemed as irritated as her hair was red. I studied her outfit: a blue skirt hiked high to display plump thighs she thought slender; a white silk blouse a size too small, to highlight a pair of odes to silicone; and an Evan Picone jacket, to show she didn't have to wear the big box knock-offs worn by the women on the lower floors.

Darlene said, "The Chief is very busy today."

"He asked Lieutenant Mason to send me up here."

"You're not in the Chief's appointment book."

"Perhaps I'm in the footnotes."

She tapped a button on her phone. "Chief?" she said. "Detective Ryder is out here." She listened for several seconds, put the phone down. "He's on the phone to the Mayor. It'll be a few minutes."

Every time I'd come here, I'd waited out a call to the Mayor. I once compared notes with Harry, who'd been here twice. Both times Harry cooled his heels while the Chief finished his consultations. Harry, ever the detective, had noted Baggs's phone line wasn't lit, but perhaps he communicated on a secret line like the Batphone.

Darlene returned to penciling a magazine page as I studied the walls, laden with photos of Baggs shaking every political hand in four states, including such Washington stalwarts as Alabama senators Jeff Sessions and Richard Shelby. Both men's eyes seemed to say, *Who is this geek at the end of my arm?*

Though the degree in Police Administration was framed near center on the Wall of Baggs, most prominent was the law degree. The name of the institution was unknown to me, perhaps a correspondence subsidiary of Harvard or Tulane. While the bulk of the photos and certificates were in simple black frames, the degree was in a baroque gilt rectangle. It seemed a shade over-wrought, but who was I to judge, being *sans entrée* into the world of police administration.

The ambition-prone Carleton Baggs was late to the top floor. Though he and a cabal of like-minded admin-istrators had been headed upstairs several years back, Baggs had cast his lot with an ambitious manipulator named Terrence Squill who eventually ascended to Acting Chief. Squill's career had slammed a wall when he'd been murdered by an even more ambitious manipulator.

Since Harry and I – me particularly – played a major role in the incident, we were not beloved of several old-timers in administration, feeling we had delayed their ascension to the uppermost ranks, thus costing them time and money. When the former chief retired last fall, enough years had passed for the scandal to have become history. Baggs, twenty years in grade and boasting well-framed degrees in law and police administration, got his shiny new Chief hat.

Darlene's phone buzzed. "You can go in," she said, not looking up from her pencilings. I shot a downward glance and saw Darlene was taking a quiz: "Test Your Hotness in Bed".

I mumbled *Somewhere between death and dry ice*.

"What?" she said.

"I said you look lovely today."

Chief Baggs was staring out his window, his back broad and blue in summertime seersucker. I could smell his cologne, one of those over-musked concoctions advertised by ageing jocks wearing towels. He turned, snatching a memo from his jacket pocket.

"Your lieutenant recommended you for a citation," he said. "I want to present the award in a department-wide ceremony to let the public see what their taxes are paying for."

The situation wasn't about me, it was about the department's image. Baggs pursed his lips and studied my clothes: green tee, cream linen jacket, jeans, black running shoes. "You'll wear a uniform or a suit," the Chief said, recalling the time I received a citation dressed in chinos and a T-shirt touting CRAZY AL'S MARINA AND BAR.

"I'll do the department proud," I promised, holding up a two-fingered Boy Scout salute as I backpedaled.

"One more thing," Baggs said, halting me with an upraised hand. "Shumuchuru is taking a leave of absence to care for his mother. He can't teach his class series at the police academy. We need a replacement, starting tonight. It appears, Detective Ryder, that you've never done a teaching stint."

I resisted a groan. "The classes always seem to be at times when I'm indisposed, Chief."

"The last time the academy asked, you said you had

22

to visit a sick brother. Didn't you tell me you were an only child, Detective?"

I had a brother, but not one I admitted to – for various reasons. Thus I had long fostered the only-child story. "A misunderstanding, sir. It was, uh, an uncle."

"You've also claimed your house had fallen into a sinkhole. Do they allow sinkholes on Dauphin Island, Detective?"

"Uh, more like quicksand, Chief. The stuff can be treacherous if—"

"I don't know why you're dodging the academy, Ryder," he scowled. "People like you usually jump at the chance to pontificate before an audience."

I shrugged. "I don't know what good I could do, Chief. They're raw recruits. Kids, basically."

"Meaning what exactly, Ryder?"

I shook my head, Baggs just wasn't getting it.

"It's a total waste of my time, Chief," I said. "Pearls before swine."

4

"Class is about over for tonight, folks," I announced. "Any final questions?"

I set aside the projector's remote and studied the recruits, surprised to discover the class wasn't entirely made up of dolts. Several *were* complete dullards, of course, a red-faced mouth-breather named Wilbert Pendel coming to mind. No matter what I said, Pendel wanted to talk about guns. The other students began telling him to shut up. He muttered, stamped a foot on the floor like a mini-tantrum, then sulked in silence.

But on the whole the class seemed several notches above my expectations. They were fast learners, too. A cell phone had gone off early on. "Don't think of that as a phone," I'd said. "Think of it as a warning bell. When the next phone rings I will stomp it into its components. Thank you."

Not an electronic peep since. I'd explained various homicide cases solved by Harry and me – with histories, photos, news stories – and the recruits now regarded me with eyes both admiring and envious, which wasn't offensive in the least.

In response to my call for final questions, a tentative hand climbed into the air. "I have a question, Detective."

"What was your name again?"

"Wendy Holliday, sir."

Initially, I hadn't been well disposed toward the auburn-haired Holliday, her slender frame, piercing gray eyes and pursed lips reminding me of a temperamental college girlfriend, but the long-legged recruit was one of the night's best surprises: observant, analytical, and inquisitive, making intelligent – if wrong – conjectures about cases presented.

Intelligence took brains. Right took years.

"Your question, Holliday?" I asked.

"I'd like to know your most nightmarish scenario, Detective Ryder," she said. "Real or imagined."

I started to wave the question away as frivolous, but when everyone in the class leaned forward with interest, I considered what truly frightened me and reached into my briefcase for the rolled coins I kept forgetting to take to the bank. I broke open a tube of pennies and poured them into my palm.

"Here's my nightmare scenario," I said, flinging the coins skyward. They tinkled down across the floor, spinning, rolling into corners, dropping at the legs of desks and chairs.

"Penny-ante crime?" said a recruit named Wainwright, buying a round of laughter.

"Come on, kiddies," I said, stepping in front of the lectern. "What inference can be made from the pattern?"

Several recruits stood to better survey the floor. I saw a tentative hand.

"Yes, Miz Holliday?" I said. "Have you discovered the pattern?"

"I don't think there is a pattern, Detective Ryder. The coins fell at random."

"Bingo," I said. "Imagine a purely random victim selection process: the killer walks down the street with closed eyes, opens them and sees someone – cab driver, elderly woman, shopper, child in a playground. He tracks and kills that person. Without a motive – monetary, sexual, psychological, power, vengeance – the detective is never sure one death is connected to another. It's my idea of a nightmare situation."

"What about evidence at the scene?" a recruit named Terrell Birdly asked.

"I was purposefully simple for the sake of the answer," I said. "If the perpetrator leaves his prints behind – or blood or semen or the mortgage to his home – the case gets easier to solve. But let me enhance our scenario by giving the killer three traits: high intelligence, a basic knowledge of police procedures, and an awareness of the confusion he's causing. Now you've got big trouble."

"You've dealt with random killings, sir?" Birdly asked.

I shook my head. "I've never personally seen a killer

without some form of motive, though it eludes the killer himself. Even with severely deranged minds, I've always found a motive behind the madness."

I was making that information up on the fly. But it felt right.

"Seeing all the cases you and Detective Nautilus solved," one young woman gushed, "I figure if anyone could catch a random killer, it would be you, Detective Ryder."

She was cute and her breathy words sent a pleasant blush to my neck. "I expect you're exactly right," I said, bouncing on my heels. "And on that note, class is dismissed. . ." I held out my cupped hand, fingers making the *gimme* motion. "After the pennies have come home."

Gregory had done a half-hour's worth of faces followed by two strenuous sessions on his Bowflex, pushing to his limits as he watched his sweating body in the mirror, muscles shining and rippling.

Frail, Ema? I'll show you frail . . . I'll turn into the fucking Hulk next time.

He'd followed with a shower, then gone to his office to write code. He worked in a suit, but after being on the job four hours allowed himself to hang the jacket over the back of his chair and roll his sleeves to mid-forearm.

Gregory took a break, sitting in the dark with honeyed tea and graham crackers covered with organic peanut butter. He winced at the yowl of a horny feline outside his window. He had called the Animal Control department twice in the past week, but the cats eluded the nets.

After his recent breakfast with Ema, Gregory had considered her comments, then grudgingly purchased a Havahart Cat Trap and Rescue Kit, the most humane way to trap cats, according to Ema. He'd set the ridiculous cage-like contraption in his backyard at dawn. Probably time to check it.

Gregory changed from suit into chinos and a polo shirt. Tucking a flashlight into his pocket, he stepped into the backyard, the steamy air smelling of the pine straw at the base of the trees.

Feeling a delicious shivering in his loins, Gregory tiptoed to his burlap-camouflaged trap at the rear of the long yard. He snapped the fabric away and shone his flashlight down.

He had a cat.

5

"*. . . risking his life disguised as a convenience store clerk, his surveillance and backup team across the street, Detective Ryder heroically. . .*"

Chief Baggs's memo had pulled a third of the force to my award ceremony. I figured he'd had a PR person write his speech, since he never said anything similar to me.

"*. . . talent of the MPD marksman who took out the woman perpetrator as Detective Nautilus simultaneously incapacitated her male counterpart. . .*"

I'd asked Harry to share in the award, but he refused, claiming he'd been beside me for a half-dozen other citations and this time I was on my own. Cal Mallory, our senior marksman, declined as well, not wanting to remind his neighbors his livelihood included shooting people in the head.

". . . *ladies and gentlemen of the force and guests, I present Detective Carson Ryder. . ."*

I strode to the dais as Janet Wing tracked me with a camcorder. Wing was a student intern in the PR office. Our main PR person was Carl Bergen, a retired cop supplementing his pension. Ask Carl what he thought of the New Media, and he'd say he really enjoyed cable TV. Wing, on the other hand, had the department on Facebook from day one and trumpeted the MPD across venues most cops would never see. I figured the net effect was near zero, but Wing was a determined type.

"*. . . known to everyone in the department. Ladies and gentlemen, Detective Carson Ryder.*"

Chief Baggs recited a few more words and handed me a framed certificate that would look nice in the closet with the others.

That's when things got weird.

Everyone stood, hands pounding as if I were Hank Aaron at his retirement game. Not knowing how to respond, I held the cheesy plaque high, strutting like a card girl at a prize fight. The applause turned to cheers as I sashayed across the stage, some cops singing a tuneless version of "I Fought the Law (and the Law Won)".

A perplexed Baggs dismissed the gathering. I went to the foyer, where cheers turned to good-natured insults. Most folks headed to Flanagan's, a loud and rowdy cop bar. Harry and I booked to a quieter joint a few blocks away. I was still pondering the surreal action at the ceremony.

"Jesus, Harry," I said, "it was like everyone made me king for two minutes."

My partner tried to hide the smile, couldn't. "I take it you didn't read the memo sent out by the new PR intern?" He reached into his jacket pocket for a copied document, slid it across the table.

The award ceremony for Detective Carson Ryder will be held tonight at seven p.m. in the City Building's auditorium. Past ceremonies have been sedate and we'd prefer to present a more positive face to the public. Thus when Det. Ryder receives his award I encourage everyone to be upbeat and demonstrative. . .

"Upbeat and demonstrative," I sighed. The whole thing had been a big joke and Wing – now introduced to cop humor – would be more measured with her words in the future.

A week passed, and I survived the next two academy classes, Wendy Holliday remaining the standout, the sullen Wilbert Pendel her counterbalance. I came to work later on post-class mornings, figuring each two-hour class cost me seven hours in actual time and prep time. I was crossing the room at half-past ten when Tom called across the floor.

"Carson, see you a moment?"

I turned to see him hanging up his phone. Tom was

leaning back in his chair with his cowboy boots on his desk, hand-tooled, silver-tipped, lacking only spurs to complete the effect. He picked up his Stetson and spun it on one finger, a puzzled expression on his face.

"Please don't tell me Baggs has set up another award ceremony," I said.

Tom grinned, looking like an amused basset hound. "I heard the guys were planning to have a little fun."

"Uh-huh," I said. "Little."

He went serious. "Listen, Carson, what was that thing you told me about psychopaths and animals? The markers?"

"A huge per cent of serial killers have three markers in their history: pyromania, chronic bedwetting, and cruelty to animals."

Tom sighed. "The dispatcher got a call from Al Hernandez in Animal Control and it got bumped to me. Can you spare a few minutes to talk to the guy?"

I called Hernandez. What I heard had me in my car five minutes later, roaring to northwest Mobile, up where the auto graveyards and carpet outlets turned into farms and woods.

Hernandez was on a small county road, against a white van with DEPARTMENT OF ANIMAL CONTROL, MOBILE, ALABAMA on its side. A rope-skinny guy in a brown uniform, sleeves rolled up, sinewy forearms, he had a high forehead, inquisitive eyes and a neat mustache. He led the way to a slow-flowing muddy creek below the bridge, a shallow pool on the upstream side, sandy hummocks downstream. Trash thrown from above was everywhere.

Swatting insects from my face, I followed Hernandez to the downstream side and smelled decomposition. Scattered across the ground were four small carcasses, cats. All were burned and split open, like they'd been gutted. Three lacked tails. Hernandez had the right instinct: the hairs stood up on the back of my neck.

"Couple kids from a farm down the road found 'em," he said. "I figure the carcasses got flung from a car, expected to float away. Some probably did, but these landed on high ground."

I studied the stinking ruination at my feet, sighed and ran to my cruiser, back thirty seconds later with latex gloves and a twenty-gallon trash bag.

"What you gonna do?" Hernandez asked.

"Get myself on the pathology department's shit list for about a month," I said.

6

"Autopsy a cat?" Clair Peltier said, frowning at the lumpy bag in my hand. "Is that what you're trying to say?"

She was assembling instruments for a procedure. With her coal-black hair and outsize arctic-blue eyes, Clair Peltier, director of the southwest division of the Alabama Bureau of Forensics, was the only person I knew who made formless surgery garb look sexy. She flicked a switch, testing the high-powered light above. I made the mistake of looking up.

"Actually, several cats," I said, blinking away shapes floating before my eyes. Clair thumbed a button and water washed down the table. Satisfied with the flow rate, thumbed it off.

"For what case, specifically?"

"You know how the maniacs start, Clair. Bedwetting, fire—"

Clair nodded to names on a whiteboard: four post-mortems scheduled for today alone. "Autopsies are backlogged, Carson. The human kind. And I'm short a pathologist."

"Please, Clair?" I lifted the bag of dead cats and tried to appear needy.

She shook her head. "There's not even a case file to assign to the work."

"Clair. . ."

"Sorry, Carson."

I was three steps gone when I turned and emptied the bag onto the gleaming table. Clair's eyes flared. "What are you. . ." A tailless carcass caught her eye. She frowned and leaned closer to the charred husks that had once been living creatures, reading every mark and torment on the pathetic remains.

"Put them in cooler eight," she said. "I'll invent a case number."

Gregory's fingers tapped the keys of the computer on his desk, developing software for precision heat delivery in ceramic coatings applications. It was supremely boring. The company was located in Birmingham, but there was no need for Gregory to work on-site. In fact, he'd only visited the headquarters once, when he interviewed for the position. Because of his unusual health history, he'd undergone a trial period, but surpassed his employer's expectations several times over. He worked an average of a dozen hours a week, though he billed for thirty. And was still lauded for his productivity and "elegant" shortcuts.

He stood from his chair, stretched, ran a few faces found in a recent magazine – *Congestion-free at Last; Travel Opportunities Await; Concerned About Inflation?* – then went downstairs to find fuel.

The carpeted stairs led to Gregory's living room, low black-fabric couches and chairs with burnished-steel frames, the floor polished oak parquet, the lamps mere stalks with globes. The entertainment center held a large-screen television and the latest audio devices, including surround sound. The other rooms were decorated in the same spare and sleek fashion.

Gregory had bought the house after qualifying for his inheritance. The first month his sole furnishings were a mattress on the floor, table and chair in the kitchen, an overstuffed reading chair and lamp and a television to provide items to talk with the morons about.

Life had been simple and perfect.

Three weeks after Gregory's arrival Ema had visited unexpectedly. He inspected his visitor via the door lens, seeing a pink pendant floating between a double chin and milk-white cleavage. For a split second his knees loosened and his breath seemed to stick in his throat. Inhaling deeply, he'd opened the door with a broad expression from a dishwasher-soap ad, *You'll Say WOW at Sparkle-Clean Dishes!*

"I knew it'd take you for ever to invite me over," Ema

said, already apologizing. "I hope you're not angry with me dropping by and—"

"It's a wonderful surprise. I've just been working."

Ema entered the living room. "Goodness, where's the rest of your furniture?"

"I, uh, haven't had time."

"You brainy types. We'll start at the stores this weekend."

"I . . . have someone helping me already," Gregory invented, aghast at the prospect of spending hours in Ema's company, his face going into spasms with the effort of matching her enthusiasm for each color and pattern and item of furniture.

Ema clapped her hands. "You hired a decorator!"

"He's coming this week," Gregory said. "I can't wait to get started."

Cursing his fate, he contacted a decorator minutes after Ema padded away. The man arrived the next day, a leather-trousered robot that walked as if it were dancing. Gregory's instructions had been simple: "Make it look like someone lives here."

"Don't *you* live here?" the decorator replied, puzzled.

Gregory felt his intestines begin to constrict as his mind raced to find the solution. Then the deco-robot clapped its hands and laughed as if in appreciation of a joke. "Oh, wait . . . I get it. You want a lived-in quality. Something comfy. No problem. I just need your preferences in style, colors. . ."

Gregory retreated to his Faces room, digging through

37

magazines and expelling gases from his painful tubes. Five minutes later he handed the man a page from a magazine. "This is it."

The deco-robot studied the page, puzzled again. "Danish *ultra*-Modern. Not what I picture as old-shoe comfy."

"That's what I want," Gregory said, tapping the photo. "It looks easy to care for."

"I'll contact sources, show you photos. I'll call soon with choices in—"

"No," Gregory said. "You do it. Colors, furniture. Everything."

The man showed confusion again, but Gregory spoke four words he'd found helpful in dealing with the robots.

He said, "Price is no object."

The decorator said, "Whatever you want, sir."

The empty spaces had been filled with couches, chairs, sleek floor lamps, accessories such as the red glass vase on the mantel. Above the mantel hung a huge, multi-colored mish-mash the decorator had called "an abstraction redolent of Kandinsky".

Interested in the odd phenomenon of hanging someone else's scribbling on one's walls, Gregory had borrowed books on modern art from the library. He now knew what Kandinskys were, but couldn't understand why. The only works he understood were by Andy Warhol. Products, packages, people, faces, all reduced to flat simplicity and repeated endlessly in different shades. . .

Warhol knew.

Gregory continued to his kitchen and blended organic power bars with almond milk, honey, protein powders and vitamins, drinking the foaming concoction. He felt a rumble in his bowels as the food filled his stomach, a sharp pain in his tubes, the new food pressing vapors from his body. His knees loosened and his face went slack. His hands began to shake and long-gone voices filled his mind.

"*You have splendid vodka tonight. And such food!*"

"*Carnati, piftie, mamaliga. Tuica made from plums as sweet as your mouth. Call Petrov and Cojocaru. And, of course, sweet Dragna. Tell them time grows short and we must enjoy our remaining nights to the fullest. Hurry, then we'll go select tonight's robots.*"

Gregory leaned against the counter and caught his breath.

What happened?

It was the remnant of a dream, he knew. He had built a wall between him and his dreams, but on rare occasions images pushed through. He must have dreamt last night, a piece of dream finding a crack in the wall. He looked around the room, needing to focus on something beyond unbidden voices and pictures.

Bong bong bong. . .

Gregory heard the alarm ring on his computer upstairs: time to go out and check his trap. The dream disappeared within a quickening pulse and he swiftly changed into outside clothes. He had another cat, skinny and white with brown spots. It mewed plaintively and pressed

39

against the furthest corner of the wire mesh, shaking with terror.

"Don't worry," Gregory grinned, the bad dream eclipsed by his new acquisition. "Everything's going to be all right."

7

"What was that, Detective Ryder . . . did you say lack of effect? What kind of effect?"

I was starting to think Wilbert Pendel would never graduate from the academy. The kid wasn't stupid, he just seemed unable to listen or focus.

"I didn't say *E*-ffect, Pendel," I explained. "I said *Af*-fect. A common characteristic of someone suffering antisocial personality disorder – sociopathy – is a lack of affect. Can anyone tell me what I'm talking about?"

Class was nearing its end and again the students had drifted to homicide investigation. Though most homicides were depressing sagas of love gone wrong or gang avengement or drug-driven slayings, everyone seemed fascinated by the Mansons and the Bundys and the Gacys.

My question launched a smattering of hands, the majority of students pretending to study the array of cell phones, laptops, iPads and other electronic wizardry on their desktops. On my first day I had questioned the need for the gadgetry. It was politely noted that I had compiled digital photos and words in PowerPoint and was writing on a five-thousand-dollar interactive digital whiteboard.

I indicated the nearest palm. "Yes, Miss Holliday?"

"Doesn't affect mean, uh, showing your feelings? So wouldn't lack of affect be showing no feelings?"

I nodded. "Affect is emotion displayed by facial and body gestures, laughter, tears. Show most people a fluffy puppy and they'll ooh and ahhh and gush about cuteness. A sociopath views only an object captioned *Dog*. A puppy, a choking baby, a blind man in traffic, all carry zero emotional weight. Lacking a conscience, a sociopath feels neither guilt nor shame. Ditto for morality, responsibility, compassion, love . . . all as foreign as the topography of Pluto."

"Having zero conscience sounds like complete freedom, in a way," Terrell Birdly said quietly, his legs crossed in the aisle. "There's nothing to keep you from doing anything you want."

The skinny black kid with the heavy-lidded eyes could cut to the heart of an issue. "No boundaries." I nodded. "It's what makes the violent ones so dangerous."

"Aren't they all violent?" Jason Kellogg asked.

"Most are content to disrupt the lives of those nearest them through lies and manipulation. Only a few develop homicidal leanings, thankfully."

"Do they feel fear?" Birdly asked; another good question.

"Heart-pumping, fight-or-flight adrenalin?" I said. "Most shrinks don't think so. What socios do have, the bright ones, is a powerful drive to avoid negative results, such as incarceration."

"If sociopaths show no emotion, how do they get by?" Amanda Sanchez frowned, her round face framed by close-cropped chestnut hair. Her silver hoop earrings seemed large enough to pick up broadcast signals.

"They can be superb mimics, training themselves to display correct emotional responses. Sociopaths are self-preservation machines and the better they blend into the crowd, the more they can accomplish. False emotions are their currency."

Wendy Holliday's hand rose haltingly. "I might have once heard a notion, called functionalism or something like that, which says emotions are an evolutionary response to stimuli and are designed to keep people safe. Like smiling when meeting someone to show you mean no harm. Or displaying sympathy to create a bond. Sociopaths don't only learn the rules of emotion to blend in, it's essential for manipulation."

"Exactly," I said, my voice curt. "See me after the class."

A moment of uncomfortable silence as eyes turned to Holliday, now shrinking in her desk. Another hand lifted.

"Miss Lemlitch?"

"I was just thinking that it seems a lonely life. Being a sociopath."

"The closest they probably come is feeling a lack of someone to manipulate. What we call loneliness can't occur in a sociopath."

"I don't get it. Why not?"

"Normal humans define and mingle interior and exterior relationships. We experience the idea of Me, plus the broader concept of Us, the world of relationships and commonalities. Knowing the world of Us, the normal Me can feel loneliness when Us is lacking. Sociopaths exist solely in the realm of Me. When you are your own universe, there's no place for Us."

"But they have to deal with the Us," Amanda Sanchez said. "Doesn't that pull them into the real world or whatever?"

I said, "Take it, Holliday."

Confusion in her eyes. "Excuse me, Detective?"

"I'm ceding the floor. Answer the question: How do sociopaths deal with the concept of Us?"

Holliday swallowed hard. "Uh, I guess in their world it's not Us, it's Them. Me versus Them. Me is inflated via pathological megalomania or narcissism, while Them is demoted to insignificance, a collection of idiots and fools."

"Good," I said. "Us is an inclusive collective, Them isn't."

"My head's spinning," someone said, sparking laughter.

"Are such people born or made?" Jason Kellogg asked.

"Some might be born that way. An anomaly in the brain. The ones I've seen – the homicidal – were created, often by childhoods that made the Spanish Inquisition seem pleasant." I shot a glance at the clock. "That's it," I said. "We're outta here."

I began stuffing material in my briefcase, then heard metallic clicks and saw an anxious Holliday approaching. "Why are you clicking?" I asked, looking at blue shoes crisscrossed with zippy white detailing.

"I'm wearing cleats. Bike shoes. I forgot my regular shoes. You wanted to see me, Detective Ryder?"

"Your comments on affect and emotion were phrased to sound like errant facts grazed somewhere," I said, leaning against the lectern and looking her in the eye. "But later remarks suggest you know the lingo, perhaps through study. How am I doing?"

Embarrassment colored her long neck. "Psychology was my major, along with law enforcement."

Two majors. I closed my eyes. "All right. See you at the next class."

She turned and hustled toward the door. "Holliday?" I said to her back.

She turned. "Yes, Detective Ryder?"

"Don't pretend uncertainty in my classroom, kid. If you know something for a fact, say it. And be goddamn proud you took the time to learn it."

She nodded and left the room. I left seconds later. Leaning against the hall wall was a familiar man in a puce shirt, lavender slacks and blue running shoes. All he seemed to lack were purple socks, which I noted when he stepped from the wall.

I hadn't told Harry I'd been hijacked into servitude, but police departments held few secrets. A regular academy instructor, Harry had been trying to wrangle me into a classroom stint for years. "I heard the great Carson Ryder finally deigned to teach," he grinned. "You enjoying the experience?"

I shrugged, *no big deal*.

Harry laughed and clasped my shoulder. "Bullshit, Cars. You love it. Where else are guys like us gonna find a roomful of people to hang on our every word? Let's go grab a beer and—"

My cell trilled. The screen showed *C. Peltier*.

"What's up, Clair?" I asked, seeing motion outside the window, Holliday blowing past on a bicycle, hair trailing from an orange helmet.

Clair said, "I finished that extracurricular project of yours."

The cats. "What'd you find?"

A pause. "I've been in the morgue for fourteen straight hours. How about you buy me a cocktail at Tango?"

8

The Sex Itch commandeered Gregory's head. He'd been making discoveries with his new cat, but when the Itch got this strong nothing was a distraction; he needed to empty into a woman. It was Ladies Night at a lot of local bars, desperate women everywhere, and Gregory knew if he wasn't choosy, he could be in and out of one in a couple of hours.

Gregory shaved and showered and tried a new moisturizer he'd created from olive oil, honey, retinol and a dab of Preparation H. The oil smoothed, the honey nourished, the retinol restored, and Preparation H drew out the tiny crow's feet at the edges of his eyes, a flaw in the smooth perfection of his face.

He wore the concoction as a mask, saturating his flesh as he selected his wardrobe: blue oxford shirt *sans* tie, a russet linen sport jacket, chestnut-brown slacks and cordovan loafers. Gregory washed off the moisturizer while peering in the magnifying mirror, noting how small and delicate his pores were. He stared into his eyes, pleased at the subtlety of hue, and winked. He started to turn away, but realized his wink had gone unacknowledged, so he returned his wink for closure.

Gregory and Me, he thought. Us.

Just before opening the front door, he reviewed his condition. Stomach calm. Breath relaxed. Bladder empty. Gregory moved his consciousness to his groin and found a problem: He was semi-tumescent with the prospect of releasing his fluids inside a human body. He unzipped his fly and, staring at the ceiling, gave himself an orgasm in under a minute, careful to ejaculate on the mat by the door. This would make later sex last longer.

Gregory stepped into a blue dusk, turning to see his elderly neighbor watering tall red things in her front yard. *Millard, Agnes. Seventy-seven years of age, retired CPA for Austal Inc. Husband Lyle Graham Millard, former insurance actuary, died three years ago, heart attack on a plane in Mexico* (Idiot; who would visit Mexico, much less board a plane there?). *Sister Carla, brother James, sixty-nine and eighty, respectively. James in Birmingham, retired optometrist. . .*

The data streamed through a lower channel of Gregory's consciousness, accessible in case the wrinkly old bitch wandered to the fence to blather. Millard, thankfully, continued sprinkling the lawn, flicking a wave. Gregory climbed into his car and made a check of all systems: fuel, oil pressure, water level, doors closed, seat belt engaged, gasoline level of seven-tenths. His odometer read 6,235.2. Plus his intestines were calm and he'd ejaculated.

Everything as it should be.

Gregory wound toward the hotel bars in the Airport Road area, shadowy bunkers with an ever-changing cast of locals, transient businesspeople and pianists no one listened to. He picked one and sat on a barstool, ordering a glass of wine, more prop than libation. Too much alcohol made his faces inexact and increased the likelihood of mistranslations.

Gregory noticed a woman at the far end of the bar: fortyish, spray-lacquered blonde hair, a button nose and eyebrows penciled in swooping arcs. Her chin was doubling. She wore a red dress showing more leg than the legs were worth. The woman was talking with wide gestures and an overloud voice and Gregory judged her to meet his three criteria for prompt sex: Ageing, Homely, and Buzzed.

"I'd like to buy the lady a drink," Gregory said to the bartender, watching its delivery. The woman smiled broadly and lifted the glass his way, *Thanks*. A connection made, Gregory shot the woman faces as he sipped his wine, starting with *It Feels Good to Relax* and inching up to *I've Got a Secret Just for You*.

Ten minutes later she was leaving her stool to walk to him (one of Gregory's rules: never go to them). A half-hour later she was walking out the door after him, squeezing his arm. The woman followed Gregory home in her own vehicle; another rule: Gregory wasn't a taxi service.

Clair lived in Mobile's Spring Hill neighborhood, a beautiful and wooded enclave of historic homes. Tango, an upscale bar-restaurant at the edge of Spring Hill, offered a quiet walnut-and-brass ambience preferred by the wealthy denizens of the community. I'd been to the joint three times and never saw anyone tangoing.

Harry and I entered and saw Clair in a back booth. The dinner crowd had been replaced by inebriated businessmen. One, a fortyish investment banker-type in a black suit with wide pinstripes, stood beside Clair's table with a lascivious grin below a hundred-buck haircut. He was tall and relaxed and had the look of a man who specialized in bored housewives.

"Come on," he was saying. "Let me buy a pretty lady a drink."

"No, thank you, I'm waiting for friends."

"If they're as pretty as you," the Scotch-fueled lothario winked, "I'll buy them drinks, too."

Harry tiptoed to Pinstripes. "Sounds good, buddy. I'll take a Sam Adams. Carson?"

I slipped past Pinstripes and sat across from Clair. "Same."

"Two Sammys, then," Harry said, big hand squeezing the man's shoulder like he was an old friend. The guy was paler by two shades, staring three inches up into

Harry's eyes. "I, uh, I really didn't mean that I was going to, uh, buy you—"

Harry's smiling eyes tightened toward scowl. "Are you saying I'm not pretty?"

I tugged the guy's sleeve. "Tread lightly," I cautioned. "My friend is hurt he wasn't chosen as Junior Miss again this year."

"Guys. . ." Clair admonished. But her eyes were having fun.

Pinstripes glanced toward four similarly dressed men at the bar, his colleagues. They'd probably been betting on his success with Clair, but had turned away when Casanova stepped in it. "Bartender!" Pinstripes barked with a frozen smile. "Two Sam Adams over here."

"Thanks, brotha," Harry said, releasing his grip on the guy's shoulder. "Nice to know I still got it."

Pinstripes backpedaled like a sprinter in reverse, banged his ass on a table, spun and disappeared from our day.

"Get many drinks like that?" Clair said as Harry sat.

"Not nearly enough."

Clair's smile faded as she removed a file from her briefcase and studied it as if reluctant to flap it open, a Pandora's box of manila. "And now, on to your latest project, Carson. . ." She pulled out pages, put on reading glasses, and detailed her findings in detached and clinical verbiage. I winced at the repetition of the word "vivisection".

When she closed the file no one spoke.

*　　*　　*

Gregory was laying in bed and stroking himself. "Come back to bed," he said. "We're just getting started."

"I'm not in the mood," the woman said, pulling on her panties.

The woman had been a poor choice, Gregory thought. First off, she had more native caution than he'd judged, always a problem. Secondly, she was a Kisser, Gregory enduring ten minutes of lips slopping over his, biting, tugging, running her tongue over his teeth as if feeling for a snack.

When Gregory'd finally tugged her clothes off – did the bitch ever stop talking? – he needed oral sex, but the woman only used her hand. When he pushed her head toward his groin she'd grumbled he was messing up her hair. When he'd given up on a blowjob, he mounted her and put her legs over his shoulders. He was rubbing her anus with the tip of his penis when she nixed that one. So he'd settled for pussy and was finding his rhythm when the woman complained the position was cutting off her breath.

And now the bitch was standing up and putting on her dress.

"Come on," Gregory said.

"Not gonna happen." The woman stepped into her shoes. "I'm not there."

"There? Where the hell is *there*?"

"Like I said, in the mood." She spelled it out, "m-o-o-d", as if talking to a third-grader. Gregory felt his jaw clench in anger, both at her condescension and because he wasn't sure what she was saying.

"A mood is happy or sad," he explained. "We were fucking."

"OK, then," the woman said. "I'm happy we stopped fucking. How about that?"

Gregory let his face go slack, no need to waste any more energy. He could at least learn something. "Just what is it you want?" he asked.

She frowned. "Want?"

"You hang around bars to meet men who want to fuck. If you don't want to fuck, what do you want? You're not attractive, you're not young, you're not smart. You can't want much, because you don't have anything to trade."

The woman picked up her purse and left the bedroom. Gregory stood at the top of the stairs and watched her descend the steps to the front door. She put her hand on the knob, then turned to him.

"You fart while you screw, you know that? Little ones that leak out. What's that about?"

"Get out of my house."

"You should see a doctor. Maybe get a cork put in."

"GET OUT!"

"And not only do you leak stinky farts, buddy. . ." she said, a smile crossing her lips, "you fuck like a fifteen-year-old."

She walked out. Gregory's red-faced anger turned to cramps in his intestines. He doubled over in pain and ran to the bathroom, leaking gas with every step.

*   *   *

53

I arrived home at midnight and checked my e-mail. Clair sometimes followed late-night conversations with thoughts on the topic, using e-mail in case I'd gone to bed.

I sat on the couch with my laptop. Nothing from Clair, just the usual spam assuming I was a lonely man with erectile dysfunction who needed pictures from hot Russian women, a fifteen-inch penis, and a Rolex knock-off. I was deleting the crap when I noted a post from *Wholliday*, the subject line a simple *Sorry*.

Detective Ryder,
There was a girl in my high school history class named Nancy Sullivan. When the teacher asked a question, Ms Sullivan not only answered it, but added everything she'd ever learned about anything. She was a bore and no one liked her.

I think I was afraid of becoming Nancy Sullivan if I kept referring to things I'd learned in my Psych classes. I'm sorry, and in the future I'll always chime in when I can. I will also be proud that I took the time to learn it, which hadn't occurred to me before.

Your class is my favorite, and I think the favorite of most of my colleagues.
Thank you,
Nancy Sul . . . I mean Wendy Holliday
(Student in your Overview of Investigative Techniques class)

I laughed at the sign-off and re-read the letter. My mind presented me with a picture of Holliday snapped at the last class: exiting after our talk, her high, round hips ticking side to side and metered by precise clicks, the cleats of her bike shoes tapping on the hard floor.

It was a delightful picture and I studied it for several gratifying moments. Then I closed down the computer and went to the deck to sit in the dark, trying to understand a mind that would find pleasure in mutilating helpless animals.

9

Gregory was driving to the quiet and expensive whore-house he sometimes patronized. It had taken an hour for his anger at the woman to subside. He had almost followed the pig out the door and to her home, thinking of wiring the slut to her goddamn bed, slicing her open and running his fingers through her guts while she watched.

But he'd gripped tight to the staircase and run the data: he didn't know her house, her neighborhood, what he'd do with the body. To kill a human was probably easy if you planned correctly, but he hadn't planned. One misstep and he'd go to prison, a place where they put you in a box and fed you slop and everyone waited for night to come so they could hurt you.

He knew how that worked.

So he'd cursed the filthy slut, made a promise to

never visit that rat-trap of a bar again, and set out to find relief in a prostitute. Whores weren't as satisfying as hunting your own women, but whores did pretty much what you wanted and never asked questions about where you worked and what movies and restaurants you liked and all that ridiculous shit. They sure as hell didn't insult and lie to you. And they never wanted to kiss.

The light at the upcoming intersection turned red. Gregory saw no other vehicles near, no reason to stop. He passed a small corner bar, wondering why the bar's neon lights seemed to fill his vehicle. No, not the bar's lights, he realized . . . the blue-and-white flashers of a cop car on his bumper. Gregory pulled beneath a streetlamp, anger curdling in his belly. Goddamn cops . . . people getting robbed and shot all over Mobile and here they were, bothering him.

Gregory squinted into the rearview and saw two faces in the flashing lights, the passenger-side face obscured by a brown bag. Was the cop drinking? A cop in his twenties exited the driver's seat, putting on his cap and walking toward Gregory's car. The other cop leaned on his open door and watched.

"I need to see license and registration, sir," the young cop said.

"What did I do?" Gregory sighed.

The cop said, "License and registration."

Was the cop a parrot? It was a simple question, so Gregory repeated it, enunciating each word carefully.

"What – did – I – do?"

"Hey, asshole," the older cop barked. "Do like you're goddamn told."

Gregory felt his anger ratchet up a level, but caught himself. *It's a routine traffic stop,* he reminded himself. *Just one more moronic ritual. Put on the faces of concern.*

"I'm sorry. What's this about, officer?" Gregory handed over his license as a small crowd gathered to watch, drawn to the flashing lights. Gregory saw three whores plus two bone-skinny guys in outsize white tees and sideways ball caps and two grinning old drunks from the corner bar. More gawkers were pushing out the door.

The young cop shone his flashlight in Gregory's eyes, blinding him. The world turned white, like a sea of snow. The whiteness condensed into a ball that tolled back and forth like a bell. Gregory could actually *hear* the flashlight.

"What is the light, Grigor?" the cop said.

Gregory's mouth fell open. His heart turned to ice. It seemed as if time stopped.

"Uh, what did you say?"

"What are you doing here this time of night?" the cop said.

Gregory blinked. The young cop was staring from behind the flashlight, now scanning the rear of the car. The light returned to his face.

"I asked you a question, sir," the cop repeated. "Why are you here this time of night?"

"I couldn't sleep, officer," Gregory replied quietly, though his jaw was tight with anger. "I was driving to relax."

"Get him outta the car, Mailey," the older cop bayed. "I wanna look at him."

"Step out of the car please," the young cop said, pulling the door open as though Gregory was some kind of criminal.

"Is there a reason why I—"

Again the sound of the damned light. Gregory winced.

"GET THE FUCK OUT OF THE GODDAMN CAR!" the older cop yelled. Gregory exited his vehicle and stood with his hands at his side. The audience on the sidewalk started laughing as though this was a show they'd seen before. The older cop walked toward Gregory, the younger several steps behind. Gregory felt a rumble in his belly. For one strange and breathless second, the cops seemed to split into two pairs, one team walking left, the other walking right.

Behind him, someone said, "What happened next?" Gregory turned and saw only the giggling whores. When he turned back, the big cop had reappeared a foot from Gregory's face. His uniform seemed to pulse and shimmer in the soft light, like it was woven from dreams.

"Breeeep," the older cop said.

"What?" Gregory said, frowning.

Gregory felt a sharp poke in his side, looked down to see a shining black nightstick.

"Breathe, dammit. Like I just told you."

Gregory heard gas bubbling in his intestines. A voice in his head said, *Your guts are upset, Grigor; be careful.* He exhaled. The cop stuck his nose in the outflow, made a big deal out of grimacing. The onlookers giggled. They had moved closer.

"His breath stinks, Mailey," the cop grinned. "But I don't smell booze." He turned back to Gregory. "Only two reasons people come down here at night, mister. Drugs and pussy. Which one are you after?"

The whores giggled and chanted, "*Pus-sy, pus-sy. . .*" It was almost like they were singing. Gregory felt a trembling in his guts, moving lower. He heard squirting noises, bubbling.

"I'm not looking for a woman," he lied, "and I don't use drugs."

"*Pussy . . . pussy. . .*"

The older cop grinned and waved the girls into silence. "Check inside his pretty car, Mailey."

The young cop stepped close. His uniform was glowing in the light. "You don't mind if I take a look inside your vehicle, do you, *sir*?"

Gregory was seething but forced a nonchalant shrug. The pressure in his belly was starting to hurt.

"Suit yourself, officer."

The cop leaned into the car, patting beneath the seats, opening the glove box, pulling down the visors.

"Can I go now?" Gregory asked the older cop. His words seemed to come out half-sized and plaintive, like those of a frightened child.

"I say when you can go, *sir*," the cop said, tapping Gregory's shoulder with the black baton. "But I haven't said that yet, have I? Check the back seat, Mailey."

The young cop leaned into the rear, sliding his fingers between and underneath the cushions, reaching into the seatback pouches. He retreated holding a glossy magazine. Gregory felt his insides slosh and grind as the pain grew sharper.

"What is it, Mailey?" the old cop asked.

The cop named Mailey held up a page opened to a shot of a naked woman hanging upside down in chains, black clothespins clamped to her nipples and a red ball gag filling her mouth. Gregory stared in horror: How had he left the magazine in his car?

"It's one of them pervert magazines, Horse," the young cop said. "Something called *Women in Agony*."

"Freak!" one of the women yelled, a gold incisor glinting.

The older cop pulled reading glasses from his pocket. "Lemme see."

"I purchased that legally," Gregory stammered, feeling a hot cascade through his intestines. He clenched his sphincter. "There's . . . nothing wrong . . . with it."

"You're a freak!" the woman yelled again. The others took up the chant. "*Freak, freak, freak. . .*"

The young cop handed the magazine to the older one, who shook his head and *tsk*-ed through pages, reading glasses perched on the bulbous tip of his nose. "You like to tie ladies up, sir?" he asked in mocking sincerity. "Put those rubber balls in their mouths?"

The drunks joined in the chorus. "*Freak, freak. . .*" They were getting louder and louder. Gregory couldn't answer the cop, his intestines were squirming like cut worms. He felt his control slipping away.

"You know, if you jam rubber balls in their mouths," the cop grinned, "it doesn't leave room for your dick."

"*Freak, freak. . .*"

"I really . . . need to. . ."

"You need to shut the fuck up and stand still," the cop said, tapping Gregory's belly with the stick. He went back to turning pages and *tsk*-ing loudly.

What happened next?

Gregory felt his bowels explode, a hot flood filling his pants and sliding down his legs. The stink rose as the liquid fell. The cop stared at Gregory's pants, his eyes following the stain to the pavement.

"Christ, Mailey," the cop laughed, "the pervert just shit himself."

The audience exploded into hoots and catcalls. Several onlookers began chanting *Shit boy*. One of the drunks started a rap in the middle of the street, grabbing at his crotch and pointing at Gregory. "*Look at the boy with his face inna trance, got shit dripping down the legs of his pants. . .*"

The cop named Horse didn't seem to walk toward Gregory, but simply appeared in front of him like magic, a tower of threatening blue, his grin fierce and horrific. The cop put his huge callused hand over Gregory's face and pushed him backward toward his car. He stumbled several steps before his legs tangled and he fell to the ground. When he tried to regain his legs, the cop's big foot came down on Gregory's chest and pushed him to the pavement, back into his own filth. The chorus of catcalls and laughter almost deafening, the big cop leaned over Gregory, grabbed his collar and jammed the magazine in the front of his shirt.

"You stink like a sewage factory, poopy," the cop laughed as he stood and pulled his boot from Gregory's chest. "Go home and learn how to use a toilet."

What happened next?

10

"You know, if you jam rubber balls in their mouths, it doesn't leave room for your dick."

Gregory screamed and kicked the pail of soapy water across the floor of his garage. It was useless to try and clean his car seat. The brown stain had not only set, it spread as he rubbed with the detergent solution.

"You stink like a sewage factory, poopy. Go home and learn how to use a toilet."

Gregory had nearly crashed twice on his return, once driving through a stop sign, the second time almost missing a curve. His drive took him past Ema's house and for some wild reason he pulled into her driveway, wanting to go to her door, make up an excuse, anything, *anything*.

Help me, Ema. I'm sick.

It was as if he saw himself walking her drive with his face contorted in misery, his body reeking of itself as his nails scratched in agony at her door. But no, that couldn't have happened. Because when Ema's lights came on at the sound of a car, Gregory had panicked, cutting the steering wheel and flooring the accelerator, whipping into a U-turn across Ema's yard and back into the street, his heart wild in his throat.

What happened next?

Home minutes later, Gregory had torn off his clothes – designer khakis, linen shirt, silk socks, Italian walking shoes – jamming everything inside a garbage bag, and another and another, until a dozen bags surrounded the disgraced clothes. He'd showered until the water ran cold.

Gregory howled and kicked the pail again, sending it into a rack of rakes and brooms. They tumbled from the wall, clattering to the concrete.

I will kill them both, Gregory thought, kicking aside the implements as he paced inside the hot and reeking garage, hands wet with shit-stained water. *Cut out their eyes. Slash their bellies and pack them with starving rats . . . nail their ballsacks to a tree and snip their carotids with pruning shears. . .*

Harry and I were in early the next morning. I called Hernandez and filled him in on what we'd discovered. "Have you had any other instances of animal bodies lately?" I asked. "Tortured, I mean."

"None. Same for the rest of the folks in the department. I'm not including neglect, a kind of torture, but. . ."

"Yeah. This was methodical and likely the highlight of this freak's day."

"Could you stake out the bridge?" Hernandez asked.

"We don't have the manpower. And the pathologist is fairly certain the carcasses had been frozen. The perp probably froze the cats when he was, uh, finished with them. So he may well have driven across the bridge just the once."

"Uh, listen, Detective Ryder . . . I did some reading on the Internet. I'm sure you know that people who torment animals can a lot of times turn into, uh. . ."

"Yep," I said. "I know."

I hung up and heard a throat being cleared. I turned to see a pretty young woman three paces back wearing a light summer dress with a backpack slung over a bare shoulder. "Hello, Miz Holliday," I said. Harry turned, his eyes lighting as always when he saw a lovely woman.

"We've studied several of your cases, Detective Nautilus," Holliday said after I'd made introductions. "Detective Ryder is always talking about you."

Harry raised an eyebrow my way.

"It's the other Harry Nautilus," I said. "The pretty one."

Harry shot me a strange grin and stood. "I'm gonna pull some uniforms to canvass the block below Bienville," he said, referring to a current case.

"What brings you to HQ, Wendy?" I asked.

"Our class in police administration heard lectures from administrators. Departmental structure, chain of command, work flow, efficiency analysis, public outreach—"

"Did you manage to stay awake?"

"Let's just say I'll take one of your classes any day."

"Very diplomatic. Chief Baggs . . . did he talk to the class?"

"We saw his office. His secretary said he was busy."

I pressed my fingers to my temples and closed my eyes like a Las Vegas mentalist. "Something about the Mayor, right?" I divined.

"How did you know?"

I winked. "I'm a detective, Wendy. I detect. Where's the rest of the class?"

"Dismissed a few minutes ago."

"And up you snuck."

"I was just going to peek through the door. Then I saw you and Detective Nautilus. And, uh, sort of kept walking."

"Here's the homicide floor. Peek away."

She turned to look across the room, a full floor of cubicle offices. I almost avoided lowering my eyes past the knee-top hem for a mental photograph of the long, sun-browned legs, the slight front bow of her shins perfectly complementing the swell of calf.

"It seems kind of dark compared to the other floors," she noted, turning my way as my head snapped up.

"Good catch," I said, hoping she hadn't caught me ogling. "When the building was put up, before my time, the latest in high-intensity ceiling lights were installed. Within two weeks the dicks had removed the fluorescent bulbs and brought in floor and desk lamps, creating an atmosphere better suited to solving mortal crimes."

"Chiaroscuro," Holliday said. "The juxtaposition of dark and light."

"Nice vocabulary, Wendy."

She blushed again and turned toward the door. "I guess I'll see you in class, right?" she said over her shoulder.

"Looking forward to it," I nodded, fighting to keep my eyes level.

11

Gregory was sleeping when his cell rang from the bedside table. He tried to ignore it until his eyes caught the clock: 10.17 a.m. He never slept past eight . . . *why did I* . . .

The horrors of his night flooded into his head.

You fart while you screw, little ones that leak out.

The goddamn woman, the slut who'd insulted him. It was all her fault, making him need a whore, leading to getting stopped by the goddamn cops. Then the filth, shame, humiliation.

Step out of the car please. . .

The smell of shit was everywhere.

Officer—

. . . no not here no not now. . .

What happened after that?

GET THE FUCK OUT OF THE GODDAMN CAR.

My pants—

Officer, please, I can't—

What happened next?

It's one of them pervert magazines, Horse. Something called Women in Agony.

Gregory moaned. The phone rang a third time.

If you jam rubber balls in their mouths, it doesn't leave room for your dick.

You stink like a sewage factory, poopy. Go home and learn how to use a toilet.

What happened next? What happened next?

The phone rang again. The answering machine came on. "*Leave a number and I'll get back to you.*"

"*Gregory?*" a voice said, worried. "*Gregory? Are you all right?*"

Ema.

"*Gregory? Are you there? Please pick up if you are. I'm so worried that you—*"

He grabbed the phone. Pushed the thoughts of last night from his head. Ema was the current problem.

What happened next?

"I'm here, Ema. What the hell's wrong now?"

A pause as his sister swallowed hard. She hated it when he cursed. "I've been . . . worried about you. We had breakfast scheduled for nine-thirty. I waited a half-hour and left."

"Why didn't you call from the restaurant?"

"I was afraid you might be ill. I didn't want to wake you."

"I simply forgot to set my alarm, Ema. I'm fine."

"You never oversleep."

Gregory felt his guts cinch up. "I never tell you when I oversleep because you'll fucking think I have sleeping sickness."

"I couldn't eat at the restaurant," she said. "I just had coffee. Why don't you come over and I'll fix us a healthy breakfast."

"I can't, Ema. I have so much to do today and—"

"Grigor, you have to eat. And you know you won't unless I—"

"It's Gregory, Ema. G-r-e—"

"It pops out when I get worried. I'm sorry, Gregory. I worry about my little brother too much; it's stupid."

Christ, Gregory thought, *Grigor.* The fucking name was a dozen years gone, but poor addled Ema still used it several times a year.

"You're not stupid, Ema, you have a big heart," Gregory said, wishing she had a brain to match. He did a high-speed inventory of his systems, finding hunger: if he didn't eat he'd get a headache. And if he didn't see Ema this morning, she'd want to make up the missed meal tomorrow at one of her goddamn restaurants. If he ran over now he'd be free of her for days.

"Let me get dressed," he said. "I don't want a big breakfast, Ema. Toast and honey, right?"

He went to the garage. His car stank of shit. And the brown stains were soaked into the fabric of his seat. He went back in the house and called a cab.

Fifteen minutes later Gregory's taxi was winding past

71

brick and wood structures with large front windows and decorative plastic doors, Ema's suburban housing complex.

Ema lived but two miles distant from Gregory. When he had received his inheritance, she had tried to get him to buy a home on her street, but he had shot that idea down immediately, knowing Ema would be visiting every day, plates of cookies or stuffed cabbage rolls in hand.

She was at the door as he arrived – *probably watching for me since I hung up the phone* – and he submitted to another crushing, smelly hug, her pendant pressing against his belly. But he endured, smiling through every second.

"Why did you come in a cab?" she asked. "You weren't in a wreck, were you?"

"Just some mechanical problem."

Ema's living room was a warehouse of girly-type things overlaying the simple Colonial furniture; rag dolls on the couch, a throw pillow on a rocking chair, the words LOVE CHANGES EVERYTHING embroidered on its multicolored surface, a dozen kinds of cutesy magazines. There was a pink bookshelf of mysteries, biographies of Hollywood celebrities, and several running feet of true-life crime books. The television was on, though muted, Ema incapable of life without TV. She had a set in every room, an endless display of talent competitions, cop dramas, cooking programs and home-shopping options.

"I'm so happy you're all right," Ema said. "I was worried when you didn't show."

"You worry too much. I'm a grown-up."

"I know. But it's like I always told Dr Szekely: Even when Gregory's fifty, he'll still be my baby brother."

Gregory fought to keep from rolling his eyes. Ema nodded toward the rear of the house. "Let's eat in the kitchen as it's so sunny."

"Just toast and honey for me," Gregory said. He'd said it earlier, but telling Ema not to cook was like telling a fish not to swim.

Gregory followed Ema to the kitchen, too bright for his eyes, sun streaming painfully through the window. He looked to the table and saw tomato slices, onion slices, link sausages, biscuits from a can, and a blue porcelain bowl full of thick yellow goo. He stared, feeling his stomach begin to foam.

"Is that mamaliga?" he whispered. The pendant glistened between Ema's fat breasts as she picked up the bowl and brought it near, as if offering Gregory a gift. He smelled fumes coming from the pile of cheap, filthy and inescapable Romanian porridge.

He turned away. "Get rid of it. I can't look at that shit." Gregory's hands clenched into fists and blood roared in his ears. He slapped the bowl from Ema's hands. It spun to the floor and shattered, the thick cornmeal porridge breaking into pieces.

"IF YOU WANT ME TO STAY YOU'LL GET THAT SHIT AWAY FROM ME!"

"I'm s-sorry," Ema said, her voice trembling. "S-so sorry, Grigor. I only wanted to make you happy. I only w-want—"

"STOP WITH THE FUCKING GRIGOR!"

Bawling as if her world had exploded, Ema turned and ran from the kitchen. Her toe caught in the rug and she stumbled to the floor and lay there crying.

"I'm so sorry," she said. "I'm so sorry. . ."

Gregory ran his options. He had to tell her he was sorry. Ema had made the sickening slop, but now he was the one who would have to apologize. The Moron World went by rules that were inside-out.

He walked to his sister and leaned to touch her back. "Are you all right, Ema?"

A shiver ran through her body. "I'm so sorry I made you mad. I always do stupid things. I'm so ashamed."

"I'm the one that's sorry, Ema," Gregory said, his expression blank since Ema's face was in the carpet. "I shouldn't have gotten angry."

"Hold me, Gregory," Ema wailed, trying to roll to sitting, the pendant flapping across her skin, into the folds of her breasts. Tears streamed down her cheeks. "Please hold me, Gregory. No one ever holds me."

Gregory felt his skin crawl, but lowered himself to the rug and wrapped his arms around his sister as far as they would reach. Her body heaved with sobs and her odor rose to his nose and mingled with the smell of the mama-liga splattered across the kitchen floor. The smells turned to the stink of shit and Gregory fought the urge to retch.

"I never want to hurt you," Ema wailed in English, then the same in Romanian, the old native tongue rising unbidden through tears and fear. "Hold me, Grigor," Ema bawled, clutching at Gregory's surrounding arms and making him wish he could disappear into the air.

What happened next?

Gregory escaped after a depressing half-hour. The smell of Ema and the mamaliga and all the female odors of the house had fired up a shrieking pain that pounded his temples. He returned to his house to try again to clean his car, but grew livid with anger once more: the stains had set and the smell had gotten worse in the heat of the garage.

There was no sign of the porn magazine the cops had found and brandished, as if it never existed except as a whip to flay him with. That seemed odd, and Gregory looked beneath the seats, in the glove box. The fucking thing was nowhere to be seen, nothing in the car but a stench as thick as cold mamaliga.

He had to sell the car, his beautiful creamy Avalon. He could never get the stink out. A thirty-five-thousand-dollar car turned to dross by the morons. The two cops were subhumans from the robot caste and Gregory would grind them beneath his heel as if he was stepping on ants.

Striving for calm in his writhing guts, he made himself walk to the utility sink in the corner to soak his hands in de-greasing soap. *No,* Gregory revised as his palms rubbed beneath the water. It wasn't the ants. The real problem was the anthill. It wasn't the two morons who had savaged him, it was the process that had created them, made them feel invincible. They were a Blue Tribe. Their own form of dress, symbols, rituals, special pledges and codes . . . all tribal.

Gregory returned to the cool of his house and recalled lessons from history. When one tribe wanted to inflict great hurt on another tribe, they killed its chief, a symbolic beheading of the entire tribe. Behead your enemy and jam his head on a pike, a dripping and fly-encrusted trophy that said *I Win, You Lose*.

Gregory suddenly felt a delicious calm in his tormented belly. He would humiliate the police, the Blue Tribe. It would take work, it would take planning, but he would behead the Mobile Police Department.

He would kill its Chief.

Moarte. Death.

12

"I think I have all the information I need for my article, Dr Szekely," the young reporter said. She clicked off her recorder and closed her pocket-sized notepad. "Is there anything else you want to add?"

Dr Sonia Szekely stared across her paper-strewn desk at her questioner: blonde, blue-eyed, skin the hue of a spring peach. The reporter wore a loose and flippy mini-skirt, tank top, pink running shoes over short white socks, and represented the newspaper of a local university. *I've got plenty to add*, Szekely considered saying. *If you've got the stomach for it, which I doubt.* Instead, Szekely looked down at her age-wrinkled hands, fought her need to light a cigarette, and regarded the reporter with bemusement.

"How old are you, my dear?" Szekely asked. Her eyes wandered past the reporter to her overloaded bookshelves holding such titles as *Ceauşescu's Orphanages: a History of Hell*, *The Pathology of Fetal Alcohol Syndrome* and *Psychic Damage in Early Childhood*. Other titles were in Romanian.

"I'm twenty, Doctor. Almost twenty-one. Why?"

"The worst of what I'm telling you happened before you were born. The wretched Ceauşescu regime in Romania, the plight of the orphans, the decades of horror and human wreckage—"

"I got that, Doctor. About how Cacesku—"

"Ceauşescu," Szekely corrected. "Nicolae Ceauşescu."

"Sure," the reporter nodded, flipping open her notepad to glance inside. "Ceauşescu wanted to grow the country's workforce so he outlawed birth control and demanded large families, but the country was so desperately poor the children couldn't be cared for and were placed in state-run orphanages." The reporter wrinkled her button nose. "Nasty places."

"Yes," Szekely nodded, thinking, *They were more than nasty, miss, they were hell on earth, a dark bloom of evil that poisons to this day.*

"But what does my age have to do with that nasty moment in history, Doctor?"

Szekely felt her legs propel her to standing. Heard her voice grow loud.

"It's not history!"

The reporter's eyes went wide. Szekely waved her hand in apology and sat down again. Took a deep breath.

"Forgive me. My work means reliving events of that

time almost daily. Plus I'm a bit fearful you'll view these orphanages as having no more hand in our present lives than a faded newsreel from World War II. Yet they're with us today. That's the real story."

The young woman frowned. "But if the Romanian orphanages have been changed and the children saved—"

"Physical salvation differs from psychic salvation. Physically, the children may have been removed from conditions of horror, but in many cases the horrors have not been removed from the children."

"Sure, Doctor. Some poor kids probably have nightmares and things. I know I would if I'd started life like that."

Szekely began to speak but closed her mouth. The intern reporter had most likely grown up in a bright home with a green lawn and white picket fence. Enjoyed large and healthy meals each day. Generations of adoring family would have surrounded and coddled her. Her bedroom held toys and dolls and lace curtains, cool in summer and warm in winter. She would have spoken at two years of age, walked at three, been in school at five. Interacting with her fellow humans would have been as natural as giggling.

Could the young woman in any way comprehend what happened to children who grew up in a box with no human interaction? Wallowing in their excretions? Feeding on slop, like hogs? Could the pretty young thing ever envision what some of these broken children became as they aged? It was an impossible task. Szekely knew;

she had been studying such children for years and was herself still capable of awe at the horrors inflicted on the innocent.

Szekely looked into the eyes of the reporter, the woman's pencil now tapping the notepad. She was impatient to get to her next assignment, something to do with a circus in town.

"I'll see you to the door," Szekely said, standing.

They strode along the hall to the reception area and out the door into a bright Gulf Coast morning. A faux-wood plaque on the side of the red-brick building said *Coastways Behavioral Medicine, LLC*. Beneath it were the names of several psychologists including Dr Sonia Szekely. Under Szekely's banner a small sign proclaimed EEOSA.

The reporter thanked Szekely and promised to send a copy of the article when it was out, a month perhaps, or more, depending on how much of the paper would be devoted to sporting triumphs.

"Remember," Szekely called to the woman's departing back, "it's not history. It lives with us today."

But the reporter had already hidden inside her iPod. Szekely shook her head and watched the woman's tiny silver Honda buzz from the lot. She was turning toward the building when her eyes fell across a familiar face in an automobile near the front of the lot. The face suddenly looked embarrassed and sank two inches, as if trying to hide below the dashboard.

Szekely waved and walked close. "Goodness, Ema, what are you doing here?"

"I, uh, was out driving and—"

"Needed to see me about something?"

The woman's fingers drummed a nervous tattoo on the wheel. She started to speak, swallowed.

Szekely frowned. "Is anything wrong, Ema?"

"No . . . I mean, I uh . . . guess I just need some reassurance." A sigh and a self-deprecating smile. "Like always, Doctor."

Szekely grinned and nodded toward the offices. "I've got a group session at one, Ema. I'm yours until then. How about we grab some coffee and have a nice girl-to-girl chat? That should make things better."

13

Night had fallen. Gregory sat in his living room surrounded by pages he'd gathered from Google, copies of everything available on Chief Baggs, mostly mentions in newspaper articles. The data focused on Baggs the cop, which was fine, but Gregory wanted more: what centered the entity known as Carleton T. Baggs? Where did he live? How did he live? What patterns could be discerned in his life?

If it's seven fifteen on a Tuesday evening in summer, Gregory thought, making notes as he went, *where, statistically, would I expect to find Carleton T. Baggs?*

When he'd pulled all the newspaper data on Baggs, Gregory frowned at the paucity of his file and considered where other information might be found. On a whim he tried YouTube, entering *Baggs, Chief, Mobile, Alabama, Police.*

Nothing.

But there was a hit on *Mobile Alabama Police*, one titled *Det. Carson Ryder Lauded for Bravery*. It had been logged into the system a couple days before by someone named Janet Wing. Gregory expanded the screen and hit Play.

He leaned back in his chair as the camera panned ranks of cops in a large room, some in uniform, others in street clothes, slack-jawed droolers getting taxpayer money to sit on their asses. The camera zoomed in on a slender, suited man standing from a front seat as someone called his name, *Detective Carson Ryder*. Ryder seemed about six feet tall, dark hair falling over his ears.

Gregory whispered "troglodyte" as Ryder approached the podium, his suit looking like it had cost fifty bucks with tie and shoes thrown in. The haircut was a ten-minute, ten-dollar job by a barber named Mort or Ralph. The knot of the Ryder-ape's tie would have been more at home on a bowline.

But when the man forswore the step-stairs to the stage and took the half-meter jump as a natural extension of his stride, *troglodyte* suddenly didn't fit. The man moved with a fluidity Gregory had noted in athletes, though nothing about him seemed particularly athletic save for shoulders a bit wider than the norm.

The man stepped into white light beside a podium. The camera panned left and Gregory's breath froze in his throat. Baggs was the voice who had summoned Ryder to the podium. They touched palms in an imitation handshake and Baggs handed Ryder a framed certificate.

Gregory froze the video and studied his adversary, Baggs, a large man with veiled eyes and mottled skin, attempting to hide encroaching baldness with a comb-over, which merely served to highlight the condition. He looked stupid, which Gregory had expected, needing only a line of drool down his chin to complete the picture.

This is my quarry, Gregory thought as his heart increased its rhythm, burning the image in his brain. *This man is dead*. Gregory re-started the video, hoping for additional footage of Baggs.

But he found something more interesting. When the Ryder-cop took the certificate, the camera image widened to show an audience leaping to their feet with hands pounding. Ryder studied the crowd, then commenced what seemed to be a ritualized step-pattern, holding the award aloft. *Was Ryder dancing?* His action further inflamed the crowd. Somewhere in the room chanting started, the words indiscernible but clearly known by everyone.

Braka ros n'da hasun. . .
I faw telawan telawon

When Ryder finally stepped from the stage he was enveloped in a sea of cops. Baggs stood alone on the stage, looking shrunken, uncomfortable and even more stupid.

Puzzled by the contrast, Gregory did a Google search on Carson Ryder, discovering he'd been the youngest patrol officer to make detective, recipient of a dozen commendations for bravery and resourcefulness. He'd been an Officer of the Year when in uniform, had twice been Detective of the Year. Archived photos showed Ryder receiving commendations from the last four mayors, three chiefs of police, and two citizens' groups.

Gregory closed his eyes and saw Ryder holding his victory citation high. He added the applause. The cheers. The chanting. The rush of the crowd when Ryder stepped from the stage. There could be only one conclusion. . .

The man named Carson Ryder was the Blue Tribe's Warrior.

Though the Chief was the MPD's head, Gregory realized, a warrior was the department's heart. Baggs himself was meaningless, as replaceable as a hat. It showed in his face when the crowd ignored him to pay cheering tribute to Ryder.

It was Ryder who was irreplaceable. Thus it was Ryder who had to die. But Ryder couldn't die in battle. That would turn him into a martyr. He had to die in the worst way possible for a warrior . . .

In shame.

Gregory turned his attention back to YouTube, saw

one remaining video under Mobile Police Department. Four minutes and thirty-nine seconds in length, it carried the title of *Random Nightmares*. Gregory pressed Play.

Five minutes later Gregory had a perfect plan to destroy Carson Ryder.

Heart racing like he'd just found a cat in the trap, sweat glistening across his palms, Gregory stood and held his hands high, mimicking Ryder's dance steps at the ceremony and aping the MPD's praise chant.

"*I faw telawan telawon . . . I faw telawan telawon. . .*"

Harry and I spent several days working a case, trying to put the hammer down on a dope dealer who thought a nine-millimeter was the best way to deal with competition, a not-uncommon career move in the illicit-substances biz. We'd returned at six to read the newspaper. Alcohol was not allowed in the shop, which was why our beer cans were hidden in foam jackets.

Footsteps behind me turned into the Buddha walking our way in a three-piece suit, a smile on his round face, his head as bald as a melon: Don Shumuchuru.

"Don," I said. "Great to hear your mom's doing better."

"They adjusted her meds and she's like a new person. Thanks for handling the classes. And don't worry, I'm back in the saddle again."

"Pardon?"

"I'll pick up on the sessions." He grinned. "You just got two nights a week of your life returned, buddy."

"Uh, thanks Don. . ."

Don shot me a thumbs up and retreated. Harry was staring at me across his coffee mug, an eyebrow cocked in interest.

"What?" I said to my partner.

"Looks like school's out," he said.

14

Gregory was cross-legged on his living-room floor. He'd done an hour of Bowflex and taken a shower. Supper was protein powder with honey and three slices of organic wholewheat bread.

Beside him was his favorite object, a compound bow, its profile resembling a mechanical bat with outstretched wings. It had a sixty-pound pull that fired an arrow at over two hundred miles an hour. Gregory had asked the decorator if the bow might be hung over the fireplace in place of the scribble-painting, but the man's face had told Gregory he was in one of those areas where he lacked understanding.

The bow had been a thirteenth-birthday gift from his stepfather so the two could enjoy deer season together. Gregory's stepfather had grown up on a farm in central Alabama and when his parents died had inherited the six-hundred-acre tract. By that time he was living and working in Mobile, but he'd kept the farm, leasing it to tenant farmers and hunting in the two-hundred-acre woods. Whenever they went out together, the old man was always blabbing about how much he enjoyed hunting, loved the woods, loved the streams.

Over there, son, is where my father bagged a fourteen-point buck. How I loved to walk these woods with him, Gregory, and I wish I could have just one of those days back. . .

A tear rolling down the old man's cheek, weird.

Gregory was fascinated by the word *Love*. The morons used it as if it meant so much, but also to mean very little. People said they loved other people. Some said they loved their automobiles. Others used the exact same word about canaries, or cats or dogs. People loved Mexican food. Or their shoes. Or a paint color. It was another trait of the morons that they had no solid meaning for a word they used like water.

Gregory had been to funerals where the word seemed to dominate . . . *yayaya loved his children, yayayaya, a lover of humanity yayayaya we will miss his love yayayaya* . . . and all the morons who had *loved* the piece of dead stuff laying in the box would cry and howl and moan and act like death had happened to them. The person was gone: find someone else to do what they did for you.

But no, it was *Love, death, pain, love death pain . . .* which was really pretty interesting when you thought about it.

Despite its liquid character, *Love* somehow had a big influence on the idiots, and Gregory knew whatever the word meant to the morons, it must have been something like what he applied to the bow. Probably even more: people said they would die for love, but there was no way Gregory would fucking *die* for the bow. It was, after all, just wood and metal and plastic. If it was him or the bow, the bow would be out the window justlikethat.

Gregory stopped thinking about Love – an ununderstandable concept – and picked up his bow. He and his new gift had been inseparable for weeks, the boy caring less for hunting with his stepfather – and listening to all those stories – than waiting for the old man to go on some errand so Gregory could hide in the woods and shoot at everything that came into view: birds, rabbits, groundhogs, dogs. . .

Gregory had come close to being in trouble once when he shot a neighbor's dog, but claimed he'd thought the yellow Lab was a coyote.

"*Yellow Labs don't look nothing like a coyote,*" the neighbor had said. "*That boy's lyin' through his teeth.*"

"*You hold it right there,*" Gregory's stepfather said. "*Anyone can make a mistake.*"

"*My dog got shot twice, once in the hindquarters and once in the head. I think that boy crippled him for fun and killed him when he got bored.*"

"*You hold your tongue, now—*"

"*That dead-face kid may be some kind of mental wizard but that don't make him right in the head,*" *everyone in the county knows it too. You owe me five hundred bucks for the dog or I'm bringin' the sheriff in."*

Gregory's father had said nothing, but the bow disappeared. Gregory regained it two weeks later by telling his stepfather how much he loved hunting, *especially with you and could we do it some more real soon? Please, Daddy?*

He grinned at the memory. Call the limpy old fucker *Daddy* and Gregory could get anything he wanted, kind of like pulling Ema's strings.

Kayla Ballard shook her strawberry-blonde hair over her shoulders and patted her face with a bandana, the air in the university's greenhouse dense with humidity. She studied rows of five-inch-tall cotton plants in individual planters, making notes on their size and health. Each plant was graded on eight points and turned into statistical models.

"You getting all this, Kayla?" fellow student Harold Barkley asked.

"My 4-H project was more involved," Kayla answered, hefting a heavy tray of plants like it was a shoebox. "This is simple."

Barkley shook his head as he studied columns of figures he'd spend all night crunching. "Your senior 4-H project took this much math?"

"It wasn't the senior project, Harold, it was the junior one. The senior one was a lot more complicated."

Barkley pretended to make sobbing noises. Kayla's cell

phone rang and she plucked it from the back pocket of her jeans. She noted the caller and the smile broadened on her face.

"Hi, Daddy." She covered the phone with her hand. "Run along, Harold. I'll catch you tomorrow."

"In class it's *us* who are trying to catch *you*, Ballard."

Kayla grinned and returned to her cell phone. "Yep, I'm here in the greenhouse, Daddy. Guess what? I got voted president of the ag club and I wasn't even running. . ."

The pair talked for ten minutes and would talk again near ten p.m., before Kayla fell into bed. Kayla missed her father terribly. They had been inseparable since her mother passed away when she was seven, the victim of a drunk driver.

". . . all right, Daddy. I'm heading to the dorm to start calculating all this stuff. I love you."

Harold Barkley walked toward the dorms. Kayla would beat him on her bike, riding the wide sidewalk that served both pedestrians and bikers.

She rounded a bend to find the same curious sight she'd noticed for the second day in a row: a man staring into the trees with binoculars. A birdwatcher, she figured, goofy-looking in that big floppy hat and sunglasses. Yesterday she couldn't tell if it was a guy or girl until she got closer. A guy, could have been twenty, could have been fifty, from all she could see of him.

Had a game leg, too. Favored it and carried a cane, sticking it under his arm to scan the terrain. All that to watch birds, which meant a person with dedication. As Kayla closed in, the glasses seemed to turn her way, then drift back to the trees. Kayla felt a camaraderie with the birder, out practicing his hobby on a hot evening like this.

Good for you, buddy, she thought, smiling and waving as she sped past.

15

I looked at the classroom clock, almost nine already. How did the time fly by so fast? "OK, let's wrap things up," I said. "Questions?"

"Can we go back to the sociopath issue a bit?" Jason Kellogg said.

We'd spent two hours on securing crime scenes and its protocols – vital information, but nowhere near as tasty as discussing motivations of the Hillside Strangler or the Night Stalker. When you've eaten your cauliflower, you've earned a slice of pie.

"Sure," I said. "Go ahead."

"You mentioned the sociopath's need for control. Why is control such a big deal?"

"Holliday has book learning in that area," I said. "Let's give her a shot."

"Get it, girl," Sanchez grinned. "School us."

Holliday swallowed hard. She was in the front row and turned to address the bulk of the class. "Uh, well, many professionals think that by being controlling and manipulative, sociopaths reinforce their sense of superiority."

Holliday looked at me. I said, "Keep going."

"They're in charge, ergo they're the most powerful person in the relationship. Conversely, by being stupid enough to be manipulated, the other person is diminished."

Jason Kellogg spoke up. "Why don't people get tired of being jerked around?"

"The manipulation can be so subtle it's not noticed, especially with intelligent socios. It's an interesting problem to them – a project – pressing someone's buttons without leaving fingerprints on the buttons."

"Let me step in," I said. "I watched a sociopath named Bobby Lee Crayline be hypnotized. He was dangerous to the extreme, guards in attendance. A guard ordered Crayline to sit for the procedure. He didn't. When ordered to sit again, Crayline crouched slightly on bended knees. Without a second thought, the guard pushed the chair beneath Crayline's butt and he sat."

"So?" Pendel yawned. "The guard ordered the guy to sit and he sat."

"It's diffcrent," Terrell Birdly said. "Crayline made the guard slide the chair under his ass."

Pendel scowled. "Again, so what? The guy sat like he was told."

A tittering, most of the class getting it. "You're missing it, Wilbert," Birdly said. "Crayline didn't sit until the guard was manipulated into repositioning the chair."

I nodded. "It was a tiny moment of meaningless control, but in Bobby Lee Crayline's mind, it proved his superiority."

Pendel shook his head and crossed his arms, refusing to believe it. Kellogg had his hand up. "You can hypnotize a sociopath?" he asked.

"Almost anyone is subject to hypnosis by a professional, though it's easier to hypnotize subjects who want to be hypnotized or who have been prepared through a previous suggestion. Hypnosis isn't something sociopaths generally like, because it's putting someone else in control. Still, it can happen." I shot a glance at the clock. "OK, good job. See you next time."

Everyone started putting away their texts and electronic thingies except Holliday, who ambled towards me. She passed Pendel, who gave her a lascivious grin and whispered, "Gonna go suck teacher's dick for an A?"

I heard every word; the poor geek couldn't even whisper right.

"Grow up, Willy," Holliday said, not looking at him. Two seconds later she was in front of me.

"You learned your lessons well, Wendy," I said. "Good answers."

"Thank you. Uh, listen Detective Ryder, I mean Carson, I was wondering if you might want to—"

"Well, well," a big voice boomed. "I'd heard there was

96

an encore performance." Harry was leaning in the doorway, a Cheshire-cat grin on his face.

"I'll get back to you," Wendy said. "Next class maybe." She scooted past Harry, saying hi. My partner spent a couple of self-indulgent seconds watching Holliday glide down the hall before turning to me.

"School's still in session?"

I shrugged. "I figured I started it, so I should finish it. That's the way it's supposed to go, right?"

"I saw Shumuchuru in the property room laughing like he'd hit the daily double. He said you'd promised to take his next two all-night stakeouts if he let you finish teaching the course."

Snitch. I said, "Um. . ."

"So how much of your return to the classroom is due to that pretty little lady who just walked away?"

Harry had been my best friend for a decade. He knew everything about me, including things I either didn't know or didn't acknowledge.

"Ten per cent," I sighed. "Maybe fifteen."

"And the other eighty-five to ninety per cent?"

"I actually enjoy the class."

"Which should be celebrated," Harry said. "I'm thinking beer."

We settled on a cheapie bar a few blocks distant and I finished putting my materials away. We were heading out the door when my cell trilled, screen showing *Tom Mason*.

"You still at the academy, Carson?" Tom asked.

"I've been arguing pedagogical theory with an fellow academician, Tom," I said, winking at Harry. "What can Professor Nautilus and I do for you?"

"Harry's there? Good. A body was just found along a bike path near there, by the university. . ."

16

Harry'd parked in a lot one building over so we jumped in my truck and stuck the flasher to the roof. Three heart-pounding minutes later I sailed past a pair of cruisers, uniformed officers setting flares to divert traffic.

A hundred feet further I saw scene techs circling an object on the ground and pulled over. The area was lit by headlamps from the cruisers and we felt a rush of relief at seeing Holliday at the periphery, looking unsteady but alive. She had a bright orange helmet in one hand, the other was holding up a bicycle.

"I found her," Holliday said as we ran up, her voice barely above a whisper.

"Who?"

"The victim. I was riding home – I live a mile from here. I rounded the bend and. . ."

She teetered, the helmet falling from her grasp. Harry

was at her side in an eye-blink. "Easy there, girl," he said, putting a big hand under Holliday's arm. "Take a couple breaths."

Holliday complied. "She was beside the path, not moving. I called 911. I tried first aid, but . . . couldn't find a heartbeat. Then I looked at my hands." Holliday held up her hands. I saw blood. "When the medics arrived they said she was dead."

"Go to the ambulance, Holliday," I said. "Get your hands cleaned and disinfected."

Holliday was still loose on her legs. "I'll walk her over there," Harry said.

I went to the body, arriving at a sprawl in blue shorts and white top. The victim was in her late teens or early twenties. Her eyes were open, as if surprised by death.

I didn't expect you for sixty more years.

I made a fast check of the body without moving it, looking for ID. There was no purse around, suggesting robbery. The ME's van rolled to a stop with Clair Peltier jumping from the passenger side. As director of the Mobile branch of the Alabama Forensics Bureau, Clair rarely went out on runs. But this was less than a mile from the AFB. She lifted the scene tape and walked over, Harry in her wake.

"You're working late," I said to Clair.

"I've been at a conference in Seattle the last couple days, so I'm playing catch-up."

Used to be I'd know Clair's whereabouts to the hour and would have driven her to the airport, fetched her upon return, probably spending a welcome-back night at her home. Overnight visits rarely happened these days, but it didn't mean Clair and I had drifted apart; in a way we might have been closer. There were two people in the world I could talk to without reservation, and they were both beside me at that moment.

Clair was still in the white lab jacket she wore at work, beneath it a burgundy pantsuit. An art pin held her lapel, a mother-of-pearl creation that glittered in the hard light. Clair's black hair shone. When the photographer signaled completion, Clair crouched beside the body.

"The wound's on her right side. I need a closer look."

A tech rolled the body. Clair recorded some observations before her gloved hand patted a saucer-sized blot of blood.

"Cut away the blouse, please."

The tech handled the task, revealing an inch-long shaft protruding from the right rib cage, three feathered vanes encircling a notched base.

"What the hell's that thing?" the tech whispered. "A dart?"

"I saw one before, a hunting accident," said Clair. "I think it's an arrow from a crossbow. For some reason they're called bolts."

"A crossbow?" I pictured a dark knight crouched in the shadows, flame-red eyes glowing behind the slits of a iron helmet. Clair nodded for the attendants to run the body to the morgue and I went to study the bicycle in the grass.

101

"Wendy Holliday!" I yelled into the crowd gathered outside the lights. "Yo, Holliday. You still here?"

She stepped into the clearing. "Yes, Detective?"

"Walk a straight line to me."

She ducked under the scene tape and walked as if treading a tightrope. I nodded to the fallen bike. "No one here knows diddly about bicycles. Tell me what you see."

Holliday knelt beside the bicycle. I was ready to tell her not to touch anything, but she knew better. "It's an inexpensive bike," she said. "A couple hundred bucks. A lot of students own them."

"What about the damage?"

She pointed to the front wheel. "Broken spokes suggest something got jammed into her wheel while she was moving. It would have stopped the bike as dead as hitting a wall."

I liked that Holliday didn't conclusively say an object was jammed in the wheel, only that visual evidence suggested the event.

I waved Clair over. "We've got a theory. Picture this . . . The vic approaches on her bike, brakes to make the corner. The perp is on the path, maybe dressed like a runner or jogger. When she passes by. . ." I looked to Holliday for completion.

"He thrusts an object into her spokes."

"The rider falls," I continued. "Maybe she knows what happened, maybe she's disoriented. . ."

Clair nodded. "In the van I saw abrasions on the arm and the side of the head. What next?"

"The perp produces a crossbow and fires."

Clair crossed her arms and studied the setting. "Except for this short stretch, the bike path is well lit. Wouldn't someone carrying a crossbow arouse attention?"

I shrugged. "Hidden, perhaps." I thought back to crossbows I had seen, all of them large and unwieldy. To successfully hide one on your person would probably take a Batman-sized cape.

We heard an engine fire into life, the van that would carry the body to the morgue. A medic slammed the gate open. "I'm following the deceased," Clair said, patting my forearm. The three of us walked toward the street where Harry was talking with the tech staff. "I want to get a preliminary work-up tonight."

"Which means I'll see you first thing in the morning," I said.

Gregory drove slowly down the dark avenue, traffic at a crawl, the smell of exhaust thick in the humid Alabama night. He was driving with care, unused to the brakes and accelerator of the new Avalon, two days from the lot. He'd taken the other to a detailer for a complete cleaning before trading it in on another Avalon, exactly the same but untainted. Gregory figured the exchange had set him back over five thousand dollars. The Blue Tribe *owed* him.

"What happened in here?" the man at the detailing shop had asked, nose wrinkling as he opened the door and looked inside.

"My dog had diarrhea," Gregory said.

"Must be a big dog," the man said, taking Gregory's keys.

The line of traffic passed a flare laid in the right lane, pushing the stream of vehicles into the left lane. A cop car was to the right, a cop beside it, arm flapping as he yelled "Keep moving."

Gregory's heart stopped as the cop turned his head into the line of traffic, the face spotlit in the bright headlamps like an actor on a stage.

It was the cop named Mailey. *Gregory's foot pressed the accelerator to the floor as he spun the wheel hard, aiming the bumper into the cop's knees, pinning him between the cruiser and Gregory's bumper, Mailey screaming like a little girl as his kneecaps turned to bloody slush. . .*

Gregory averted his face and moved past. He saw dark step-vans with logos stating MPD COMMAND AND ALABAMA DEPT OF FORENSICS, SW DIVISION. An ambulance had its rear doors wide open and waiting. Men and women were peering behind trees and bushes, writing on clipboards. Hand-held communications crackled in the air – "*Tech Command one, we need more evidence bags up here.*"

Hearing the communications was like eavesdropping on his enemy. The tape was an interesting idea, a bright yellow *Keep Out*.

He paralleled the trees he knew so well, having spent hours parked nearby or walking the bike and pedestrian trail with a birder's field guide in one hand, camera around his neck. He'd bought a fabric foot brace at a pharmacy, his sprained-ankle gait making him seem particularly innocuous, perhaps slightly pathetic, an injured birdwatcher, one more in the stream of people who used the path.

It also allowed him to carry a cane.

"Area now illuminated and waiting to be gridded. . ."

Gregory drove by a break in the trees and again his heart stopped in his throat. Twenty paces away was the warrior.

Carson Ryder.

Ryder was leaving the scene with a woman at his side. She was in her forties and stunning, even in the strobing light. Her long white jacket flowed behind her in the breeze as if she were a cloaked queen. Gregory hated that Ryder could walk through his scene of death and destruction and come out with a beautiful woman at his side.

17

Ten-year-old Tommy Brink rolled past the small grocery, his wheelchair bumping over the uneven pavement and making his knees rock back and forth in his white shorts. He looked at his watch, Donald Duck pointing at the eight and eleven. The sun was just now topping the brick tenements on the other side of the street.

"Hey, Tommy," he heard over his shoulder. "Get over here, boy."

Tommy spun to see Mister Teddy, the owner of the grocery, its door and windows barred to keep the crackheads out. Tommy grinned and rolled close.

"Mornin', Mister Teddy."

Ted Simmons was a tall and skinny black man in his forties with an outsized smile. He was wearing a white tee and blue uniform pants, a butcher's apron around his waist. He'd been in his store wrapping sandwiches, his hands in clear plastic mittens.

"What you doin' out here, boy?" Simmons said. "Ain't you s'posed to be at school?"

"School's out," Tommy grinned. "I won't see no more school 'til August."

"You lyin' to me, boy," Simmons mock-scowled. "I'm gonna call that truant officer and he's gonna slap your skinny butt back in your desk."

"I'm gonna call the truant officer and make him put *you* in your store," Tommy said, mimicking Simmons's scowl. "Ain't you s'posed to be working and not out here botherin' me?"

Simmons leaned back his head and laughed. Tommy lifted his hand and the two slapped palms. "I been fixin' san'wiches, Tommy Brink," Simmons said, "an' I made too many. What kind you want?"

"You got that Cajun egg salad?"

Simmons dove inside his store and Tommy studied the street, always the same this time of day. Ol' Man Wombley rooting through the gutter trying to find decent-sized cigarette butts he could finish. Teritha Mapes on her stoop, a bagged forty of Colt in her hand. By noon she'd be passed out. Down the street Wesley Johnson was sweeping outside his little second-hand shop.

All of the furniture in Tommy's room had come from Mr Johnson's store. It might not be new, but it was strong and good. His bed, his chest of drawers, a big soft chair to sit in and look out the window. A radio, a television, a ukulele to strum his fingers on and make music, all were from the store.

His aunt, Francine Minear, had gotten the good things for him. They'd made a big deal out of looking at the stuff in Mr Johnson's store.

"Slip up into this chair over here, Tommy," his aunt had said. "It looks soft."

"It cost a hundred-twenty dollars, Auntie."

"Whose money gonna buy this chair?" his aunt frowned. "Yours or mine?"

Mister Teddy stepped outside and Tommy's thoughts of his aunt disappeared, leaving only a smile. She visited every weekend, and sometimes during the week. Tommy knew the surprise visits kept his mother closer to home.

"Here's your san'wich, boy," Simmons said, handing Tommy a bag. "An' apple juice to wash it down."

"Thanks, Mr Teddy," Tommy said.

The pair slapped a high five again and Tommy wheeled toward home with the bag in his lap. Yep, everything about the same on the street this morning, just like always.

'Cept maybe over there, Tommy noted, looking down to the corner. That white guy in sunglasses and a big, low-cocked hat parked outside the laundrymat and reading a newspaper like waiting for his clothes to get clean. *I ain't seen him before.*

* * *

"The bolt punctured the artery that supplied blood to the liver," Clair said. "Dead within three minutes, but conscious for one at the most."

I leaned against the morgue wall. Clair had run home at three in the morning to grab a few winks, returned at seven thirty to meet me. Harry was interviewing friends and colleagues of the victim. Despite almost two decades as a detective, Harry never felt comfortable in the morgue, with its astringent air, shining walls and tables, the long wall holding the cabinets of the dead. I always experienced a quiet thrill as I entered: this was where questions were answered.

"No helmet," I said. "Not that it would have guarded against an arrow."

"She was nineteen. At that age they feel invulnerable. I've seen bicycle accidents where someone tipped over and hit his head, dead of aneurysm in minutes. Don't get me started on helmetless riders – bikes or motorcycles."

Clair got a call and excused herself. The door opened, Gillian Fortner moving my way. She was a new evidence tech, in her mid-twenties, short and spiky 'do, huge green eyes behind frame-heavy glasses. She wore black jeans and black tee under the white lab jacket. The former head of the forensics unit had demanded dark slacks, white shirts or blouses and, for the men, ties. The current head, Wayne Hembree, didn't care, hiring the best young minds he could find, dress and eccentricities be damned.

"What's up, Gilly?"

"Scraps from the scene." She tossed plastic evidence

bags onto a white marble counter. "Got a couple bottle caps, a rotting hair band, probably been there a year. Pieces busted off the bike. Crumpled cigarette pack that's weeks old. A few coins. The usual detritus."

I sorted through the findings, the coins at the bottom of the pile. Two nickels, a dime, a quarter. One shiny penny.

"You printed the coins, of course."

"Smudged partials on all the coins except the penny. It was as fresh as from the mint."

"No help from the coins," I said. "No help from anything."

Gilly returned to her department, one building down the block. Clair entered, her face serious. Behind her was a slumping man in his sixties, his mahogany face bespeaking a lifetime in the sun. He was big-boned and wearing a gray work shirt and Levi's tucked into battered Wellingtons. Though strong and fit, sorrow had shrunken him and his clothes could have been hung over strands of vapor.

"Carson, this is Mr Silas Ballard. He's come to. . ." She caught herself, the words *identify the body* harsh and final. "To tell us what he can," she amended.

Clair led the man to the coolers. I saw his knees tremble and stepped to his back. When Clair opened the door Ballard went down, slowed by my hands under his arms. He began weeping and I helped him to a chair.

The standard meme is, *I'm sorry for your loss*. But years of repetition on cop shows and the like have turned it into parody, same as asking someone *How are you?* then turning away because an answer isn't expected.

"You're from Shuqualak, Mississippi, sir?" I said, taking another road. "Is that what I heard?"

For a moment the man did nothing. Then he seemed to hear my words and nodded at the floor.

"I've been through that area," I continued, trying to picture the region, to make it my link with the broken man beside me. "I hear it's some of the richest land to be found in the whole Delta. That seeds will sprout just being waved over the dirt."

Ballard cleared his throat. "My great grandaddy bought a eighty-acre parcel there in 1887. He planted fifty acres and Ballards been working that land ever since, adding a few acres here and there."

"How many acres is your place today, sir?"

"Over a thousand." Even through his grief there was pride in his words.

"Do other family members work the place?" I asked.

Ballard lifted his eyes from his hands. "It's been said the Ballards could grow anything 'cept more Ballards. I got one brother gone twelve years. A couple cousins up north, no interest in farming. All I had was Kayla. But we had each other."

"Kayla was going into farming?" I asked.

"She loved. . ." His voice broke and he swallowed hard. "She loved making things grow, was here getting her agriculture degree. I know all the old ways, Kayla was studyin' all the new. We figured together we could, we. . ." His voice broke.

"Did Kayla have a boyfriend, Mr Ballard?" I asked. "A special someone?"

"Tyler Charles, as fine a young man as you'll find. They was gonna get married when they got out."

"Where's Mr Charles today?" I asked. The boyfriend always got the first look. Often it was where we stopped.

"He's been three months in England. A place called Middlesborough College in North Yorkshire, wherever that is. Tyler got a prize . . . got to go there free. . ."

"A grant?"

Ballard nodded. "Ty's studying botany. He and Kayla was gonna get married in the Fall. I been building them a house on the land. Four bedrooms to handle the kids they wanted." He looked up. "Finally we was gonna have a bumper crop of Ballards."

"I'm so sorry," I said.

"It's all over," he whispered to the air.

"Pardon me, sir?"

Ballard swiped tears from his eyes with thick and callused fingertips. He pushed to his feet and shuffled to the window, staring into a wall of gray rain.

"I'd gotten to looking out over the land and seeing the future: fresh crops pushing up year after year. Grandkids playing, a big party at harvest time. Now all I'm ever gonna see is dirt."

There was little left to say. Clair and I walked Mr Ballard to the door and watched the rain wrap his form.

He seemed oblivious to the downpour, shuffling into the forever wreckage of his dreams.

"You all right, Clair?" I asked.

"The worst part of my job," she said. "Watching lives change for the worse." She nodded out the door and into the rain, Silas Ballard's form a dark smudge disappearing into gray. "Everything in that poor man's life is gone, Carson," she said quietly. "It's like the killer got him, too."

18

For two days Harry and I dug up anyone who might deliver insight into the last days of Kayla Ballard. She did not drink. Was terrified of drugs. She drove home every other weekend. The rare social forays were to church, campus movies and sporting events. Her number-one topic of discussion was farming.

No one had anything approaching a grudge toward Kayla Ballard. There was no hint of anything sexual. The purse I'd missed at the crime scene was in her dorm room, not generally carried, and I pretty much nixed robbery as a motive.

I contacted the chief of police in Ballard's hometown. *It's a small community*, he said, *everyone knows every-one's business.* Kayla Ballard was without enemy, without any kind of dark side. *Whatever went wrong,* was the unspoken conclusion, *it was based down there in your damn city.*

The next day I was parked a bit north of downtown, engine running to keep the AC flowing in the ninety-degree heat. Harry and I had split our duties, me dealing with the Ballard case, Harry pushing on the more quotidian killings that crowded our desks. The radio crackled with the dispatcher's voice.

"We've got a kid in the backyard at 423 Mason, Detective. Paramedics report a knife in his side. Lieutenant Mason says to boogie."

I knew the area: poor, tough, crime-ridden. I fired up the screamer and light show and pulled behind the forensic van alerted to the same call, arriving at an end-of-street house with a listing porch and torn-sheet curtains. It sat at the end of a line of similar houses owned by slumlords who charged the government outrageous sums to enclose the downtrodden. Behind the ragged boxes of despair stood rooflines of warehouses and factories.

I jogged past the house, jumping a rusting fence. I found a uniformed cop named Mailey who I'd never formally met, one of the first on the scene. When I asked, "What we got?" he nodded to the rear of the dirt backyard. I looked ahead, felt a punch in my gut.

A small form lay on the ground, a kid, black, aged ten or thereabouts. Two paramedics were above the body, one doing chest compressions as the other held an oxygen mask over the boy's face. They got him stabilized and onto a gurney, the handle of a hunting knife protruding from below his right ribs. In the liver.

"How's he doing, Wade?" I asked Wade Delacroix, pulling the front of the gurney.

"Wish us luck, Carson," was all he said, racing to the bus. I was left with the two first responders, the youngster named Mailey and his hulking partner, Horse Austin. Austin was in his fifties, old school, a too-large percentage of his collars visiting the emergency room for stitches, Austin claiming resisting arrest as the reason. Austin also loved citing people. If a kid got hit by a car and his mother ran into the street to help, Austin would cite the mother for jaywalking. Harry and I didn't much care for Austin, nor him for us.

"What was happening when you got here, Horse?" I asked.

Austin stifled a yawn, showing huge yellow teeth that could have crowded Secretariat's jaw. He scratched one of the big canines with a fingernail, flicked something away, and turned to me like an afterthought. "A neighbor came sneaking round the back looking for the mother and saw the kid. Lucky for the vic, since he was all alone here."

"Where's Mama?"

"At any one of a dozen bars. Or holed up in a crack house. You know the type, Ryder, all the motherly instincts of a clam. Squirt 'em out, collect the welfare."

I ignored his jibes, figuring Austin would be retired in two or three years, sitting in his living room watching football and polishing his cirrhosis. I'd seen him sneaking nips from a bagged bottle he kept in his cruiser kit.

"Why was the kid in the wheelchair?" I asked.

Austin put his hands in the small of his back, stretched, broke wind. "Hell if I know."

"You didn't think to ask, like maybe it could have been important to the medics?"

"The neighbor wasn't making much sense, Ryder, jabbering like a magpie. She wouldn't know nothing."

I looked to Mailey. "You didn't ask why the vic was in the chair either, Mailey?"

He shot a glance at Austin, like a kid hoping Daddy would save him. "Don't look at Horse," I growled to Mailey. "Look at me. Why was he in the chair?"

"Didn't think to ask."

"Next time get your head out of your ass. You see a vic has a medical condition, you ask what it is. You got me?"

Austin was in my face. "Get the fuck away from my partner, Ryder. Save your righteous bullshit for someone who cares."

"Detective Ryder?" called a voice from behind me.

I saw Jim O'Reilly walking up, beside him a rope-skinny middle-aged black woman in a pink housedress. O'Reilly was twenty-eight, one half of what the department called the O Team. "Here's the woman who found the boy," O'Reilly said. He headed to the rear of the lot.

The woman glared at Austin. "That big cop treat me like dirt, tell me to get outta the way."

"What brought you back here, ma'am?" I asked.

"The boy's mama is bad news, so I come to check a few times a day, make sure Tommy got food in his belly. Tommy a good boy, smart in school. Ain't no one want to hurt him."

"Why is Tommy in a wheelchair?"

"He got some disease where his body eat on his body. An audamune problem, something like that."

"Auto-immune?"

She nodded. "That's it."

I looked over Austin and Mailey, Austin jutting his equine jaw, Mailey studying the dirt at his feet.

"How hard was that?" I said.

I called the info to the hospital as O'Reilly came up from the backyard, a tumble of scraggly bushes. "There's an alley past the brush," he pointed. "One-way east to west. The fence is trampled to the ground."

I pushed through the brush, finding the windowless sides of warehouses and defunct factories, a tunnel of brick. "All the perp had to do was stop in the alley. Attack and retreat. Get every available uniform out on the street, O'Reilly, door to door, wino to wino. Find out if anyone saw a car back here, or anything suspicious."

"On it." He ran off.

"Detective Ryder!"

I turned and a hundred feet distant saw Ron O'Herlihy, the other half of the O Team, waving from the alley's intersection with the street. I ran his way, finding a horizontal yellow strip strung between a fence and drainpipe fifteen feet from the alley entrance. I ducked beneath the strip – a three-inch-wide plastic ribbon – and turned to the familiar repeated phrase:

POLICE LINE – DO NOT ENTER

O'Herlihy read my mind. "Not ours, Detective. We strung tape around a robbery scene on Edison Street last night, but someone else put that stuff up."

The tape made my blood run cold. "Don't touch it, Ron. Don't move – I need to get the techs over here."

I grabbed two scene techs and showed them the tape. They looked puzzled until I said, "It's not ours."

A glance passed between the techs. "The perp made certain he'd be alone," one said.

"Looks that way."

"Devious motherfucker," the other tech said. "All the perp had to do was pull a car-length into the alley, jump out and set the tape."

"Gave him his own private drive," the first one nodded.

As the techs carefully removed the tape for analysis, I headed back to the house, finding O'Reilly.

"I put the guys on the door-to-door, Carson. What now?"

I stared into the dirt backyard. "Pray the kid got a look at his attacker and lives to tell the tale."

Gregory padded across the call girl's floor in nothing but canvas slippers, not wanting his bare feet to touch the green carpet, a cut-pile petri dish culturing a hell's broth of biological hazards. The sex robot was in the bathroom washing with the hospital-grade antibacterial soap Gregory had provided. The regimen was simple: shower in the soap, rinse, repeat. Hair too. The next step was a potent mouthwash. Not that Gregory's lips would get near the robot's lips – most of the time it'd be turned away anyway – but he wanted to know nothing was festering in its food-hole.

Since Gregory had started his new life, he'd been too busy for all the bullshit associated with picking up regular women. Plus the recent event with the bleached-blonde bitch – *Do you always fart like that?* – had proved that the more expensive fuck-machines were superior to regular women. The only fun there was the hunt, and his latest adventures were fulfilling that need by ten thousand per cent.

Everything in his life seemed to have changed the night the two cops dragged him from his car and humiliated him in the center of the street. Or did his life actually change four days later, when little Kayla dropped to the ground whispering, *Daddy?*

Gregory heard the shower shut off and put his ear to the door, satisfied to hear the robot gargling. He returned to wandering the room, his hand dandling his genitals. The furnishings were simple: a king-size bed with small tables on either side, lamps on each table, a chair in the corner and a large bureau. He saw a packet of white powder on the bureau, picked it up and flicked it with a fingernail.

The robot emerged from the bathroom, a small black woman with flat breasts, slim hips and muscular, heavy-calved legs too large for her frame. Her close-cropped hair was bright yellow and her sole adornment was a slender ankle chain.

Gregory held up the packet of powder. "What's this?"

The woman stretched her arms and reclined on the bed. "Coke, baby. Primo quality. You wanna taste? Ten bucks a line and I guar-un-*tee* it'll set your brain free and put steel in your pecker."

"I don't use narcotics." Gregory started to replace the packet, but paused, again lifting it to his eyes. "What does it feel like?"

"Like you're a hundred feet tall," the robot purred, "and nothin' can get in your way."

Gregory saw his image in the full-length mirror. He flexed his biceps, showed his teeth, *Kristal-White Tooth Gel for that Sun-Bright Smile.*

"I feel a hundred feet tall now."

The robot rolled to the bedside table to pour some

cheap, sweet wine into a glass. It downed half the liquid and winked.

"Then it'll make you feel like God."

Gregory bounced the packet in his palm. It wouldn't hurt to try a bit of the powder, would it? But not now. Today had started busy and he still had much to do.

Reluctantly, he set the bag back atop the bureau.

19

Harry and I hit the streets and banged on our snitches as if they were bells, hearing nothing in tune with the case. At seven p.m. we heard Tommy Brink was drifting in and out of consciousness, his condition precarious. We found a small face with closed eyes. Chrome stands hovered by the bed like alien sentinels, on their arms the bags of pharmaceuticals filling Tommy's body. Arletta Brink sprawled in the bedside chair, Tommy's mother, late twenties, silver shorts as tight as paint, her green halter top displaying cleavage and tattoos. Her pink high heels were as bright as they were cheap. We entered with badges displayed, me in the lead.

"What you po-lice want?" she snapped.

"We need to talk to Tommy when he comes around."

"He don't wanna talk. Leave me be."

"Can we speak out in the hall, Miz Brink?"

An elaborate eye-roll. "What's wrong with here?"

"I don't want to disturb your son."

She sighed and followed us into the hall, leaning against the wall with arms crossed and one toe tapping her anger. Arletta Brink was maybe twelve years old emotionally, a fact highlighted by her rap sheet: shoplifting, public intoxication, assault, drunk and disorderly, resisting arrest.

"Where were you when this happened, ma'am?" I asked. "The attack."

The eyes went evasive. "I was visitin' a friend down the street. Jus' a few minutes. You can't say I did nothin' wrong."

"I wasn't making any inference, ma'am, I'm trying to establish the events."

"Events is what I say they is."

"Do you have any idea who would want to hurt Tommy?"

"How the hell I gonna know that?"

"Has Tommy received any threats?" I said, keeping my voice even. "Gotten into any trouble at school?"

"Trouble?" she cawed. "That boy spend his life in a wheelchair. I gotta stick the food in his mouth some of the time. And clean it away when it come out. How he gonna get in trouble?"

I'd been watching Brink's eyes, saw the pupil dilation. "Are you under the influence of anything, Miz Brink?"

She wobbled on the heels and jabbed a scarlet fingernail my way. "Who the fuck are you to talk to me like that? How about you kiss my—"

A shrill, piercing sound cut Brink short. I winced and turned to Harry, pinkies in the sides of his mouth. Harry could whistle the dead from their graves. Nurses were leaning out of rooms and looking our way. Harry walked to Brink, stopping one step away with his hands in his pockets.

"You spent good money on that buzz, Miz Brink, right?" he asked, his voice as pleasant as springtime birdsong.

"Hunh?"

"Some wine. Something for the pipe. I figure you got twenty, maybe thirty bucks invested in that buzz."

The chin jutted. "I doan know what you talkin' about."

"You spent good money on that high, Miz Brink. Be a shame to haul that buzz to a loud, smelly jail. Especially when you could make nice and let that sweet buzz bloom in this quiet hospital."

Harry was brilliant as usual, threatening not the woman, but the quality of her high. He looked past Brink and into the room. "Tommy's awake again, Missus Brink," he said. "May Detective Ryder and I please speak with him?"

A pause. "G'wan inside," Brink said.

"You coming in, ma'am?" Harry asked. "To see how your son's doing?"

"Hunh-unh," she said, digging in her purse for a crumpled pack of Kools. "I need a smoke."

We stepped into the room and I studied the monitors. I'd been in a lot of hospitals and knew when things seemed stable. The kid's eyes followed us.

"Where's Mama?" asked a paper-thin voice.

"She had to take care of something, Tommy," I said. "She said to tell you she'd be right back."

Tommy seemed dubious. I introduced us and pulled a chair close. "Do you remember anything about the attack, bud?"

"I was watching a big jet way up in the sky and wondering what it would be like to go through clouds. I heard footsteps behind me and felt a terrible hurt in my side and got knocked over."

"Did you see who it was?"

He shook his head. "I tried to git to the house but tipped over. I think I kind of passed out. I could hear, but it was like from far away. I heard a voice."

I scooted closer. "Man or woman, Tommy? Could you tell?"

He paused. "It seemed like a man."

"What did the voice say?"

"It wasn't words, just sounds. Like laughing. Then that Indian thing."

"Indian thing?" I asked.

"You know. . ." Tommy Brink pulled one hand from beneath the covers, cupped it over his mouth.

Went "*Woo-woo-woo.*"

Tommy Brink's eyes started drifting and Harry and I tiptoed quietly away, hoping the kid could turn sleep into healing. We headed down the corridor toward the elevators. Harry frowned at me.

"Woo-woo-woo?"

"Kid could've dreamed it," I said.

"Or the perp said something and it got garbled."

I flagged a nurse at the floor station. "Tommy Brink – he'll pull through, right?"

Her eyes went blank and she did the voice that tells you things are bad without saying bad. "Infection's a major concern since he's immuno-compromised. We're hoping for the best."

I nodded and walked away, seeing Arletta Brink step off the elevator like the hall floor was six inches higher. I figured whatever she was on, she'd had another taste.

In the lobby we headed to the main door, passing the information desk, almost bulldozed by a sixtyish black lady in a flower-print dress, a bag the size of a shopping sack under her arm. Her face was drawn.

"What room is Tommy Brink in?" she asked the blue-haired lady at the desk. "I need to see my poor sweet baby."

"Granny, you think?" Harry said.

I shot a look at the woman, shuffling toward the elevator with fear in her eyes.

"Or an aunt. At least Tommy's got someone who cares."

20

Morning arrived with dawn rain chased off by hot breezes from the southwest. Gregory pulled into the lot of a restaurant near the bay, gulls shrieking above like bleached rats with wings. The overpriced venue was the current favorite of Mobile's moneyed types and the lot was already crowded. He muttered about having to park at the rear and trudge through the soupy morning heat in a wool blazer. A dozen summer-weight blazers hung in his closet, but the wool was a particular iron-gray Gregory felt was the perfect complement to the subdued gentian in his irises, and he'd never been able to duplicate the color in a lightweight jacket.

As he passed the first rank of parked vehicles, head craning for a spot, Gregory saw a blue Dakota leaving a space in the row nearest the restaurant, another driver angling for the prime slot. Gregory squealed through a turn and raced down the front row. The other vehicle was in the oncoming lane, indicator signaling the driver's intention to enter the space.

Using the reversing Dakota as a shield, Gregory zipped into the spot. He grinned and shot a glance into the mirror as the loser cruised past his bumper, two blue-haired old women giving him the frosty eye. Gregory had recently seen a news clip suggesting exercise might improve memory in the elderly, and he figured the desiccated hags should thank him for the opportunity to hobble a couple hundred feet.

Exiting his vehicle, Gregory glanced at an open side door to the kitchen, two youngish men taking a cigarette break, one in waiter garb, the other in a stained dishwasher's apron. The pair puffed as Gregory walked the two dozen paces to the door.

He entered and crossed the floor, the restaurant at capacity, plates of food on the starched white tablecloths, the population heavily skewed to middle-aged and elderly women in designer clothes. Gregory knew most would be regulars, their weekly gobble-and-gossip session the highlight of useless, wastrel lives.

Ema was looking at her watch as Gregory walked up. A cup of tea sat in front of her, napkin centered on her wide lap. He tapped the back of her neck and she turned, startled.

"There you are, dear. I was, uh, getting worried again." An attempt at a smile. "Only a bit, though."

Gregory said nothing, wanting Ema to worry, punishment for all she'd put him through the other day.

The waiter arrived, a slim male robot in his mid-twenties with a mouth like a wet rose, his close-cropped black hair looking more painted-on than grown. His eyes were an emerald green. The man verged on being pretty and Gregory disliked him on sight.

While Ema scoured the menu, the wait-bot metronomed its pen against the order pad, probably to rush them. Was the moron too blind to note Gregory's jacket cost more than the man earned in a week?

Ema ordered an asparagus and chèvre crêpe with a side of hash browns, except here they were called pommes frites. The waiter turned to Gregory, the pen doing the tapping again. The robot's brass nameplate had greasy thumbprints on its surface.

"And you, sir?" the machine said.

"Bring me a simple spinach salad, no eggs, bacon, onions or mushrooms. Vinaigrette dressing. Wholewheat toast, dry." Gregory ate nothing that grew underground, or pushed from the unspeakably filthy interior of a chicken.

"Basically a bowl of spinach, then. And to drink?"

"A pot of tea and a small pitcher of honey."

The waiter nodded at honey packets in a basket centering the table. "There's honey in the basket, sir."

Gregory felt a surge of anger and pushed it down his throat. Had he not requested a goddamn *pitcher* of honey?

"There's honey in the kitchen. It's used to cook. Pour some into a small pitcher and bring it to me."

A nod. "Very good. I'll see what I can do."

The ridiculous excuse for a man was back in two minutes, a small pitcher in hand. He set it on the table, said, "There you go, sir, honey."

The man went to serve another group of diners. Gregory scowled at the man's small and high derriere until Ema's voice broke into his thoughts. "Was that man being short with you, do you think?" Ema asked.

"I don't think so, Ema," Gregory said, watching the man take the order of the other group. Looking as though he was actually *serving* them.

"He seemed rather dismissive," Ema said, resettling her napkin in her capacious lap.

Gregory took the pitcher of honey, inspected the contents carefully, and poured it into the carafe of tea, stirring with a butter knife as Ema watched in fascination. "When did you develop such a taste for honey?"

"The majority of microorganisms can't reproduce in honey," Gregory said. "It involves the water index, an indication of the energy status in an aqueous system." Gregory pulled a silver pen from his pocket and began writing on the white linen napkin. "I can show you the exact formula, taking p as the vapor pressure and. . ."

Ema reached across the table and stilled Gregory's hand. "I'll take your word for it, dear. You know I don't have a head for numbers."

Gregory held his flash of anger. Every time he tried to teach Ema something important, she demurred. How was she to ever become more than she was?

Ema's meal arrived and she shoveled with delight, her mouth showing the glistening slop ready to be squeezed into a bolus. The pair traded small talk, Ema carrying ninety per cent of the conversation as always, Gregory nodding assent or assuming the faces Ema liked to see, all the time conscious of the insolent waiter, seeing his slender form flash by at the edge of vision, two tables away, one table away, three. . .

Never quite close enough.

Ema finished her breakfast and studied Gregory as a busboy robot cleared the dishes. "There's something different about you today. More assured. More intense, like you're suddenly. . ." She struggled to frame her words.

"Alive?" Gregory said quietly, a smile ghosting his lips.

Ema chuckled nervously. "That's an odd choice of word."

"It seemed the direction you were going."

"I'm not sure where I was headed. You seem . . . bigger. Like you take up more space." Ema paused to listen to her own words, then shook her frilly curls. "That's silly, right?"

"You're never silly, dear Ema." Gregory reached across the table to take her hand, a simple gesture she seemed to relish. He was pleased that even Ema recognized his new energy. He showed *Minty Fresh* smile, but his eyes scanned the floor for the waiter . . . *There!* One-handing a silver tray of dishes above his head and moving in their direction.

Closer, you insolent fool. . .

The waiter paused to answer a question from a diner, then continued. When he was about to pass the table, the waiter shot Gregory a glance and they locked eyes. Turning his head the opposite direction, Gregory threw his leg out. The waiter tripped over it, his body slamming the floor as the tray came clattering down, bacon, eggs, sausages, coffee, juice . . . all splattering across the carpet. Every head in the restaurant turned.

The waiter sat upright, his eyes flashing at Gregory. "You . . . did that on purpose," he whispered. "You saw me and you stuck your leg out."

Gregory's eyes bored into the eyes of the robot. "I'd be damned careful what you say, moron," he hissed. The waiter started to respond, but several staffers arrived to assist and he turned away to gather the strewn items.

"The man . . . accidentally tripped over your leg?" Ema asked, her face anxious.

"The man never touched my leg," Gregory said. "He stumbled over his own feet. It's easy enough to understand why. He's obviously on drugs."

"You can tell?" Ema said, eyes wide.

"His pupils were dilated," Gregory explained, a note of condescension in his voice. "I'm surprised you didn't notice, given all that crime TV you soak up."

"You're amazing," Ema said. She looked toward the waiter, now disappearing into the kitchen. "Shouldn't you mention it to the management? The drugs?"

Gregory sighed. "It's a difficult job market and I can't

bring myself to be the cause of a man's termination. What if he has a family dependent on him? Babies?"

Ema gazed at Gregory in wonder. "You are a saint, dear," she said. "I never would have considered such a thing."

They parted soon after, Gregory washing his hands for several minutes before leaving. Arriving at his car he saw someone had spat on his windshield, a thick retrieval from the deepest recesses of someone's lungs. Gregory fought to keep his food contained in his belly. Averting his eyes, he entered his car and turned on the wipers, forgetting to hit the washer button. When he glanced up, the wipers had smeared phlegm across the entire driver's-side window. Unable to hold himself any longer, Gregory leaned from his door, vomiting.

He pulled himself upright and groped for the washer button, spraying until he heard the grind of an empty reservoir. When he finally looked at the window, it was clear. Still, he visited a car wash on his way home, passing through twice.

It wasn't until he pulled up in his own drive that he recalled the men smoking outside when he'd parked in the lot, idly watching Gregory enter the restaurant. He focused his mind on the memory. One of them was the robot Gregory had punished.

The waiter had known his car.

21

When I arrived in the morning, Harry was hunched over his keyboard, coffee mug to the side, staring into the screen. He was wearing an orange shirt, lime tie, strawberry jacket, plum slacks. I didn't know whether to greet him or harvest him.

"Am I interrupting your morning porn session?" I said, Harry still immersed in the monitor.

He pushed away from his desk. "You think there's any possibility the Ballard killer and Tommy Brink's attacker are one and the same?"

I sat and perched my chin on tented fingers. "The attacks were brazen: Ballard on a well-used pathway, the Brink boy in his own backyard. Using crime-scene tape to shut down the alley shows a creative mindset, using police tools to help foil discovery. The Ballard killing probably required a disguise. The difference in weapons is what's keeping me from a full yes. Freaks like consistency."

"What if the guy doesn't need a particular weapon, his only need being one that best fits his attack mode?"

"That's a nasty thought," I said. When tracking psychos you wanted set patterns that might be used against them. A killer with a fluid and ever-changing methodology was much harder to profile, much harder to find.

"Still, I started thinking how a knife is easy to conceal. When you mentioned the crossbow being a strange thing to carry, hard to hide, I got to wondering. I did a little research, found this. . ."

Harry turned the monitor my way and I saw what appeared to be a typical crossbow, save for a pistol-style grip. It was also, judging by the arm in the photo, about half the size of a standard crossbow.

"A pistol crossbow?" I said, reading the text. "One-handed use?"

"A spring-steel bow," Harry said. "Check the dimensions. You could hide it in a backpack or beneath a jacket. Whip it out, wham off a shot, jam it under cover. I'll bet it could be done in five seconds."

"Jesus," I said, reading deeper into the text. "The damn thing can drive a fiberglass bolt an inch deep into a pine board from ten feet."

Harry brought up a page offering a dozen pistol crossbows ranging from twenty-buck models to the hundred-and-seventy-five-buck Handhunter Pro. *Stalk and Shoot with Deadly Accuracy,* the copy claimed in blood-red typc.

I stared at the screen as Harry put on his gun, heading out to grab a couple of uniforms and hit Tommy Brink's neighborhood again, trying to leverage sympathy for the kid into information.

I reviewed interviews with the friends and associates of Kayla Ballard, one question foremost: if thc cases were linked, how was a farm girl from middle Mississippi connected to a wheelchair-bound kid from inner-city Mobile? The disparity of their worlds was apparent in their parents, the broken Silas Ballard and Arletta Brink, the party girl who treated her son like an afterthought. It seemed the killer had dealt one a blow beyond measure, provided the other with a favor.

I was moving from one stack of paper to another when the phone rang. I picked it up and listened, then closed my eyes. For a minute I sat there, numb. Then I pulled my cell and displayed Harry's number, taking a deep breath before pressing Call.

"Nothing yet," he answered, thinking I was hoping for a lead. "But we've just started down the street at the corner of the block and—"

"The kid's dead, bro," I said.

"What?" A whisper.

"Tommy Brink took some kind of infection last night and the antibiotics couldn't handle it. He passed an hour ago, Harry."

"You OK, Carson?" he said, hearing my voice.

"I'm fine," I lied.

I hung up and sat at my desk. Detectives jogged the floor around my cubicle, spoke on phones, pecked at computers. I couldn't hear a thing, my ears consumed by a roar so loud it closed my eyes and made my hands clench tight in my lap.

22

Brrrrrring . . . brrrrrring . . .

The sound of my landline phone in the kitchen. My eyes snapped open, saw the half-moon above, a pale ghost in a twilight sky. I was in a lounger on my deck, Tommy Brink's case file on my chest and two empty beer bottles at my side.

Brrrrrring . . .

I shot a glance at my watch: 7.40 at night. My phone connected to an ancient cassette tape answering machine with all the electronic sophistication of a doorbell. I kept it for the audio quality. Cell phones could tell you your position on earth, but not the gender of your caller.

"Hello, Detective Ryder. This is Wendy Holliday. From the academy? I don't mean to bother you but I was in the area . . . I mean, on Dauphin Island. Actually,

I was looking for a place to grab supper, wondered if you had any recommendations. I guess I'll see you in class. Bye."

I ran for the phone but arrived too late. Holliday hadn't left a number and my Clinton-era machine didn't record them. *It's no big deal*, I told myself, tapping the phone with my forefinger. I'll see her Tuesday with the rest of the class.

But she was so close – and so obviously hungry – that it seemed uncivil to not try and reach her. *Aha!* I thought. As an Academy instructor I had received all of my students' addresses and numbers. I dug to the bottom of my briefcase – finding several loose pennies from my example in class – and located Holliday's cell number.

"Detective Ryder? I hope I didn't bother you."

"No bother at all. And outside of class it's Carson. What brings you to our friendly little island?"

"Biking. I got here an hour ago, put in twenty miles, stopped for some fuel and thought you could give me a tip on a decent meal."

"Where are you?"

"By the ferry dock."

I thought a moment. "Listen, Wendy, if all you want is fuel for the belly and not tinkly-piano ambience, I've got roast beef in the fridge. I can knock out sandwiches."

A pause. "How do I get to the restaurant du Rydair?" she said, a smile in her voice.

Suddenly wide awake, I gave Holliday the directions, then showered. I traded shredded cut-offs and my CRAZY AL'S MARINA AND BAR tee for green cargo pants and a fresh blue shirt, stepped into brown moccasins and switched to anti-disarray mode. Files and pages hiding the dining-room table were whisked into a single pile. Dishes in the sink went into the dishwasher, shoes piled by the door got kicked into the closet.

The place looked reasonably clean. I checked the neatness of my bookshelf – *Whoops* finding a condom package rising from the pages of a recent read, a bookmark. I tapped it down and stepped to my small porch overlooking the street. The sun was a sedate orange orb in the low western sky, filling the wind-rippled sand of my yard with blue shadows. The nearest dwelling was to the west, a stilted Cape Cod-influenced house owned by a couple from Ohio who wintered there.

A small blue SUV was moving my way. The vehicle turned onto my brief street of crushed shells, stopped, backed into my driveway. Holliday drove a well-used Toyota RAV4 with a bright yellow bicycle on the roof, a super-skinny model with turned-down handlebars and a seat whose width I could have covered with my palm. Holliday exited, waving as I stepped down to meet her.

A limited amount of women can wear Spandex in a complimentary fashion, but Holliday pulled it off, her top white, tight, and short-sleeved, festooned with colorful logos. Purple shorts reached her knees and glistened as if wet. Her auburn hair was tied back with a hank of red fabric.

I nodded at her top as I walked up. "You look like a NASCAR driver."

She grimaced. "I won it in a race last year. They come with crap written all over them. Still, the things retail for a hundred bucks, so I use it."

We stood silent for a second, both trying to find something to say. She looked beneath my house where my kayak hung between pilings.

"My God, a Whisky 16. What a great boat!"

"You paddle?" I asked.

"I've got a Dagger Axis. Inexpensive, but I love it." She ran to my boat. Behind it was a shoulder-high cinderblock enclosure of three walls with an opening covered by a black plastic curtain. She smiled. "If I remember beach houses, that's a shower."

"Your memory's fine."

She pinched the damp fabric between her modest breasts. "I've been pedaling pretty hard. Would you mind if I, uh. . ."

I opened a plastic tub beside the shower enclosure and pulled out a fresh towel, hung it over the curtain rod. She ran to her RAV and grabbed a backpack. I started upstairs.

"Drink, Wendy?" I called over my shoulder.

"Whatever you're having."

I heard the squeak of the faucet followed by the shower running and stepped into my living room. When I realized one meter beneath my feet water was rushing over Holliday's unclothed body, I reddened and tiptoed to the kitchen to give her privacy.

Ten minutes later, she was stepping through the front door, the *Tour de France* garb replaced by multi-pocketed tan hiker's shorts and a white, scoop-neck tank top. The missile-sleek bike shoes were now sandals.

Mix-up rocketed into the room with his wide tail whisking like a broom. He was a big dog and every part of him seemed from a different breed, hence the name. He somehow understood I'd saved him from the euthanasia needle with minutes to spare and made each second count, joy-wise. Holliday dropped to her knees and scruffed Mix's massive head and thumped his shoulders. When he dragged his tongue over her face she seemed unfazed.

"That's Mr Mix-up," I said belatedly. "He's on his way outside." I opened the door and he thundered down the steps to play Whack-A-Mole with the sand crabs.

"Feeling cooler?" I asked Holliday when the canine uproar had passed, handing over a tall and lime-inflected Tanqueray and tonic. I know the vodka-tonic has gained ascendance, but vodka has all the magic of rubbing alcohol; good gin has sorcery in its soul. Holliday sipped and shot an enthusiastic thumbs up.

"What I needed: cold water down, firewater up."

She inspected the art on my walls and gravitated to an oil painting two feet tall, almost as wide. At first glance it seemed abstract, hard edges trailing into soft-ened forms, tinted glazes stacked on colors. The casual viewer saw only the colorful surface, but the painting invited a select few into its depths and I waited to see if she saw the deep end.

"My God, Carson. It's you."

"Painted by a friend named Nike Charlane," I explained. "It was a gift for helping her niece out of a jam a while back."

I saw the standard question in her eyes, not prompted by the painting, but by the whole package: a beachfront home on one of the area's most-desired – and therefore most expensive – communities, Dauphin Island.

"I didn't get the place on a policeman's salary," I explained. "My mother left an inheritance. Not big, but enough for this."

Not long after my mother's death, I had been fishing the surf on the Island. Passing by a tidy house standing on tall stilts, it seemed I had two choices in life: use the newly acquired money to live a simple, bohemian life, or take Harry's advice and enter the police academy. I noted that the house had a For Sale sign and when I inquired on a whim, found buying the house would use up all of my inheritance and make it necessary to find employment.

I dreamed of the house for days, waking in my cheap inner-city apartment with the sound of surf outside my window. When I opened my curtains I saw a white and gull-studded strand, not the grumble of city traffic. A lifted window didn't pull in the smell of fried food and truck exhaust, but sea breeze and the saline scent of tide pools evaporating into the blue sky. A week later I was in the academy signing the roster. Ten days later I was pulling into the drive of my new home with an eight-foot U-Haul holding all my worldly and battered possessions.

Most days I thought I'd made the right choice.

As Holliday continued her viewing, I pulled a roast from the fridge, plus a wedge of stilton and a crock of dark, whole-seed mustard. The breadbox held a dense loaf of rye bread and my veggie basket offered a Vidalia onion.

"I've got chips," I said. "They're probably not what a tight, fit cyclist snacks on, right?"

"We usually eat nuts and berries," she affirmed, entering the kitchen, taking the bag, and pouring a pile of chips over her sandwich.

We sat on the deck with the sun just below the horizon and lighting the western sky with an amber glow, turning the sea to shimmering gold as the pleasure boats drifted homeward. Holliday nodded at the pedestrian beach traffic, perhaps a dozen folks wandering the quarter-mile of visible beach. A football field away a young mother shooed her three children indoors as she picked up sand pails, swim floats, beach chairs.

"Do most of these people live here year-round?" she asked.

"Mostly tourists this time of year. You can always tell the tourists by their sunburns."

She grinned, pointing a hundred feet distant. "That one looks scared even dusk will give him a sunburn."

I saw a man in khakis and boat shoes, an outsized Oxford hunting shirt above. His hat was white and floppy, his neck strung with binoculars. He had a camera slung around his wrist.

Holliday chuckled. "Probably coated with sunscreen, at least the three square inches of skin that are showing." As if hearing us, the man aimed the field glasses toward the deck. Resisting the urge to wave, I turned back to Holliday, a much more interesting view.

"So," I said, tilting my glass for a sip. "What made you want to be a cop?"

She frowned. "My motivations aren't something I usually talk about."

"We can talk about the weather."

Holliday went to the railing and studied the golden sea for a full minute, then looked to me, her eyes troubled and her voice as low as if in a confessional.

"My father manufactured methamphetamine, Carson. Selling to biker gangs, where it was distributed across the country. I guess that's how the story starts."

She had left her drink at the table and I carried it over. The tourist was angling toward the public-access point for this stretch of beach and craning his head our way again. Reluctant to leave, he produced a blanket from his backpack and sat in the sand at the edge of the sea grass.

"This was when?" I asked.

"Eighteen years ago. The lab was in the country and got raided one afternoon. My mother and I were in the living room of an old farmhouse, Daddy was in the barn, where he made his meth. I was reading a book, Mama was staring out the window, pretty much what she always did. I heard her say something and looked up. I said, 'What, Mama?' But she just got a strange smile on her face and said, 'Free.'"

"Free?" I asked.

"Seconds later a cop on a bullhorn said the house was surrounded. I think Mama smiled when she saw the cops taking position outside."

"Her only hope to be shed of your father?"

She nodded. "I remember how quiet it was for the next five or ten seconds, then all hell broke loose. My father ran into the room with an automatic rifle. He had about twenty guns stashed around the house."

"Paranoid."

"That day was even worse. Not only were there cryptic calls on our police radio – he was never without one – Daddy had also been sampling from his meth batch."

"Bad circle," I said, having seen it plenty before. He'd freak at what he was hearing on the airwaves, hit some meth, the meth making him even more paranoid about the radio. . .

She nodded. "I'd been reading a book about mummies and remember how his eyes looked like the eyes of a sarcophagus, all shiny and empty. Daddy started laughing and fired out the window, full auto. One of the cops was hit in the face, killed instantly. A second died at the hospital. A third took a round to the throat but lived, though he had to retire."

I felt my mouth fall open. I'd heard the story, a decade before my time as a cop, but I recalled the photo from the newspaper and TV: a wild-eyed man crouching in a doorway, one hand pulling a young girl in a white frock to his body, the other holding an automatic pistol to her head.

Between the photographer and the crazed man a body lay sprawled in the grass – the mother, shot to prove to the cops the man would kill his daughter unless the cops retreated. I recalled the confused face of the little girl, like she wanted to turn to her father for a hug. A second later a police sharpshooter terminated the stand-off.

"Your father was Virgil Haskins," I said.

She nodded. "I started the day with two parents, ended as an orphan. I was headed to foster care, but one of the officers took me under her wing – Angela Welles."

"State police," I said. "Welles operated out of the Birmingham HQ."

I had met Angela Welles twice, once when she addressed a law-enforcement convention in Huntsville six years ago, the other at a similar event in Birmingham. She was a committed street cop and early promoter of now-fashionable concepts like community-oriented policing, cops paid to learn second languages, and improved computer modeling of criminal activity. A tall and gangly woman with a salty tongue and ready smile, Welles was homely as a mud hut, but smarter than most of her superiors and not afraid to tell them so.

"After all I'd been through, I was a mess," Holliday continued, "but Angela alternately schmoozed and brow-beat people in the social-service system until I received the best counseling and therapy. She was there at every session. Three months later she took me in."

"Didn't Welles retire a few years back?" I said.

"A medical discharge," Holliday affirmed. "Ovarian cancer. Angela died two years ago."

I let my eyes show my condolences. "I had no idea Sergeant Welles adopted . . . the little girl in the news-paper photo."

"I was always a foster. She never legally adopted me. Angela's life-partner was a woman named Laurie Leger."

I understood. This was Alabama and lesbians attempting to adopt would have pulled every fundamen-talist shrieker and political hack to the nearest micro-phone to decry an abomination in God's eyes. It always amazed me how many spiritual myopics claimed access to God's vision.

"So that's why you're not Wendy Welles."

"I took my mother's maiden name when I turned eighteen. It was part of a long process."

Shedding the past, bit by injurious bit. I'd done the same to escape a family name encompassing the death of my abusive father and a crime spree involving the deaths of five women, the killings attributed to my brother, Jeremy Ridgecliff. I had come to believe his participation in the women's murders was secondary and unwilling, though Jeremy never denied killing our father, claiming it as his finest moment.

I turned to Holliday and started to speak, cut off by a raised hand. "Can we switch to a different subject, Carson? It's still painful. Not the childhood stuff, which seems like something that happened on the other side of the planet, but losing Angela."

Again, I sympathized. My childhood hadn't retreated to the far side of the planet, more like ninety degrees. I could always see it from the corner of my eye.

"Let's avoid cop talk altogether," I said. "You pick the subject."

She thought a moment. "How about favorite kayaking location?"

"Sounds safe," I said.

An incredible evening, Gregory thought, kicking the sand from his shoes. The MPD's computer system had the security of a wet cardboard box and he'd found Ryder's address in seconds. He'd made two trips past the single-story stilt-standing home in two days, taking pictures and studying the neighborhood. Dauphin Island was expensive; that Ryder could afford to live there meant he was paid far more than a regular policeman.

Gregory had parked two hundred yards away, one more anonymous tourist shuffling along the beach and kicking at shells and seaweed. When Gregory saw motion beneath the house – two human forms! – he had pulled a towel from his backpack and sat down at the edge of the dunes a hundred feet from Ryder's house. No one was near, so he'd angled his vibration-damped Nikon binoculars toward Ryder and a woman with wind-blown hair and bicycle clothes so tight Gregory could see nipples pressing the fabric.

But the joy of watching Ryder and his woman got even better: Ryder ran upstairs and the woman got naked in the shower under Ryder's house. Gregory couldn't see much with the curtain across the shoulder-high enclosure, but he watched her rub suds into her gleaming hair, a smile on her face. When he visualized Ryder mounting and penetrating the woman he grew hard in his pants.

The woman had pulled on fresh clothes and climbed the steps. Minutes later they exited the house carrying plates. Gregory walked nonchalantly past the house and sat a hundred feet away on a blanket, aching to move closer. But both Ryder and the woman had glanced at Gregory several times and he had known it was time to leave.

No problem . . . he was getting comfortable in the neighborhood.

23

Two days passed with no further insight into the killings. The media broadcast the attacks, but without anything tying them together, other stories dominated. The upcoming fishing derby in the Gulf was a major annual event, the renowned Southern chef Paula Deen would soon make an appearance in Mobile, and a fire at a large warehouse quickly pushed our cases from public note.

The third morning found me awake before dawn, sitting on the deck as a storm front dragged toward the land, smelling rain well in advance of its arrival in howling sheets that beat the gray sea into a froth. By the time the front had passed, leaving low dark clouds that drizzled erratically, I was in my bedroom pulling on my darkest suit.

Today was the day of Tommy Brink's funeral.

Given Ms Brink's attitude toward police, I probably

wasn't welcome, but killers sometimes attended the services of their victims, enthralled by their handiwork. Harry would be there, as well as two guys chosen for their ability to spot unusual behavior while blending into a crowd. I'd hoped to enlist a woman, but all were on other assignments.

I thought a moment, tying my tie for the fourth time, and reached for my phone.

"Hello?"

"Wendy, this is Carson Ryder. Doing anything for the next two hours or so?"

"I was going to study for your class. Got another offer?"

I was on my way to pick her up ten minutes later. She stepped from her apartment in a pitch-perfect dress, charcoal gray, mid-calf, with dark hose and black pumps. She carried a small black clutch purse and an umbrella.

When we arrived at the cemetery, the rain had returned, the sky as gray as slate. Harry was standing by his old red Volvo wagon, hiding his surprise when Holliday exited my truck.

"Are we ready?" I asked, looking toward the white tent in the distance.

"As I'll ever be," Holliday said.

"Once again into the breach," I said, taking a deep breath and pushing my feet forward.

I'd always felt the funeral of an elderly person should be on a bright day where the sun shone down and the world resolved into tight detail, a day for celebration, since a person who had made a long passage – long and healthy, hopefully – should shine hope across the attendees and lighten their natural sorrow. But I also felt the funerals of children were best served by days of rain and chill, dark clouds hovering, since a life drawn short was an ugly thing, and for the sun to warmly and merrily illuminate such an occasion seemed far too harsh an irony.

But I was reconsidering my thoughts as I walked to the gravesite, Harry and Holliday at my side, our umbrellas beaten by rain. Bright and open days are best for all such events, I thought, with cloud-free skies of depthless blue and our sorrow wide in the light of a blazing sun as we balance life against grief. Low gray skies and a mocking rain serve only to compress us into ourselves, perhaps the worst place to be at such moments.

I kept my eyes moving as we walked among others heading toward the gravesite. But the poor and ragged folks I saw had no hint of the madman or killer in their eyes, only grief.

There were perhaps four dozen in attendance, more women than men, the women mostly past fifty. I saw Arletta Brink at the graveside, staring blankly as a young and suited man from the funeral parlor held an umbrella above. No one had told her to dress in black or, if so, she'd ignored or forgotten it, her scarlet dress short and with a low neckline. Beside her was the sixtyish woman we'd seen at the hospital, her face a mask of sorrow, a tissue at her eyes.

I let my eyes wander the encircling marble monuments, many holding baskets of flowers real and false. My focus drifted across the open grave to Harry, hands crossed at his waist, his eyes scanning. To the right I saw Preston Fuller, a lifelong beat cop who'd seen everything and could spot an out-of-place person the way most people could tell blue from red.

When the service was over and the simple box had descended into the earth, Harry and I crossed to pay our respects to Miz Brink as she stood leaning against a tree and smoking a cigarette. The older woman was six paces away, staring into the open grave. I saw that she was shaking, though the morning was becoming hot.

"What you po-lice doing here?" Brink asked as we walked up.

"We came to pay our respects, Miz Brink," Harry said. "We're sorry for your—"

"I doan need y'all's respect. Ain't nothing but a lie anyway." She stomped away and I approached the woman beside the grave.

"Excuse me, ma'am. You're Tommy's grandmother?"

I don't think she heard. I felt a hand on my arm and turned to a frail and elderly woman in her eighties. The hand drew me from the woman at the grave, a few paces away. "That's Miz Francine Minear, Tommy's aunt on his mama's side," the woman whispered. "She's all tore up inside. That boy was her whole life."

I heard a soft wail and looked to the woman at the grave. Tears were racing down her cheeks and dropping from beneath the veil.

"Do you have any idea why someone would try and

hurt Tommy, ma'am?" I asked the woman at my side. "Has anyone said anything about why?"

She shook her head. "That boy was pure joy, never made an enemy. Arletta prob'ly didn't tell you Tommy was set to get a new operation where they change the insides of your bones. It makes your body fix itself. Five more months, Tommy would have been fixed."

"How could I do that?" the woman at the grave whispered.

"Excuse me, sir," the woman beside me said, stepping to Tommy's aunt, who was shaking as if she was being ripped asunder from within.

"I could have taken that boy as my own," she said to herself, voice growing louder. "God knows Arletta gave me reason enough. But I failed him, always hoping Arletta would learn what a fine little angel she'd been blessed with. It should be me down in that ground, but it's an innocent lamb never did nothing but love people."

I'd seen stress hysteria before and knew she was slipping fast. The elderly woman by my side waved for the other mourning women then threw her arms around her distraught companion. But Francine Minear tore free and dropped to her knees beside the hole, head craned toward the sky.

"Take me, God," she screamed. "And bring Tommy back! Kill ME!"

A half-dozen women in black raced to the aunt, the minister running in as well. "KILL ME INSTEAD," Tommy's aunt begged the clouds, her make-up dissolving

157

down her face, her hat and veil tumbling from her head and into the grave. "PLEASE KILL *ME!*"

"I think we're done here," I said.

It was late afternoon when Gregory pulled into the cemetery, the recent rain rising as steam toward a clearing sky. Assuring himself the path was clear – five hours now since the service – he parked and strode the grass with a bouquet in hand. He passed the mounded dirt of a fresh grave, the small stone engraved with the name of Thomas T. Brink and the ten-year span of his existence.

Gregory continued to a large slab of marble commemorating the Weisses, Johanna and Howard, dead for over a decade and their grave flanked by two flower-filled urns. Gregory reached into an urn to retrieve a video camera the size of a pack of cigarettes. Aimed at Tommy Brink's service, the recorder had vacuumed two hours of data.

He was on the road minutes later, taking another surveillance run past a house on the southern side of Mobile, one inhabited by a pair of men. He'd added it to his list of potentials a few days ago, and was now making observations several times a day.

I returned home at five and walked Mr Mix-up along the strand, weaving through tourists and letting giggling kids pet my odd-looking pooch, a hundred-plus pounds of patchwork parts and colors. Mix-up responded by rolling in the sand, his tail whipping circles and his tongue darting at every face that neared.

But it was more than children who found fascination with Mix-up. His impromptu admirers included a number of women in their late twenties and thirties who studied Mix-up's jaunty saunter for several moments before running over to lavish attention.

It didn't escape me that many were tourist ladies in swimwear, the newly purchased suits too abbreviated for casual poolside at their northern apartments or swim clubs, but perfect for coastal beaches where sun sought skin and the anonymity of a one-week stay kept bright shreds of cloth flying from the shops of Dauphin Island. In the past – and here I'm going back weeks – I might have allowed Mix-up to lead me past laughs and explanations about his name into drinks on my deck as the sun hid under night and the white moon turned pleasant talk to husky whispers.

Instead I let him lead me away, down the beach and home, my only deck companions my dog and the hiss of low waves on wet sand. I was too benumbed by the day to seek anything but quiet and, truth be told, the one woman that seemed to fit in my mind was Wendy Holliday.

24

"*Grigor?*" A man's voice. "*Are you hungry?*"

Gregory was dreaming. He rarely dreamed or, if he did, a special wall in his mind never let him see himself dreaming. When he'd first come to America, he had terrible dreams. Dreams he could walk through, as if a path had been installed within the dream. When nothing stopped the dreams, Gregory heard a voice in his head. "Build a wall," the head-voice said. "A wall between you and the dream. They can't hurt you when you don't see them."

"*You're here late tonight . . . Doctor.*" A woman's voice. "*And you look sad.*"

"*Ceauşescu's time has been over for four years, Nurse Vaduva. We've been too far from prying eyes, but it's all dissolving. Our time is nearly over. Are we alone?*"

"*Until dawn . . . Emil.*"

160

"*Who sits at the guard desk tonight, Sorina?*" the Doctor said. Gregory couldn't see his real face, it was behind a mask turned inside out. He couldn't even see the mask, just its rippled and yellow backside. Over the mask the Doctor wore opaque metal glasses. Sometimes a slit opened in the mask and displayed three silver teeth, two canines up, one incisor down. They filled the quivering slit with vampire light.

"*Big Petrov and Cojocaru,*" Sorina Vaduva said. All Gregory saw of the nurse's face was a pair of high and angular cheekbones that resembled bat wings. Her body was full within the gray uniform.

"*Ah, our very good friends and midnight companions. But what about the, uh, oversight?*"

"*Tonight's Securitate officer is old Anatolie Lungu. Give him a few leus and a bottle of vodka and he'll go home and get drunk. Who else might be invited?*"

Dr Popescu scratched his chin and pretended to think. "*How about that hot dish of spice from the records staff?*"

"*Little Dragna Negrescu? The one who looks like a girl?*"

"*And who has the appetites of a woman. Several women.*"

A nervous chuckle. "*Dragna Negrescu scares me. A records clerk makes a few strokes of a pen and I might drop two grades in pay. Or disappear.*"

Popescu laughed. "*Even your paranoia is sexy, Sorina.*

Plus Dragna Negrescu can't scare you too much – I've noticed you and Dragna enjoying one another."

"I enjoy many things, Emil. Especially your little robots."

But the wall hadn't worked tonight. If Gregory knew he was dreaming the wall had failed. He had no choice but to step onto the path and be propelled through his dream. The step pulled him. . .

Into a cavern of shadows. A small lamp flickered from a corner. Gregory knew this place; the large supply room behind the kitchen, stocked with cans of food, barrels of cooking oil, metal bed frames for the floor, mattresses, light fittings and bulbs.

"You have splendid vodka tonight," the nurse named Sorina said, raising her glass. "And such food!"

"Plus tuica made from plums as sweet as your mouth," the Doctor said, taking the woman's hand and licking her fingertips. "There must be food: carnati, piftie, mamaliga. Call Petrov and Cojocaru. And, of course, sweet Dragna. Tell them time grows short and we must enjoy our remaining nights to the fullest. Hurry, then we'll go select tonight's robots."

The room spun to show the far side, a broad set of double doors. The Doctor appeared beside the doors and they opened with a sound of thunder. Gregory watched a white trail drift into the room with a slinky, feline grace. The trail was the smell of food. It began to fill the room like fog.

The Doctor made his way to a bed where a young

boy with huge eyes and pale lips sat, his nose inspecting the scents in the air. The boy's eyes did not register the man beside him, his face held no expression. It was the face of the orphanage.

The Doctor leaned until his mouth was at the boy's ear.

"*Grigor?*" he whispered. "*Are you hungry?*"

From the far side of the long room another door opened, the one from the girls' dormitory. Four small balloons floated behind Sorina Vaduva. They drifted into the fog and disappeared.

The dream-path delivered Gregory to the supply room. Several adults were there now, and the balloons were children. The Doctor led the children to the kitchen, where plates of food awaited.

In the supply room a huge man and a smaller one were pulling mattresses from a stack by the wall and setting them on the floor. They wore blue uniforms. The uniforms were wrinkled and poorly washed and Gregory could smell the men's bodies. The nurse took another drink from a bottle and went to the bathroom, an open pipe that led to a trough in the basement, from there to the river.

A second woman watched from a small desk. She had a petite body and was eating from a plate of sausages and licking her fingers. Her mask was a doll's face held in place with string, pink cheeks and lips as red as apples. The eyes were bottomless holes. Her name was Dragna Negrescu and she had unbuttoned her official tunic. Gregory saw her breasts bobbing within the folds.

Dragna Negrescu stood and went to the door to the kitchen, observing the children as they smeared their faces with food, eating without a word, as if alone. She walked to the Doctor and sat in his lap.

"*Like perfect little machines waiting to serve us. How do you do it, Doctor?*"

"*I studied with Blaskov, Dragna. And Blaskov learned from Milovitch.*"

"*I don't know such names. Your education has me at a disadvantage.*"

"*Does it, Dragna, my wily little mink?*" the Doctor grinned. Gregory saw liquid drip from his mouth-slit with every word. "*Your delicious wiles have me at a disadvantage.*"

"*Please Doctor, tell me how you learned such magic.*"

Gregory looked on as the Doctor lit a cigar with a match, smoke roiling as the red ember waxed and waned. "*President Ceauşescu recognized the importance of the trance state in unlocking information from some minds, burying it in others, and using advanced techniques to manage person-alities. Milovitch, a genius, had been doing the same work for Stalin. When Khrushchev imposed his ridiculous reforms, Nicolae convinced Milovitch to work for us, and he taught Blaskov and myself. We refined the techniques.*"

"*Do you do it with a swinging watch, Doctor? The way they do in the movies?*"

A deep chuckle. "*Parlor tricks aren't needed. It took*

several months of training, but. . ." He gestured toward his creations. "*They come to this room and the smells relax them, the food fills them. They hear a few words from me, in my voice, and they become our sweet little robots.*"

"*They become robots just like that?*"

"*Such a state builds from special cues,*" the Doctor said in a boastful voice. "*The most potent are smell, followed by event references. Finally an object. That can be the swinging watch or a purple beret or an egg-beater – whatever you stick in a mind.*"

The woman named Dragna crossed her arms over her floating breasts and smiled. "*Look at their faces. Like little machines.*"

"*It's not faces I want,*" one of the mattress-throwers said, the hulking one. Everyone laughed. The light flickered and the children were no longer in the kitchen but the supply room. They stood naked in the vibrating luminosity, tattered clothes at their feet. The smell of food mingled with the smell of bodies. The children's eyes were as black and shiny as obsidian. Their faces were smeared with gruel.

"*Mamaliga,*" the children in the dormitories began to murmur. "*Mamaligaaa. . .*"

The word became a chant that echoed through the building. "*Shut the fuckers up,*" the Doctor told Sorina Vaduva. She nodded and strode out the double doors. A screaming voice, the crack of leather over skin. Squeals of pain.

Then silence.

165

The nurse returned. There was a candle on the table now, beside it several glass vials and a hypodermic syringe. The vials glittered like black stars. Gregory heard a sound beneath the chanting and felt his head turn to the window. A white cat was sitting on the outside ledge, scratching at the glass. "*Go away,*" Grigor felt his mouth say to the cat. "*Go away, it's not safe to be—*"

"*What's that noise?*" the man named Cojocaru said. He was naked and smoking a flat cigarette that smelled of burning broom straws.

"*Nothing,*" the Doctor said. "*Some idiot cat climbed the fire escape.*"

"*Leave it to me,*" the woman named Dragna said, now dressed only in her panties, her doll's face craned toward the window. She set aside a bottle of tuica and opened the window, multiple panes grated with steel.

"*Here, kitty kitty,*" she coaxed. "*Nice kitty kitty. . .*"

She grasped the cat by the skin of its neck, her other hand under its thin belly, pulling it inside the room and holding it high like a prize. Dragna Negrescu's hands moved to the cat's neck. They made a fast twist and a cracking sound. The cat went limp as a wet dishrag and she threw it out the window.

"*Shall we work on tonight's projects?*" she laughed, turning back to the room. The man named Big Petrov clapped his hands and studied the row of children. He walked to them and licked his right forefinger with a lolling, lizard-like tongue. Gregory felt a wet finger glide over his forehead. Big Petrov lowered his voice to a

166

sing-song whisper. *"Pretty little robot with its pretty little lips."*

The Doctor's mouth opened and silver vampire light poured out. *"What will you have the pretty robot do for you, Petrov?"* the light said, pooling on the floor like mercury.

"Ema," Gregory heard his mouth scream. *"Ema come save me."*

But Ema knew how to hide in the girls' section. She was never seen here.

25

Driving to work the following morning, I was preoccupied by the killings of Kayla and Tommy, wondering if they were random. It seemed strange to wish they were tied together by some unseen factor, but as I had explained to my class on the first day, random, motive-less crimes were my worst nightmare.

I found Harry at his desk, feet up, in a purple shirt and green slacks, sipping coffee and scowling at a file on his lap.

"What you studying?" I asked.

"I'm trying to make some connection between the cases. Kayla and Tommy."

I shook my head. "I've got nothing, bro. Two separate worlds. You?"

He tented his fingertips and rested his chin at the apex.

"I'm thinking Kayla was involved in a lesbian relationship with Tommy's mother. Kayla's boyfriend found out about it, texted by Tommy, who was angry with his mother. Tommy probably got Kayla's number off her phone when she left it out. The boyfriend, safely alibied in England, arranged for a hired killer to do the women, then when the killer arrived at the Brinks' house, Mama was out. But he had to kill Tommy anyway – the kid might squeal that he'd tipped off the boyfriend – so he got the knife. The killer's laying low and waiting for things to die down so he can knock off Mama."

"A bit, uh, convoluted. You believe it?"

He looked at me as if I was crazed. "Of course not, it's ridiculous. But it makes more sense than anything else I've come up with."

My intercom buzzed, replaced with the voice of Tom Mason. "Carson, the Chief wants to see you. I got no damn idea why."

I experienced the first luck I'd had since Baggs had taken over the camp: Darlene Combs was passing by in the other direction, off on an errand. "Knock and go in," she snipped. "He's expecting you."

"The Mayor sick today?" I asked.

She pretended deafness. Baggs barked *Enter* in response to my knock, as if he was angry at being his own Cerberus. It fit, the SOB had multiple faces.

I stood with hands behind my back, a good soldier for the cause. "You wanted to see me, Chief?"

He got to his feet, flicking a file with his fingernails. "I want to discuss your recent citation. I just read your Lieutenant's recommendations and saw, to my chagrin, that—"

"You didn't read it the first time?"

His eyes tightened. "I misspoke myself. I *re*-read it."

I looked out the window and saw a flash of silver from a jet pulling a fluffy white contrail across the blue sky. I didn't care where the plane was going, Azerbaijan to Zambia, I wanted to be aboard. Or hanging from the landing gear by my teeth. Anywhere but in this prissy space reeking of furniture polish and high-school cologne.

"And?" I said.

"I'm nullifying it."

I took a second for the word to make sense. "Nuli— What? Why?"

"The male perpetrator – Noblin Maggard? It appears you let him slip under your radar, Detective. He was hiding in the bathroom, right?"

"It's a C-store, Chief. People are running every which way."

Baggs crossed his arms and jutted his chin. "Had you noted his absence, you might have alerted backup units prior to the perpetrators getting the drop on you. Am I not correct?"

I stared.

He said, "Do I get the courtesy of an answer, Detective?"

"I think I missed the question."

Baggs shook his head as if he was sorry to have to tell me a terrible secret. "You let a subject armed with a shotgun slip past you and hide in the restroom of a store you had supposedly secured. Remember, Detective, a citizen lost his hand."

I felt my own eyes narrow and my jaw clench. Ham Neck's stupidity had cost him his hand. "Are you saying it's my fault that—"

Baggs did shocked, holding his hands up to stop me. "Don't use the word 'fault', Detective," he said, talking like he was protecting me from myself. "It's too harsh. There's no real fault here."

"You just said—"

"I'm simply saying your inattention to an important detail cancels out your fine work on other fronts. A citation has to mean something, right?"

I stared at Baggs, his throat within reach of my hands.

"Do you ever eat anything but greens and whole grain toast, tea and honey, dear?"

"I like them, Ema. Obviously."

Gregory and Ema sat in a restaurant in Daphne, on the Eastern Shore of Mobile Bay. The drive had taken forty minutes in the morning traffic and an irritated Gregory wondered why Ema couldn't have breakfast on the Mobile side. He figured the restaurant must have advertised pretty pictures of food on television, evoking a Pavlovian need in Ema. She probably stood in front of the screen and drooled.

Ema was ridiculously suggestible, and Gregory had once fantasized about hypnotizing her, perhaps with a watch or some form of amulet. He'd get her under the first time and insert a cue into her mind, a word or action that would make the process easier in the future. Then he realized inserting such an action would be unnecessary, since his one and only command would be: *Leave me alone.*

And, Gregory thought, I remember a bit about hypnosis.

Gregory had considered avoiding the get-together, but recalling the endless hours Ema spent soaking up television, he realized she would have followed the two killings on local news. Her opinion would represent that of the average dolt, and he suddenly wanted to know her thoughts. "You know . . . I was watching the news the other day, Ema. It seems a young black fellow was killed. Tragic. Did you hear about that?"

"The poor child died the other day," Ema corrected. "But he was attacked two days previously."

Gregory affected mild curiosity, *Can I Get a Fiber Cereal that Doesn't Taste Like Fiber?* "Why wasn't he killed during the attack?"

Ema looked up from a ham and strawberry omelet covered with gelatinous goo. "I heard the attacker was clumsy in his attempt – a great fortune for the boy because

172

the paramedics saved his life, bless them. Unfortunately, the child had a weak constitution. A disease." Ema swallowed hard, her voice softening to a whisper. "He must have suffered so."

Gregory prickled at the word *clumsy*. He'd slammed the goddamn knife into the little bastard, but it hit a rib and didn't sink to the hilt. You learned by doing: It wasn't as if there was a class in this stuff.

"Perhaps it was all for the best, dear," Gregory said, nipping an edge off a toast point. "His suffering ended."

Ema stared at Gregory. "That's a strange thing to say."

"Have you never been to a funeral, Ema? It's a common expression."

"The way you say it seems so—"

Gregory raised his hand to signal his displeasure with the current dialogue. "Wasn't there another killing recently?" he said. "A college girl?"

Ema set her fork on her plate and frowned in thought. "The girl on the bicycle? Stabbed as well, I think. Or was she shot?"

"I don't believe anyone has said, Ema. The police are being coy."

Gregory was irritated the cops were concealing his pistol crossbow, an inspired choice. His beloved bow had been too large to hide successfully, so he'd found its little brother online, ordering the weapon from a Canadian sporting-goods store. How many people were killed by a crossbow? Ryder must have been greatly impressed.

Gregory said, "Have you heard if the cops have any . . . what do they call it? Information that helps solve crimes?"

"Leads," Ema said, delighted to know something Gregory didn't. "I don't think so. At least, not that I've seen on TV."

"Killings like these seem to happen all the time," Gregory sighed. He added a shake of his head, as if disturbed by the knowledge.

Ema paused with her lips pursed in thought. She held the pose for almost a minute.

"Are you in there, Ema?" Gregory finally asked. "Hello?"

"I'm thinking."

A sigh. "Give me an overview."

"Both killings seem so strange, Gregory. Like there was something underneath the surface."

Gregory kept his face impassive. Ema was four feet from the man who had made both deaths happen. He could have reached across the table and taken her life as well. Or, to be more realistic, followed her out the door and killed her at whim, making sure not to be beneath her as she went down. *Boom.* Seismographs clacking across the South.

From nowhere a thought crossed Gregory's mind: *I'm in Ema's will. If I killed her, how much would I make?*

"Gregory?" Ema said.

"What?"

"What are you thinking? You looked so far away."

"I was absorbing what you were saying, Ema. That, based on your observations from television, the killings seemed strange."

"You're making fun of me."

Eye-roll. "For Christ's sake, Ema." *Sigh.* "You won't let me joke and now you won't let me think? Why do we even meet?"

Ema's pout face. "I'm sorry."

"Tell me about the killings."

"I can't put it in words," Ema said. "But no matter . . . I'm pretty sure the police will catch the perpetrators."

Gregory frowned. "Why so certain?"

"I watch police reality shows: *Cops, America's Most Wanted* . . . Plus mystery shows. So I know a lot about these things."

Gregory feigned nonchalance, displayed as *Why Should I Care Which Margarine Has Fewer Calories?* "How do you think they'll catch him, Ema? I mean *them.*"

"By tiny bits of evidence. Logan's rule."

"Whose rule?"

"Logan's rule says evidence is always exchanged at crime scenes."

"That makes no sense, Ema."

"Of course it does, Gregory. Killers leave evidence they don't know about. Tiny things. That's Logan's rule."

"Evidence like the mortgage to his home?" Gregory kept a straight face, inwardly chuckling at stealing a line from Ryder's classroom video.

"You ask my thoughts and then you make jokes when I tell them."

"I'm only teasing, Ema. Please, continue. I promise I'll be serious." Gregory did the *Cross-My-Heart* truth gesture, a recent addition to his repertoire.

Suddenly in her element, Ema began quoting shows named *Quincy*, *CSI*, *Inspector Morse*, *Wallander* and a half-dozen others, dwelling on inane minutiae about crime scenes and evidence and profiling.

". . . surveillance cameras are everywhere these days, Gregory, and you'd be amazed at how many people don't . . . *CSI* episode where a suspect was identified by her . . . cyanoacrylate fuming is even able to raise fingerprints from human skin. I think Kay Scarpetta was one of the first to use the trick back in. . ."

When Ema finished, Gregory thought she was about to faint away in joy; she had the same look on her face she got when entering any restaurant with an all-you-can-eat buffet. Gregory snapped his fingers for the waiter.

"Thanks for all the information, Ema," he said. "Fascinating."

"I'll e-mail you when the programs are on. I think you'll enjoy them."

"I'm sure I will," he lied, knowing he'd spend the next week dragging e-mails to the trash.

"Oh," Ema said, tapping a pudgy and over-powdered cheek. "I just thought of one other way the criminal could get caught. Or not really caught, but stopped."

"How's that, dear?"

"An attack of conscience. He might turn himself in."

"Always a possibility, I suppose," Gregory said, reaching for his wallet and feeling an unsteadying glimmer of fear in a far corner of his mind.

"He actually took away your citation, Carson?" Harry asked. I'd managed to jam my hands in my pockets and make my way back to my desk after my go-round with Baggs. I'd shifted files for an hour, stewing all the while. Harry had trotted into the department seconds ago, following a morning meeting at the DA's office. I had just finished the thirty-second synopsis of my encounter with Baggs.

"No. He *nullified* it. Like he'd made some magical incantation and the certificate turned to ash. I should check my closet. Maybe it did."

Even Harry's big body couldn't contain his irritation. He paced circles in our cubicle. "You risked your life in that store. You could file a grievance with the union."

I stared silently at my partner. Filing grievances was like hiring a third party to punch someone you had a beef with. A punch didn't mean anything unless it came from you.

"Yeah," Harry sighed, knowing it too. "It's the cheap way out."

* * *

On reaching home, Gregory peeled off his clothes, exchanging them for a wardrobe that didn't stink of bacon and sausage. His ears ached from Ema's ramblings and his face was tired from the workout. He turned on the television, CNN, and lay down on the couch to give his head a rest while he absorbed the day's headlines.

But in the back of his head, Ema's nasal babbling.

Logan's rule says evidence is always exchanged at crime scenes. . .

She'd seen or read something and the information had, as usual, gotten garbled. Gregory went to his office to Google the phrase, finding nothing concerning crime detection. He tried similar names, coming up dry again. Struggling to remember words Ema used, he tried *crime scene, evidence, exchange.*

Bingo! he thought, looking at the screen. *Locard's Exchange Principle.*

The principle, boiled down, was that any violent crime scene held evidentiary minutiae from perpetrator and victim: fingerprints, footprints, hair follicles, blood, fibers from clothes, dirt particles from shoes, sputum . . . and within a few years such things as skin cells, sneeze droplets, perhaps even human scents lingering in the air or trapped in nearby fabrics.

Gregory stood from his desk with his heart pounding. He'd been lucky. No, make that smart, exercising care in hiding his identity, wearing gloves, throwing away his shoes. But the Blue Tribe had techniques and procedures he'd overlooked.

Another thing Ema said – quoting a show called *Missing* – was that successful killers become too secure in their success and get caught when they grow lazy. Gregory would have to watch out for this in his duel with the police. These were pieces of data worth considering. And they'd spilled from Ema.

Was the obese, babbling gourd actually good for something?

26

Paul Lampson took a long drag from the joint and set it in a blue ceramic ashtray shaped like an elephant. A bottle of red wine sat on the table beside the couch. Paul saw he'd forgotten a glass. He padded to the kitchen in bare feet, his socks and work shoes kicked off. He was dressed in green nurse's scrubs, baggy and wrinkled after a twelve-hour shift, his fourth in as many days. But now he had three blessed days off.

Even better, Terry had two days free; maybe they could go to the beach, spend a day in the sun, giggling as tan men strutted by in swimsuits.

"*I give that one a five-point-eight.*"

"*Five-five. The hair is so 2006.*"

"*Oooooh. Over there in the green cut-offs. Six-five?*"

"*Girl, that's a full six-nine.*"

All talk, Paul thought as he opened the cabinet and

retrieved a wineglass. He and Terry had been a . . . Jeez, a couple? . . . for months now. Other men were on a *Look-but-don't-touch* basis. And the arrangement seemed as good for Terry as it was for Paul.

Paul returned to the living room, picked up the iPod remote and pressed play, Tony Bennett singing through the stereo system.

"*I left my heart, in San Francisco. . .*"

The corny old song was both a joke and a vision. The plan was to move to San Francisco in the fall, a city where they could be themselves.

Terry had grown up in rural Alabama, wounded by a macho culture – beaten up in school as teachers looked the other way – and a father that tossed him out when he was seventeen. Paul had come up in Atlanta, still southern, but more progressive. Plus his parents had accepted his sexuality.

But San Francisco was the New World. Terry had been there twice, and knew it was where he needed to be. Where *they* needed to be.

Paul reclined on the couch and relit the dead joint. Moving would be tough. But as a nurse specializing in cardiac rehabilitative care he was highly employable; by working extra shifts he might pull seventy grand a year. Plus he was taking classes to become a nurse practitioner.

Terry was another story, waiting tables not so lucrative. But at twenty-four it was time for him to find his life's work. Until then, a waiter at a toney place might pull over thirty if he hustled.

181

Paul smiled to himself. Terry certainly had hustling experience, though of a different sort, a rough little piece of trade when the pair met at a bar, a hard-partying druggie more confused than malevolent. But under that kiss-my-ass exterior was a sensitive kid who sought stability.

Paul walked to the window. The sun lit the long canebrake across the street and a mockingbird called from the brush. There was a FOR SALE sign on the lot with the canebrake, thickly overgrown with bramble. Their house sat alone, past a marsh, a wide culvert, and a suburb that died aborning, a few rotting stakes marking lots never sold. The nearest dwellings were a third of a mile away.

Though the area was decrepit and an eastern wind brought the scent of the swamp, the house was near the highway, the rent was right and they'd been allowed to decorate as they pleased, which meant bright paint on every inside wall and flowers in the yard. When Terry had moved in – two months ago – he'd insisted on paying half the rent and had taken responsibility for keeping the yard in good condition, finding peace in working with flowers.

The only fear Paul had in moving was placing new temptations in front of his partner. Terry was a hard drinker by the time he was eighteen, with a heavy reliance on pills as well, OxyContin, Lortabs, Percocets. He'd been a monster when they'd met, offering drunken, shrieking anger one night, crying jags the next.

But the pair had discovered kindred angels within one another, slowly engaging Terry's demons and – if not fully vanquishing them – pushing them toward the horizon. *As long as I'm there*, Paul thought, watching a wavering line of pelicans glide across the tops of the cane, *Terry will be safe. And as long as Terry's with me, I'll be happy.*

Gregory pulled down the small lane, past the marsh where yesterday he'd reconnoitered the house. The gray Corolla was gone. Gregory knew it would be, a simple phone call having established the other man would be working for at least another hour.

Gregory looked for nearby eyes and saw none. He wasn't in his daily vehicle, but a beater truck he'd purchased for his work, nondescript, the license tag obscured with mud. If stopped by the police, he'd simply claim the mud came from driving past a construction site and he'd wash it clean as soon as possible.

Thanks to Ema's television-inspired ramblings on police procedures, Gregory had spent ten hours of the last twenty-four studying online law-enforcement sites. The amount of information was incredible.

Plus he'd started recording the TV show *Cops*. On some cable channels it ran for hours at a time.

Gregory pulled into the driveway beside a battered red Honda Civic. He flipped a cheap plastic messenger bag over his shoulder, the current choice for style among the hip. Gregory liked it because the unzipped top allowed immediate access to his necessaries and its plastic manufacture shed no fibers. He'd made a few other changes as well.

Tumbling a penny in his gloved hand, he approached the door. Just before pressing the doorbell, he dropped the coin into his bag. He had a wonderful idea for the penny.

It was going to make a statement.

27

Bong.

Paul was dozing on the couch when the doorbell rang. The meter reader? That was usually Tom Jenkins, who read the meter at the back of the house and never said a word unless the door was open, when he'd call inside to say he was in the yard.

A salesman, then, hoping to put siding or a new roof on the house. Or another of the congregation from the nearby Baptist church, wanting to press a tract into his hand.

Bong.

Paul's bare feet slapped the floor. He smelled himself as he stood, having fallen asleep on the couch in his scrubs, too tired to shower. He shot a glance out the window as he padded to the door, saw a nondescript black truck in the drive, not a salesperson's vehicle. Churchies probably.

He replayed the last conversation he'd had with the Baptists, the one he figured would keep them from the door for ever.

"Thank you so much for the information. We'd love to join a church that's welcoming to people like my partner and myself."

"Partner?" one of the two stout ladies had said, frowning.

"We're queer. My boyfriend's a Muslim, but he loves to sing the Christian hymns."

Ten seconds was all it took to see their rattletrap Buick retreating from the drive.

Bong.

"Coming," Paul muttered.

He went to the door and pulled it wide to see a bald man in full-length black tights like a dancer. His feet were in tennis shoes, but for some reason the fronts had been slit to let his toes poke out two inches. The toes appeared to be in plastic wrap. He wore surgical gloves.

But it was the man's head that dropped Paul's mouth open: The guy was wearing diver's goggles. His covered hand was holding a long-handled hammer. No, not a hammer, a goddamn tomahawk, or something similar.

"What the fu—"

"Woo woo woo," said the mouth beneath the mask.

"Do you think the killings are connected?" Tom Mason asked. He'd pulled us into a meeting room after reviewing our files. He seemed upset at the lack of progress, which wasn't making us very happy either.

"We haven't found anything tying the Ballard girl and the Brink boy," I said.

"But you think it's the same killer."

I shrugged. "No idea."

"Not what I need to hear," Tom said.

"Two different weapons," Harry said, stepping in. "Both blind attacks, well-planned and executed – pardon my choice of word. But the vics were from two different worlds."

"The Chief's wanting something quick here, guys," Tom said. "The college community's spooked that a coed was killed minutes from campus."

"I imagine the folks in Tommy Brink's neighborhood are worried as well," I said, looking up.

Tom sighed. "They have less weight than college administrators. The female students are withdrawing from night classes, afraid they'll be next."

"We're at a dead-end, Tom," I confessed. "There's nothing resembling a motive. Nothing at scenes but cigarette butts, coins, trash, the usual detritus. No prints on anything."

"The goddamn pistol crossbow or whatever?"

"Seven sold at local outlets this year. We checked the buyers, nothing there."

The phone on the table rang and I picked up. "Carson?" the desk man asked. "There's a man here, says you told him to stop by if he was in the area, a Mr Ballard?"

Kayla's father. My heart dropped. "Tell him I'll be right down."

I took the stairs, opening into the lobby. Mr Ballard was slumping in a chair and stood when I entered.

"Hello, Mr Ballard. Why don't you step over here and we can talk in quiet."

He didn't move. "Have you been able to find my little girl's murderer?"

"No, sir, not yet. There's a lot to look at."

He pushed himself from the chair and we stood eye to eye. "But isn't this what you do, find bad people?"

"It's been seven days, sir. It takes time."

"Eight days," he corrected.

"Of course."

"Tyler's about torn up. He left school. I don't think he'll go back."

"I'm sorry," I frowned. "Who?"

"Tyler Charles, Kayla's boyfriend. He was in school in England. I told you all about him. Didn't you listen?"

Tyler Charles, five time zones away, had been dismissed as a suspect from the first day and the name hadn't stuck in my forebrain, which was busy juggling a hundred facts that might have been pertinent. There was no way to convey that distinction to someone not in law enforcement.

"Yes, sir, we listen very carefully."

He stared into my eyes. "Kayla wasn't from here. That wouldn't make a difference, would it?"

"Kayla was the victim of a horrible crime in Mobile, Mr Ballard. That's my jurisdiction. Where she lives is of no consequence."

"Where she used to live," Mr Ballard corrected. "My girl's dead, remember?"

"I meant that—"

"Carson," the desk man said. "You're wanted upstairs. It's important."

"Just a second—"

"They said to get up there, pronto."

"You better go, Detective Ryder," Ballard said. "Someone important needs you."

I ran upstairs to the detectives' room. The meeting room had cleared and Harry was pulling on his shoulder rig. "We've got another, Carson. A killing on the south side by the bay."

We raced to a small house on an isolated strip of worn asphalt, one of those places where industrial mixed with residential and the houses were coming down so more industry could go up.

Inside the house was the typical investigative action, chaotic to casual bystanders, but tightly controlled to an insider's eyes, choreographed movement to put the

Rockettes to shame. Uniformed cops kept the onlookers at bay, the photographers had captured the position of the body before the pathology folks – led by Clair – moved in. Evidence techs worked everywhere.

I went to Elmore Baskin, who had been coordinating the scene until Harry and I arrived. "Who found the deceased, El?" I asked.

"Meter reader said the front door was open, he saw blood on the floor, called 911. That was. . ." he checked his watch, "twenty-seven minutes ago."

Harry and I entered. Two couches made an L-shape against the far wall, tables at both ends. An overstuffed lounger was in a corner, as was a five-foot lady palm. But our eyes didn't linger on the furniture, it was the pale yellow carpet that caught our attention. Outside of three dime-sized dots of red a couple meters past the threshold, the center of the rug had a concentration of blood spatter, a ragged circle with fewer droplets at the periphery. The blood had been stepped in repeatedly, the footprints aiming every direction, as if someone had gone amok with red paste-on dance steps.

"Weird," I muttered, seeing only one trail of spatter not contained within the rough circle, leading down a rear hallway. "The body's back there, I take it?" I asked Elmore.

"Bedroom on the left. Doc P's in there."

The body was on the floor in a pool of blood, Clair kneeling beside it, her gloved hands making gentle discoveries. "Blunt-force trauma," she said. "The victim – male, late twenties I'd guess – took a series of blows to the head and body."

The body looked as though it had run a gauntlet. Light flashed as final photos were taken. The victim was lifted to a gurney and rolled from the house. I found Hembree in the kitchen, fingerprinting the refrigerator handle.

"You finished in the living room, Bree?"

He nodded without looking up, too busy brushing on powder. "Do what you need."

Harry was tearing the bedroom apart. I stepped into the living room. Clair was studying the scene with quiet intensity. "What's your take?" I asked her. "What does the floor say to you?"

She said, "I listen to bodies. What's it telling you?"

"Lampson is on the couch," I said. "He's kicked off his slippers, at ease. The killer knocks, rings the bell, whatever. Lampson opens the door. I figure he received a blow to the head, took several steps backward and fell to the floor, but got up."

"What makes you think he got up?"

I pointed to three red circles three yards inside the door. "These dots of blood could be fingertips. He's pushing himself to standing."

"But there's so much blood."

"Because I think our killer was doing something like this," I said, raising an invisible truncheon and acting as if I was keeping the bleeding Lampson centered in the room, stepping in his way when he tried for the front door or the rear.

"Jesus," Clair said, tracking my motion against the blood and footprints. "You think the killer was corralling Lampson? Keeping him in the center of the floor?"

"Cat and mouse," I nodded. "Playing with his food."

Shaking her head, Clair headed back to the ME's offices. John Lippincott was in a corner on a mobile phone. I heard him say, "Can you let me talk to anyone else who worked with him?" John was a new-made dick, thirty-seven, getting his investigative feet under him. He wasn't great on a scene yet, but knew how to dig up background. He snapped his phone shut and slipped it in his suit jacket.

"I found pay stubs on the bedside table, Carson. Mobile Memorial Hospital. Lampson was a floor nurse there the last four years. I talked to his supervisor and two nurses who worked with him on a regular basis. Good work history. A couple arguments with supervisors over hours and assignments, no big deal. All three said he cared about his patients."

"Threats?"

"Not that anyone knew of. He'd work someone else's shift if they needed, which made him a friend to all."

"Relationship?"

"He's been in a relationship for several months, a guy named Terry."

"Terry who, Terry where?"

"Not known. More nurses come on shift in an hour. They know Lampson better."

Harry entered the room waving papers. "Found a

Verizon bill for one Terry McGuiness. I'll call the number, tell him there's a problem."

Harry made the call, speaking, hanging up. "Damn phone's off. I left a message."

The window was open to vent the murder-scene smell of the victim's released bowels and I heard tires screech out on the street, followed by a metallic *whump*. We sprinted out the door, seeing a slender man in dark slacks and white shirt leaping from a battered gray Corolla, the nose of the car against the crumpled trunk of a cop cruiser. He'd driven in too fast, misjudged braking distance. The man's eyes were wild and he ran straight into two uniformed cops who, unsure of what was happening, grabbed him and put him on the ground.

"PAUL!" he screamed toward the house. "PAULIE!"

"Calm down!" one of the uniforms was yelling, trying to pinion the man's clambering arms.

I was there in two heartbeats. "Terry?" I said. "Are you Terry?"

"Where's Paul? What's going on? LET ME UP!"

"If you stay here and let me talk to you. That OK?"

"WHERE'S PAUL? WHAT'S WRONG?"

"Listen to me, Terry. There's been a problem."

"WHAT PROBLEM? WHERE'S PAUL?"

"It's bad, Terry. Paul's dead."

"NO! NO! NO!"

The man was decompensating fast. He was restrained and put into a gurney, then sped to the hospital, his screams carrying down the street. There would be no interviewing Terry McGuiness today.

I stayed until everyone else had left, sitting silently on a dead man's couch and trying to fathom the mindset of a man who had – from our conjectures – wounded his victim with blow, then played with him like a toy. If this was the same guy who'd killed Kayla and Tommy, he was learning to enjoy his time with the victim.

After a half-hour I pulled my cell and tapped the second number on my speed-dial list.

"Hello, Carson," Clair said. "You're still there, right?"

"I'm ready to leave. Guess I'll head on home and stare at the walls."

"How do you feel?"

"Alone."

"I'm about to call it quits, too. I'll do the procedure in the morning when I'm awake." A long pause, a softer voice, almost whispering into my ear. "Why don't you stop by that Thai place on Dinmont, Carson? Grab some take-out."

"You don't want to go out somewhere?" I asked, knowing what she intended. "A quiet restaurant?"

"Let's just close the door and pretend the world went away. At least until tomorrow morning."

The black truck chugged past the house for the third time in an hour, twilight dimming the air from yellow to blue. The first two passes revealed sightseers in the street, neighbors hovering like carrion birds. But they'd retreated to the comfort of *Inside Edition* and *Wheel of Fortune*, Gregory knew, things they could understand. What had happened here was so far beyond the morons it might have been on a distant planet ruled by mathematics and justice.

Gregory stopped across the street, beside a FOR SALE board half-hidden in the cane. His video camera was taped to the signpost and peeking just above the metal sign. He'd thought about planting a camera inside the house, but ruled it too risky. The warrior would almost certainly be in attendance, and if anyone could spot a hidden camera, Ryder would.

Gregory dropped the recording device into the leg pocket of his painter's pants and congratulated himself on another perfect slap to the face of the Blue Tribe.

28

I awoke alone in Clair's bed, recalling a kiss laid on my cheek in the pre-dawn light. She had risen early to head to the morgue. I had called my dog-sitting neighbor last night to have Mix-up's needs tended, no need to rush home to fix his morning plate of kibble and grits.

Through the window the golden light of a new sun blazed over the leaves and limbs of the live oaks in Clair's deep yard. My shoes were still in the paper booties worn at crime scenes and I now understood the odd looks I'd gotten at the Thai restaurant. I'd kicked my shoes off immediately inside Clair's door and we'd fallen into an embrace, finding our way to supper an hour later.

I kept clothes in Clair's closet and changed into jeans and a beige blazer over a white dress shirt. Clair had tossed the paper inside and I read it with my coffee. A headline below the fold stood out:

POLICE SILENT ABOUT THIRD STRANGE KILLING

The subhead read, *Won't Rule Out Random Attacks.*

Uh-oh, I thought, three reporters had contributed, meaning the media was smelling something. A quote stood out, Silas Ballard: "*They [the MPD] kept drilling me about who Kayla knew and associated with, like trying to lower her reputation, like she did bad things and got killed because of it.*"

I felt irritation, though I couldn't fault Ballard's intentions, only his naïveté. All we'd done was ask the same questions we asked day in and day out. Ballard had the rural dweller's suspicion of the city.

Asked if the attacks were related, the standard "departmental spokesperson" basically said anything was possible. Asked if the attacks were random, the spokesperson said no relationship had been established between the killings, though that didn't mean none existed. It was a masterly job of weasel-wording.

There was also suspicion about the postmortems, Clair's office specifying results as "preliminary work-ups awaiting toxicology and other tests". That allowed us to keep them vague for now, but the clock was ticking.

I was heading to the morgue when a thought hit. I pulled my cell and pressed the newest number on my list.

197

"Detective Ryder?" she answered. "I mean, Carson?"

"It's Detective Ryder today, Holliday. Business. You think you're ready for the morgue?"

There were two distinct categories of answers Wendy Holliday could have given. One was, *Do I have to?* The other was, *I can't wait.*

She said, "I'm out the door."

Holliday was pacing out front when I rolled up. Four men were in the waiting area, one hunched over in a chair as the others made consoling sounds. Terry McGuiness was here to make the official identification of the body, looking far better composed than the last time I'd seen him.

Holliday followed me down the long and marble-floored hall denoted by a sign saying ADMITTANCE WITH AUTHORIZED ESCORT ONLY. We passed Clair's office, the door open to a desk topped by a vase brimming with floral pyrotechnics, the product of Clair's gardening prowess. The chair was empty and we walked to the main autopsy suite, a white room, cold and smelling of disinfectant.

Clair stood at the table checking the lights, recording system, instruments; such a stickler for order, one might think she was preparing to operate on a living body. When Clair saw Holliday beside me, her eyes moved to me and held a question.

"I thought I'd bring a student," I said, my hand on the small of Holliday's back. "You two met the other night."

Clair's eyes remained on me for two beats then she turned to Holliday. "You ever see an autopsy before, Miss Christmas?"

"It's Holliday, Dr Peltier. Wendy Holliday."

"My mistake. A senior moment, perhaps. Have you ever attended a postmortem?"

"I've seen one on videotape. So I know what to expect."

Clair said, "We have one thing to do first. The hardest part."

"I'll fetch him," I said, returning to the lobby, pondering Clair's *senior moment* remark. She was barely forty-seven. When Terry McGuiness saw me he wiped his face and walked my way, his steps tight and mechanical.

"Your friends can be with you, Terry," I said. "You don't have to do this alone."

He swallowed hard, struggling to hold it together. "It's OK. I don't want them to remember Paul like . . . he is."

I guided him into the suite. Holliday had retreated to a respectful distance, letting Clair center the situation. She brought McGuiness to the cooler drawer, me at his back. He wavered but stayed up, maybe his last piece of strength.

"It's him," he confirmed, tears streaming down his cheeks. "It's my Paul."

I walked him toward the reception area. "We have to talk soon," I said. "But I need to know about anyone who had a beef with Paul. Former friends, co-workers, ex-lovers. Anyone. We want justice, Terry."

He stopped, leaning against the wall for support and

wiping tears from his eyes. "Paul didn't make enemies. That was me, making cracks, pissing people off. The old me, mostly, a nasty little bitch. But then I met Paulie and . . ." his voice trailed off. He looked at me. "We were going to San Francisco." He said it as though it was important for me to know.

"Paul had no enemies?"

"P-Paulie helped everyone. He worked their shifts, remembered their birthdays. When friends with kids wanted a night out, he'd be their sitter. He needed to do things for people . . . even people like me."

"Excuse me?"

"When I met Paulie I was a whore with a hundred-buck-a-day coke habit, a real fuck-up. He looked past all that and saw inside me, what I wanted to be. He pushed me into a program, stayed with me every step. I've been clean for four months, mostly."

"Where you working?"

"The Crane's Roost restaurant in Daphne. I put in sixty hours a week waiting tables." He paused. "Saving for San Francisco."

We continued to the lobby, no sound but heels on the white floor. The lobby was empty, McGuiness's friends smoking outside, the receptionist taking a bathroom break. We were alone.

"I need you to consider who might have had a grudge against Paul," I said, handing McGuiness my card. "It's hard right now, but it's necessary."

But Terry McGuiness wasn't listening. He was staring

200

into a place he'd thought forever full, now forever empty. McGuiness looked at me, a sad realization in his eyes.

"That person I've been? I don't think I can be him any more. Not without Paul."

"You said it's who you wanted to be, Terry," I said, tucking my card in his shirt pocket. "Plus you gotta do it for Paul, right?"

"For Paul," he echoed. "Right." But his eyes belonged to someone different. He turned away and slumped toward a changed world.

I trudged back to the autopsy room, the body now on the table. Clair reached for the scalpel. "So you know what's about to happen, Miss Holliday?"

"The Y-incision. Like I said, I've seen a videotape."

Before my first autopsy, I too had researched the procedure, soaking up photographs, fearful I would perform poorly, blanch or faint. After the initial shock of a body opened under light as white as snow, I had been transfixed by the oddly haphazard arrangement of tubes and tanks, pumps and bellows, that carried our consciousness in its journey from nothingness to wherever. I recalled the elderly pathologist, Dr Earnest Grey, opening to my interest and telling me wondrous things, explaining how the stomach's process of digesting a piece of steak would require over a hundred books crammed with chemical equations.

I retired to a chair in the corner to study cases, but Holliday remained beside the table, her attention as rapt as mine those many years ago. I studied files and made notes for a half-hour, until I heard Clair say, "What's this?"

I walked over and saw the resected stomach draped over Clair's gloved palm like a deflated sack. She had a pair of forceps inside the stomach, removed them with an object clasped in the jaws.

"The victim seems to have swallowed a penny."

Clair dropped the coin into a small metal bowl. It rattled in a circle and I realized I'd recently seen dozens of pennies spinning and dropping. I recalled a fresh bright penny found within a meter of Kayla Ballard's body. Another penny atop the dirt beside Tommy Brink's wheel-chair.

Not in the dirt, on top of it.

And now a penny swallowed by Paul Lampson.

"I think the killer may be someone from class," I whispered, hearing my heart pounding in my ears.

The Fed-Ex man rang Gregory's doorbell at nine. He unwrapped two books on forensics, three on police proce-dure. Gregory reclined on his couch and started reading.

Ema had been basically correct about Locard, Gregory discovered, finding additional references to the forensics scientist and his lauded principle. Her nattering had sparked his study of police procedures and helped him create his Event Skin. Drab little Ema was making him better. He should schedule more time with his sister and pull everything about cops from her head before. . .

Gregory froze. He sat up, a book falling from his

hand to the floor. *Before?* Had he just thought the word *Before?*

Before what?

"Before I kill her," he said slowly, feeling his lips make the words real. *There!* He'd said the word aloud and heard himself say it. Voicing the thought didn't necessarily mean he'd end Ema's life, merely that the possibility had entered the programming. It meant he could formalize his research: What was her property worth? What was the range of her investments? How much time would he have to spend with an idiot lawyer to claim her estate?

Gregory stood and studied himself in the full-length wall mirror. Could the man in the glass kill the only constant in his life? It would be an incredibly dramatic move, one that would put him in direct contact with the police.

"Mr Nieves? I'm so sorry to have to inform you that your sister was found. . ."

My God . . . what if Ryder showed up at his door? Gregory paced the floor. He was entering a new realm, but every realm he'd entered since that night had made him better. More alive. More master of the world. He was even beginning to understand the painting above his mantel: it was about assembling order from chaos.

As he paced, Ema's voice called out. . .

"I just thought of one other way the criminal could get caught. . ." she said, sounding as vivid as if she were standing in the room. *"An attack of conscience."*

Gregory froze. *Conscience.* Like Love, the word seemed

everywhere. But Love could be understood in a basic fashion: you had something you wanted. If someone took it away, you felt shitty. Love was simple math.

What he didn't understand, exactly, was what a conscience was or did, though he assumed if he had one, it was a much better one than the morons had. Yet when he closed his eyes, stilled his head, and went looking for it in his skull, it stayed hidden.

Hello? What do you look like?

The more he considered the concept, the more upset he became. Was it actually possible something in his head could send him to the police to confess?

"I killed people. Put me in jail."

It was irrational. Senseless. Macabre. But above all, it was totally unsettling that he might have something so horrible within his head.

A conscience!

29

We arrived at the academy minutes later. When students wanted to discuss lessons I tried not to stare into their faces and claimed a tight schedule. Wilbert Pendel was sucking on a cigarette. He saw me and veered down a side path. Inside, I passed Public Relations trainee Janet Wing, who snapped a photo of me with the digital SLR around her neck.

"The star of the academy," she grinned. "I'd like to feature you on the MPD website, Detective. How are you on time?"

"Tough for now. I'll get to you when it's clear."

"You could be a great recruiting tool, Detective. You have stage presence, a natural. Loved the analogy."

I had no idea what Wing was talking about. I opened the door to my classroom, empty. Holliday followed, puzzlement in her eyes. I closed the door and set the lock. "This is all in strictest confidence, Wendy," I said. "Three of the recent murders are related: Kayla Ballard, Tommy Brink, and Paul Lampson."

"The penny?"

"They've been left at all three scenes. Does anyone in the class strike you as different? Remarks made, questions asked? Is anyone strangely quiet or strangely talkative? Who doesn't fit?"

She crossed the room, brow furrowed in thought. "Gerry Wainwright jokes a lot, but he's our class clown, funny and harmless. I'm sure he's not a killer."

"Who else sticks out?"

"I don't like Pendel because he can be mean and arrogant."

I nodded. "I heard Pendel diss you one day because you were coming to talk with me."

"The blowjob remark. That's Weird Wilbert, as he gets called behind his back. But dangerous? If I blew a kiss at Pendel he'd turn and run. Can I ask what you're getting at?"

"There's a commonality to the crimes. It's the scenario for my worst fear. Do you remember it?"

"Sure. You tossed pennies across the floor to demonstrate random murders. Everyone in the class talks about it."

"Still? How?"

"Like we'll have drinks after class and the waitress brings our change. Someone always points to the pennies and yells 'Dead people!' It's an inside joke."

"Who's the most likely to yell about dead people?"

"Anyone, really. Me. Is it important?"

"We've found pennies at every murder scene, Wendy. That's not unusual, coins are everywhere. But a penny inside the victim's stomach goes beyond coincidence. He was probably forced to swallow it, a message."

She frowned, adding it up. "So the killer. . ."

I nodded. "My penny shtick was spur of the moment. Only the eighteen people in class saw it."

A strange look from Holliday, unease mingled with embarrassment. "Uh, maybe eighteen is an underestimate, Detective Ryder. We better go to the computer lab."

My turn for confusion. I followed Holliday to a room of computer carrels and stood at her shoulder as she navigated to YouTube, entered my name in the Search field, tapped keys. A video loaded onto the screen. The title was *Random Nightmares*.

I felt a sinking feeling and sunk deeper through an edited, multi-angled compilation of the class, primarily the final minutes when Holliday asked about my worst nightmare as a detective. Several cameras had caught the toss, pennies falling from different angles, spinning, rolling, zipping between one another as my voice droned over the scenes.

Imagine a purely random victim selection process: the killer walks down the street with closed eyes, opens them and sees someone – cab driver, elderly woman, shopper, child in a

207

playground. He tracks and kills that person.
Without a motive – monetary, sexual, psycho-
logical, power, vengeance – the detective is
never sure one death is connected to another. . .

A final shot of dozens of pennies dead on the floor. The scene faded to black.

"Who the hell would do such a thing?" I said. "Tape me?"

"You didn't know? You mean, we're not supposed to take notes?"

"Of course you can take notes. What are you talking about?"

Holliday reached in her purse and retrieved a black rectangle that could have been concealed in the palm of a hand. "Some people use recorders like mine, others use phones. Some write down the major points. But most of us record the class so we can review it at home."

I fought to keep from slumping forward. I was a ridiculous throwback to video recorders with hand straps and proboscis lenses. Meanwhile, they'd evolved to cigarette-lighter size. I recalled student desks strewn with mobile phones, iPads, Kindles, miniature laptops, all manner of e-doohickies. Even when I was in college, back in the Paleolithic Nineties, I'd taped lectures with a recorder using micro-cassettes I'd invariably misplace. But video had been added, along with hundreds of online venues for storing and displaying the results.

"Who edited the video? Stuck it on YouTube?" I said.

Her face fell and she looked on the verge of weeping. "Me and Jason and Amanda Sanchez. Terrell. All sorts of videos are put up by police departments, none half as informative as yours, Detective Ryder. It was an homage. We didn't mean to do anything wrong. I'm terribly sorry."

"You didn't do anything wrong, Holliday," I said. "I was just too stupid to see what was happening."

It took her a moment to realize I was angry at me, not her. "Do you still think it's someone in the class?" Holliday asked.

I returned to study the YouTube screen. Beneath it were the words *860 views*.

"Probably not. Are there any other of my classes on here?"

"We were going to put up a version when the class was over, a highlight mix, like a super-intense class in detective work. There is another video of you on here, but not from the class."

She started a video titled *Mobile Police Detective Cited For Bravery*. I saw it had been put up by Wing, the PR intern. The three-minute clip wasn't as popular as *Random Nightmares* – only 216 views – but it lacked a provocative title.

The show kicked off with Baggs doing ninety seconds of Pride-Honor-Achievement followed by me jumping to the riser, grabbing my plaque. Then the sudden, wild applause as I lifted the ridiculous certificate and danced it across the stage as if it were the World Cup trophy, then left the stage to "I Fought the Law" sung so out

209

of time and tune it sounded like an Apache chant on LSD.

The video ended. I was relieved that a student probably wasn't responsible for the deaths, but unhappy that my killer list was as vague as ever. I had, however, discovered a common denominator in the killings.

Me.

Gregory set aside the book he was reading and stood from the couch, picking a speck of lint from his blue oxford button-down. He walked to the window and opened the thick curtains, letting his eyes roam the sunlit yard and street beyond as if needing added space in which to think.

A morning spent studying conscience had left him both fascinated and puzzled. It seemed a conscience affected a mind like the governor on an engine, keeping it operating within reduced boundaries. What idiot would want an engine that performed beneath its capabilities? Why cripple yourself that way? But the morons did, mostly through the operation of their consciences, or at least that's what they claimed in the company of others.

Was a conscience the same as religion, with people yowling their belief in nonsensical doctrines like Love the filthy poor, Don't get horny for someone else's wife, Truth will set you free? All the while shitting on the poor at every opportunity, fucking their neighbors when they had the chance, and lying whenever it helped, which it usually did.

Gregory recalled a church he'd been dragged to as an adolescent arrival in America. The purse-lipped, shoulderless minister reminded him of the strange machines dotting the green lawns of his neighbors, hose-fed devices that flicked water in all directions. The minister was a non-ending spray of *Love* and *Truth* and *Conscience*, the words soaking the head-bobbing adherents to the bone. The minister often nodded toward his wife as he spewed *Love, Fidelity, Trust, Faith* throughout the room.

Then one fall day the minister was no longer there. Nor was a woman who caterwauled in the choir. They'd run off to Mexico together.

Everyone at the church seemed astonished by this turn of events. One woman even stood, fat tears rolling down her cheeks, pleading for someone to explain how anyone in good conscience could do such a thing?

Gregory remembered how he'd almost laughed aloud at the idiot bitch, the answer naked before everyone's eyes: the minister's wife was a dowdy sack of lard with thick ankles and a hairy mole on her eyelid, while the singer was hot, comparatively speaking. It should have been blatantly obvious the minister had traded up, improving himself and his life. The man had made a logical decision.

The reality was the poor were poor because they were even stupider than most, sex felt good, and telling the truth could invite trouble or jail (the goddamn cops again). Surely everyone knew this and only pretended otherwise because . . . well, because for some strange reason the morons loved nonsensical and meaningless pronouncements.

In all things, moderation.

Money is the root of all evil.

Let your conscience be your guide.

Standing at the window and looking down the trim suburban street lined with oak and sycamore, his neighbors coming and going at the same hour each day, repeating the same ridiculous statements – *Hot again today, sure hope we get a break soon* – Gregory realized the pronouncements weren't just empty babblings, but verbal algorithms the rabble built to discourage themselves from reaching full potential, like crabs trying to escape a bucket but always dragging one another to the bottom of the pail.

Under our skin we are all the same.

Live for the day.

The average person – the moron – wanted to remain inferior. They preferred life in the bottom of the bucket. To aspire higher only reminded the morons that they were scuttling crabs, which shamed and angered them when confronted with the glorious few who climbed from the bucket.

Conscience, therefore, was a fiction designed to keep the majority of the moron species happy in the bucket with the other morons. Ema would have a conscience. A fat one.

The mailman passed by on the sidewalk. He glanced

toward Gregory's house and saw the face in the window. The postman puffed his lips and pulled on his shirt to indicate, *Hot again today, sure hope we get a break soon.* Gregory nodded and mimicked wiping his brow, drawing a smile from the moron, who moved past, oblivious to the fact Gregory had moments ago, in one sizzling intellectual concatenation, solved a major puzzle in his life: Why the vast majority of people acted contrary to their own interests.

It was the Lie of Conscience.

Gregory turned from the window and stared at the new books on his coffee table. What further revelations waited within?

Wilbert Pendel was prone on the couch of his apartment, his breath coming in ragged gasps. The room was furnished with a lounge chair, a wooden cable spool for a table, a rack for CDs and DVDs, a chipboard entertainment center with a sound system and television. In one corner was a stack of free weights. The carpet was a patchwork of stains.

The shades were open and there was a porn DVD playing on Pendel's television, a heavily tattooed muscle-builder type screwing a wild-haired woman with basketball breasts and scarlet shoes, the six-inch heels as thin as ice picks. The woman was digging at the guy's cannonball shoulders with nails an inch past her fingertips, purring, *Fuck me that's right fuck that pussy don't stop push hard baby fuck that hot pussy. . .*

Pendel was masturbating, his eyes closed, his police academy T-shirt pulled up and his jeans bunched at his knees. Inside his eyelids he was seeing Wendy Holliday, her long legs wrapped around his waist as her wet mouth howled *Fuck me Willy that's right fuck that pussy don't stop push hard Willy baby fuck that hot pussy. . .*

He knew the show-off bitch had the hots for him. Holliday played up to Ryder, but all hot bitches used the promise of pussy to get good grades or drinks or supper. She pretended to not care, but he'd seen her looking at him from the corner of her eye. It was *that* kind of look.

Fuck me Willy that's right fuck that.

The phone trilled, its ringtone identifying the caller. Pendel pulled up his pants, snatched the remote from the floor and switched off the video. The phone was on the table beside him, flanking a can of cheap beer and a greasy box holding half a pizza.

He grabbed the phone. "Hi, Ma. What's going on?"

"Are you all right, Will? You sound winded."

"I was lifting weights. What you need, Mama?"

"Just checking on my boy. Your father and I haven't heard from you for a week."

Pendel brushed sweat-matted hair from his eyes. He'd been fucking Holliday for half an hour. "Jeez, Ma, I'm twenty-four."

"You know how moms are, Willy. We like to hear from our sons."

Pendel laughed.

"What's funny, Willy?"

214

He looked out the window. Rain was falling.

"I dunno."

A pause. "How are you doing in your academy classes? Everything going along fine?"

Pendel felt a piece of food stuck in his tooth, spat it on the floor.

"Willy?" his mother said. "How are your classes?"

Pendel reached for the beer, took a sip and grimaced. Warm.

"Classes, Willy?"

"The people are ignorant. But whenever I get some thing right in class they look at me like *I'm* some kind of retard."

"We've talked about that a lot, Willy. Perception. A lot of it's in how you treat people. You're treating them with respect, right?"

"Hell yes. I wish they do the same thing back." Pendel stood and walked to the bathroom with the phone to his face. The toilet was clogged and he didn't want to deal with it. He pulled out his penis and urinated in the bathtub.

"Willy? Are you still there? What's that sound?"

Pendel grinned. "It's raining here, Ma."

"I talked to Dr Szekely yesterday, Willy. She hasn't seen you at group sessions for quite a while."

"I hate that shit. Group. It's not like I have to go."

"Sometimes people with difficult childhoods need to hear from people with the same experiences. It's a way of knowing you're not alone and that you always have a place to go and people to talk to."

Pendel zipped up and returned to the living room. "It's not talk, Ma, it's a bunch of assholes yelling and whining. They're sick, a lot of them. I'm not sick."

"I'm not saying you are, Willy. But the sessions help you to better relate to people, to work on control issues."

Pendel ejected the disk, *Max and Yolanda's Afternoon Delight*, from the DVD player and replaced it with *Buttfest III*. "I don't need to work on control issues."

"Remember when you hit that fellow in the group? That was—"

"He insulted me, Ma, said I was a moron."

"That was his fault. Yours was slapping him and calling him names back. But that was a year ago and you're beyond that kind of behavior, Willy. Why? Because of going to the group every week. I'm sure the other fellow is doing better, too."

"He doesn't go to group any more. He got to leave."

"Probably because he showed he could control himself, Willy. That's what group sessions are for. To discuss your feelings, get control of them, and live a happy life doing what you want to do."

"I'm doing that now, Ma. I'm gonna be a cop. Can we talk about something else?"

A pause. "What's your favorite class so far?"

Pendel's face brightened. He did a karate chop with his hand. "Street tactics. The self-defense stuff. Yesterday we went to the gym all day. The first thing we learned was the straight-arm bar takedown. How it works is you grab a guy by his wrist and put your forearm above his

216

elbow. Then you push down and step back and the guy goes down, *bang!* right on his fuckin' face as you—"

"Language, Willy."

"Sorry Ma. Then we learned three types of wrist locks. It was really cool. In the first kind you grab a guy's wrist and twist it so he falls down and. . ."

30

"Incredible," Harry said, watching my YouTube moment on the meeting-room computer. "And scary as hell."

"You're sure this is a connection, Carson?" Tom Mason said. "Not coincidence?"

I was pacing a tight circle, too agitated to sit. "I reviewed the forensics," I said, holding up three fingers, closing them down as I made the points. "One, the pennies at the Ballard and Brink scenes were atop the ground and clean of dust or debris, meaning recent placement. Two, the coins were within a meter of the body, easily planted when the attack occurred. Three, the Ballard and Brink coins were mint condition."

"The Lampson coin?"

"Stomach acid discolored the coin, but I expect it was as bright as the others when he was forced to swallow it."

"Each penny represents a killing?" Tom asked.

I shrugged. "Unknown. In my example they were only a symbol of randomness."

"You're saying we've got a guy out there killing at random because of a class you taught?"

My hand slapped the table, hard. "He's not killing because of the class!" I closed my eyes, breathed out. Lowered my voice. "He's killing for his own reasons, Tom, and there's no way to tell if it's random. But yes, he's patterning at least part of his murder system on my penny analogy."

Tom stared at me. "This is gonna fry the Chief's hat. Any idea why the perp picked you, Carson?"

"None. Nada."

"But you're going to review every case where you pissed someone off, right? Not only perps you sent to prison, but people you just irritated in passing."

"That could be hundreds of people, Tom," I said.

He slapped his knees and stood, meeting over.

"Then you best get started."

Gregory's new books continued to provide revelation and expert guidance. He'd moved from his research on conscience to the book on famous killers, taking notes as he went, fascinated by the process of killing. Many of the noteworthy characters in the books were drooling half-wits like Ottis Toole and Henry Lucas. Yet, Gregory noted to his satisfaction, these lumps of barely sentient protoplasm had eluded the Blue Tribe for years, demonstrating the intelligence level of the cops was actually below the dull throbbings of Toole and Lucas.

Some, like Ed Gein, were what Gregory termed "hobbyists", killing without cause or philosophy. Others were clearly insane, yowling about God or demons or talking dogs, like the Jew-boy nutcase David Berkowitz. . .

He paused and frowned. Ryder didn't consider him in either of those categories, hobbyist or madman, did he? That would be a serious mistake on Ryder's part. Though a warrior, Ryder was also a cop, thus not overly bright. It was actually conceivable that Ryder might be seeing Gregory as a Toole or Lucas, a Gein or a Berkowitz. And what if they'd missed finding the penny?

No matter. An easy fix. He went to his cabinet and withdrew an envelope.

I was surrounded by files. Desk. Floor. Lap. Cases past, cases present. Some were opened to photos of killers and rapists and general monsters. I hoped the photos might spark memory of a threat.

Harry walked up, jingling the change in his pocket. "Reunion with old friends?"

"A lot are in prison," I said. "Or dead."

He reached to the far side of my desk and tapped a photo. "How about Norbert Scaggs?"

I pulled the file close. Saw a face long and pitted from acne, the left eyebrow broken by a scar. Black hair drizzled down in ringlets that resembled dreadlocks, but were formed by sweat and clotted skin oil. Scaggs's sneer showed filthy, ragged teeth and I grimaced at the recollection of his breath.

Scaggs had a rap sheet stretching back to childhood, but he'd always skirted serious prison time, never quite within reach of my rope. When I'd heard he and his biker buddies were running a prostitution ring, I turned a guy who hung at one of Scaggs's favorite bars into a snitch, or Confidential Informant for the files.

It was a poor choice of informant, the guy deciding to freelance both sides of the street and telling the bikers he was ready to deal me any misinformation they wanted. When the bikers decided they couldn't trust the guy, a drugged-up Scaggs beat him to death with a baseball bat.

It was one of my first cases as a dick and the killing of my CI – though the guy basically committed suicide by trying to double-dip – seriously pissed me off. I went after Scaggs with personal heat, banging on his door in the middle of the night, showing up at his bars, tailing him in broad daylight. I'd haul him into the station for minor infractions like parking tickets. One day I pulled him downtown for a U-turn and was firing questions at his ugly face when he snapped, just as I'd hoped.

"*Yeah I beat your little squealer, Ryder. I busted his brains across the floor.*"

The recorder was running and I had the bastard. The jury nailed it down and Scaggs headed to Holman on a twenty-fiver, no parole.

221

Three years later a bottom-sucking mouthpiece named Preston Walls maneuvered the case into appeals court, arguing I'd "*relentlessly harassed pitiful, brain-damaged Norbert Scaggs, making him uncertain of what was reality and what wasn't.*" I'd also "*elicited a confession in circumstances that would make Don Corleone flinch*".

The case was re-tried. With a key witness dead under suspicious circumstances and another in the wind, Scaggs not only walked, he sued the state for three million dollars and settled for a quarter mill. He did the same to the MPD and got seventy-five thou. Walls got most of the largesse, his plan all along. "Scaggs would be a prospect," I admitted. "He blames me for his prison time."

"Think he's bright enough?"

I held the photo with my nails, not wanting to commit flesh to the touch. "Scaggs actually had native smarts, though Walls portrayed him as retarded."

"That's Walls," Harry said, looking as if he was smelling week-old fish. "Whatever lie works. Where you think Scaggs is hanging these days?"

"He'll be with his biker crew, the Steel Gypsies. They still meet at that hovel by Citronelle, right?"

We pulled into the lot of the Gypsies clubhouse twenty minutes later, a signless single-story mason-block building suggesting a bunker. The joint was windowless to keep rivals from shooting inside and had a red steel door, the words *Private Club* painted over it in foot-tall white letters.

I had the license tag for Scaggs's Harley and we scanned

the line of steel and chrome. "Thar she blows," I said, pointing to a ponderous black machine resembling a mechanical rhinoceros. "He's inside."

"Into the valley of the shadow of death," Harry said, pulling his nine, checking it, returning it to the holster.

We stepped into a room smelling of stale beer, cigarettes, and last-night's vomit, waiting out a worrisome moment of semi-blindness until our eyes adjusted to the dim light. There were maybe a dozen bodies in attendance, mostly male, a couple women. Most were in booths to the rear, two men clicking pool balls across a table.

"There's our boy," I said, nodding to a leather-covered back hunched over the bar, a shot and a Dixie longneck before him. A red bandana wrapped his skull, greasy strands of hair snaking down his neck. Scaggs was alone, maybe composing Elizabethan sonnets in his mind. I walked over, Harry right behind me.

"How's it going, Norb?" I said.

His head craned around and his red eyes stared. "Ryder? What the fuck are you doing here?"

I nodded at the pile of beer-soaked change at his elbows, coins and a few sodden bills. "Got some pennies there, Norbert. Anyone in mind?"

"What?"

"Like on YouTube, right? *Random Nightmares?*"

The eyes tightened to slits. "What the fuck are you talking about, Ryder? Get away from me. You ruined my life."

223

"Three years of prison ruined your life, Norbert? It was the easiest a jerk-off like you ever had it . . . free food, free bunk, and all the twinks you could poke. Or maybe your life was ruined from the day you slid out of your mama. Probably kept her from turning tricks for an hour."

Scaggs's eyes blazed, but he said nothing. Scaggs's biker buddies were fine-tuned to us now, standing. The two greasebags at the pool table moved closer, cues in hand. Harry opened his jacket to show an edge of shoulder holster.

"Private conversation," he said. "Sit down and tend to your business."

I put my hand on the bar and leaned close to Scaggs. "You never liked blacks and gays, Norbert. I got that. But what about the girl, what did you have against her? Getting an education? Was that it? Or maybe she made your pecker hard and you knew she was eighty worlds above you."

"Girl? I don't know nothing 'bout what you're talking about."

"Sure you do, Norb. We got prints at the house on Blake Road, the Lampson place."

"Fingerprints?"

I wiggled my fingers in his face. "Clear as the stars on a winter night." Scaggs was a loosely wrapped collection of dirty thoughts and erratic impulses, and I hoped to push any button that would give me a reaction.

He grinned into my eyes. "Stop busting my balls. You got something on me, show it."

I leaned lower, my mouth almost in his ear. "Don't like cops either, do you, Norb?" I said. "Me in particular? Maybe you've been out long enough you figured to take your shot at me. It's chickenshit, Norbie. You got a problem with me, you come to me. Or does direct action give you the shivers?"

"I got a lawyer you can talk to," Scaggs said. He turned away and emptied the beer glass. "But you know that, don't you?" He fake-yawned, closed his eyes and pretended to fall into a doze. It appeared he'd learned restraint the past few years.

I felt a tug on my sleeve, saw Harry nodding toward the door, *We're done here*. Scaggs chuckled wetly and I felt like bouncing his face off the bar. Instead I said something stupid along the lines, *We're watching you*.

Crossing the lot, we heard jeering laughter from inside. When we got to the car a door opened behind us and I turned to see Scaggs grinning from the shadows.

"Sounds like someone's got a personal beef with you, Ryder," he called.

"Leave it be, Carson," Harry said quietly.

"They digging in your head?" Scaggs continued. "There every time you try and sleep?"

"Let's roll," Harry said. I walked around to the passenger side, slid into the cruiser.

"But you don't know how it's gonna end, do you?

Hell, Ryder, you don't even know who it is, right? Not a clue."

Harry put the car in gear, started away. I shot a glance at Scaggs, his hair hanging in filthy ringlets, his middle finger upthrust, a victorious grin on his ugly face.

"How does it feel to be on the other side, Ryder?" he yelled.

Harry pulled into the street and looked into the rearview. "Jesus, I think I got plague just from breathing in there. How many more times we gonna have to do this, Carson?"

I thought of the files stacked on my desk. Even if one in twenty needed to be checked, it was. . .

"A lot," I said, closing my eyes and slumping low in the seat.

Harriet Ralway was in the air inside a tire. She could smell the warm rubber as her arms hugged the black circle. The ground passed by below her, back and forth, the red clay exposed by thousands of foot-scrapings. The tire hung on a yellow rope from the thick horizontal limb of an old live oak in her front yard. Her daddy had made the tire swing just for Harriet and her sister, Odelia. Odelia was eleven, four years older than Harriet.

Harriet did the math as she pumped her legs and made the swing push higher into the warm south Georgia sunlight. Harriet was seven years old.

That made the year 1943.

"Harriet, *Mama*, Harriet. . ." Odelia called. Harriet turned to the sound and there was Odelia floating right in front of her. Was Odelia flying? How did she do that? "*Mama?*"

"You have to wait your turn, Deel," Harriet lectured Odelia. "I just got in the swing. It's my turn."

Odelia frowned and flew away, over the tree and into the woods at the edge of the yard. "My turn," Harriet giggled.

But as fast as she'd gone, Odelia was back, her face as near as if she were in the swing with Harriet.

"*Mama*," the voice said again. No, not Odelia. Who was that voice? "*Mama, it's me. . .*"

Odelia melted away, replaced by another face. It was so familiar, it was—

"Mama, it's me, Patricia. Your daughter, remember?"

The tire swing dissolved, making a musical note like a chime as it vanished. Harriet felt her feet touch the ground and she was off balance, falling backward into white. A pillow surrounded her head, crisp and cool. The air suddenly smelled less of grass and more of liniment. Harriet studied the face before her. Round, with ringlets of bright blonde hair. She held up her hand and felt another hand clasp her fingers, hold them gently. It felt good.

"Patricia?" Harriet whispered. "Is that you, girl?"

"Yes, Mama, it's me. I'm right here by your bed."

Harriet felt a wave of sorrow pass through her body. It was as if she'd become surrounded by pictures from a long time ago. She had to push at them to make them retreat, but they never seemed to go far. Sometimes it seemed they were painted inside her eyelids, there every time she closed her eyes.

"Hi, baby," she said, squeezing back at the hand around hers, feeling its strength and affection. "I'm sorry."

"Sorry for what, Mama?"

"I got confused again. I thought you were Odelia."

"You weren't confused, Mama. You were just dreaming. You always know who I am."

"Just dreaming?" Harriet said, taking in the small room, her bed, the television on a table by the wall. The photos push-pinned into a cork board.

"Everybody dreams, Mama. You were dreaming of Odelia."

Harriet saw a dark hearse and smelled fresh dirt.

"She's dead, isn't she?"

"Yes, Mama. Aunt Deelie passed a dozen years back."

A tall black woman in white went by the door, stopped, looked inside. Harriet forced thoughts to the front of her head. The woman's name was Selma. She was a nurse. She was nice.

"Howdy, Miss Harriet," the nurse named Selma said. "How you doin' this lovely morning?"

"I'm good, Selma. I was dreaming again."

Harriet saw Selma pass a look to Patricia, then a broad smile. "You're a lucky woman, Miss Harriet, to have a daughter like Patricia here to care for you almost every day."

"She's my baby," Harriet said, new thoughts flooding her head. "I took care of her, now she takes care of me."

"We take care of each other, Mama," Patricia said, leaning in to kiss Harriet's brow.

"Are you crying, Odelia?" Harriet asked. "Are those tears in your eyes?"

31

It was past six when I dropped Harry at his car and headed home, too worn out to think any more. It was a quiet drive to the Island, me trying to figure who might be insane enough to murder people to get back at me. Since we moved as a team, Harry was probably making his own list, though I tended to make more enemies, by and large.

The worst problems arose from two primary quarters, Honor and Madness. The first, honor, was big with gang types. Having nothing normal people would claim as worthy, they develop honor codes as a gauge for self-worth, always using hyper-inflated currency. People who've never done anything remotely respectable bristle at the slightest signs of disrespect from others.

Dissing someone, in gang parlance, could get you killed, probably by a twenty-year-old dropout who sells drugs, fathers children he doesn't acknowledge, beats his girlfriends, steals anything within reach, all the while ignoring and evading every attempt to bend him toward becoming a productive member of the human coalition.

Yet somehow his sensitivities are so finely tuned that if you look sideways at him, he'll shoot you dead in the street to assert his honor.

The other side is more nebulous: madness. I figure of every thousand human beings, sixty are broken beyond repair from a psychological standpoint. Twenty go to prison by their mid-twenties and stay in or near the penal system. Ten become their own victims, homeless, drug or alcohol-ravaged, institutionalized for hallucinations, or they sit in a corner of a relative's home and melt into components.

This leaves a pool of thirty souls. They hold jobs, appear to be decent neighbors, speak normally on the street. But closed doors find them hunched over the vilest of pornography, or imagining ugly things to do to people of different gender, racial make-up, or contrary political views. Most stay wrapped up, their inner torments rarely breaching the containment vessel. Some are undoubtedly sociopathic, but aren't physically violent, instead manipulating those closest to them, stealing company funds, running Ponzi schemes, and so forth.

Five of these people eventually act out in a violent and generally unforeseen emotional explosion, often injuring others in the process. They reach some kind of limit and combust.

Two simply disappear. No one will know where they went, ever.

The final one is the person who not only manages his or her sickness, but draws strength from the disease, becoming more and more twisted, yet simultaneously stealthy in its concealment. These distillations of human misery are invariably megalomaniacal, their sense of self-worth inflated past all limit. They view social and cultural structures as barriers to their development, but become exceptionally adept at fitting in, emotional chameleons who can jiujitsu others with a word or gesture.

Oddly enough, they hold something in common with the Honor types: insecure at their deepest, unacknowledged core, they can be sensitive to every slight. Insult or humiliate one of these people and you could create an enemy whose sole goal in life is your destruction. And you might never even know it until it was too late.

I aimed the headlights toward Dauphin Island, looking forward to retrieving Mix-up from my animal-activist neighbor, though she would gladly keep him a week if asked; he was her favorite pooch in a house holding six dogs, three cats, and one strutting, Napoleonic parrot. But I was feeling neglectful and guilty about my late hours.

Still, my recent overnight respite with Clair played warmly through my head. I had to go home, but I didn't have to go home alone. I picked up my cell, dialed her directly.

"Hi, Clair. You home or at the shop?"

"Here I am surrounded by dead bodies. A girl's lifelong dream, right?"

"I was thinking . . . how about I pick you up and we'll head to the Island? We can grab 'cue or sandwiches on the way, sit on the deck and watch the water." I lowered my voice. "Maybe take a moonlight swim."

"Swim? But I don't have a suit at your place, do I?"

"You've not needed one in the past," I crooned. "At night, at least."

"And moonlight doesn't weigh as hard on an ageing body, does it?"

"Pardon me?"

"How's young Miss Holliday? Will she be there?"

"What do you mean?"

"Two of the last four times I've seen you have been with her."

"She's a student, Clair. I'm trying to broaden her experience."

"Broaden her experience? Is that what it's called now? I'm so out of touch with youthful slang."

Since the beginning the conversation had seemed off-kilter, like walking a path tipped three degrees sideways. But I suddenly saw things straight.

"Jesus, Clair, you think I'm, I'm, I'm. . ." I couldn't find the right words.

"I've never heard you stutter before, Carson. You're what?"

"Sleeping with her," I finished.

"Sleeping with who, Carson?"

"Holliday."

"You're sleeping with Holliday?" Clair asked.

"NO! I didn't say I *was*, I said I *wasn't*."

"I know you're not," Clair assured me. "She doesn't have that look yet. How many times has Little Miss Christmas been to your home, Carson?"

"Once, Clair. She was biking in the neighborhood and briefly stopped in. A couple hours is all."

"Two hours is brief? I think of two minutes as brief, two hours as—"

"It was perfectly innocent, Clair. She stopped by, showered, changed, then I made sandwiches and we—"

"My ears must be in terrible shape. I thought you said she showered."

"Downstairs. She'd been biking, remember?"

"Vaguely. It's my dimming geriatric mind."

"Clair, the girl is eleven years younger than I am."

"Lawd, eleven years. How much younger are you than I am, Carson?"

I mumbled something.

"I probably should look into hearing aids," Clair said. "What did you say?"

"About eleven years. But that's different. We're, uh. . ."

"Older? Wiser?" she interrupted. "I am. Older, that is."

"We're friends, Clair. Wonderful friends."

"Friends?"

"Exactly. Great friends."

A two-beat pause. "Who is this calling again? I can't remember a thing these days."

She hung up.

Gregory had put in an hour-long workout, showered, changed into gray cords, cream dress shirt, a maroon linen jacket. The sky was dark outside his office window, the moon hiding under clouds. Streetlamps lined the avenue, the trees nearest the lamps glowing white, the shadows long and stark. Gregory saw a white cat vault from a parked car's roof to its hood, then to the ground, disappearing into black. *I have to check the trap tonight*, he thought. *It's been two days.*

They had been a very busy two days, the most exciting days of his life, *electric* days, as if lightning was powering Gregory's mind, the thunder reverberating through his body with orgasmic intensity. He was exercising ultimate power. What was it Oppenheimer had said after the first successful atom-bomb test? *I am become Death, destroyer of worlds.*

What is Ryder's world like now?

Gregory sat and navigated to YouTube. No new videos had been loaded. A pity. Knowing what he now knew, would Ryder still pitch the pennies?

Gregory's eyes scanned the room and fell on the brown manila envelope on the cabinet top, his upcoming contact with Ryder. Beside the envelope folded black fabric rested atop a pair of dark Converse sneakers. An Event Suit, ready to go.

The body stocking kept his hair and skin cells on his body. He'd shaved his head as well, but wore goggles so he didn't have to shave his eyebrows. He could easily explain a shaved head to Ema, eyebrows another story. He'd bought cheap tennis shoes far too tight for his feet and opened the fronts to fit; if he left footprints they'd be three sizes too small.

When he'd left the tragic little fairy dying on the floor he'd simply stepped into the coveralls that had been folded inside his messenger bag and traded his event shoes for boots. In the old truck he was one more anonymous painter or carpenter on his way to a jobsite.

A smart man prepared for every eventuality. The cops weren't smart, but they were dogged, and a single misstep could be costly. Only after learning that from Ema had he conceived and developed his Event Suit. Use it, burn it, wear another. He'd bought a dozen body stockings and sneakers. And could always buy more.

But now to check his traps. He could use a little furry company before the cats moved to the next stage of their existence.

32

When I returned to the department at eight a.m. the files were still on my desk, though I could now re-file the Scaggs material. Both Harry and I had felt it: Scaggs wasn't the perp.

There was something new on my desk: a letter-sized manila envelope. Across the front was a taped square of paper, printing on its face.

OFFICIAL POLICE MATERIALS
If found please return to Detective Carson Ryder,
Police Department, Mobile Alabama

"What the hell's this?" I said aloud.

Al Perkins, the detective at the next cubicle, stood and looked over the divider. "You don't know?"

"Never saw it before."

"Some woman brought it in a few minutes ago, said she found it on the sidewalk a hundred feet from the parking garage. I figured it must have fallen out of your briefcase or something. Seemed odd. Didn't you just get here?"

I undid the metal clip and opened the envelope, shook it over my desk. Three bright pennies dropped out. Followed by a strip of paper much like those found in fortune cookies, bearing one brief line:

Selected by a chance in time, pennies pay for all your crimes

"Where's the woman?" I said, my heart in my throat as I jumped to my feet, chair rocketing into the wall.

Perkins shrugged.

"WHAT DID SHE LOOK LIKE?" I yelled.

Perkins gawped at me like I'd blown a circuit. "For chrissakes, Carson, she didn't walk up here. She left it at the desk."

I took the steps three at a time, bolted across the lobby seconds later. Big Jim Lott, the desk man, pointed out the door. "Sixty maybe. Polite black lady, grandmotherly type. Gray hair, stout build. Blue dress. Big purse. She walked out of here two minutes ago."

I hit the street at a run, looking both ways, nothing. I sprinted to the end of the block. *There!* Getting into a silver compact. "Excuse me, ma'am," I said, puffing in behind her. "You just left an envelope at the station?"

She studied me: jeans, black T-shirt, blue running shoes. I produced my ID, held it up. "I'm a police officer."

"I was walking down the street, there it was in the middle of the sidewalk. I took it to the police station straightaway."

"Where was the envelope lying, ma'am? Can you show me?"

She backtracked two dozen feet, stopped. Pointed to the pavement. "Right about there, I guess."

Nothing but sidewalk. No pennies. No notes. Sparse traffic blew past.

"You didn't see anyone leave the envelope?" I asked.

"I turned the corner and there it was." She thought a moment and got wide-eyed. "It didn't have a bomb or nothing like that inside, did it?"

"No ma'am, nothing like that."

She breathed a sigh of relief, looked at me over tortoise-shell glasses. "You're the one who dropped it?"

"Yes, ma'am. It was a mistake. Thank you for bringing it to the department."

I nodded and moved away. "Sir?" the woman called to my back. "Officer?"

I turned. "Yes, ma'am?"

"You should be more careful with things in the future, sir. It said 'Official'."

I nodded. "Yes, ma'am. I promise to do better."

Harriet Ralway was sitting in the sun on the long side lawn. There were planes in the sky, the soldiers returning from the war. Daddy wasn't coming. Harry James was playing a trumpet somewhere nearby. A little girl ran to the edge of the Gulf waves and picked up a shell. When she returned she was an old woman.

"Odelia?" Harriet said. But when she reached out Odelia was gone. The planes flew by and the air was quiet. Harriet closed her eyes and listened to Harry James. He was playing "Muskrat Ramble", a fun tune.

A little boy ran past, that boy from next door, Jerry Ralway, a scamp. She would fall in love with him in high school. They'd get married young and have a pregnancy that ended in a miscarriage. She would not get pregnant again for many years, a daughter named Patricia. The marriage would last twenty-four years until Jerry died in a car crash outside of Dawson, drunk on Southern Comfort and Coke, drag-racing that old Dodge Charger even though it was 1988 and he was forty-six years old. Racing, hunting, fishing all the time . . . he never really grew up, that Jerry Ralway.

Harriet sighed, heard a crackly sound and opened her eyes, dreaming again. She was in her usual place when she'd go outside, the bench at the far corner of the lawn, the brick building at her back. Many of the residents couldn't come here because it was distant and old legs couldn't walk so far. Plus you had to cross grass and walkers and wheelchairs didn't work well.

The sound again: feet over dried leaves. Harry James played softly in the distance, the notes punctuated by crunching leaves.

Harriet opened her eyes and turned to the woods bordering the property, a tall fence separating them. A shadow stared back at her, a black shadow in the shape of a man. The shadow was leaning against a tree.

The Shadow's name was Lamont Cranston and he fought crime on radio when Harriet was a little girl. The Shadow knew the evil that lurked in the hearts of men. Harriet was thrilled to be visited by a man who'd kept her company on many a youthful afternoon.

No, wait . . . there was a diving mask over the man's eyes. It wasn't the Shadow. It must be Lloyd Bridges, that actor she used to love to watch on TV in the sixties, *Sea Hunt*. Such a handsome man, unruly hair and sparkly-crinkle eyes.

Harry James began playing the *Sea Hunt* theme, so thoughtful. Mr Bridges was getting ready to take a dive. He had one of those things in his hand, metal and rubber. Jerry had one of those things too, used it to bring home supper sometimes, red snapper or mackerel. Spear-fishing, Jerry called it.

"Hi, Lloyd," Harriet whispered, waving hello with her fingertips.

Lloyd Bridges smiled and waved back.

Ten minutes later we were in the meeting room adjoining Lieutenant Mason's office. The far wall held a TV monitor and video player. A whiteboard stood in the corner. One wall was all windows and I saw gulls darting through a cumulus sky.

"It was sitting on the sidewalk?" Tom Mason said, spinning the envelope his way with the eraser of a pencil.

"I called Forensics. They're looking for trace on the pavement."

"Anyone witness anything?"

"Probably nothing to witness. Hell, you could have the envelope in your pants. Shake your leg as you walk and out it falls."

"*Selected by a chance in time,*" Tom said, studying the message. "You figure that means the victims? Random, like you said in class?"

"Seems to fit."

"*Pennies pay for all your crimes.* Dead people pay for your misdeeds, I guess. Where the hell is this coming from?"

I upended my hands, *no idea.*

"A random killer," Tom said, closing his eyes. "Jesus. What you gonna do from here, Carson?"

I was considering that thought when Tom's desk phone rang. He picked up, looked at me. "Gotcha, Darlene," he said. "Tell the Chief we'll be up in a minute."

Evidently the Mayor wasn't in need of the Chief this time, since Baggs was standing at his open door. We filed past. Tom sat, I leaned against the wall, waiting.

"What have you done, Ryder?" Baggs said, glaring at me.

"I don't understand."

"Seems simple enough. Somehow you've inspired a lunatic to start killing citizens at random."

I heard a cleared throat from Tom and looked his way. He bent his fingers downward and mouthed the word *Calm*.

"We don't know if that's the case, Chief," I said evenly. "It's true he's grabbed the coin analogy from the website and—"

"Why the hell was it there? Did you start the Carson Ryder TV network?"

"A few of the recruits put the video up. Without my knowledge."

He scowled. "Why?"

"They, uh, thought it was interesting."

"What's next, a film showing how to poison someone?"

I started to explain how the video had been created from class notes, but stopped. If I hadn't grasped the newest tech wave, there was no way Baggs would've.

"If word of a random killer gets out, we've got a PR nightmare on our hands," Baggs said. "Especially if it's thought a member of the force influenced it. I want that goddamn film pulled off FaceTube or whatever."

I nodded, not the time to argue. "You got it, sir."

"How nice of you," Baggs said, his voice thick with sarcasm. "Now, what are you doing to nail this bastard?"

I detailed what we had in progress: canvassing, working the snitches, the forensics people going over every inch of the scenes, processing the evidence we had. Baggs shook his head.

"Running in circles. What are you planning that will work?"

I jammed my hands in my pockets and pretended to think for several seconds. "Maybe we could take a tip from the Wizard of Oz and hire a skywriter to scrawl SURRENDER above the city."

Tom Mason maneuvered between Baggs and me. "I'll call in part-timers and some retired dicks, Chief. Move cold-case cops to the present cases. Everyone not engaged in a pressing case is getting involved."

"FBI?"

"No indication of anything crossing state lines. Half the FBI is on homeland security, stretched to the limit. They'll stay away as long as they can, so for now it's ours."

"OK. . ." Baggs said, clapping his big pink hands together. "You think it's random, right?" he said. "Like the fucker said in his note? Chance?"

"Seems to be, Chief," Tom said.

Baggs looked my way, same question. The question had been nagging at me day and night.

I said, "I don't know if they're random or not."

"Then what the hell's the motive? How are they connected?"

I had nothing. Baggs shook his head. Tom cleared his throat.

"What is it, Mason?" Baggs said. "Speak up."

"I'd like to activate the PSIT, Chief. Give the guys more authority."

The PSIT was the Psychopathological and Sociopathological Investigative Team, known internally as *Piss-it*. The entire team was Harry and me plus any specialists

244

we might call in. The major advantage was having a single hand on the investigative wheel. That and, as Tom mentioned, we had experience with these people.

Unfortunately, Baggs looked as if the Lieutenant had suggested putting circus clowns in charge of the investigation.

"You actually want Ryder to run an investigation of the crimes he kick-started? A man who doesn't know if they're random? Doesn't have a motive? Who wants to use the Wizard of Oz to catch the perp?"

Tom ignored the barb, his face serious. "Carson and Harry know psychos better than anyone this side of Quantico. If they coordinate the investigation, it'll produce. You've got to trust me on this, Chief."

But Baggs wasn't in a trusting mood.

"It makes no sense to me, Lieutenant. The idea is ridiculous and I don't want to hear it again."

Tom thought quietly for a moment. Shot me a glance I couldn't decipher.

Said, "Can I talk to you in private, Chief?"

33

Gregory approached Ema from behind, weaving through the tables of diners. Even though he'd already had a busy and exciting morning, his guts were gloriously quiet. He looked at his watch, 10.06 a.m. Despite the morning's full agenda, he was only six minutes late to meet Ema.

It was amazing how much a superior man could accomplish with a bit of planning.

Gregory paused to flick lint from the lapel of his black silk suit, feeling the approval in the other diners' eyes. *What a strikingly handsome man!* When he finally arrived across from Ema, her eyes popped wide.

"Gregory? My Lord, what did you . . . where's your hair?"

He shook his head as he sat. "Don't ask, Ema. Just don't ask."

She put on pout lips and downcast eyes. As if all was

normal, they ordered, a seafood omelet for her, stripped-down salad for Gregory, spinach and walnuts with chick peas. The waiter brought a small pitcher of honey without turning it into an ordeal.

Ema masticated in silence, occasionally daring a glance at Gregory's shining cranium. After five minutes Gregory performed a complex expression – heavy sigh through fluttering lips and a raised left eyebrow morphing into a head-roll with closed eyes – then set his fork aside and looked at his sister.

"I don't know where to start, Ema."

Ema clapped her chubby hands like a seal. "At the *beginning*, dear."

"A couple weeks ago I was at a grocery near down-town. A sign on the bulletin board asked for volunteers at an elementary school down the street. I don't know what came over me, Ema. I, that is. . ." Gregory pulled a face found in a magazine ad: *I Never Believed Tiles Could Get This Clean.*

Ema's mouth dropped wide. "You went in and volun-teered?"

"You've always nagged me to get out and meet people. I signed up for the after-hours program. It's nothing really, assisting with math skills, reading. . ."

"You're using your knowledge to help children," Ema gushed. "And you know so much."

Gregory frowned. "I'm not teaching quadratic equa-tions, Ema. It's addition and subtraction."

Ema looked ready to tip over from joy. They'd have

to rent a crane to get her upright. "You're making the world better, Gregory. I'm so proud." She paused. "But how does that explain your hair?"

"The children are lower-income," Gregory said. "Some don't live in the most sanitary conditions. We sit close for our studies."

Blank confusion filled Ema's face. "I don't get it."

"I caught head lice, Ema. I had to shave my head and apply medicine. Don't look at me like that, I'm fine."

"But you have to keep your head . . . bald?"

Gregory sat back. "Don't be ridiculous, of course not. But I'm going to. At least for a while." He patted his dome. "Sort of a badge of honor. And it's certainly easy to care for."

Ema giggled. "No shampoo. No combs or brushes." She moved her own head side to side, checking Gregory's shiny pate. "Now that I'm getting used to you like that, it's actually kind of cute." She tittered. "Maybe even sexy. Are there any ladies in the volunteer program?"

"It seems men are at a premium. I'm the sole male."

A sly grin. "Any ladies of your age?"

Gregory rolled his eyes. "Ema. . ."

"Oh, all right," she trilled. "Be coy. You should call Dr Szekely and tell her you're helping children. She'd be delighted."

Gregory's eyes darkened. "I'm not required to see Szekely any more, Ema."

"I know that, silly. But you should tell her. It's a huge

step, Gregory. You're a community volunteer." Ema looked at Gregory and tears came to her eyes.

"No waterworks, Ema," Gregory sighed, "it's only a couple hours a week."

"Two hours or two minutes, I'm so proud of you."

"Can we talk about something else?" Gregory said. "Now that you know my secret."

"Anything, dear. Like what?"

Gregory knit his brow and stared at the ceiling, as if searching for an idea. "Oh, I don't know," he said. "Maybe you could tell me more about police shows. That was mildly interesting."

While I waited for Tom Mason to return from Baggs's office, my cell rang. I checked the screen, saw *Hernandez*. The name didn't register for two beats, then I recalled the slim, mustached guy who worked for Animal Control. I pulled the phone to my ear.

"Tell me you're only calling to see how I'm doing, Al."

"Wish I could, Detective. I'm back under the bridge. Four more feline carcasses that I can see. You want me to bag them?"

I thought about what Clair'd say if I brought her another sack of mutilated cats. "I doubt there'd be anything new to discover, Al. We know what's happening. At least the body count seems to be slowing."

"There's that, I guess. These people, Detective Ryder . . . they ever become normal again?"

"Not that I've seen."

"I was afraid of that. I'll keep you informed."

I looked up and saw Tom crossing the floor, his meeting with Baggs over. I was in his shadow two seconds later and we went into his office and closed the door.

Tom said, "Piss-it is up and running, Carson. You and Harry decide who does what. I'll send out departmental notification."

My mouth fell open. "What did you say to Baggs? He was dead-set against it."

"Baggs is ten per cent cop, forty per cent lawyer, fifty per cent politician. I explained if you and Harry were running the case and it went off the rails, he could point to you and say, 'Not my fault. These guys assured me they could do the job.'"

I jammed my hands in my pockets and stared out the window. "Harry and I get the shitstorm and Baggs lives to fight another day."

Tom's lean brown hand squeezed my shoulder. "Just get it done, Carson. Baggs is right about one thing: it's a nightmare in waiting."

I nodded half-heartedly and went to our cubicle. Now in control of the action, at least in a titular fashion, we could call in specialists.

"I want Doc Kavanaugh to consult on this one," I told Harry.

He shot a thumbs up. "See if she can get here yesterday."

Dr Alec Kavanaugh arrived a half-hour later. She was a psychologist who had done exemplary work with the MPD in the past. Doc K was in her early forties, willow-slender, with huge brown eyes in a pale oval face. Her prematurely white hair fell to her mid-back when unleashed. She moved like a kite in a gentle breeze and reminded me of a female wizard, lacking only a glittery wand to complete the effect.

"He's intelligent and educated," Doc Kavanaugh said after studying the YouTube video, envelope, and message. "Word choice is clear and precise, comma placement exact. There's rhyme and a sense of meter. I also doubt the fortune-cookie-sized message is accidental."

"He's predicting the future?" Tom said. "More to come?"

"I hope I'm wrong. You say this guy – and I'd bet my shrink license it's a male – killed three people you know about?"

I had the case files in front of me, pushed them her way. She lofted reading glasses from the beaded lanyard around her graceful neck and read the overviews.

"Crossbow bolt?" she said, wincing. "Plus a knife and a . . . what did it say in the ME's report? Ax or hatchet-type blade with sharp-edged side and a blunt side. Did any of the deaths occur where a gunshot wouldn't have been heard?"

"The last one – Lampson. It was isolated."

"If the killer is choosing weapons to fit the conditions, a handgun would have been the obvious choice." She reached for the pre-autopsy photos of Lampson. "The victim was over six feet tall and obviously worked out, potentially formidable. Yet the killer chose a blunt ax or club. Why?"

"He also played with the vic, Doc," I said. "At least, that's how it looks from blood spatter."

Dr Kavanaugh stared at the ceiling for several moments, assembling the facts in her head. The calm exterior was deceptive, her lightning-fast mind calling up previous experiences, weighing facts, consulting reference books, hearing expert testimony. All heavily dosed with intuition.

"He's liking what he's doing," she finally said. "Or perhaps I should say he's getting comfortable with it. The first attack was an arrow shot from distance. The next time he went close enough to use a knife."

"And now he's going berserk with a freaking hatchet," I said. "Chopping his victim in the living room, chasing him into the bedroom for a slow kill."

"I'm intrigued by the weaponry," she said. "Arrow, knife, hatchet-slash-ax. It has meaning."

"Strangest assortment I've ever encountered," Tom said.

"Woo-woo-woo," Harry said, patting his lips.

"What?" Kavanaugh said.

"It's what Tommy Brink thought his attacker said. 'That Indian thing,' is what the kid said. 'Woo-woo-woo.'"

Kavanaugh stared at Harry. The phone rang and Tom picked it up. Listened.

Whispered, "My Lord."

We were at the scene fifteen minutes later, a wooded field beside a white complex with a long and broad lawn, the sign by the street proclaiming MAGNOLIA VILLA – A FULL-SERVICE RETIREMENT COMMUNITY. The forensics van was there, as was an ambulance and three patrol cruisers, another pulling in – Horse Austin and his young partner, Mailey. The kid exited and I watched Austin turn away and bring something to his lips, then jam it beneath the seat. When he got out I caught a glimpse of brown bag on the floorboard.

"A bit far from your beat, Horse," I noted as Austin slapped his hat on his head. "I thought you worked the second district."

Austin chomped a heavy wad of gum. "Goddamn brass hats keep moving us like a game of fuckin' checkers. I been on three beats in five years."

Current wisdom preferred cops working regular beats to improve relations with the citizenry. I figured the blustering, ticket-plastering, quick-to-his-nightstick Austin had quickly worn out his welcome in the districts.

Harry pointed to an old school bus painted blue, the MPD logo on its side. "What you think they brought the bus for?"

"Probably the police-academy types," Austin grumbled. "They been using 'em on searches alongside the Civil Air Patrol cadets."

"It's a good idea," I told Austin. "The recruits may need to coordinate searches in the future."

"Buncha meddling kids." Austin arched his back and belched. The duo turned and trudged toward the command vehicle ahead, but Austin stopped dead in his tracks, as if something had entered his mind. Mailey kept walking, but Austin headed back to me, one eye narrowed.

"I heard some weird scuttlebutt, Ryder. Even knowing you, I can't quite believe things I'm hearing."

"Can't believe what, Horse?"

"That you caused these killings."

"*What?*"

"You did some fool thing that got this fucker riled up, pushed his buttons. You make out like you're the big expert in psychos and you go and set one off."

I walked to Austin and looked him in the eyes. "No one could believe that," I said, "unless they were simple-minded."

He cracked his chewing gum and shrugged. "Just repeating what's in the wind, Ryder."

Harry walked up. "You got a job to do somewhere, Austin?"

Austin grinned and turned away.

"I wonder who's spreading that story?" I said to Harry, watching Austin make his lazy way to the command post.

"Who cares?" Harry said. "No one's gonna believe it."

We veered toward the woods, seeing activity behind the trees. I pushed through the brush and crossed a dry creek bed. The woods thinned out and I saw a form sprawled on the ground. It resolved into a woman's body, elderly, gray hair, wrinkled skin on her arms. She was turned away from me, shoeless, blood on the back of her blue dress, two inches of blood-covered metal sticking out of the fabric.

Clair was kneeling beside the body. She looked up and saw me, showing no emotion. Whatever issues divided us at present, they held zero sway here.

"There's some kind of metal point emerging from the

victim's back," she said. "And a wire device hanging from a wound in her upper abdomen. Any ideas?"

I knelt and took the wire in my gloved fingers. "It's from a fishing spear, Clair. The kind shot from a gun."

"Where's the shaft?"

"With the perp, I imagine. The shaft detaches to make it easy to remove from the fish."

Clair shook her head. "A spear gun. I thought I'd seen everything."

I walked twenty densely wooded feet to the fence, on the other side of which was the mown grass of the facility. I found the victim's shoes snagged in briars. A dozen feet on the far side of the fence was a trio of trees and a low-cut hedge, a cast-iron bench at the foot of the trees. I pulled at the base of the hurricane fence. Two vertical cuts had been made in the mesh, a yard apart, a couple feet high. The fence opened like a top-hinged doggie door.

I figured the killer had been hidden on the woods side of the fence, his victim on the other. He'd fired the spear and she'd dropped, the impact like a ball bat swung by Barry Bonds. Hopefully she'd been unconscious when pulled across the grass and through the fence, her shoes snagged by branches or vines as he hauled her into the woods.

I explained the scenario to a forensics tech, then walked to the street where Harry and Tom were talking to a trim, fiftyish woman in a white uniform. A card on her breast gave her name and title, JENNY WILKES – DAY SUPERVISOR. Her face was puffy from crying.

"We called as soon as we missed Harriet," the woman said.

"You let a patient with Alzheimer's wander alone?" Tom asked.

"Harriet always visited the same places. You can see everywhere from the building. The entire property is fenced. And it was early. Harriet was usually more clear-headed in the morning."

Harry said, "The last anyone saw her was. . ."

"Right after breakfast. She was going to take a walk and be back before nine, like always, as regular as a clock. When no one saw Harriet at nine, we sent the staff out. When we couldn't find her we called the police."

I pointed to the bench beneath the trees. "Ms Ralway liked to sit there in the morning?"

"Every day the weather allowed."

I jogged a couple hundred feet, stopping short of the building. The area preferred by the victim was at a slight incline. Harry was beside the bench, but I couldn't see below his calves, the effect of the incline. I ran back.

"Look at the building from the ground," I told Harry.

Harry lowered to his hands and knees. His head was shaking as he stood.

"On the ground is out of sight."

"The perp used the fishing line to pull her across the grass and into the woods."

"Fishing line could handle it?"

I'd spear-fished reefs in the Caribbean, knew the gear. "Five-hundred-pound test is a fairly standard line," I said.

"You can get big-game lines that handle a couple thousand pounds."

We heard a sound like a human siren powered by grief and turned to a stout blonde woman in the distance, screaming, held back by a pair of cops and a paramedic.

"Next of kin, I figure," Harry said.

34

I met with Tom and Harry after they'd taken statements from facility personnel. The pair were heading to the DA's office to discuss a court case and I said I'd take the cruiser downtown. The Medical Examiner and forensics workers were still swarming the woods and grounds.

There was no report of the penny yet, but I knew it would appear.

The recruits were being led from the woods by Captain Alvin Leighton, the academy's director. They broke into small groups and swung wide of the official vehicles, wandering toward the blue bus. I saw Holliday alone in the street, eyes vacuuming every detail, studying while others relaxed.

I walked over. "Hello future-officer Holliday. I heard you were getting in a little SAR without the R."

"We were at the jail studying intake procedures.

Captain Leighton loaded us onto a bus and we were here fifteen minutes later."

If I'd been teaching intake procedures I wouldn't have the class on a weekday morning but around midnight on a Friday, when payday coincided with the arrival of government checks. Shrieking whores, puking drunks, blood-soaked fistfight participants, people babbling on a cornucopia of drugs . . . If you're teaching religion, it's best to provide a vision of Hell before you open Sunday school.

"So I guess it's back to jail?" I said.

She nodded at the battered old bus, torn and creaky seats and D-rings in the floor for prisoner transport. It rode like a cattle truck. Wilbert Pendel was hanging out the window of the bus and shooting a classmate the finger. Holliday moaned.

"You really don't care for Pendel, do you?" I said.

"It makes me feel guilty, but I don't. There's the maturation issue. Plus it's like he's . . . I don't know, watching you through some weird crack in space-time. You can see him, but you can't make contact."

"Sounds creepy."

"It's not so much creepy as sad, somehow."

"I'm heading downtown," I said. "The ride isn't a whole lot softer, but the company's a step up."

She was delighted to escape the dilapidated bus and we wove slowly through three cruisers, forensics van, command van, ambulance, and the door-open Ford Fiesta I figured belonged to the screaming woman.

I pulled past the Fiesta as the bagged body emerged from the woods, Clair walking behind with her kit in her hand. She looked up and saw Holliday and me. I kept facing forward. When I glanced into the rearview mirror she was beside the forensics van with her head turned our way.

I set a course for HQ, Holliday asking questions about the scene as we drove. They were intelligent questions, but then she was the foster daughter of a cop. I was in full lecture mode when my cell rang: Harry.

"The woman at the scene, next of kin? It was the daughter, Patricia Ralway. Chaplain Burgess transported her home. When he told her to expect a visit from MPD detectives she said, 'Let's do it today.' Tom and I are at the DA's, trying to postpone some court cases so I can go full time on Penny Man. Can you maybe. . ."

Gregory pulled into Ema's flower-lined drive, knowing she would be out until early afternoon. Today was Hair Day, when Ema and a robot hairdresser named Traci flapped tongues for an hour. His next meal with Ema would be dominated by Traci's diet-childcare-boyfriend woes.

After spending fifty bucks for whatever – Ema's hair never changed – she'd waddle from shop to shop in Fairhope, nattering with shopkeepers and buying ridiculous things like floral potholders. With only two hours gone since breakfast, she'd plop down in a restaurant and eat again. The woman was an eating and shopping machine.

Gregory wondered if Ema was burning through her inheritance. She made money writing her little newsletters, but enough to cover her eating and shopping tabs? Gregory had studied math and computers at Auburn University. Using natural abilities teachers noted as far back as middle school – *"He came from where? When? You're kidding!"* – he excelled. At least until things got a bit difficult.

Brother and sister shared everything, her idea   the woman had bonding issues or something – so he used her spare remote to pull into the garage. Neighbors saw a white Avalon at least once a month. The couple in the nearest unit were in Wisconsin for the summer anyway, visiting a bunch of squalling grand-brats Ema knew by name.

Once, while Ema was babbling about the kids, Gregory asked how she could tell them apart. Ema had sung, *"Katie is the youngest one, Willy is the oldest son, beneath Willy stands Joanelle, then comes Twyla and Daniel. Three and twelve, eight-six-four."*

"The numbers being how old they are?" he had asked.

"Yes," Ema replied proudly.

"Don't the creatures age?"

"I set it two years ago when I moved here and met the Pedersens. Of course now the children are—"

"Never mind, Ema, I get it."

Gregory opened the door from the garage into Ema's

kitchen. For a moment it seemed he could still smell mamaliga and he froze as a whirlwind of images and words blazed between his synapses.

. . . share food with us, Grigor. Isn't he a pretty one, Petrov . . . if you jam rubber balls in their mouths . . . Carnati, piftie, mamaliga and tuica . . . You stink like a sewage factory, poopy . . . what happened next. . .

Gregory steadied himself against the wall and willed the images from his brain. He felt a sudden weight in his bowels and had to empty them, which meant using Ema's dreadful bathroom. He entered to a smell of flowery potions so thick the air should have been a gel. It was a large contemporary bathroom with hard white light streaming from the ceiling, as bright as a freaking operating theater. The room was in the center of the house, windowless.

The counter was white stone and three meters long including the sink. A large Jacuzzi dominated the room and Gregory didn't dare let himself think of Ema floating in a foaming tub. The toilet wasn't a standard model but a bidet, probably so Ema didn't have to reach around her vast bulk to cleanse herself.

After evacuating – not too bad, a bit of gas – Gregory went to the pink-inflected living room with its dolls, stuffed animals, throw pillows, cutesy knickknacks . . . a child's room that over-ran the entire house. Then there was the reading material: magazines filled couch-side racks and were spread out on the coffee table, articles and recipes sticky-tabbed. Gregory snatched up a *Cooking*

Light magazine and turned to a blue-tabbed page, seeing a blonde model with a questioning smile under half-closed eyes. She was holding up a plate of wilted lettuce. The article asked *Do Your Greens Go Brown Too Soon?* and offered suggestions for keeping vegetables fresh, as well as recipes for low-calorie salad meals.

Gregory tossed the magazine back on the table. He'd never seen Ema eat a salad without a plate of fat and sludge beside it. Then there were the celebrity magazines and true-crime paperbacks, a bookcase of the damn things, the bookcase pink, of course. *My Father the Mob Boss* rested against *Princess Di in Her Own Words. The Killer in the Next Room* flanked *Madonna: The Myth and the Magic.* Gregory shook his head at the waste of mind and money.

He found his sister's records in a pink metal case on the floor of her bedroom closet. Gregory carried them into the dining room, opening the case on the table and immediately spotting a folder inscribed in Ema's wide, childlike handwriting: *Financial Stuff, May–June.* This year.

Bingo!

He pushed aside ceramic candlesticks festooned with smiling cherubs and spread the pages across the glossy oak tabletop: A report from Ema's accountant, the June statement from her investment fund, similar pages from her SEP-IRA fund. His eyes found the bottom lines and added as he jumped sheet to sheet. One minute later he was putting the paper back in the case.

Two minutes later, he was on the road, his face one borrowed from a man on an outdoor board he'd passed seconds before.

How Would You Feel If You Won This Week's Lottery?

35

"Ms Ralway?" I was on the porch of a blue bungalow, trim and fresh and part of a fifties-era suburb not showing its age. "My name is Carson Ryder and I'm—"

"I know who you are," she said, pushing open the screen door. "Please come in."

Patricia Ralway's eyes were rimmed with red, her fingers clutching a tissue. She was a plain-faced woman at best, dressed in Levi's beneath a rumpled T-shirt that said THE BEST DAUGHTER IN THE WORLD. The shirt a gift from her mother, no doubt.

I said, "We'd like to ask you—"

"Some questions. I know, I watch a lot of police shows. Please, sit, make yourselves comfortable. Can I get you a glass of sweet tea?"

Holliday started to decline the offer, but I said, "Thank you. That would be nice, since it's such a hot day."

"Yes," Ralway said, as if suddenly realizing there was a day going on. "It's a scorcher, isn't it?" She went to the kitchen and I heard the refrigerator opening, ice clinking in glasses.

"I'm sorry," Holliday whispered. "I didn't mean to—"

"In a situation like this I usually accept any offering. Tea, coffee. Cookies. Sometimes a simple human interaction helps break down the wall."

"Noted."

The libations arrived. I apologized again for the interruption and pulled my notepad from my pocket. "I guess my primary interest is any enemies your mother might have had, Ms Ralway. People angry with her, though she might not have realized it."

Patricia Ralway shook her head. "I've thought and thought about it. No, none. Oh, there were women she quarreled with now and then, but they were at the home. You don't suspect anyone there, do you?"

"Not really."

"Then she had no one that would wish her harm."

"Is your father—"

"Gone for decades. Dead."

"How long was your mother in the home?"

"Five months. It wasn't her physical state but her mind. She had Alzheimer's, as you know. She'd seem fine earlier in the day, but afternoons and evenings she would often have trouble recognizing me, or confuse me with my late aunt. It was g-getting difficult . . . I'm s-sorry." Tears fell from her cheeks to her

266

lap. "It hurts," she apologized. "It hurts worse than anything."

"I've been there, ma'am," Holliday said quietly. "Take all the time you need."

Ralway nodded her thanks to Holliday and took some deep breaths. A couple of elderly women at the home had pulled Harry aside to whisper in his ear. He'd passed on the info, what I figured was the gossipy meanderings of those with too much time on their hands.

"I hate to bring this up, ma'am," I said, "but a couple of the folks at the home said you and your mother fought on occasion."

"A bunch of eavesdropping biddies. Mama and me quarreled once a month or so. She was on me to settle down, have children – like that would ever happen. Sometimes she'd gnaw the topic like a dog on a bone and I'd tell her to drop it."

"Sounds like typical mother stuff," Holliday said.

"She'd get irritated when I said I'd been at a bar. She'd say, 'Now, Patty, you know full well a barroom's no place to meet a decent man.' I'd tell her, 'Mama, I ain't lookin' for a decent man . . . I want a good one.'"

I couldn't help myself and smiled. So did Holliday. "That was how we argued," Ralway continued, "two hens clucking at one another. Five minutes later I'd be laying beside her as she told stories from her youth. She was spending more and more time in her past. It was sad, but it made her happy and that was a kind of reward."

Tears came to her eyes again.

"Forgive me if I'm overstepping any boundaries, ma'am," Holliday said. "But I lost my mama two years ago next month. We were very close." She reached out for Patricia Ralway's hand. "The good thing is that my mama's death was the worst thing that ever happened to me."

Patricia Ralway canted her head at Holliday.

"I don't understand, miss."

"I've seen people who barely sniffled when they lost a parent because they didn't have a good relationship. When I hurt – and that's every day – it underscores the depth of the love my mother and I had for one another, and how so few people get to experience anything so wonderful. My pain also tells me our love."

Ralway's face twitched. Tears came hard and Holliday stepped to Ralway and held her tight. After a minute they separated, Patricia Ralway's hand squeezing Holliday's shoulder.

"Thank you so much. I know that will be of help."

"I'm obliged for your time, ma'am," I said. "I'm sorry to have disturbed you."

Mrs Ralway walked beside Holliday as we went to the door. I had become extraneous. We stopped at the threshold. Ms Ralway thanked Holliday again, stepping back to scan her from tip to toes.

"My, my . . . I'll bet a pretty girl like you has your pick of men when you're out on the town," she said.

I waited for Holliday to ignore the comment or offer

an embarrassed thank you, but she surprised me yet again by going for sisterhood.

"We both know how it is," Holliday said, winking. "The best-looking men are either gay or have more mommy or daddy issues than a decade of *Parents Magazine*. Or, of course, they're not really single." Holliday mimed pulling a wedding ring off and dropping it in a pocket.

Like a moment of sun breaking through storm clouds, Ms Ralway chuckled. "Isn't that the God's truth about men. I met a guy a couple weeks back I swear had both mommy and daddy issues and maybe granny and grampa thrown in as well."

We climbed into the cruiser and drove a few miles in silence. I turned to Holliday. "All good-looking single guys have issues? Really?"

"You weren't listening, Carson. Not all do."

I nodded. "That's good."

"The others are gay."

My head spun her way, she was grinning. "On a more serious note," she said, "there's something I'd like to talk about, though now's probably not the time."

"Go ahead. I'd—"

My cell phone rang. I fumbled it from my jacket.

Clair. She got to the point. "If you're not too busy, you might want to know I found the penny during the visual exam, tucked in the labial folds. I'm starting the post now. Can I expect to see you and little Miss Christmas at the procedure?"

"I'll have to send a sub, I'm too busy."

"No Miss Christmas? Damn. I wanted to look at someone the same age as my daughter."

"You have no children, Clair."

"I'm ageing *and* childless? Shit."

She hung up. I kept my face expressionless and I told Holliday about the penny's location. "Didn't you want to talk about something?" I remembered, distracted by the last minute with Clair.

"It can wait."

I dropped her at the jail and proceeded to the office, meeting up with Harry. He'd managed to get six weeks' continuance on his upcoming trial to allow him full-tilt boogie on the Penny Man case. Neither of us mentioned that, if the killer continued at his current rate, another ten people would be dead by then.

My next step was to call in Doc K, who had assembled conclusions from our last meeting. The initial cast was the Doc, Harry, Tom, and me. We had just closed the door of the conference room when it pushed open: Baggs. "This is a meeting on the current situation?" he asked. Assured it was, he said, "I'd like to sit in."

"Good to have you, sir," Tom drawled, playing the game that had kept him in charge of the homicide division for over a decade. "We'd enjoy your input."

"Somebody's got to do it," Baggs said, starting the meeting off on the perfect note.

We handed the talking ball to Doc Kavanaugh, who gave an overview on the weapons used by the perp. "It

seems probable the killer imagines he's doing battle,"
Kavanaugh said. "Given his choice of crossbow, knife,
ax or club, spear . . . I think the weapons have been
selected for overall symbolism, not adaptation to any
particular manner of killing."

"Does he know this?" Harry asked. "The symbolism?"

"All he may know is that the selection feels right
and—"

"Everyone keeps saying how smart this bastard is,"
Baggs interrupted. "Now you're saying he isn't bright
enough to know why he's picking his killing tools?"

"He knows many things," Kavanaugh said. "But the
last thing he knows is himself. He exists behind a veil
of delusions."

Baggs snorted his disbelief. Not big on veils, I guess.

Harry said, "You think the killer's specifically at war
with Carson, Doc?"

Kavanaugh shook her head. "Evidence suggesting a
direct antipathy toward Carson is sketchy."

"What's anti-pathy?" Baggs said.

"An intense dislike. Hatred."

Baggs shook his head. "Then why not just say *hatred*?
Why do you people hide everything behind psycho-
babble?"

"I'm sorry, Chief Baggs, but antipathy is a widely used
word that—"

"The killer leaves pennies like in Ryder's video and
sends messages to Ryder. Maybe I'm not acquainted with
how shrinks think, but how is it the perp doesn't hate

Ryder? Isn't at war with Ryder? For Christ's sake, Doctor, he's killed four people to prove he hates Ryder."

I caught Kavanaugh's glance. This was the first time she'd been exposed to Baggs, but she'd already figured complexity wasn't his specialty. She wheeled her chair to face him, legs crossed, her fingers tented beneath her chin.

"Exactly, Chief Baggs," the doc said evenly. "Four people dead. And yet Carson sits among us, alive and breathing. If the killer has a personal vendetta against Carson, why didn't he simply kill Carson?"

All heads turned to Baggs for his answer.

Baggs glared at Kavanaugh. Having no answer, he changed the subject.

"Do you believe the killings are random?" he challenged. "Or is that unprovable, too?"

Kavanaugh spun back to me and Harry. "You've found no ties between any two victims?"

"Nothing cultural, geographic, job-related," Harry said. "We've made lists of friends and acquaintances of the victims, talked to those folks and their friends and acquaintances. Not a single case of overlap. Kevin Bacon never showed."

Kavanaugh turned to Baggs. "Then yes, Chief. It's quite possible the killer drives around town, sees someone, decides right then to murder them. That's your take, right, Carson?"

I studied my interlocked fingers, tapped my thumbs together.

"I can't say that yet. Maybe if we—"

"Stop thinking like that!" Baggs barked, his hand slapping the table. "Fuck lists and acquaintances and navel-gazing over motive. It's *random*. The bastard drives around town, counts down five-four-three-two-one and whoever he sees at zero is dead. You've got to get a fucking description of this perp and get it distributed."

"I wish I'd thought of that," I said to myself.

Baggs's face went red and his thick forefinger jabbed my way. "I wish *you'd* thought before you started up the Carson Ryder random killer contest. And if I hear another goddamn insubordinate remark like the last one I'll—"

A knock. Baggs yelled, "Come in!"

The door opened to Sergeant Nate Gibbons, an envelope in his hand. "This just got dropped at the desk. You said if anyone left anything for Ryder I should run it up as fast as—"

"Gimme that," Baggs said, grabbing the envelope from Gibbons and starting to tear it open.

"Gloves!" I yelled.

Baggs realized what he'd nearly done and angrily threw the envelope to the table. I put on latex gloves and studied the address, the same as the first example.

"How'd it get here?" I asked Gibbons.

"Guy said he was paid twenty bucks to tote it over from the corner of Conti and Royal. He's downstairs."

I was out of my chair and moving, Gibbons calling, "You ain't gonna get anything, Carson. The guy's—"

But I was already thundering down the stairs. I pushed into the lobby and saw a patrolman standing beside a

273

heavy-set black man in a worn blue seersucker suit over an orange-heavy aloha shirt. He wore obsidian sunglasses and a top hat with a plastic daisy poking up. I stopped and resisted the urge to scream.

Beaten again.

I walked across the floor, said, "Howdy, Blind Jim."

"Howdy back, Carson," said the panhandler. "You get what I brought?"

"Yep. How'd you come across it?"

"I was heading down to the square when a fella steps close, says he needs a letter delivered to the po-lice. I said, 'They right up the street, mister.' He says he can't go there without trouble an' I figure, you know. . ."

"The guy's got a warrant on him."

"Sure. But maybe he still needs to give you something. He gimme twenty bucks, so I didn't really care what his problem was."

Gibbons said, "How you know it was a twenty and not a one?"

"Be blind all your life, you learn to read voices." Blind Jim scrabbled in his pocket, pulled out a bill. "His voice told me I could trust him. It's a twenty, right?"

"Actually, it's a one," I said, plucking it from his hands. "And we need it for evidence."

"Lyin' muthafucker," Jim said. He thought a moment. "But a damn good liar, Carson. I'll give him that."

"Anything you can tell us about him, Jim?"

"Rough voice, like he had a cold, but that was fake. I put him younger side, thirty or under."

274

Harry, Tom and I pulled our wallets and brought Blind Jim up to the promised twenty, then directed a couple guys to prowl the area where the panhandler had been contacted, but didn't expect much.

We headed back upstairs, where the Doc was tapping at her iPad, Baggs staring out the window, doing their best to ignore one another. We relayed the scenario with Blind Jim. I snapped on gloves and lifted the tab of the envelope, shaking the contents to the table. Another penny. And another strip of paper carrying a message:

4–0, Detective Ryder. How Stupid is the Blue Tribe?

36

Baggs shook his head at the new message. "'*Detective Ryder*'? If we had any doubt it was personal, now we know for sure."

"Not necessarily." Kavanaugh frowned, studying the note.

"It says his freaking name, Doctor," Baggs said. "Right there and written in English: Detective Ryder."

"It also says 'Blue Tribe'. That's obviously the MPD. It's a major glimpse into his thinking. The killer's fighting a tribe."

"The envelope's addressed to Ryder," Baggs said. "The note inside is to Ryder. Any war is between this lunatic and Ryder."

"I don't see it that way," Kavanaugh said. "Although Carson is somehow representative of the MPD in the perpetrator's mind."

Baggs rolled his eyes. "A position Ryder got by boasting over the Internet that he could stop random killings."

"I can play the video for you, Chief," I said, feeling my fists clench. "You'll see that the last thing I said was—" I stopped. Both videos had been deleted. Nullified.

"I've got work to do," Baggs said, standing. "Maybe you do, too."

He left, pulling the door shut hard at his back. Doc Kavanaugh shook her head. "I was going to try and explain surrogatized anger and synecdoche, but. . ."

"Pearls before swine," I said, words that had helped put me into this mess.

We broke off the meeting, work to do. Harry and I re-consulted my list of those wishing me harm. It was not quite five and we headed out to see who else we could drop from our list of potentials. As we entered the police garage we passed several dicks from Theft who were smoking and shooting bull with some mid-level administration types. They went silent as I passed, a couple of them shooting the wet eye.

"What?" I said, stopping and turning.

"Nothing."

"You went mute when we walked past. What the hell is it?"

One of the dicks, Eddie Ondrean, took a hit of his cigarette. "I work the beat by the university," he said, smoke drifting from his mouth. "We're getting a lot of heat about the dead girl – Ballard. The campus is half-deserted at night, classes cancelled."

"So?"

Joe Arbogast, a dick from Auto Theft, took his turn. "Everyone uptown's wondering how a little crippled kid gets snuffed in broad daylight and there's no progress. Nada. They say, 'What's goin' on, Joe?' I say, 'We got our best guy on it.' They say, 'Got anyone else?'"

I stared. One of the admin types, a guy in bookkeeping named Blaine, cleared his throat. "Word has it you challenged this psycho to kill people at random, Ryder."

My mouth dropped wide. "*Challenged?* Where the hell did you hear that?"

"The usual stuff, one person to another."

"The guy sent me a letter," I said. "That's it. He could just as well have sent it to you."

"I didn't call him out. That's what you did, right? On the Internet?"

I felt my fists clench. "Look for yourself and you'll see I only—" I kept forgetting the video was history. There when I didn't want it, gone when I did.

"Only what?" Arbogast said.

"Fuck," I muttered, tugging Harry's arm. "Let's go do some police work." We headed to our cruiser, opened the door. I was about to get in when Ondrean called, "Hey, Ryder."

I looked at him over the top of the cruiser. "What?"

He took a final hit from his cigarette, flicked it to the pavement, rubbed it dead with his foot.

"Don't piss this guy off any more, will you?"

278

They stepped apart and went to their cars. No one was laughing.

Gregory was sitting in his living room with the lights lowered and drapes pulled, notes of Ema's financial records on the glass top of the coffee table. Ema was not as much of a spendthrift as he'd thought, hanging onto well over two and a half million dollars of dear ol' Daddy's inheritance. Her house had to be worth another three hundred grand.

He'd also found the wills the family lawyer had drawn up when Gregory was deemed responsible for his due. He and Ema were one another's beneficiaries. So . . . Ema represented over two-point-five million dollars, were she to die. Gregory had almost two million dollars in investments, three-hundred-fifty in the house.

For a combined total of six million dollars. Was that called a Sextillionaire? Sextuplets was six howling babies, so it had to be. Gregory Nieves, sextillionaire. It felt good, especially that word sex, hot.

Though thinking about being a sextillionaire was exciting, Gregory reluctantly pushed it from his head. He had a major project in the works: vengeance on the Blue Tribe. And another attack was due.

But first, the random selection. It was time for the next penny to speak.

The scant furniture had been pushed to the walls and the floor was bare. Gregory walked to the mantel and picked up the red vase. It clattered as he lifted it. He slowly upended the vase over a cupped palm. Dozens of pennies poured into his hand, filling it from wrist to fingertips.

Careful, careful . . . don't drop any.

He weighed the bright coins in his hand. It was the greatest feeling in the universe: holding someone's future in his hands. Closing his eyes, he flung the coins into the air, hearing the bright discs clatter to the floor, rolling hither and yon. He heard rolling coins whir to a halt, topple over.

The room was silent.

Gregory walked slowly toward the center of the room, footsteps creaking over slatted wood. He stopped and spun in a blind circle. Walked three steps, turned right, walked three more. Stopped and put his right foot a step ahead.

Opened his eyes.

Not six inches from his toe-tip was the nearest penny, head-up. He bent, picked it up, turned it reverse-side up. But he didn't see the Lincoln Memorial. He saw a dot of paper glued to the coin, on the paper a tiny, printed name. He studied the name and nodded. Then turned and looked at a floor bright with fallen coins.

Random. Exactly the way Ryder wanted.

Muriel Pendel pulled into the lot of a red-brick building, one of a dozen in the medical complex, the sign saying *Coastways Behavioral Medicine, LLC.* She patted blonde hair into place and checked her watch, early. An EEOSA group would still be in session and she decided to wait inside.

"Ms Pendel," the receptionist said. "It's been a while. Great to see you."

"Thank you, Nikki. The group still in session?"

"They should be breaking up. Go on back. You remember the room, right?"

Muriel Pendel smiled. "I've only been there a couple hundred times."

She opened the door to a broad and indirectly lit space. A dozen men and women from mid-teens to early thirties sat in chairs circled on a gray carpet. Dr Sonia Szekely sat across the room, notepad in hand, a petite woman in a sizzling orange dress. Her face was broad and Slavic, sixty-four years of history lined into coarse skin, but the facial topography suggested a life rich in smiles and laughter. The woman looked up and her bright eyes sparkled further at seeing Muriel.

"Sit with us, Muriel, we're about finished. Everyone remembers Muriel Pendel, right? Wilbert's mother?"

A gaunt and hollow-cheeked man with legs crossed tightly at the knees turned and frowned under disheveled black hair. Muriel noticed several other faces that didn't look pleased at the mention of her son's name.

"Where's Willy?" the gaunt man asked. "Is he coming back?"

"Willy's been busy," Muriel said. "He'll be back soon, I hope."

The man pulled a strand of hair down his forehead and looked at Muriel. His face was expressionless.

"Will he be nicer?"

"Willy's working on things," Muriel said with a forced smile. "Like we all are."

"You aren't working on anything," the man said. "You're too fucking perfect."

"That's enough, Nicu," the Slavic woman said. "You know Muriel is in the parents group. We all work on our issues and an apology is in order."

The man looked away. "I'm sorry, Mrs Pendel."

"It's OK, Nicu. Willy can say mean things sometimes."

"All right, then," Szekely said, dropping her notepad into a multicolored carpetbag. "We're done for today. Good work, everyone. See you all next week."

A thirtyish red-haired woman near the far corner of the circle held up her hand, waving it like a pennant in a wind. Her eyes were wide with excitement.

"I've been saving my news all session. Guess what, everyone? I finally got my degree in accounting."

A pause as minds grasped the fact, followed by cheers and applause. Someone lifted the woman's hand like a victorious boxer. Everyone gathered to hear the details.

Muriel felt a tear escape from her eye. The first time she'd seen Kristen Wallencott – née Kristen Dodrescu – the then-seventeen-year-old girl was prone on the floor outside the circle with her face in her hands, never speaking or meeting anyone's eyes. Two years later Kristen ran away from home in February and was not found until May, a dazed and dirty amnesiac selling herself on a corner in San Diego. Returned to her parents in Mobile, Kristen resumed her position on the floor of the group. But after four years of Dr Szekely's group therapy, Kristen had made an incredible leap into life.

Szekely touched Muriel's arm. "Let's go to my office and let Kristen enjoy her moment."

The pair entered the doctor's private office, the walls a warm green, the carpet a deep and relaxing umber. Muriel sat across from the desk as Szekely sat behind it, opening a drawer and withdrawing cigarettes and a lighter.

"You don't mind, Muriel?"

"God no. I'd love one myself."

Both women lit up, Szekely sliding a glass ashtray the size of a dinner plate to the front of her desk. She leaned back and exhaled a plume of blue smoke. "Willy's still avoiding returning to the group?"

"Not for lack of trying by Bert and me."

Szekely nodded. "When did Wilbert enlist at the police academy, Muriel? I thought he was taking auto-repair classes at a technical college."

"Willy's been at the police academy for three weeks. It was a whim, so . . . maybe a month ago."

"Why did he quit school?"

"He said someone fiddled with the engine he was working on. But it was just an excuse to leave."

"The usual trouble?" Szekely asked.

Muriel fidgeted with her cigarette. "Focusing, yes. Plus there's math involved. And computers. Willy's good with his hands, but being an auto mechanic is so computerized today. I can understand his frustration, but can't understand why he decided he wanted to join the police."

A sad smile from Szekely. "I think you can."

Muriel stubbed out her cigarette in the ashtray, twisting it into the glass long after it was out. "Willy thinks it'll be glamorous and let him be in charge. He'll get a badge and a uniform and a gun and put people in holds and knock them to the ground."

Szekely nodded. "Willy still feels powerless. It generates insecurities he won't acknowledge." She paused. "Willy's living on his own, isn't he?"

A humorless laugh. "Kind of. He'll come in and grab half the food in the fridge, his father's beer. But always when we're out."

"You took him off the parental dole a few months back, I recall, as incentive to finish school and find a real job. How did that go?"

Muriel studied her hands. "We, uh, reinstated it when Willy suggested he might move home again. It was . . . uh, we thought it might be. . ."

"You're feeling guilty because you don't want Willy back home, right?"

"Yes, I mean no . . . I mean. . ."

Szekely leaned forward and stubbed her cigarette out, her head wreathed in smoke. "Stop beating yourself up, Muriel. It's natural. Willy's twenty-four, he should be out making his own way. Willy's not retarded, nor does he suffer from Fetal Alcohol Syndrome like Oana and Nicu. He has relatively few of the extreme emotional problems associated with so many of the orphans. Sociopathy, for example." Szekely shook her head. "You remember Bogdan and Cezar. So sad, such a waste."

Muriel nodded slowly. "I know we have it easy compared to some of the parents, Doctor. Still, it's been frustrating. Maybe Bert and I went into the adoption cycle with too many stars in our eyes. But there were so many orphans, so many wounded little souls. . ."

37

Harry and I visited three other scumbuckets who'd threatened me. The last one we visited, Robbie Jay Turnbull, lived in a decaying trailer in a marsh, the table covered with plates of dried food, cans and bottles on the floor, rats scuttling through the walls.

The last time I'd seen Turnbull he was cooking meth and selling to gangs for resale. Harry and I had crossed paths with Turnbull on another matter and decided to take him down as a gift to society. Using personal time, we engineered a purchase with me as the buyer, then dropped the whole package into the MPD's narcotics division. Turnbull should have done a dozen years but dropped the dime on fellow sellers and bought the sentence down to two years.

He'd pledged to kill me several times.

But it appeared that in his year back on the street RJ

had progressed from cooking meth to consuming it in historic quantities. All the teeth remaining in his mouth were rotten and his tongue lolled from gap to gap, poking through like a curious adder. His sagging flesh called to mind wet newsprint without the writing. His eyes resembled flies, or maybe they were, flies everywhere in the trailer, a fog of buzzing dots.

Turnbull pretty much stayed motionless on his couch the whole time, dressed solely in stained BVDs and one brown sock, staring at a muted *Jersey Shore* with his mouth open and going "Ar-arrr-arrrr" in answer to our questions.

Actually, we only asked three questions: *How you doing, RJ? Are those rats we hear?* and *That ain't* Downtown Abbey *you're watching, right?* By then we'd determined Robbie Jay Turnbull incapable of walking a dozen feet, much less stealthily scoping out and killing other human beings.

"Have a nice life, Robbie," Harry said as we left the reeking trailer, knowing if Turnbull managed to live out the year he'd be doing pretty good.

We ended up at the garage at half-past seven. A couple cops from the floor below were leaving. They shot me glances and didn't say anything.

"Screw 'em," Harry said.

Neither of us wanting to revisit overloaded desks, we parted ways. The sun was still high, June near the summer solstice. Though I spent most of three seasons wishing for days that were three-quarters sunlit and cursing whoever mishandled the hanging of the Earth – why the tilt? – tonight I wished an early dark, perhaps providing a place to hide.

I waved as Harry drove past, heading toward home and his girlfriend, Sally Hargreaves. They'd mix a drink, fix some chow, listen to jazz. And hopefully, as Bob Dylan put it, forget about today until tomorrow.

I thought a long moment, pulled my cell and dialed, holding my breath through the rings.

"Hello, Carson," Holliday said.

"You wanted to talk about something?" I said.

A pause. "It's maybe the kind of thing best left alone."

"When talking about things that shouldn't be talked about, I find it easier to not discuss them on Causeway. How about I pick you up in ten minutes?"

I was two minutes early, yet Wendy stood on the stoop outside of her apartment, an inexpensive complex favored by students. I looked to the side and saw a swimming pool ringed by lithe and tanned bodies. Bottles of beer filled hands and tabletops. Kanye West rapped from a sound system.

"Looks like you're missing the party," I said.

"All they do is drink and play the same twenty songs. It's like they never left high school."

I studied the overeager smiles, heard the forced laughter and the loud, *look-at me!* voices. A tall kid in a dripping T-shirt yelled "*Watch this!*" before bouncing a dozen times on the diving board and cannonballing into the turquoise water, the splash pulling squeals from poolside. Someone turned the music up louder.

Most of those folks believed they were happy at that moment, perhaps as happy as it was possible to get. They had youth and drink and music and seemingly endless nights of thrilling, meaningless release in a procession of arms and beds. Music and television and movies had assured them such behavior constituted happiness, thus a fair amount of those folks would lock themselves into an unreality show called *Today at Poolside* and never venture beyond.

Yes, they would marry, have two-point-one children, buy houses in the suburbs and plant dogwoods and azaleas. But to make that sort of operation work correctly you needed to understand the broader world, allowing it to change you in places, while setting other boundaries where it could not reach. Knowing how to arrange yourself for the journey took an amalgam of curiosity, skepticism and introspection most people didn't want to touch with a ten-foot pool skimmer.

The music changed to Cee Lo Green singing the uncensored version of his hit, the poolside crowd bumping hips, hoisting bottles, and howling *So fuck you!*

"Let's get out of here," I said.

There are two ways to cross Mobile Bay in a vehicle: on the elevated Interstate 10, what's called the Bayway, and the Causeway, a slender strip of earth and pavement barely above sea level. The Bayway is a concrete flume filled with fast metal and hot fumes and with all the charm of an open sewer.

The Causeway has far less traffic. There are restaurants along its eight-mile passage, some fancy, others ramshackle fish houses. Marsh grasses grow at water's edge. Gulls, ducks, ibises, pelicans, cranes, all claim the Causeway as home. Now and then a surly gator waddles from the water and sunbathes in the road, the local constabulary having to encourage the critter back into his brackish haunts. Generations of relatives fish together from the banks of the Causeway, the occasion less about fish than family.

We passed the Drifter's Bar and pulled from the road. I reached into the cooler and produced two bottles of Bass Ale, handing one to Wendy. Without a word we leaned against my truck and let our eyes float south over Mobile Bay, the falling sun turning the water into a sea of trembling gold. After several minutes Wendy set her bottle on the hood, crossed her arms and stared across the bay.

"This has been the most amazing month of my life," she said, her voice tinged with wonder.

I nodded. "I enjoyed the hell out of my time at the academy, too. I walked in the door scared to death, but within a week knew I was where I needed to be."

"That's only part of what I'm talking about," she said. "The rest was the thing which maybe should remain unmentioned."

"On the Causeway there are no topics beyond mention," I said. "Speak your truth."

"All right, then. I recently fell for someone."

"What?" I said, my turn for surprise. "Who?"

When she turned her eyes to me I knew.

Gregory was in his office catching up on writing code, thinking it ridiculous for someone of his caliber to grind out such crap. Work was for morons and robots. If he

290

were wealthier – twice as much or so – work would be unnecessary. Even undulating markets offered ways to make money. A seven per cent return on investments would generate over three hundred thousand dollars annually. With that kind of money, he could pursue his hobby full time. There were over forty pennies in the vase.

His computer bonged. Time to check the trap and head to bed.

Gregory changed from businesswear into cargo pants and a polo shirt. Picked up the flashlight. There hadn't been any cats for the past two nights, the supply getting low.

Gregory tiptoed to the backyard and pulled the cover from the trap.

A cat! And not just any cat, a prize feline: big and shiny and black as coal, with four distinctive white paws.

"*Mow*," the cat said.

"*Mow*," Gregory repeated. He lifted the trap to his shoulder and jogged to the house, pumping his arm in victory. He didn't have much time to deal with the cats these days, but it always calmed him.

38

My phone seemed far away as it pulled me from dreams both warm and safe. I slapped the bedside table for the device. "I think you left it in the kitchen," Wendy said. I felt the bed rebound as she left the mattress.

"Ummph," I said.

"Do you want me to answer?" she asked.

"Sure." I yawned cobwebs from my brain and heard jogging feet, Mix-up's claws scratching on tile as he followed Wendy to the kitchen. She was back seconds later, holding the phone.

"Doctor Peltier needs to talk to you."

I moaned internally and reluctantly took the phone. "Good morning, Clair. How are you tod—"

"You may want to open the paper," she said. "Or you may not."

Click.

"Carson?" Wendy asked as I rolled to sitting, throwing the phone to the bed. "Are you all right?"

"I'm supposed to check the paper. It should be in the drive."

She slipped into the outsize tee I'd offered for sleeping – not needed – and padded away, her long legs whisking toward the front door. I followed, sending Mix-up out to do his business as I watched Wendy Holliday cross my sandy yard in scant ounces of cotton, the shirt's hem high enough that she had to crouch to retrieve the *Register*. I took the paper as she entered, snapping it open to page one.

Killer Claims Another Victim, read the top headline. There was a sidebar story in smaller type: *Did MPD Detective Goad Murderer?*

My heart sank as I read. The article didn't name me, referring to *An unnamed detective with over ten years on the force*, nor did it directly accuse me of throwing down a gauntlet. But it did suggest said detective might have been improvident.

The article was marred by several errors, stating the detective had put the video on the web and that he'd bragged no killer could escape his skills. I'd replayed the YouTube vid enough to remember what had actually happened. Following my penny analogy, Twyla Harper had said *I figure if anyone could catch a random killer, it would be you, Detective Ryder.*

I had replied, *I expect you're onto something*. Hardly a challenge.

I handed Wendy the paper and went to my coffee maker, needing to wake up fast. I was sucking down caffeine when Wendy entered the kitchen dressed in yesterday's clothes.

She scowled at the *Register*. "It's bullshit, Carson. We all know what you really said. Can you put the video back up? It shows the truth."

"It's gone for good," I said.

"I could put it back up. We still have our individual recordings and—"

Wendy's phone rang from her pocket. "It's Amanda Sanchez," she said, putting the phone to her ear. I wandered to the deck, my head starting to clear. What I wanted to do was sit and look over the gently rolling morning Gulf and relive the beauty of last night. The quiet talk on the deck. The midnight swim lit by a sliver of crystal moon. The whispering jog to the house.

Instead, I pondered my options. We were no nearer the killer than we'd been the night Kayla Ballard was found. Plus I was being pushed into the scapegoat role.

Wendy came to the deck two minutes later. "I say screw that guy Willpot."

Willpot was Frank Willpot, director of Internal Affairs and a toadie of Baggs.

"What does Willpot have to do with things?" I asked.

"There was a class this morning. I didn't mention it yesterday because of perfect attendance and better things to do. Amanda says Willpot stormed into class and ordered everyone to say nothing about the case or our involvement. He claimed it would be a black eye for the department and the academy and anyone talking would be immediately discharged."

"Son of a bitch," I said. Frank Willpot was helping push me under the bus. It also occurred that no one at the top of the department – meaning Baggs – had flat-out denied the story.

"The damned article makes it sound like you invited a killing spree," Wendy said, tapping the paper with a strident digit. "It's just wrong. What will you do?"

"Nail the bastard," I said. "It's the only way out."

I dropped an anxious Holliday at her apartment, U-turned in the street and booked to the department. There was a hubbub outside, news vans and reporters, the vans with uplink antennae aimed at the sky like science-fiction weaponry. I pulled into the garage and ran upstairs to Lieutenant Mason's office. He had the paper in his hands.

"First off, you're not named," he said. "That's a break. You saw the article?"

I nodded.

"Second, the department is drafting a statement countering the article and absolving itself of responsibility."

"Itself? How about me?"

Tom shrugged. "That's all happening upstairs. How do you think this got out, Carson? The news about you and the class and all?"

"You know how it goes, Tom. Someone I've pissed off in the department makes a whispery call to the media:

'*You won't believe the stupid thing one of our detectives did. . .*' Baggs himself, maybe, through a surrogate like Willpot."

"Baggs is under a lotta media pressure, Carson. You may be the release valve."

It took a second to grasp. "Baggs fuels the media with speculation, lets it build, finally names me as the guy who incited a madman to kill?"

"Yup," Tom nodded. "Then makes a media spectacle out of yanking you off the case and shutting down the PSIT. With a very public reprimand."

"You mean public hanging, right?"

Tom tipped back his Stetson and offered a flat smile. "I see you've been at the end of this rope before."

Gregory's dream-wall has fallen again. He smells mamaliga and carnati, piftie and chiftele. Hears the coarse and drunken laughter of Petrov and Cojocaru. The high cackling voice of the nurse, Sorina Vaduva.

"*Where is little Dragna Negrescu?*" Dr Popescu says, ten meters tall and standing in the center of the floor in the supply room beside the kitchen, his head wreathed in cigar smoke. His mask is still the mask turned inside out. "*Where is my tasty little tart, Sorina?*" Popescu says. When he talks, a black slit opens and closes on the mask.

"*Dragna had chores to finish in the records department,*" Sorina Vaduva says. "*Then she's running to the store for the tuica.*"

"*Call and tell her to hurry. Tell her I have great thirst and greater hunger.*"

The dream spins upside down. When it rights itself the Doctor and Petrov are roaming the halls and pulling children from holes in the wall and setting them in shopping buggies. From deep in the shadows a choir is singing for mamaliga. Dragna Negrescu pushes a cart of clinking vodka and tuica bottles into the dream. Her dark hair frames the doll-face mask.

Gregory is watching from a hole in the wall, hiding in its furthest recesses. The Doctor has a flashlight he's using to peer into the holes.

"*What have we here? Why it's little Grigor! Come share food with us, Grigor. Isn't he a pretty one, Petrov?*"

"*My favorite. Even with so many, he's my favorite little girl.*"

"*Little girl?*" the Doctor laughs. "*Did you hear, Grigor? You're a little girl tonight.*"

A sound like thunder and they are in the supply room behind the dormitories, beside the kitchen. The floor is made of mattresses and stretches to the horizon. "*Turn them into robots, Doctor,*" Dragna Negrescu laughs from beneath her baby mask, wearing only underpants and dark stockings. "*Show us the magic learned from Blaskov-Milovitch. Talk in your special voice and swing your fancy watch. Make our robots perform and forget!*"

"*I shall teach you my secrets, sweet Dragna,*" the Doctor howls, flying across the room like a hawk.

"*What's that sound?*" someone says.

The cat is back at the window.

Go away! Grigor screams. *Save yourself!* But the cat leaps into Dragna Negrescu's hands. She turns it into a dishrag, wipes her hands on its fur, throws it out the window. The baby-faced Negrescu spins to Grigor. She's singing.

"*Little Grigor, pretty one, Big Petrov must have his fun. . .*"

Gregory begins to run, but his legs turn to stone and he falls to the mattresses. The smell of mamaliga is everywhere. Gregory vomits up his insides, watching them writhe like snakes on the filthy fabric beneath his face.

NO NO NO. Save me, Ema!

But Ema has escaped the flashlight. There is no sign of her.

Muriel Pendel picked up the phone and took a deep breath. Willy answered on the fourth ring.

"Yeah, Ma? What's up?" He sounded winded.

"How was your day?"

"Ah, it was kinda a pain in the . . . Hey!" he chirped, suddenly engaged. "You see about that old woman that got killed?"

"I saw a headline, but didn't read the story."

"It was cool. We were taking a trip to the jail but got put on a bus and sent to find her. It was what we cops call an SAR, a search-and-rescue. The Civil Air Patrol people actually found her. We would have, but the chumps got in our way. I didn't even get to see the body."

"Willy, I went to see Dr Szekely today. The doctor thinks it would be good if you went back to group. So do your father and I."

"Group's nothing but a bunch of losers, Ma. I ain't a loser. I'm gonna be a cop."

"Willy, listen to me."

"NO! All the group does is piss and moan about how people think they're weird and shit like that. I don't hardly remember the goddamn orphanage. I DON'T WANT TO REMEMBER THE PLACE!"

"Calm down, son, all I'm saying is—"

"I gotta go."

The phone clicked dead and Muriel popped a tissue from the box at her elbow and blew her nose, wandering to the window to look out across the front yard, a green expanse of west Mobile lawn.

A white car passed by, a Toyota Avalon. A realtor, Muriel knew vehicles well, her favorite back-of-mind exercise the pairing of auto makes with home models her company represented. An Avalon client was not a Mercedes client, but not a used-Dodge Caravan client, either. An Avalon prospective would likely enjoy the Executive II series, $319,000 for the base model.

Muriel had seen the Avalon twice today already. Once parked down at the corner, twice passing her house. And didn't she see a white Avalon last night as she watered the lawn? The same one? Maybe it was someone looking for a home in the area, a prospective buyer. Maybe she should run out and hand over her business card.

I can help you with your needs.

Muriel checked her watch, almost eleven a.m., time to go to her job, sitting in a model of the Concord Deluxe – base price $409,000 – in an upscale community two miles away. It was a bore, the real-estate market so depressed there were days no one stopped in. It was like being trapped in a pretty box all day.

Muriel looked outside again. The Avalon was moving away.

Hope to see you again, she thought.

39

"It's looking good, Carson," Harry said, fingers flying over his keyboard as words appeared on the screen. For a four-finger typist, Harry worked fast.

Dr Kavanaugh didn't believe the killer's anger was aimed solely at me: I was a symbol for a collective called "The Blue Tribe". Baggs didn't believe it, but Baggs rejected any idea more complex than a salad fork. Harry's idea was circulating an internal flier on the chance the killer's problem with the MPD had been memorable.

Harry tapped Print and handed me the draft.

Though early reports mistakenly identified the spree killer as having a personal conflict with a single departmental member, it actually appears the killer is angry with the entire MPD, the anger likely generated from contact with member(s) of

*the department. A possible scenario: a mentally
unstable person, probably male, felt insulted or
humiliated by an encounter with the department
and is seeking revenge by demonstrating the
department's inability to solve the crimes.*

*If you've had an officer–citizen incident that was
unusually tense, threatening, strange (as in gener-
ating an over-reaction), or otherwise, please contact
us ASAP. We're especially interested in situations
where a civilian might have inadvertently been
embarrassed or put in a situation where self-respect
was lost.*

*Please volunteer any information NOW. Lives
are at stake. Call us, or leave a note in one of
our mailboxes.*

I got the flier green-lighted by Tom Mason. Within an
hour they'd be on the walls and bulletin boards at MPD
facilities: HQ, district commands, the academy, jail. Plus
it would be read at roll call before the uniform shifts
went out on patrol.

The fliers were our first roll of the dice. But cops saw
so much weirdness that asking them to cherry-pick bizarre
situations was a long-odds prospect. There was another
roll of the dice as well: shorter odds on learning more
about the killer, perhaps, but one I'd been pushing from
my head whenever it appeared: calling a seasoned expert
for an appraisal of the situation.

The expert being my older brother, Jeremy.

After his indictment for the killing of our father and five women, Jeremy had been committed to a facility for the criminally insane. He'd spent years befriending – and often, as a kind of hobby – controlling some of the most dangerous and distorted psyches of the era. With his brilliant mind and nothing else to occupy his curiosity, his abilities to gauge the depth and delusions affecting such people had become nothing short of preternatural.

I told Harry I was going to walk the neighborhood to clear my head. The day was ninety plus degrees and I jogged to a nearby museum and sat in its quiet lobby. My brother's phone number was kept in memory, not on my phone. I dialed and heard ringing, and my mind saw Jeremy crossing the floor of his isolated log cabin, a two-story structure in a mountain hollow. After escaping from a maximum-security mental institution several years back, Jeremy had found sanctuary deep in the forest of eastern Kentucky.

"Dr August Charpentier," he said, using his false accent and identity, a retired Canadian professor of psychology. His phone would not ID me as the caller – he didn't keep my number in electronic memory either.

"Bonjour, Doc," I said. "How's tricks? Or whatever that is in French."

The disguise fell away. He snapped, "What do you need now, Carson? The only time I hear from you is when you need something."

"Really?" I said. "I recall differently. Like the time

you needed me in Kentucky and tricked me there, remember?"

"I brought you here for a vacation."

"I nearly got killed."

"Bosh. You spent most of your time eating your little cherry tart."

Donna Cherry was a detective with the Kentucky State Police. We'd become friends and more.

"*Myumyumph*," Jeremy mumbled wetly, as if eating with his mouth full. "*Myumphyump*. . ." Though forty-three years old with an IQ above 150, my brother was often a sex-obsessed adolescent boy.

"Enough, Jeremy," I said. "I need to talk to you."

"Are you planning on talking long?" he asked. "More than a minute?"

"What does it matter? Yes. I have a question or two."

"Use your computer, Skype video. I need to see you."

"I'm in the lobby of the museum."

"Get out of the fucking middle ages, Carson. Skype me."

Click.

I sighed and jogged back to the office. No contact with my brother came without the requisite jumping through hoops until he felt satisfied.

I went to Harry, at his desk cross-referencing friends and colleagues of the victims for the umpteenth time. "You don't have Skype at your place, do you?"

"What's Skype?"

"I've got to go home. Make some excuses." I ran down the steps, passing two administrative grunts leaning

304

against the wall and filling out betting sheets. I nodded as I passed through the door to the lobby.

"Nice job yanking the chain of that crazy, Ryder," one called to me as I crossed the floor. "Maybe next you can get Manson put back on the streets."

I jogged to the garage, dialing my phone as I went. I'd used video conferencing last year while working with a detective for Boulder, Colorado, but she'd been the one to set things up.

"Hello, Carson," Wendy said. "Are you feeling any bet—"

"Skype," I interrupted, jumping into my truck. "You familiar?"

"Who isn't?"

We were at my home within a half-hour. For all my fretting, the process was simple. She gave me a fast primer in using the video version.

"Give me the phone number and I'll make the call," she said.

"It's kind of, uh—"

"Personal? I'll get lost. Mind if I take out the boat?"

She had left a swimsuit, which, like the sleeping tee, hadn't been used last night. The door closed behind her and feet skipped down the steps. I looked out the window as Wendy, paddle in hand, pulled my kayak across the sand. For someone who had so much to display, body-wise, her indigo two-piece was modest, and for some reason seemed even sexier. I turned from the window and went to the desk, entering the number in the computer.

Jeremy was in front of me, his room as remembered, cedar-plank walls with tall windows opening into the forest behind his log home, pines as straight as arrows, beeches, poplars, oak. My brother was in his Dr Charpentier guise: neat white beard and eyebrows to match his backswept hair – bleached, his true hair was still as dark as mine. Professorial wire-rims rode the bridge of his aquiline nose. His hand reached out and his finger swiped across my screen.

"You've got hair in your eyes," he said. Without thinking I brushed my bare forehead, then saw Jeremy's grin. He was playing with my head, a show of control.

I stared back, said, "How'd your shopping trip go today?"

A microbeat confusion became a smile. He applauded. "Well played," he said. "You can see the lines, obviously."

My brother had smooth skin that hadn't aged as far as his forty-three years, much less the fifty-plus he wished to project. In his travels through eastern Kentucky mining communities he'd observed "miners' mascara", coal dust embedded in the wrinkles of miners' faces. Before venturing into town he rubbed an oily black chalk into his skin then wiped it off, the residue darkening the slight lines in his face and adding several years to his visual age, what he called his "outside face".

"Now that we've tugged each other's dicks," Jeremy said, "what do you need?"

"We'll get there. I take it you're well, Jeremy? Still playing the stock market?"

"The market is swinging like King Kong's testicles," he replied. "But they're ejaculating money my way."

My brother believed the market had two true states: blustering drunkard or scared child. He attempted to discern which face would next present and placed his bets from there. He claimed huge profits and I had no reason to disbelieve him; Jeremy would feel no more compelled to lie about money than misrepresent what he had for lunch. My brother reserved his lies for weightier occasions.

"I'd love a car befitting my income status," Jeremy sighed. "A Maserati, maybe. I'm tired of my professorial Subaru."

"I expect it would be the only Maserati in eastern Kentucky."

"There's nowhere around here to spend money, not when I'm portraying a retired professor. Yet everywhere I put money it makes more money."

"You're cursed, a Croesus. You could make anonymous donations to charities."

He laughed, thinking such things absurd. Then leaned toward his camera, his face filling my screen. "Do you need any money, Carson?" he whispered. "I'm serious."

"Cops don't drive Maseratis either."

He sat back. "Then let's get to the reason for your call. The unusual killings of late, no? Don't look surprised . . . I read the *Register* and television-news online, knowing you're on some of the cases. It's my way of bonding."

"You haven't read today's reports yet."

"I read them at night, Carson. Or the next day. Or the day after. It's not a fucking priority."

"Any thoughts?"

"Two are obviously drug related, one is that guy who strangled his wife." He patted his mouth in a feigned yawn. "But one caught my eye . . . a chicklet attacked and murdered while riding her bike near the college community. Then a gay fellow was bludgeoned in his home. . ."

"The news reports never said he was gay."

"It wath tho obviousth, Carthon," Jeremy lisped, flicking a limp wrist. "Then an old woman gets killed with a projectile. But nowhere is it specified what kind of projectile. Why? In all of these cases the full post-mortems are 'pending'. Interesting. What's with the lack of information about the projectile? Was it a bullet, a cannonball, a Minuteman missile?"

"It was a spear from a spear-fishing outfit."

A pause as my brother absorbed the information. "Surprising and delightful," he purred. "The same with bicycle girl?"

"An arrow from what we suspect was a pistol crossbow."

"They're called bolts, brother."

"Thank you, but I knew that. The problem – mentioned in the paper today – is that the killer has a grudge against me. Or the MPD. Or both."

He grinned. "Crossbow bolts, fishing spears, a grudge against my baby brother . . . finally something interesting."

308

"Let me explain what's going on, Jeremy. First off we—"

He held up his hand. "Don't natter at me, Carson. Send everything you have."

My brother loved police files and photos. They could be graphic, salacious, and filled with sad minutiae of human lives.

"They're confidential files, Jeremy, I can't just—"

He winked into the camera and his hand tapped the keyboard.

The connection vanished.

40

I was feeding my copies of the case files into my fax machine when I heard Wendy putting the kayak back beneath the house. Then the shower. Seconds later she was stepping into my living room wearing one of my old short-sleeve work shirts over the suit.

"That is the sweetest boat, Carson. It's like paddling a teflon-coated needle."

She saw me at the fax. "I'm sending some case stuff to a friend at the FBI," I lied. "He's in the behavioral section and I want a second opinion. I'll be finished in a half-hour."

I shifted through pages, separating what I thought Jeremy might find helpful from what he'd find salacious (and therefore spend the most time with), until only a few pages remained.

Wendy was lazing on the deck in a lounger, the height

310

and cant of the deck allowing her to drop her top and work on erasing tan lines without being seen from the beach. I looked outside, sighed, and went back to feeding papers when I heard footsteps on my stairs and looked out to see a brief glimpse of dark hair pass the window.

Clair.

A knock on the door. For a moment I wondered if I could hide in the closet and wait until she left. A second knock pulled me to the door. Clair stood on the stoop in a cream blouse and dark slacks. Her face was unreadable, neither the smiling Clair of a week ago, nor the brittle and sarcastic woman of late. She simply nodded and pushed past, a green bag over her shoulder and a folder in her hand.

"I'm on lunch break and called to tell you the prelim was ready. Harry said you were here and I needed to get away from the morgue and clear my head." She fanned a hand at her forehead. "It's hotter than the hinges of hell out there. I need a drink."

My heart climbed into my throat. If Clair looked toward the deck she'd see most of Wendy Holliday. I heard Clair grab a glass from the cabinet, open the fridge, pour a gurgle of ice water. Seconds later she was back in the living room passing me the folder.

"No surprises in what I found, although it was ugly. I'll let you read the post results yourself."

"Thanks, Clair. It was really good of you to come all the way down here to—"

"There's something else, Carson. Billy Hawkins was

in Forensics checking prints on bricks of cocaine. I don't like him, a loudmouth. He spent most of his time telling everyone these killings were somehow your fault. I recalled yesterday's paper. You're the detective mentioned?"

"The whole thing is completely distorted, Clair. What I said was—"

Clair waved me silent. Her eyes were a foot away, the most beautiful eyes I'd ever seen, the blue of arctic ice reflecting a cobalt sky. They were staring past the lenses of my eyes, past the retina, somehow staring directly into my mind.

"Whatever you were going to say, Carson. I believe you. I'll always believe you. I just wanted you to have the results of the post and to tell you what people are saying. I also wanted—"

"Clair . . ." I whispered, "I think we should talk about—"

A cool finger pressed my lips still. "Sssssh. I also wanted to tell you I've been a bit of a bitch. Maybe more than a bit. I'm not going to apologize because I don't think it would be heartfelt." She paused, took a breath. "Look, I'm crossing the big bar in a couple years, Carson. Fifty years old. Sometimes I look back and think I've done exactly what I wanted to do, other times I think I've been hiding from life. The feeling is heightened when I see a beautiful and intelligent young woman whose life is spread before her like a banquet. It's further heightened when I see you attracted to that woman."

I had nothing to say, so I said nothing.

"Here's the way it's going to be, Carson," Clair said. "Exactly as it always has been. I think we've managed something – a friendship, a relationship, a . . . I don't know if a word has been invented for us, maybe shouldn't be. All I can say is, for now and for always, I'm here if you're there."

Her finger retreated from my lips. "Don't say a word, Carson. It took me a while to come to this conclusion and it's still fragile, a work in progress."

I didn't move a muscle. Clair turned away and opened the door. She started out, then paused. "Oh, and Carson?"

"Yes, Clair?"

"Make sure Miss Holliday is using sunscreen out there. The sun is brutal today."

The door closed at Clair's back as the deck door opened. Wendy stepped into the living room. "Did I just hear. . ." she went to the window and looked into the drive, "Doctor Peltier."

I waved the file. "She was dropping off the preliminary."

"She drove all the way down here? That's incredibly thoughtful."

"Yes," I said quietly. "That would be Clair."

I had to return to work and so, regrettably, did. Wendy said she had nothing to do today but study, and her notes were in her phone. Would I mind if she enjoyed the beach and had supper waiting when the day turned me loose?

We walked the two blocks to Mix-up's daycare and

brought him home – a guard dog. I'd told my colleagues at the Dauphin Island Police of my situation, and they cruised the house regularly. I didn't expect a problem, but a big, loud dog was one more layer of protection.

Harry and I resumed our pilgrimage of people I had pissed off, a sop to Baggs. We returned to the department at shift change, Harry to write reports and me to make sure our fliers had been distributed in the uniformed division. Those folks wore the blue, so chances seemed higher any conflict between the killer and the "Blue Tribe" originated with cops in uniform.

I pushed into the guys' locker room, an olfactory broth of sweat, testosterone, cologne, talcum powder and deodorant. The front was packed with rows of wide green lockers with benches between. The rear held showers and commodes. The dividing line was a wall of sinks beneath mirrors. It resembled every men's locker room I'd ever been in, like there was a master plan for the things, a Platonic Form.

There were a half-dozen guys at lockers, more in the back, obvious by the sound of showers and the steam in the air. One guy was changing clothes in the near stand of lockers – Johnny Wilkes, a lanky black guy who'd been in the academy with me. He was pulling a polo shirt on over jeans, his change of uniform cap in the open locker. Taped inside the door was a top-to-bottom montage of photos of Johnny's wife and four kids.

He said, "What brings you down here with the working folk, Carson?"

314

"I wanted to make sure everyone saw the flier Harry and I put out."

He did dubious. "I saw it. I also heard that you were the one—"

I shook my head in exasperation. "The guy's mad at me, yeah. But our shrink is pretty sure he's pissed at the whole force. I'm just the figurehead."

"I heard you were on the web inviting the guy to kill people."

He turned away. I grabbed Wilkes's shoulder, pulled him around to face me. "Look in my eyes, Johnny. Do you see anyone in there stupid enough to invite a psycho to kill people?"

"I'm only repeating what—"

"You're not looking, Johnny. How much stupid do you see in there?"

He studied my eyes, then dropped his in embarrassment. Said, "None."

I released his shoulder. "It's bullshit, John. It never happened because I'm not that stupid, and I'm tired of people thinking I am."

I was tired of it, my guts turning every time my co-workers fell into whispers as I walked by, wondering if, or worse, *why*, I had goaded a killer into action. They were wrong, that was bad enough, but there was also a tiny voice in the back of my head asking if my past actions and reputation – including a penchant for what I called innovation but others often saw as taking risks – played a role. Had I set myself up for this fall . . . at least partly? I looked up, saw Wilkes studying the flier, seriously this time.

"You're saying the perp's mad at all of us? Is that it?"

"We're convinced he's responding to an actual incident: traffic stop, arrest, roust. . ."

I saw Ronald Mailey at the back of the row of lockers, ear bent our way, eavesdropping. That meant Austin was one of the bodies in the shower.

"What is it, Mailey?" I asked.

"Ah, nothing. It doesn't mean anything."

I followed Mailey to his locker and saw Austin walking our way, towel around his thick waist, rubbing his hair dry with a second towel. His body was heavily furred and he called to mind a surly bear. He stopped at a sink and ran a comb through the graying hair.

I said, "Tell me anyway, Mailey."

"It was a few weeks back. About midnight. We stopped this dude for running a red three seconds in. When we started to check him out there was this, uh, thing with his, um. . ."

"His what?"

"His bowels, Detective. He had a bowel movement."

Austin was eavesdropping and turned to us. "The guy had diarrhea was all. Big fucking deal. Maybe we stopped him after a Mexican supper and he had to squirt some beans."

I looked at Austin's image in the mirror. "What went down, Horse?"

"Mailey just fucking told you, Ryder. The guy was

having some kind of problem. It was no big deal."

I turned back to Mailey. "No confrontation? No words, no anger, no sense of the citizen losing any self-respect?"

Mailey shot a microsecond glance at Austin. "Hunh-uh, Detective. Nothing like that. The guy, uh, ended up thanking us."

I saw Austin grimace. Something seemed off, but I had no idea what.

"That was it?" I asked Mailey.

"Come on, Ryder," Austin snapped. "We're trying to get home here. Go bang your head against the wall someplace else."

I looked at Mailey. "The guy ended up thanking you for giving him a hundred-buck citation?" I asked.

"Uh, we didn't write him up."

I stared at Horse in the mirror. Austin not writing a ticket was as rare as irony at a Southern Baptist convention. He cited everyone for everything and averaged over a thousand bucks a day in citations, one of the reasons he kept his job on the street – he was a profit center.

"Come on, Austin. You're telling me you didn't ticket a guy who ran straight through a red?"

Austin threw his comb into the sink and wheeled to me. "What the fuck business is it of yours if I let the guy slide, Ryder? I felt sorry for the silly fuck standing there with shit down his pants and a dead grin on his goofy face. And since you're so fucking interested, you wanna know what I did next?"

"What?"

"Accompanied the poor, sad fuck to his home to make sure he got there safe and sound. Maybe I shoulda kissed his forehead and tucked him into beddy-bye. There . . . now you know it all, asshole. So how's about you leave us working stiffs alone?"

"You wanna ride again, baby?" the call girl said, running a slender finger between her small breasts and down the flat, muscled stomach. "Maybe a little mouth scolding?"

Gregory reached to feel his genitals, not in the mood. "Not now."

The canvas slippers padded to the window and Gregory looked out through the blinds. Though the low sun painted the cityscape with shadows, it was still daylight, a rare time for him to seek sexual attention. But the Itch was hitting hard lately and he knew from personal experience what cops could do under cover of darkness.

You stink like a sewage factory, poopy. Go home and learn how to use a toilet.

"You still got forty minutes on the meter, baby," the machine purred. "I'm here when you need me."

Gregory wandered to the bureau. On his last visit the bag of white powder had been here, but now it was gone.

"Where is it?" he asked.

"Where's what, baby?"

"The powder."

"Open the top drawer, hon. Look on the right."

Gregory found a small round mirror, a razor blade

318

and a zip bag of white powder. "Primo quality, baby," the robot said. "Never been stepped on. Ain't nothing but the finest for my special customers."

"What did you say it would make me feel like?"

"Like God. Like you're the master of the whole fucking universe."

Gregory shot a sideways glance at his image in the mirror, his eyes pools of radiant power, his stomach hard, his biceps thickened by hundreds of hours with the bow machine. The effect seemed appropriate: he was a master of life and death.

Gregory had studied cocaine after his last visit, a stimulant. As amazing as his new life was, his surveillance cut deeply into his sleeping time – perhaps the cause of unsettling dreams of late – and caffeine didn't sit well on his sensitive stomach. Given the visibly increased police presence on the streets, he needed to be fully alert in every aspect of his new life.

Gregory picked up the bag and dandled it in his palm. He turned to the sex robot.

"How much for the bag?" he asked.

41

I got into HQ at seven the next day. Yesterday had started early and ended late – me dragging home at nine thirty – but Wendy was waiting with a thick cioppino, fresh-made French bread, and a bottle of wine she'd jogged four miles in the midday sun to get.

We had fallen asleep at two in the morning and I was slogging to my desk when a whistle pulled my eyes to Tom Mason's office. He was waving me over with an even more doleful slope to his hound-dog face.

"I think Baggs is making his move, Carson."

Tom handed me the morning newspaper, mine still in the sand outside my house. I'd figured if I didn't open the paper, there'd be nothing bad inside, my version of Schrödinger's cat.

Wrong. Another story. The head read, *Detective Who*

Taunted Killer Had Award Revoked. "It's a mish-mash of fact and fiction," Tom warned as I started reading. "It's not slanted your way."

The detective who allegedly used a YouTube video to challenge killers to test his crime-fighting skills received a major departmental award in the weeks preceding the killing spree. According to a knowledgeable source, the Chief of Police himself had problems with the detective getting the award, and soon thereafter cancelled the citation.

"Chief Baggs dug into circumstances surrounding the award and found them questionable," the source said.

A checking of the publicity releases in recent weeks shows only one MPD detective to have received a citation in that period: Detective First-grade Carson Ryder, an eleven-year veteran of the force who has received numerous previous honors and citations. The video was removed from the popular international video-hosting site when it was discovered by top MPD administrators.

Also according to the source: Detective Ryder heads the PSIT, or Psychopathological and Sociopathological Team, a specialized unit he created to apprehend mentally unstable criminals. The shadowy unit is reputedly in charge

of investigating the "spree" of random killings
now terrifying Mobile's citizenry. . .

"Jesus," I said. "It makes it sound like I'm. . ."

Tom's Stetson bobbed. "I know."

"The words alone: 'problems', 'questionable', 'shadowy unit', 'reputedly' . . . they're calculated to—"

"I know."

"It has me creating the PSIT, Tom. That's backwards. The department practically begged Harry and I to create the unit."

"I know."

"The word 'nullified' proves Baggs is behind the smear campaign. It's the word he used to—"

"I know."

"But did you know that I'm going upstairs to throw Baggs out of his very own window?"

I turned for the door but Tom grabbed my arm. "First, confronting Baggs gets you suspended or fired, Carson. Second, Baggs is at a regional chiefs' symposium in Pensacola."

"Baggs throws shit at me and runs?"

Tom closed the door and lowered his voice. "What have you guys got that you're not putting in the reports? You always have something, even if it's way out in left field."

Tom had trusted Harry and me for years because we'd always produced. But I couldn't tell him my new approach was consulting an escapee from an institution for the criminally insane.

"I'm working an angle, Tom," I said. "Something new. But it's a little strange and. . ."

He mimed putting his hands over his ears. "I don't need to hear it, Carson. Just give me results, right? Or you and the PSIT are heading down the drain."

I went to the small conference room in the corner and locked the door, pulling my cell. I dialed Jeremy. His phone was turned off so I left a message.

"Drop everything. Read the fucking material. Get back to me fast."

A knocking at the door caused me to startle and drop the phone. I heard Tom Mason's voice.

"You in there, Carson? Looks like the bastard has struck again."

Ema Nieves sat in her car outside the restaurant on the Causeway. She'd just had breakfast with Gregory, an unsettling experience. Ema had repositioned her car behind a large SUV and was sitting up so she could peek at the restaurant through the smoked windows of the SUV, waiting for Gregory to exit.

There was something wrong with her brother.

Ema knew he would spend several minutes in the bathroom, a compulsive hand washer since they'd arrived in Alabama twelve years ago, wide-eyed adoptees from a state orphanage deep in the inhospitable mountains of northern Romania, carrying only dirty, water-stained birth certificates listing Grigor Secăşeanu as twelve years of age, Ema Secăşeanu as nearing sixteen.

Peter and Pamela Nieves were the sort of people whose hearts were weighed down by the world's pain and, when unable to conceive, had taken it upon themselves to alleviate some small portion of the hurt. Ema had heard the story of how, entering the isolated orphanage in the mid-nineties, the Nieves had moved to Gregory as if drawn by a gravity of despair, his large eyes staring into nothingness as he sat cross-legged on the filthy mattress that formed his world.

"Look at that poor child, Peter. He's like a statue. I think I'm going to cry again."

"My God, Pamela . . . is he even alive?"

"Madam Fachin?" Pamela Nieves said to their guide, a reformist recently placed in charge of adoptions. *"Tell me about this poor child. . ."*

The Nieves were told Grigor Secăşeanu was basically physically healthy and had no discernible retardation or brain damage and yes, was on the list of children available for international adoption.

"He's so beautiful and so lost, Peter. We can make him whole. I know we can."

The Fachin woman had retrieved a file of tattered records, all that remained of the children's pasts, the staff fleeing when reformers took over the orphanage. Madam Fachin found what she was looking for, a typed and official-looking note stapled to a dusty file.

"*Yes, as I recalled,*" Fachin had said. "*There is another aspect, madame. The boy has a sister. She has always cared for him here to the best of her abilities. It is a condition that they be adopted together by a family in the West.*"

"*Peter?*"

"*Two children? I, uh . . . Can we meet the girl?*"

"*Of course. Her name is Ema. She is fifteen.*"

The girl was healthier looking, almost plump, her eyes bright and intense though her face was masked with fear. Instead of offering a vacant stare, the girl had crossed the room, taken her brother's hand and managed a quivering smile. "I am Ema," she whispered as the boy looked on, blank confusion in his eyes. "Please will you us help?"

Later, when the Nieves sat outside with the children, asking through the interpreter if they'd like to take the name Nieves, Gregory had simply stared. Ema had clapped eagerly and practiced saying "Ema Nieves" the remainder of the afternoon.

The restaurant door opened again and Ema thrust the past aside. But it was a group of elderly women, purses slung over frail arms as they tottered to a shiny black Cadillac.

What was wrong with Gregory? Ema wondered. First, he'd talked far more than usual, faster too, as if his thoughts were moving beyond his words and he was trying to keep up. But, even though his thoughts were racing, his face barely moved, as if anesthetized.

He'd kept shooting glances at her face, her hair, her

pendant. When asked why, Gregory's face had frozen into a cross between bewilderment and snarl. He'd stared without blinking, his eyes blazing with an inner fire.

Ema felt her heart racing as both glass doors of the restaurant opened and Gregory exploded through, moving like a man on a mission. He jumped into his Avalon and fishtailed from the parking lot in a spray of sand and crushed shells.

Ema sat up, stunned. She had to get Gregory to her house where she could cook a meal, sit him down, and discover what was happening in her brother's head.

42

The murder scene was a model home in an exclusive west Mobile neighborhood, out where the suburbs grew fast and furious and increasingly expensive. Harry and I threaded our way through the patrol cars, command van, forensics van, two ambulances and the Medical Examiner's van. Clair had been making all the runs that might be associated with our killer and I wondered how she would greet me. When I realized today was her day off, I felt grateful for small favors.

Dazed and milling onlookers were being herded away so tape could be strung. I saw Sergeant Howell Beauchamps walking from the front door and shaking his head. He gave me the two-beat appraisal I was growing tired of getting used to.

"Woman in her late forties, early fifties, Ryder. Looks like she was minding the store, a realtor. It's bad."

"The same MO as the others?"

"Guess you'd know that better than I would. I been hearing and reading how you—"

"Not now," I said, stepping inside. The anteroom held a small desk which had been upended, a chair beside it. The carpet was beige, though large swaths were blood red. So were parts of the wall.

The body was in an upstairs bedroom, sprawled across the floor. The back of her blue blouse was in strips that I knew would match the long slashes across her back displaying meat and muscle.

I didn't need to see more and headed out, careful where I put my feet. I saw Harry talking to Gilly Fortner, the young forensics tech. She was holding a curved sword in her gloved hands, its blade dappled with red.

"He left his weapon, Carson," Harry said.

"Where?"

"It was in the bougainvillea beside the driveway," Gilly said. "Stuck in the ground."

"A sword sure fits Kavanaugh's classic-battle concept."

I scrutinized the wickedly curved blade and saw small shreds of green. I turned my eyes to the front yard of the model home with its curb-appeal plantings of crepe myrtle, dogwood and azalea.

"Some of the bushes have been whacked, bro," I said to Harry. "Chopped with the sword." I slashed an imaginary sword at a lopsided myrtle.

Harry frowned. "He was doing a Jack Sparrow thing?"

"I'm picturing this." I mimicked crossing from the

front door of the house to the driveway, slashing at plants along the way. I mimed sticking the sabre in the ground and entering an imaginary vehicle.

"He's gone from *woo-woo-woo* to *yo-ho-ho*," Harry said.

"Swinging the sabre in broad daylight with no fear of being seen," I said, looking at the few surrounding homes, empty and awaiting buyers. "He either knew no one was watching or didn't care. Either way, it shows a major lack of caution. But why?"

"Decompensating?" Harry said. "Losing psychological control?"

"That's too clinical," I said, studying the beheaded bushes. "Something's pushed him into full-freak mode."

I heard my name called and saw Clarence Beekman, a scene tech, waving me to the front door. "There were some business cards under the table, plus we found her purse in the top of a closet. Name's Muriel Pendel."

I felt a cold wind blow up my spine. "I know a kid with that name. He's studying at the academy, a recruit."

"You don't think. . ."

"I got no idea," I said, pulling my cell and calling Al Leighton, director of the academy.

"What's up, Carson?" he said. "You cancelling class because of, uh, that thing in the newspaper?"

"I'm still in, Al. Could you check Wilbert Pendel's next-of-kin listing, please?"

I heard keystrokes over the phone. "Pendel lists father

and mother, Bert and Muriel Pendel, 3482 Oakmont Drive, Mobile. You want the numbers?"

Though prepared for the worst, I felt as though I'd been kicked in the stomach.

"Just the father's, Al."

I walked to a picnic table in the back and made the call. Harry had been there before so he sat beside me for moral support. Not knowing Wilbert Pendel's religious inclinations, I called the police chaplain and let him know he might be needed when we found the kid. Pendel wasn't at his apartment or studying in the academy, though I wasn't part of the search, Al Leighton stepping up to handle things.

I heard my name called again, this time by a chorus of reporters at the scene tape, yelling and waving me close.

"*Why did you challenge a psychopath, Detective?*"

"*Was it intentional? Were you trying to smoke someone out?*"

"*This PSIT . . . is it true there's no rules? You can do what you want?*"

"*I hear the reason your citation was revoked is because you lied about something. Is that true?*"

Not a single question about the actual cases. I knew the questions were based on misinformation probably fed them by one of Baggs's surrogates – Willpot, most likely – but it didn't make the frantic queries any less inane.

"*Detective Ryder, do you think you should be suspended for inciting a killer?*"

I started toward the chattering simians but felt a hand tighten on the back of my shirt. "Focus, brother," Harry whispered. "Be pleasant and make innocuous statements."

I took a deep breath, nailed a politician's earnest and joyless smile to my face, and sauntered over. "I was simply explaining sociopathic killers to my academy class," I said. "I don't know where the idea of a challenge came from."

"Why did you put the video on the Internet?"

"Class members put it up as an instructional video because informational videos are common on YouTube. I was surprised when I saw it, but not fearful, as the recording has no inflammatory content, only a factual discussion of sociopathy."

"That's not how the video has been represented."

"Perhaps you should consider your sources."

"But it sparked a lunatic into killing people, right?"

I put my hands in my pockets and shook my head amiably. "The current horrors could just as easily have been sparked by a story in the media."

That hit close to home. I glanced at Harry and he nodded *good job*.

A stiff-haired blonde woman from a local television station elbowed to the front of the herd, a pad in her hand. "But you did have a citation taken away, right, Detective? Chief Baggs gave you an award, then . . . what was the word? *Nullified* it." She gave me a *gotcha!* grin. "So why would the Chief revoke your citation if you're so innocent?"

I considered her question. It deserved a truthful answer.

"Because Chief Baggs is a horse's ass," I explained calmly as pens scribbled on paper and cameras rolled. "He's unfit to command an ox cart, much less a police department."

43

Harry moved me away from the frenetic reporters and we drove off to banging on our windows and Tom Mason calling with an update.

"Chaplain Burgess went to Pendel's parents' house, found the kid carrying away a sack of groceries and a six of beer. When Burgess told him the news, the kid totally freaked, punched Burgess, ran screaming back inside the house. The chappy tried to get the kid to come out, but nothing worked."

"Pendel's at the house now?" I asked.

"No one's quite sure. And the father is—"

"A computer salesman on a trip to Seattle. Fastest he can get here is three hours."

I U-turned in the street and headed to the Pendels' home.

"What's the kid like?" Harry asked.

"Wendy Holliday had the best description: Wilbert Pendel watches people through a weird crack in space-time. You can see him, but you can't touch him."

We were there minutes later, Al Leighton out front with the chaplain, two empty cruisers in the drive. I figured the uniforms were checking the area.

"He's not in there," Tim Burgess said. "Must have slipped out the back."

We looked up, saw O'Herlihy walking our way, a woman in her fifties at his side, her face lined with concern. "This is Mrs Calloway," O'Herlihy explained. "A neighbor. She says Pendel's behind her house. In a tree."

Mrs Calloway's home was three doors down. The backyard was centered by a thick live oak with wide-spread branches. There was a small platform in the branches, a tree fort. Whenever my family followed my civil-engineer father to a new jobsite he rented a house as far from others as possible, usually in the country. The first thing my brother and I did was build a tree fort as a place to escape our father's consuming and irrational anger.

This fort was a dozen feet up, an eight-by-four flat of plywood forming the floor. Three-foot slatted deck rails made the perimeter, a small opening on one side to allow entry.

Pendel was crouching inside, dressed in a police uniform. There were any number of places he could have gotten it using his recruit ID. He peered warily through the railing slats. He had a gun in his hand, a large-frame revolver of some sort. I waved everyone away except Harry. We inched closer until Pendel started spitting toward us, about ten paces out with enough angle to see inside.

"Where'd you get the gun, Will?" I asked.

As if all was forgiven, the spitting turned to a Jack-o'-lantern grin. "Bought it last week, Detective Ryder. I needed me a throw-down."

A throw-down was an untraceable weapon cops supposedly planted as false evidence. They existed more in the realm of stories than in real life. Pendel had probably soaked up the term from cop shows.

"How about I go call for a beaner?" Harry whispered, meaning a riot gun loaded with beanbag ammo.

I nodded, seeing where he was heading. He slowly backpedaled away.

"That's not an official gun, Will," I said, surreptitiously thumbing the magazine from my nine. "How about you take mine? I'll climb up and we'll trade."

"I like mine. I carved my name into the grip."

He showed me the scrawled grip. He frowned at something in his head, then slid the weapon's muzzle into his mouth.

"WILL!" I yelled. He didn't seem to hear, sliding the muzzle across his tongue as if fascinated by the feeling. After a few seconds he removed it.

"Your father's coming, Will. He needs you to be with him. He needs your help."

Pendel looked at me as if I were speaking Mandarin. "I'm an orphan," he said. "My mother and father threw me away."

The gun barrel found its way back into his mouth. I had no idea of Pendel's history or his relationship to his parents. The only person I'd ever seen him interact with was Wendy Holliday, and that held semi-veiled lust and a clumsy arrogance born of insecurity. I called her, spoke thirty seconds in a whisper, and returned my attention to Pendel.

"You hungry, Wilbert?" I said. "I could order up a pizza. Burgers. Whatever."

"No thanks, Detective Ryder. I think I'll just stay up here and eat my gun." He laughed, an eerie, quivering sound. Eating your gun was cop speak for committing suicide with a pistol in your mouth. Pendel would have heard it at the academy, probably as a dark joke. *If I don't get at least a B on that exam tomorrow I'm gonna have to eat my gun.*

Pendel looked like he had no idea what life meant any more, the last look I'd seen on every suicide I'd not prevented. He moved the gun close to his eyes, studied it, spun the chamber. He ran the snout over his cheek and put the muzzle back in his mouth. One touch of the trigger and he'd be gone.

I clapped my hands together hard. "Hey!" I yelled. "I got an idea. How about a few brews, Wilbert? Something cold to go with that gun."

This was at-the-edge stuff, but the barrel slid from

between his teeth and his eyes brightened. "Fuck yeah, Detective. Some brews and some Jägermeister."

"I dunno about the Jägermeister, Will," I said. I wanted camaraderie, not a boozefest in the searing summer heat.

He frowned and got interested in the gun again.

"Jägermeister for everyone!" I yelled, doing a dance in the grass, anything to get his attention.

"Rock on, Detective," he laughed. I delivered our drink order to Tom Mason, watching through binoculars from the street.

"You think that's a good idea?" he asked. "Alcohol?"

"It's all I got, Tom. But Harry and I are working on something."

"I'll send a cruiser for the drinks."

"Hurry," I said. "He's slipping fast. Anything on the father?"

"In the air, but at least two hours away."

I diddled around under the tree, playing the fool and trying to keep Pendel engaged enough to forget about the gun in his hand. I was soaked in sweat from nerves and ninety-five-degree heat. At least Pendel was in the blue shade of the wide oak. Four minutes later I heard the air-sucking swoosh of big engines and watched two cruisers pull onto the lawn, probably the first time a bottle of Jäg and two sixes of Bud ever had a police escort.

"Here comes the party, Will," I said, motioning the uniformed cop to advance slowly with the bag. I held high a six-pack and the bottle of Jägermeister.

"How about I climb up and we'll pop a few?"

"Ain't room enough for two up here," he said through the bars. "Throw me up a six and the Jäg."

He stood to grab the bottle and cans, crouched again. I watched him suck down a third of the herbal liqueur, wondering if this had been a good idea. I saw the headline: *Killer-inciting Cop Gets Suicidal Recruit Drunk.*

Pendel chased the Jäg with a whole can of beer. He picked up the bottle again.

"Easy there, bud," I said. "Save some for me."

His face became a snarl. "Get your own fuckin' bottle, asshole."

Mood swings. Bad going to worse. The gun went to his cheek again. He closed his eyes and rubbed it over his forehead.

A voice behind me called out a cheery, "Will!"

I spun to see Wendy walking my way, carefree, wearing white shorts and a cobalt blouse, running shoes. Crouched beside the house Al Leighton was holding a bullhorn and the Kevlar vest Wendy was supposed to be wearing.

Pendel moved the gun aside and stared at Holliday. "Why are you here?" he snarled. "You hate me. You think I'm gross and stupid."

I was watching Pendel's gun hand. So was the police sharpshooter in a window in the second floor of the house next door. My worst horror was Pendel going into shooting mode. At this distance the sniper, Cal Mallory, could pretty much take the kid apart. But I'd been in this land before, and was eighty per cent certain the kid was only a threat to himself.

I stepped to the side, figuring Pendel couldn't handle more than one person at a time. A dark stain appeared on Pendel's pants. He had urinated without knowing it, another bad sign. He seemed to disappear inside himself again, came back with an angry face.

"You're fucking Ryder, aren't you, Wendy?"

"Why do you say that, Will?"

"You know the answers. You get all the best grades." He moved his face to the slats and showed a leering face. "I fuck you every night, bitch." He pumped his hand above his crotch. "Like this."

Wendy cocked her head, concern on her face. "What's wrong, Will? What's bothering you?"

The angry face turned pensive. Pendel thought for a long time.

"I don't want to be here any more, Wendy."

"Why, Will?"

"Because I'm different. I got thrown away and lived in the dark. There were babies everywhere but they never cried. They forgot how."

Wendy shot me a glance, *Do you know what he's talking about?* I shrugged, *No idea.* She took a step forward.

"I don't understand, Will. Help me understand."

"Did you know I wore a diaper until I was eight years old? No one taught me how to make doo-doo on a potty."

Another *What is this?* glance from Wendy. Pendel took a swig of the liqueur and scratched his temple with the barrel of the weapon. "You want to know my real name, Wendy? It's stupid and ugly."

"Will, I'm sure it's not—"

"Haralamb Bumbescu. Can you believe that's a name?"

"It's a great name, Will," Wendy said. "You're lucky to have two whole names. Most people only have one."

Pendel scowled. "It's a stupid name, but it's the right name." His eyes floated to the sky, the ground, the tree-tops. Then, out of nowhere, "I DON'T WANT TO GO BACK TO GROUP!"

"You don't have to, Wilbert," Wendy said. I watched him reverse the gun in his hand, thumb in the trigger guard, moving it to his face, mouth open. My heart climbed into my throat. My head screamed *NO!*

But Pendel stopped, frozen, staring to my left. Wendy was slowly unbuttoning her blouse. Pendel lowered the gun, staring.

"What are you doing, Wendy?"

"I can't let this day go to waste, Will. I'm going to work on my suntan."

"Your tan?"

She undid another button. "I need sun on my body."

Pendel leaned forward, eyes wide. "Are you gonna show your titties?"

Wendy tossed the shirt aside, standing there in a burgundy bra. She pulled it down an inch to show the

340

tan line. "I have to if I'm gonna get a full tan, Will. That's the way it should be done, right?"

"You're s'posed to take all your clothes off, Wendy," Pendel said. "That's the right way."

She reached behind her and snapped her bra loose and turned her face to the sky. "Oh, Will, the sun is soooo warm."

"You have to take that off so you can get a tan."

The bra hanging loose, Wendy popped the top button on her shorts and undid the zipper. The shorts fell a couple inches, exposing a strip of white pantics. She stepped closer to the fort.

"Where are you going?" Pendel said. "Are you going to suntan?"

"Right now, Will. Here under the tree."

He frowned. "It's shady down there."

"There's a little patch of sun just the size of my body." She stepped three paces nearer, now almost under the fort. Pendel's face pressed the slats as he looked down.

"I can't see you, Wendy."

"I'm right here, Will. Almost under you."

She slipped off the bra and tossed it out where Pendel could see. He moaned and stood, the gun wavering in his hand, a line of saliva dripping from the wet hole of his mouth.

A heavy *whump*. A dark blur caught Pendel on his shoulder and sent him tumbling over the railing. I jumped beneath him with my arms locked over my head, hoping to keep him from breaking his neck. It was like having a

341

cow dropped on me and we slammed the ground together, Pendel landing on his side with his head against my ribs.

The paramedics were there in four seconds, Harry in five, the riot gun still drizzling smoke from the fat charge of the beanbag round.

"You all right, Cars? Jesus."

A moaning, babbling Wilbert Pendel was rushed away, looking as though he had nothing worse than a busted ulna and collarbone. They found nothing wrong on my end, but I knew getting out of bed would be tough for a couple days.

"Where's Wendy?" I asked.

"Here."

I craned my head around. She was standing above me, backlit by sunlight. "You were supposed to wear a bullet-proof vest," I mumbled. "And use the bullhorn to talk to Pendel from the house."

"I hate bullhorns," she said. "And I guess I just plain forgot about the vest." She paused and thought for a moment, tapping her lips with a pink finger. "You still plan to teach tonight, Detective Ryder? If so, I gotta run home and finish my paper."

Gloria Estridge's doorbell rang. She muted the court TV show and tiptoed to the door, frowning through the peephole. She stepped back and pushed a smile to her lips as she opened the door. The man Gloria knew only as Bill crossed the threshold wearing unbuttoned white painter's overalls with a skin-tight shirt under it, like a bodystocking. Billy was weird – all that shit about special soap and mouthwash – but he paid good and didn't argue when his time was up.

"Billy, baby. It's so early. Why didn't you call?"

"I was in the neighborhood. Something wrong with that?"

"Nothing, sweets," Estridge took Bill's hand. "But you shoulda called."

"I won't be long."

"Want I should take a special shower, Billy? We can have an early party."

Billy cupped his hand over his crotch, as if making an assessment, shook his head no. He strode to the bureau and opened the top drawer, looking inside.

"You got any more of those special bags?"

"I'm out, baby. But I got a friend can swing by with some in mebbe ten minutes. How much you want?"

"Remember that bag that I got the other day?"

"You want another bag like that?" Gloria asked.

"I want five of them."

"That's a lot of money, baby."

"Not really," Billy said, his eyes glittering like dark jewels. "Not to a guy about to become a sextillionaire."

44

Harry and I drove to the hospital to see how Pendel was faring. Given his erratic behavior and suicidal actions, he was under protective custody. We walked toward his room recalling how our last trip here had been to see Tommy Brink, the poor little kid whose mother treated him like a bag of rocks she'd been forced to carry.

We started into the room, almost bumping into a petite woman who was exiting. "If you're here to see Willy, I'd wait," she said in a voice tinged with Slavic vowels.

I looked past the small woman in the cream pantsuit and saw Pendel prone on the bed with his arms, legs and torso restrained, his eyes less staring at the ceiling than boring holes through the tiles. "Probably a form of psychotic catatonia," the woman sighed. "His mind became overwhelmed and he's hiding deep inside it." She studied us. "Do you know Willy?"

The three of us did introductions, Harry and I meeting Dr Sonia Szekely, a psychologist and friend of Pendel and his family.

"I was one of Wilbert's instructors at the police academy," I said.

Szekely couldn't hide a frown. "You were going to turn Will into a policeman?"

"Never would have happened, Doctor. To be frank, I'm not quite sure how he got into the academy in the first place."

"Willy can be persuasive at times. And he isn't stupid."

I saw a chance to discover more about Pendel and his family, said, "How about we go to the cafeteria for a cup of coffee, Doctor?"

A knowing twinkle in the woman's eyes. "How about we step outside for your questions, gentlemen? I need a cigarette break."

We reconvened at a picnic table beside the hospital, a place for employees to have lunch or just hang out and enjoy air free from disinfectant and disease. The area was landscaped with azaleas, myrtle and bougainvillea, here and there a magnolia tree. Birds tittered from nearby branches.

"What was your relationship to Ms Pendel, Doctor Szekely?" I asked after the doc fired up a Marlboro light.

"We met in the EEOSA group almost a dozen years ago."

"Excuse me?" Harry said.

"Sorry. The Eastern European Orphans Support Alliance, a support group, mainly for Romanian orphans. It's for children and parents, each has their own group. We work on a host of issues."

"Wilbert was adopted from one of these orphanages?" I asked.

She nodded, pushing gray hair behind one ear. "Willy was one of the lucky ones."

Her answer explained Pendel's strange comments and the foreign name he claimed, Bomblescu or whatever. It also hinted at the social estrangement he seemed to project.

"Why the geographic specialization, Doctor?" Harry asked.

"You've heard of Nicolae Ceauşescu?" Szekely's nose wrinkled when she said the name.

Harry nodded. "The former president or whatever of Romania?"

"An evil, brutal man. In 1966 he decided to enlarge the country's workforce by increasing the birth rate. He made contraception and abortion illegal and encouraged huge families. Unfortunately, Romania was a desperately poor country. Children couldn't be fed or supported, so they were abandoned. Six hundred state orphanages were built to hold the cast-off children."

"I'm not seeing a pretty picture," Harry said.

"Think of chicken coops for babies. Vast rows of cribs holding children fed with cheap, tasteless slop a couple times a day. They aged in their boxes, no nurturing, no interaction with others, no emotional bonding. They existed – *lived* is too strong a word – in filth and squalor, isolated from feeling, from discovery, from joy. The first reformers into the institutions reported children with faces incapable of projecting emotion."

Harry closed his eyes. "My God."

"That's just the surface. Get below and you find what has always plagued institutions where adults control innocents."

I said, "Pedophilia."

"Perversion of every persuasion, Detective. Physical and mental abuse. Sex parties. This is not to say all caregivers were bad, but they were uneducated, poorly paid and overwhelmed by the volume of children. Record-keeping was poor, many children unaccounted for and easily sold into the sex trade."

"When did it stop?" Harry asked.

"The horror began to abate in the early 1990s. But many orphanages continued with elements of the old ways deep into the decade."

"It's gotta be hard to enter normal society," I said, "when you have no concept of normal."

Szekely puffed on her Marlboro, legs crossed. "Many adoptees have RAD, or reactive detachment disorder, affecting their ability to express normal emotion. Others have fetal alcohol syndrome. AIDS is a problem. Anger issues are common . . . frustration at not fitting in and never quite knowing why, anger at authority figures or self-directed anger. As one might expect from barren and loveless childhoods, there are elevated levels of sociopathy."

"Why is this such an issue for you, Doctor?" Harry said.

"I'm Romanian. My parents brought me to the US in 1976 and I took a degree in child psychology. When I heard of the orphans I started EEOSA."

"I take it Willy had problems in the group?" I said, recalling his scream, *I DON'T WANT TO GO BACK TO GROUP!*

"Willy has manifestations of RAD, including problems relating with others. But he has no mental deficiency, no retardation or physical ailments from his eleven years in an orphanage. Still, he sometimes acted out in group, his insecurities manifesting."

"The struggles must seem insurmountable," Harry said.

"Many children thrive when given love and care. A woman who had a breakdown in her teens just received her degree in accounting. Others are successes in business, or as educators or healthcare workers. The sky's the limit. One fellow came here almost mute, with suppressed anger and what I suspected were sexual issues. He discovered a genius-level propensity for math and now makes a good living writing software."

348

"Sounds like a success story." I'd spent a lot of time around people wounded by their pasts and was fascinated by those who had transcended horrors. "Is the man totally normalized?"

Szekely thought a long moment.

"There are still issues. He was never socialized as a child and probably never will be. He has affect problems as well, RAD. I'm not convinced he's found a way to vent internal rage. He had a breakdown after college and spent several months in an institution. During that time his step-parent passed away, father."

"Mother?" I asked, having lost mine at about the same age.

"She left three years after the children were adopted, too much of a strain. The father was a kind man, determined to see his son succeed. He died before he got the chance, though perhaps the inheritance he left helped."

"The son left the institution a wealthy man?"

"Comfortable wealth, not major. But the son had to demonstrate the competency to manage his own affairs. It was specified in the will."

"But basically the guy made it?" I said.

Szekely nodded. "Due, in large measure, to a sister who stayed by his side. She helped him back to reality, prodded him into finding a job befitting his skills, found him a house in a nearby neighborhood so she could keep an eye on him."

"The sister was in the same orphanage?"

"Yes, though she came through in better shape."

"Why the difference?" Harry asked.

Szekely shrugged. "She doesn't talk about the orphanage. I suspect she was in a ward where the care was more humane and personal. Or perhaps female children received more nurturing because of gender."

"Is the sister another math genius?" I wondered.

A smile. "Not even close, but she may be the reason for her brother's stability. Ema makes a point of getting together with her brother on a regular basis, though I know Gregory finds the get-togethers grating."

"Grating? That seemed to be Wilbert Pendel's take on group therapy. He didn't want to go back."

"The more insecure patients sometimes mistake the sessions as judgemental and take them personally. Willy and the other fellow, Gregory, followed that model. They were in group together for several months until I shifted them to different sessions. They never got along and I figured they were probably too much alike."

"What's Wilbert's prognosis, Doc?" Harry asked.

"His mother's death will be a setback, perhaps a major one. He loved her deeply, as everyone in the group could see, but in his own way. Please be gentle in questioning him."

I nodded and leaned forward for the question I'd been reserving until the right moment. "Dr Szekely, do you think anyone in your groups could have harmed Muriel Pendel?"

She stared at the distant traffic, puffing and thinking until the end of the cigarette was dangerously near her fingers. She shook her head as she stubbed it out.

"Muriel and Bert have been members for over a decade. But I don't recall anyone ever making any threats, or showing anger toward either of them. Both she and Bert knew how to talk to the members. To adjust to their . . . eccentricities."

I looked at Harry and hid the sigh. What we had wanted more than anything was for Dr Szekely to say, *Why yes, I had a patient who fiercely hated Muriel Pendel. For some reason he hated the police as well, called them a Blue Tribe.*

No luck. "We'll bid you good-day, Doctor," I said. "Thanks for your time."

We were walking back to the car, neither bringing up the fact that it was nearing five p.m., when my comments to the media would undoubtedly be aired on the local news. "We'll arrive at that point when we arrive at that point," Harry had said earlier – his Philosopher mode – and indeed we would.

My phone rang, no caller identified. Somehow I knew. "Gotta take this," I said, ducking beneath the portico of the hospital's entrance.

"I'll be in the car," Harry said, looking away. Somehow he knew, too.

I opened the line with a tentative, "Hello?"

"Get to a computer," Jeremy ordered. "Skype me and we can—"

"No," I said, rubbing my forehead with one hand, the other propping the phone to my ear. "I'm not a television show, Jeremy. I'm tired and I need leads on our killer's psychological make-up."

"Rather testy today, Carson," Jeremy crooned. "Did you wake up on the wrong side of the bimbo?"

"All I need is—"

"I'll drop the Skype request, Carson. But you have to tell me who you're fucking."

"I'm hanging up."

"You'll miss my thoughts on your bad boy down there."

"Why do you always need to know about my love life?"

"We have different ways of dealing with crazy daddy and hide-in-her-room mommy. I now collect money. You've always collected love or whatever. It interests me."

"I date women, Jeremy. Can we get—"

"You don't date women," he pronounced. "You soak your pain in them."

I tried the silent treatment. He gave it back.

"Her name is Wendy Holliday," I finally said.

"Is she as delicious as her name?" He started the lip-smack noises again.

"Grow up, Jeremy."

"We both know that's impossible," he snickered. "Do you luuuuuv your new little Holliday?"

"Yes," I said. "I do love her."

A long silence. His voice returned, quietly curious. "You've never used the word love before, Carson. It's always, 'We're friends' or a similar dodge . . . But love?" A pause. "Have you finally grown up, baby brother?"

"I answered your question, Jeremy. That's all you asked. It's your turn to answer."

He cleared his throat and returned to his normal voice, always underpinned with sarcasm. "Your boy's quite smart but not brilliant, making things up as he goes along. The communication started after the second killing because he didn't consider it until then. I would have written every note in advance and they would have been far more literate. Think of a love child between Proust and the Zodiac Killer."

"Point, please."

"I'm not downgrading the fellow, Carson. He's eluded you, and I have to admit that takes doing. Plus he has irony, a rarity. I loved his posting you via the blind man. Though the ploy has been used before, as you know."

My brother had once communicated with me via a sightless man, thinking it a tremendous joke.

"Is he killing without motive?" I asked. "At random?"

A laugh. "You really can't see these things, can you?"

"I've never lived in an insane asylum."

"A pity. A decade in a nuthouse would make you a much better detective. The bottom line is your admirer knows something only a man with irony and an analytical mind can see."

"What?"

"A murder is too good a thing to waste, Carson."

"That tells me nothing. What do you mean by—"

"Have a nice day, Carson. Call again when you need big brother to guide you into the deep dark places. Or is your Holliday doing that for you now?"

45

I planned to teach tonight. My little media blitz would have been on the evening news, but maybe Baggs wasn't big on television. Or reading the papers. Or listening to the radio. Anyway, I'd taken on the class, so not showing up wasn't an option.

Everyone was in their seats when I arrived, faces brimming with questions though no one spoke a word. I put my hands on the sides of the lectern, eyes catching the date on my watch. It had been less than three weeks since I entered this room for the first time, my impromptu lecture taped and put on YouTube. I looked out over the expectant faces. *Whatever you do*, I thought, *don't throw pennies*.

"Wilbert Pendel is not with us tonight," I began. "You all know why, at least to a degree. If you consider Pendel a friend, be one. If you don't consider him a friend, become one. He needs support."

A general bobbing of heads.

"Tonight I'm asking you to consider a hypothetical case wherein someone is killing in what appears to be a random fashion. No discernible motive, no ties between murders. In this hypothetical case, an expert in criminal psychology looks at the murder books, the case materials, photos, everything . . . and arrives at a baffling conclusion. He simply says, 'A murder is too good a thing to waste.'"

I moved from behind the lectern and folded my arms.

"My question: What might our expert mean?"

A buzzing of voices, folks repeating the question to themselves. Chairs shifting. Terrell Birdly raised a hand.

"Perhaps the expert means a random murder has no meaning. It is simply a death, the creation of a corpse. It has to have meaning."

I nodded. "I'm uncertain what you mean, Terrell. What happens from there?"

A frown. "I'm thinking."

Jason Kellogg tried next. "A corpse has nothing to offer but dead meat," he said. "Only if there is a meaning can the murder be elevated beyond the creation of dead meat."

"What if the killer hates humanity?" I scoffed, Devil's Advocate. "Is not a dead human the perfect goal to such a person?"

"But just killing anyone?"

"If someone hates humanity, killing at random might be a way of saying, 'I hate you all, it doesn't matter who you are.' The goal is simply dead humans."

"It's a goal if the killer is simple-minded," Amanda Sanchez added, her outsize earrings bobbing in and out of her dark hair. "Hate people, kill people, goal. But in your first class you postulated an intelligent and creative killer. Is that what we're dealing with here? Hypothetically, of course."

"Excellent question," I said. "And the answer is yes."

Deborah Bournet was shaking her head, skeptical. "Simple-minded or intelligent, a sociopathic killer needs to kill. It's like eating. Whether a meal is planned or unplanned makes no difference when it's all food."

A murmur of assent. Wendy had her hand up and I nodded at her.

"It's not satisfying," she said. "I'll continue Deb's analogy. It's not a thrilling, delicious, meaning-fraught meal."

A chuckle through the class. I batted downward with my head, *shhhh*.

"Satisfaction, Miss Holliday?" I said. "That's your premise?"

"Killing to kill would not satisfy a higher-level mind. A chess-level brain would be bored stiff with checkers. More is demanded from a death than just death."

I thought for a long moment. "Maybe the more that is demanded is simply control and pain, Miss Holliday.

He kills at random, causing pain. Pain equals goal reached."

"Then I would suggest the pain has meaning beyond its infliction."

Something in her answer gave me pause. "What sort of meaning?"

"Retribution for a wrong, perhaps."

I lifted a skeptical eyebrow. "But if the killings are random, Miss Holliday, the killer is incapable of being wronged by the victims because he's never met them. How can you have retribution without a wrong?"

I'd thrown a wrench into her concept.

"Maybe the pain is meant to, uh—"

The door banged open. Frank Willpot stood in the entrance flanked by two uniformed cops, his cold blue eyes boring into mine. "Class over, Ryder," he announced, stepping into my space. "Chief's orders. Pack up and git. You're suspended for insubordination. That little conversation with the media? I expect that's the swansong for your career."

Confused and angry voices at my back, the recruits out of their desks and demanding answers from Willpot.

What are you doing? . . . This is our class . . . Detective Ryder never put up those tapes . . . This is crazy . . . Detective Ryder never said anything wrong . . . Who said you could do this?

Willpot hadn't expected a student protest. His eyes blazed with anger. "This is a departmental matter, and none of you are in the department . . . yet. If you want to fuck your careers before they've even started, then go ahead and question my authority."

"Stop being an asshole," Wendy said.

Willpot glared at her. "You're threatening your future, little girl."

"It wasn't a question."

Willpot couldn't find a friendly eye in the room. He waved his arms at the door. "All of you out! Class dismissed. Go home. Detective Shumuchuru will be taking over again next week."

46

"You can fight it, Cars," Harry said, setting his beer on the hood of my truck. "The insubordination charge. . ."

"Three TV stations and two radio outlets have me telling the world what I think about Baggs. Maybe my future's elsewhere."

I'd retreated to the Causeway to lean against my truck, drink beer and consider my future in a department where colleagues could suspect me of a ridiculous action. A department where the Chief of Police hated my guts. Where my best prospect had me busted back into uniform, years of hard work turned to dross. Harry'd figured out where I was and joined me.

"Don't even begin to think like that," he said.

To the west a container ship pulled from the Mobile River into the bay, a dark shadow against the shimmering lights of the city. I wondered if I could somehow stow away inside a container marked for delivery to a murder-free zone, Antarctica maybe.

"I'm on tape again, no way to deny what I said. Maybe I could put my Baggs appraisal up on YouTube."

"Not funny." Harry paused. "Or maybe a little."

I stared into black water lapping at the reeds and traded dark future considerations for even darker ones from the recent past. "What's not funny is four dead in two weeks and not a single place to look."

"The killer's falling apart. You said so yourself . . . going batshit with a sword, throwing it into the bushes. We'll get him."

"How many people will he take down first?"

Harry pitched his emptied can into my pickup bed. "You'll be barred from the department tomorrow, Cars. What can we put in motion before the ax falls?"

"We need to update Kavanaugh. We've got to run Muriel Pendel's friends and associates through the wringer, and we've got to ensure every cop has seen the flier." The word *flier* prompted a memory. "One more thing has to be cleared."

"Which is?"

"Mailey mentioned a traffic stop where a guy shit himself after he blew through a hard red. A flat-out violation."

"What's the big news? I had a guy crap himself once, an old wino who—"

"Austin didn't write the guy up, Harry."

Harry did a double-take. "The same Horse Austin who empties ten pens a week writing tickets?"

I nodded. "If something bad happened during the stop, Austin wouldn't have written a ticket. No ticket says no incident, no need to keep the recording in case the offender contests the citation."

Harry crossed his arms and watched the blinking light of a jet high in the black sky. "I'd love to see the recording of the stop. Think Mailey'd tell you day and time?"

"He brought the incident up in the first place."

"How do we get the recording?"

"They're filed in Temp Records for a month, right? Sergeant Lizzy Baines sitting atop the pile?" I made kissy sounds. "Baines has the more-than-slightly-warms for you, Harry."

"Be that as it may, I'm with Sally now."

"You don't have to move into a Motel 6 with Baines, bro. Just blow in her ear and give her a glimpse of leg."

While Harry mumbled unrepeatable phrases, I pulled my cell and had the dispatcher patch me through to Mailey. It was a B week, meaning he was on night shift.

"Mailey? It's Carson Ryder. Horse around?"

Hesitant. "Not right now. He went to get, uh, a cup of coffee."

Sure, I thought, recalling Austin stashing the brown bag under his seat at the retirement home. *With vodka replacing the creamer.* "The stop with the guy who had the scoots? Harry and I need to see it. No big deal, just another part of the investigation."

362

"If Horse thought I gave you that he could make my life—"

"For chrissakes, Mailey, it'll look like we found it on our own. What's really on that recording, by the way?"

A pause. "Watch it yourself."

Mailey told us enough to find the recording and I promised we'd never tell Austin where the information came from.

"All right," I said to my partner as I slid my phone into my pocket. "All you need to do is get the tape from Baines. First thing tomorrow would be nice." I threw my empty can in the bed of the truck and shot a look at the container ship, angling closer as it turned for open sea.

It seemed to be saying, *Last chance for Antarctica, Carson.*

Gregory leaned over the coffee table and inhaled more of the white powder, an explosion of white sparkles in his head. He closed his eyes and marveled at the clarity in his mind. In the past, his only clear thoughts had been about math and software code, the numbers and symbols etched black against a snow-white background, clear and dynamic and understandable in every permutation. Even when the numbers zipped through his head at supersonic speeds, transmuting into new structures and giving revised answers, they were easy to follow.

It was everything else that was so difficult to understand. Love. Conscience. The ridiculous and antithetical pronouncements of the morons.

But now it seemed he could see through the morons like windows. See their halting and faulty machinery. His trouble was having to exist at their level. To translate their chimp-like language and find faces to meet their faces. But the white powder gave him the ability to fly above them. To see in perfect clarity that which had always been denied to him. Why was something that opened one's mind so widely illegal?

The fucking cops again.

Gregory was naked because it felt so good. He brushed white powder from his chest, leaned back against the couch, and thumbed the remote for the fifth time tonight. He'd stashed his video camera in the flower bed of the empty home across the street from the model home and it was providing the best movie so far: a couple entering the home for a showing, exploding out the door seconds later, the woman vomiting, the man fumbling at his cell. The cop cars racing up, the useless ambulance, the dark vans pouring out geeks and freaks like circus clowns.

And then, Ryder, the big negro at his side. Ryder looked ten years older than the night of the Ballard girl's event. Slumped, pale, worn. He was wearing a light jacket over jeans, the jacket looking as if he'd slept in it for a week.

How do you like your warrior now, Blue Tribe?

Gregory delighted when the sword was found in the bushes, though he couldn't quite remember why he'd left the weapon – a spur-of-the-moment decision. No matter, his Event Suit kept him safe, covered from crown to toe. The suit, crafted after Ema's comments about crime-scene evidence, made him invisible.

The phone rang again. Ema, no doubt. She had called over a dozen times, left texts, voicemails, messages on his answering machine.

"We should have supper tomorrow, Gregory. Give me a time, dear. I'd like to see you."

"Gregory, are you there, dear? Pick up, please?"

"Gregory, are you well?"

"How's the volunteering, Gregory? Are you busy tomorrow?"

Listening to the drone of Ema's voice was like bees buzzing: *Bzzz. Bzzzz. Bzzzzzz.* Gregory realized he was making buzzing sounds. They tickled his lips. He wavered to his feet, laughing, and put his arms out at his sides as if he was flying. *Buzzzzzzzzzzz,* he hummed, flying through the house like a bumblebee. *Buzzzzzz.* Six million dollars on its way, a sextitextijillionaire! *Buzzzzzzz-fucking-buzzzzzzzzzz!*

Gregory flew into the kitchen, swooped down to the refrigerator and drank from a bottle of apple juice, feeling it run down his throat as it ran down his neck and chest.

When he replaced the bottle on the shelf he saw the Tupperware container used to store sardines, the bait for his cat-catcher. He remembered he was a master trapper of cats, a pioneer in feline entrapment. Only yesterday old lady Millard had remarked on the dwindling number of cats in the neighborhood.

I got them, Gregory Nieves had wanted to scream in her face. *I have taken away the dishrag cats!*

I picked up Mr Mix-up on the way home, entering my house to find the answering machine blinking like a strobe. Wendy stood from the couch as Mix-up ran to his bowl. She was wearing blue shorts and a white tank top and was hands down the best thing I'd seen all day.

"Can I get you a beer?" she asked. "Or would you prefer—"

I nodded. "Something stronger."

She fetched the Maker's Mark, poured a double shot over ice. "I see I'm in demand," I said, nodding at the phone as my bourbon arrived.

"All except two are reporters asking you to deny or expand on your comments about Baggs." She'd heard the messages as they arrived.

"And the two?"

"One's from a guy named Roy McDermott. He wanted you to call when you got a chance."

McDermott was a former investigator for the FCLE or Florida Centre for Law Enforcement who'd recently jumped into upper-level administration. We'd worked together when Bama criminals headed to Florida or vice versa. We'd also fished together for snook, a sleek and powerful fish species found in mid-Florida and points south, my favorite gamefish. I figured he was passing through and wanted to meet for a brew. Another time, Roy.

"That leaves one call," I said to Wendy. "Chief Baggs, I expect."

"A very loud and angry Chief Baggs."

"I take it he used the word suspended?" I asked, sipping my drink.

"Until further notice, which he claims will never happen. Do you want to listen?"

"No, I want to take a container to Antarctica."

She watched in silence as I emptied my glass and considered my options, arriving at one I thought perfect. I went to the answering machine and pressed *Erase All.*

"There's nothing I can possibly do tonight," I said. "So I'm declaring a moratorium on killings and case histories and politics and general human idiocy. This house is now a free space, as distant and inaccessible as Antarctica." I twiddled buttons on my sound system. Beethoven's Sixth Symphony, the *Pastorale,* filled the room as I replaced electric light with candlelight.

Wendy went to the front window and peeked between the blinds. Said, "Wow, look at that."

"What?" I asked.

"It's snowing."

Gregory sat astride his Bowflex, pumping furiously, watching his shining muscles in the mirror. The white powder let him work out harder than ever before. He was sweating away toxins from food and the bacteria that infested his insides. Bacteria that had hidden in his muscles, in his guts, in his spine, all were being washed away.

He was becoming pure.

The alarm rang on Gregory's computer: time to check the trap. He dismounted the Bowflex and wiped his body with a towel. There were no more faces on the wall, he'd stripped them away after returning from the model home.

A pure man didn't wear the faces of others: he built his own.

Gregory walked to his office to disable the alarm. He'd put several teaspoons of the powder on his desk, spoons of it in every room. Gregory sniffed from a mound of powder and felt it sparkle across his neurons. He walked downstairs and outside, no need for clothes. If old lady Millard saw an Adonis in the dark, she'd not be offended, she'd want to fuck him.

Gregory strode to the rear of his yard and stripped the burlap from the trap. The half-moon dropped enough light to see a small and frightened creature huddling in a corner and mewing plaintively: a kitten. Gregory returned to the house with the trap held high above his head.

"*Braka ros n'da hasun. . .*" Gregory chanted as he walked, stealing even Ryder's song from him. "*I faw telawan telawon.*"

47

The next morning came too fast. *Persona non grata* in my own department, I met Harry in a coffee shop a few blocks away. He held up a black flash drive. "Austin's and Mailey's midnight stop."

"What'd you promise Baines?" I asked.

"If you see someone looks like Baines and me at that fancy new seafood joint in Daphne, it ain't us. Where we gonna look at the thing?"

Plugging it into my or Harry's computer was out of the question. Baggs probably had snipers focused on my desk. We jumped in my truck and I drove seven blocks to a small store off Government, the sign saying *Grant's Security*.

Nicolas Grant was Welsh, an ex-Royal Marine who'd fought in the Falklands and did tours of Northern Ireland in the tougher days. A few years back he'd visited the

States, found the coastal sunshine to his liking, and made the jump, opening a security and surveillance-oriented shop. The tech types at the MPD sometimes rented equipment from Grant.

We went inside, saw shelves of video cameras, monitors and other electronic gimcrackery. The proprietor pushed through curtains from the back, six-two, goateed and tatted and with a head shaved bald as an egg.

"If it isn't the terrible twosome," Grant said in a gruff brogue, fixing a blue eye on me. "I saw you on the news last night, Carson. Telling the world the Chief of Police wasn't fit to command an ox-cart. How are you still working?"

"It's a fluid situation, Nick," Harry said, holding up the drive. "You got a player can handle video from a cop cruiser?"

"Digital CCTV? Sure. Encrypted?"

"Doubt it."

Nick held the curtains wide. "Step into my parlor." He set us up at a bench holding a computer and monitor, plugged in the drive. "I expect you want me somewhere else, right?"

"Thanks, Nick," I said. "We owe you."

"A couple whiskies would be nice," Nicolas Grant grinned. "But the full story would be even better."

Nick disappeared and I pressed the forward button. A shiver on the screen was replaced by a nighttime street scene, Austin and Mailey's cruiser beside a building for concealment while providing a full view of an intersection. We watched the lights turn red on the north–south side. Three seconds later a white Toyota Avalon blew through the light as if it were invisible.

Austin's voice: "*Look at that muthafucker, goddamn light was so red it was almost green again. Let's roll.*"

Headlights led the cruiser into the street a half-block behind the taillights of the violator. Mailey's voice next, calling the department to run the license of a white Toyota Avalon.

Then Austin on the tape. "*Let's pull the asshole over on the next block, up by the Empire Bar. I like these hoo-hahs to know we're on the streets.*"

Lights flashed. The cruiser raced up on the bumper of the Avalon as it pulled to the curb just past the neon-lit Empire Bar.

The female dispatcher over the radio: "*Got a read on that plate, Horse. Registered to a Gregory T. Nieves of 2367 Parchwell Drive in Mobile, twenty-five years of age. Clean record. Not so much as a traffic ticket.*"

"*We're gonna give him one, hon,*" Austin laughed. "*A hundred-buck cite for Disregarding. Wish I got a commission on these things.*"

"*I'll bet you do too, Horse,*" the dispatcher yawned. "*Have fun.*"

Both cars were stopped now. In the periphery I saw shadowy forms and figured they were denizens of the Empire Bar, out to ogle the action.

Austin's voice. "*You take it, Mailey. I'm busy.*" I heard a rustle of what might have been paper and a wet sound.

It could have been an ass on the seats or a sip from a bottle.

Mailey addressed the driver over the loudspeaker: "*Stay in your car, sir. I'll come to you. Please shut off the engine and place your hands atop the wheel.*"

I heard the door open as Mailey stepped out. The cruiser-cams were sensitive to both image and sound. The head of the stoplight runner was craned back and I caught a glimpse of an impassive face as Mailey walked to the Avalon, stopping by the window.

"*I need to see license and registration, sir,*" Mailey said.

"*What did I do?*" the driver said.

"*I need to see your license and registration,*" Mailey repeated.

"*What – did – I – do?*" the driver repeated, petulant, speaking as though Mailey was a child. I heard Austin's door open, his voice trumpeting into the dark.

"*Hey, asshole! Get the fucking license out and do like you're goddamn told.*"

I heard chuckling from the side and figured it was the audience from the Empire.

"*I'm sorry,*" the driver said, affecting a conciliatory tone. "*What's this about, officer?*"

"*What are you doing here this time of night?*" Mailey said, his big Maglite scanning the rear of the Avalon, coming to rest on the driver's face. The guy just sat there like a robot.

"*I asked you a question, sir,*" Mailey repeated. "*Why are you here this time of night?*"

"*I couldn't sleep, officer,*" the driver said. "*I was driving to relax.*"

"*How much you had to drink?*"

"*A couple beers, sir. But that was hours ago.*"

Austin yelled, "*Get him outta the car, Mailey! I wanna look at him.*"

"*Step out of the car, please,*" Mailey said, pulling the door open.

"*Is there a reason why I—*"

Austin again: "*GET THE FUCK OUT OF THE GODDAMN CAR!*" I pictured him bellowing out the window. The guy still sat there. I heard the cruiser door open and Austin's big feet hit the pavement. He entered the picture, lumbering toward the car with his nightstick in his hand.

"*OUT OF THE CAR,*" he bellowed.

The man exited the vehicle. Harry and I could see a dark wet sheen spreading down the man's tan gabardines.

"*Jesus, Horse,*" Mailey said. "*The guy's shitting himself.*"

The driver clutched his belly and fell to his knees. I could actually hear his bowels squirting fluid. "*I – can't – help – myself,*" he moaned.

I heard the audience begin to laugh, followed by derisive comments.

"*Look at the boy shittin' hisself.*"

"*Hey, mister, you need some Imodium.*"

One of the bar drunks stepped into the light, hip-hopping toward the man on his knees, pulling giggles from his buddies.

"*Look at the boy with his face inna trance, got shit dripping down the legs of his—*"

The man stopped with a *whoof* as Austin's nightstick jabbed his sternum. He grabbed his belly and staggered away.

"*Get back to the bar, buncha goddamn drunks,*" Austin snarled. 'NOW!" I heard muttered words and receding footsteps.

"*The driver drunk, you think?*" Austin asked Mailey.

"*I didn't smell alcohol, Horse. I'm sure he's sober.*"

Disregarding what must have been a terrible stench, Austin crouched beside the stricken driver and put a hand under the guy's bicep, the bull-strong Austin bringing the driver gently to his feet and making sure he had his pins under him before releasing his grip.

"*It's all right, buddy,*" he said. "*Happens to the best of us. Think you're gonna be OK?*"

"*I think so—*"

"*Tell you what, my partner and I will follow you home, make sure you get there in good shape. That cool?*"

"*Thank you,*" the man said. "*Thank you so much.*"

Harry and I watched as the man pulled away, Austin and Mailey on his bumper. We heard a final line from

Austin, a threatening rumble: "*You tell anyone about me babysitting a guy home, Mailey, you and me are gonna tangle ass.*"

The cruiser-cam went dead.

"Nothing bad there," Harry said, pulling the zip drive. "A dead end, like Mailey said."

"Zilch," I agreed. "But we had to check."

48

We returned to HQ and parked in the garage as a black Dodge Ram pulled in a half-dozen slots away, Horse Austin, late as usual for his shift. "I can't help it," I said, jumping from the cruiser. "I gotta find out."

Harry and I were there when Austin's black boots hit the pavement. "Well, look who's here." Austin tipped back his Braves ball cap. "You better get a TV-union card, Ryder, you're spending so much time on the screen. Guess this is the last I'll see you at HQ, though."

I smiled. "Took us some doing to find the traffic stop," I said for Mailey's benefit. "But luck was on our side."

Austin's jaw muscles clenched. He knew we'd seen the tape.

"Jeez . . . You cut a guy slack, Horse. Not only that, you escorted him home. I'm gonna get the recording

376

played at roll call as a testimony to quality police work."

"You'll wind up in the ER," Austin snarled, raising a knuckle-heavy fist.

"I just want to know why you let the guy off, Horse," Harry prodded. "You ticket people when you don't like their haircuts."

"The guy had a problem, Nautilus." Austin slapped his lower belly. "His guts were all tangled up and he couldn't hold it back. I'll say it slow so even you can understand: he–couldn't–fucking–help–himself."

Austin started to juke past us toward the elevator. I replayed the recording in my head – *happens to the best of us* – and before I knew it my lips said, "I know what happened, Horse."

"You don't know anything, Ryder."

"You've been there before, Horse. Is that it?"

"Get outta my face, Ryder, or I swear I'll. . ."

"We won't hold it against you, Horse," I said. "And I'll make double sure the recording gets buried."

Austin looked between us. He sighed, pulled off the cap and dry-washed his face in his palms. "You two assholes ever hear of something called IBS?"

"Irritable bowel syndrome," Harry said. "My aunt's got it. When she goes on a long trip she marks maps with every rest stop."

"You never know what's coming next," Austin sighed. "Cramps, constipation, diarrhea. You fart a lot. My IBS is better controlled since I started eating freakin' yogurt two meals a day. Still, I gotta brown-bag a big goddamn bottle of Imodium while I'm working." He shook his head and stared at his boots. "A couple months back I was driving up to Montgomery and cramps slammed my guts. I ended up shitting my pants like a baby, the worst fucking day of my life. I guess I let the goof in the Avalon go because I knew what he was going through."

Austin gave us the tight eye. "This story goes nowhere, right?"

Harry and I simultaneously held up our hands in the *I swear* motion. Austin nodded and turned toward the door.

"You know why Horse doesn't want anyone to know he gave the guy a pass, don't you?" I said. "He doesn't want to tarnish his hardass image."

"Be that as it may," Harry said, "Horse Austin was sensitive to someone else's misery. It must be the delayed dawning of the Age of Aquarius."

Harry stared at Austin's back as if waiting for it to turn into a mirage. When it didn't, he grabbed his briefcase and started toward the door, checking his watch. "I figure it'll be a half-hour or so until I'm back out," he called over his shoulder. "We can keep working and stay off Baggs's radar. You waiting here?"

"I'm gonna wander over to the Square," I said. "Come by when you get free."

I walked toward Bienville Square, the block-sized park forming the heart of downtown Mobile, taking a bench beneath a live oak by the fountain. Street people wandered the area, young and old, many bleary-eyed with last

378

night's intoxicants. My mind returned to last night's class, and my question about random killings.

Interrupted by Baggs, we'd not made much progress, not that I'd expected anything: it was a Hail Mary pass.

Motion caught my eye. Twenty paces distant I saw a slender young man stumble to one knee, then push to standing. His brown hair hung over his eyes and his clothes were disheveled. I watched his stomach shudder in dry heaves and his hand came to his mouth, vomit spraying into his palm. He fell again and I jogged over. It wasn't unusual to find druggies sleeping off excesses in the square.

He was face-down and I grabbed his arm. "Come on, partner, roll over and let's take a look at you."

"Fuuugyew," he said, trying to slap my hand away and missing by a foot.

"Right," I said, rolling him over to check his carotid for heart rate. He tumbled and his unfocused eyes stared past mine.

Terry McGuiness. His eyes were dilated, his skin as white as lard. I put my fingers to his neck and couldn't count fast enough. I pulled my cell and called for medics. He started dry heaving again.

"What'd you take, Terry?" I said, pushing him to sitting so he wouldn't aspirate vomit.

He batted at my face with his hands. "Go 'way an' lemme die."

"Hang on, Terry." I heard a siren in the distance, we were just blocks from a firehouse.

"I'M A WHORE. LET ME DIE!"

I held him sitting as passers-by gave us sidelong glances and moved away quickly, fearful of the human drama playing out at the edge of their worlds. The ambulance approached. I put my knees behind McGuiness's back to keep him upright and waved frantically until the medics raced in with gurney in hand.

"He's OD-ing," I said. "Pulse has to be over 160."

"EVERYTHING'S GONE," McGuiness pleaded. "LEMME DIE!'

Within a minute Terry McGuiness was heading to the hospital. I leaned against a tree and wiped my brow with my bandana, Terry McGuiness's pleas still ringing in my head.

"EVERYTHING'S GONE, LEMME DIE."

Then an echo of the words, almost, but in a different voice. . .

"KILL ME INSTEAD. PLEASE KILL ME!" It was the voice of Francine Minear, Tommy Brink's aunt the day of the funeral, when all she had in the world was taken away. Minear's voice was replaced by the voice of Silas Ballard. . .

"I'd gotten to looking out over the land and seeing the future . . . Now all I'm ever gonna see is dirt. It's all over."

Patricia Ralway speaking of her beloved mother: *"It hurts worse than anything."*

And finally, Clair on the rain-gray day Silas Ballard slumped from the morgue after identifying Kayla's body.

"Everything in that poor man's life is gone, Carson. It's like the killer got him, too."

I heard the sound of angry car horns, then realized I was running down the middle of the street, sprinting toward the department.

49

A circle of police administrators were smoking by the entrance, Frank Willpot sucking the tip of a wet cigar. At first they just stared, then Willpot stepped into my path, hands out.

"Hold the fuck up, Ryder, you're not allowed in—"

I tried to juke past the blowhard but forward momentum slammed my shoulder into his outstretched arm, spinning him to the ground. I ran in the door with loud cursing at my back, the guy at the desk wide-eyed as I sprinted to the stairwell, taking steps two and three at a time.

I got to my cubicle, scrabbling for my list of telephone numbers. I spun the chair beneath my ass and put the list in front of me. Footsteps crossed the floor behind me. I turned to see Baggs puffing my way.

"Get out of here, Ryder!" he yelled. "You're suspended. You're going down."

"I need to make some calls."

Tom Mason appeared at the door of his office. Baggs heeled up a dozen feet from me, jabbing a finger my way. "Lieutenant Mason, get this man out of this room by any means you feel necessary. That's an order."

I looked at Tom, my eyes pleading. "I need to make some—"

"Get him gone," Baggs hissed, retreating to the sanctity of his framed doohickies. I looked at Tom Mason.

"Tom. . ."

He shook his head. "Chief says you can't be in this room, Carson."

"It could be important, Tom. Can I just—"

"Though he didn't say anything about that room over there." Tom pointed to his office, the blinds drawn. I shot a thumbs up and ran inside, locking the door. My first call went to Silas Ballard, no answer, probably out in the fields. I tried Arletta Brink and got her voicemail. My third call made it through.

"Ralway residence."

"Miz Ralway, this is Detective Ryder. I need to know if anyone has threatened you, either recently or perhaps even in the past. It's important."

Long seconds passed as her nails ticked on something. "No," she finally said. "I've had other girls threaten to pull my hair out, stuff like that. But that was in high school, forever ago."

"How about any situations where someone might have come away feeling insulted or humiliated?"

She paused. "Well . . . there was that thing I mentioned to Miss Holliday. The man with issues? We, uh, met at a bar, the Oasis Lounge by the airport a couple weeks ago and I . . . followed him to his home."

"What happened?"

"Um, it's rather personal."

"Frankly, ma'am, brief, uh, romances are not unfamiliar to me. I sort of understand the dance."

Another pause, then a chuckle. "All right. The guy seemed nice enough at first, but got progressively stranger. When we were intimate, he seemed odd and inept. Almost mechanical. When I put the brakes on, he became extremely rude. I kept my cool until getting to the front door, then said some things that could be construed as insulting. Hell, they *were* insulting."

"What's his name?"

"Bill Sieves."

"Where does Sieves live?"

"I had a few drinks at the bar and followed his tail-lights. I got lost when I left his place, but found Dawes Road after a few minutes."

There were stretches of Dawes surrounded by subdivisions. Hundreds, perhaps thousands of homes. "Where on Dawes?" I asked.

"It's fuzzy. I'm sorry."

"What does Sieves look like?"

"Short brown hair, brown eyes. Sort of angular face with thin lips. He's well built. Not bodybuilder mass, ropey muscles. He's pretty strong."

"He never mentioned anything violent?"

"No. But when I told him he, um, fucked like a fifteen-year-old I could see hate in his eyes. He started yelling and I left."

I told Ralway to keep trying to recall the location of Sieves's home then found a William T. Sieves in the license-bureau database. Mr Sieves was seventy-three, six-four, and bald. Was Bill Sieves a fake name? Maybe, maybe not. Bill Sieves might be a recent arrival to the area. I tried Ballard again, nothing.

The office doorknob turned and I froze.

"Carson, it's me," Harry whispered. "Open up."

I glanced into the detectives' room as I let Harry in. A half-dozen of my colleagues were at their desks, not one of them looking our way, pretending we weren't there.

"No one's gonna snitch to Baggs," Harry said. "They're beginning to think this thing smells political. Tom says you told him you were onto something."

I nodded. "Terry McGuiness . . . Lampson's partner? He was in the square, wasted. I think he fell into old ways, got the guilts, ate every pill he could grab. He started screaming about letting him die."

"And?"

"It's how Tommy's aunt was screaming, remember? The sound of complete loss."

Harry stared at the wall, but I knew the inside of his head was racing. "You're thinking pain is the bottom line, Cars?"

"The infliction of pain. And what greater pain. . ." I let it hang.

"Than the death of a loved one," Harry finished.

"A couple weeks before her mom's murder, Patricia Ralway told a guy named Bill Sieves he fucked like a fifteen-year-old. He didn't much care for it."

"We have to find out if Sieves touches the other cases."

"I can't get Silas Ballard or Mama Brink yet."

"So we go to the hospital."

Harry drove. I tried to get a call through to Wendy to tell her she had been on the right track the other night: the killer got his satisfaction from pain. Not from the immediate victim, but the person closest to the victim.

Her cell was shut off, a first. I wondered what she was doing, dropping my phone in my pocket as we reached the hospital.

Terry McGuiness looked as though he'd been run over by bulldozer. Twice. He'd had his stomach pumped and was receiving hydration. His arms and legs were restrained. When Harry and I entered the room his head turned away.

"Tough night, bud?" I said, putting my hand on his arm. "Everything came crashing down?"

"P-pretty much."

"I'm not gonna sell you anything, Terry. No lectures. It's your life."

His head rolled to me. "Then why are you here?"

"I don't think Paul was killed at random. I think he was killed because you crossed someone. Probably someone you never saw before. I think it was recently."

Tears welled in McGuiness's eyes. "I killed Paulie by pissing someone off?"

"No. A psychotic killed Paul because he thought it would be an amusing form of vengeance. You know a guy named Bill Sieves?"

"Never heard the name."

"Who have you recently angered, humiliated or insulted? One or all. Who, Terry?"

A one-shoulder shrug. "I used to piss people off all the time, the old me. Now I just serve food and. . ." He froze, eyes flicking back and forth as they scanned memories. "There was this couple at the restaurant. The guy had it in for me from the start. I was walking by with a full tray for table seventeen, a six-top. He put his leg in my path on purpose. Everything went flying."

"What happened then?"

"He called me a moron. I went to put on a fresh uniform and grab a smoke. When I came back they were gone."

"You never said a thing to the guy?"

McGuiness looked between Harry and me. "I'd seen the asshole pull into the parking lot so I ran outside and hawked a fat one on his windshield. Maybe he saw me do it."

"What was he driving?" I asked.

"An Avalon, I think. White."

"Jesus," Harry whispered.

"You ever see the guy before that day, Terry?" I said. "Or since?"

McGuiness shook his head. "He's not memorable. Brown hair and eyes, kind of a round face. A tight, pissed-off little mouth like this. . ." McGuiness pursed his lips. "The guy was in his mid-twenties."

We milked every bit of information from Terry McGuiness, then headed up one floor to Pendel's room, surprised to see Dr Szekely sitting by a sleeping Pendel and reading a book.

"They gave him an opioid," she said. "I don't expect he'll be around for several hours. His father went to make funeral arrangements. When he returns I have to leave to give a lecture in Atlanta."

"For EEOSA?"

She nodded. "We're starting a chapter there." Szekely looked at Pendel with concerned eyes, the kid motionless, his mouth open. She reached out and patted his leg. "Sleep is the best thing for Will now. The waters of Lethe."

"The peace of oblivion," Harry said.

"I wish I could dispense such water selectively, Detective Nautilus. If I could wash away the memories of the orphanages . . . Are you here to check Will's progress?"

"We came to check a theory with Wilbert. That his mother's death was reprisal for something Wilbert did. An insult, perhaps."

A raised eyebrow. "That could be hard to narrow down. Any interaction with Will could result in an insult. Have you tested your theory, Detective Ryder?"

"We have a vehicle similarity, two incidences of someone being insulted, and the name Bill Sieves."

"Sieves? That's with an S?"

"From what we know."

Szekely frowned. "I mentioned the math whiz? The one who didn't get along with Will?"

"Too much alike, you said."

"Will used to make fun of Gregory's emotional issues, including Gregory's difficulties in expressing himself. In return Gregory would make disparaging remarks about Will's intellect. It turned physical, Will slapping Gregory in the face and telling him to make it readable."

"This Gregory isn't named Sieves, is he?" I asked.

Szekely looked anxious. "It's Nieves, with an N. That's really pretty close, isn't it?"

50

Harry called Sally Hargreaves, his girlfriend and a detective in the Missing Persons unit, for a quick search. She reported a Gregory Nieves in the listing. He lived in West Mobile, not far from Dawes Road.

"We're not in the cruiser, girl," Harry said. "No computer. Gimme the guy's particulars."

"Average Joe," Sal said. "Five nine, one seventy-five, brown and brown. Twenty-five years old. Looks as dangerous as a vanilla milkshake."

My phone went off and I turned on the external speakers. "This is Silas Ballard, you wanted me to—"

"Gregory Nieves," I blurted, adrenalin taking over. "Know the name?"

"Jesus . . . I ain't heard that name in years. A decade or more."

Harry threw a jubilant air punch. We had the tie.

"How do you know the name, sir?" I asked.

"His granddaddy – step-granddaddy, actually – owned a farm beside ours. Gregory's stepdaddy quit farming, but kept the woods. Nieves used to bring the kid up here to hunt. The kid was always spying on people. Had the damndest expression, like always saying *Huh?* without saying it. The little bastard killed my dog."

"Pardon me?"

"Bruno. A big friendly ol' Lab. I came home one day, no dog. Found Bruno in the woods, an arrow in the hindquarters to cripple him, one in the head to finish him off."

"Arrow," Harry whispered.

"Did you in any way insult Gregory?" I asked Ballard.

"I prob'ly cursed the kid out. He was a mental genius, but messed up bad in the head."

I promised Ballard I'd get back to him quickly and turned to Harry. "That just leaves a motive for Tommy."

"To punish Arletta Brink?" Harry frowned. "For what?"

"Not her. The killer would have been getting back at Tommy's aunt. She was the one who loved him."

Francine Minear lived six blocks from the hospital so we did that one in person. Her apartment was on the second floor of a pre-WWII brick building, at the end of a long hall smelling of fried food and cabbage.

Miz Minear was wearing a bright yellow pantsuit. A school photo of Tommy centered a piece of circular silver jewelry on her lapel. She waved us into a pin-neat living room with antimacassars on the couch, doilies under lamps.

She gave me a dark look verging on anger. "The newspaper said you're the man started all this trouble."

Harry pointed through the window at a dazzling blue sky. "The newspaper also said it was going to rain this morning, Miz Minear. I assure you the paper is wrong on both counts"

She looked between Harry and me. "What you need?"

"Gregory Nieves," I said. "Ever heard the name?"

She shook her head and sat. "I cleaned for the Nieves about ten years back, father and two adopted kids from Armenia or something. The kids were learning to talk American. The girl I got on good with, the boy was creepy. That was Gregory."

"Creepy how?"

"I'd be washing and feel a touch on my backside. I'd turn and he'd be licking his hand like seeing how I tasted."

"Can I ask if you ever did anything to anger him, ma'am?"

Her eyes tightened in memory. "I was doin' laundry and heard something in the closet, one of those with wood shutters you can peek through. I yanked open the door. That boy had his pants 'round his ankles and his you-know-what in his hand. I got so mad I slapped him up side his head an' called him a nasty li'l freak. Then I quit, walked out the door."

"And the last time you saw the kid?"

"Staring out the window when I left. His face was blank as pudding, but I could smell his hate."

Gregory climbed into his car, wiping a powdery residue from his nose. The sun blazed above, a ball of yellow fire that lit the world in crisp and perfect detail. Colors didn't just seem brighter, they seemed enlarged.

He was going to Ema's, though he hadn't called. "*Gregory dear!*" she'd chirp as the door opened. "*What a surprise! What brings you here?*"

"*FOR FUCK'S SAKE, EMA,*" he'd scream into her fat face. "*YOU'VE BEEN CALLING ME EVERY GODDAMN HOUR!*"

He laughed and put the car in gear. An errant thought crossed his mind. What if no neighbors were around? What if everything inside Ema's house was perfect for an Event? What if the universe showed him the time was right?

My God . . . What if it happened today?

Gregory ran back inside his house and put on a black bodystocking, just in case. And in case today wasn't the right day, he went to the garage, grabbed what he needed, put it in the trunk of his car.

One way or the other, something would get accomplished today!

What happened next?

We roared back to the department, sprinting to our floor. Baggs and Willpot and several of the administrative cabal

393

were clustered around Tom Mason's door. I saw worried faces. Everyone turned to look at us, Baggs's eyes popping wide in surprise.

"Please don't shoot Baggs, Carson," Harry whispered.

"I just have to get my phone list."

"Don't punch him, either."

We kept moving toward our cubicle, waiting for someone to make a move. I watched as Chief Baggs pushed a freakish grin onto his face and started our way. Several dicks were watching from their cubicles. I could see into the cubicle of Larry Hartwell, his computer showing the YouTube home page.

I turned to Baggs, hands up in surrender, my voice set to full-plead.

"We may know the killer, Chief," I said. "Let us get things in motion and I'll get gone."

Baggs stopped two paces away and cleared his throat. "We'll deal with this like professionals, Detective Ryder. Mistakes were made on both our parts. But high ideals can sometimes mean high emotions, and that's what we're dealing with here, right? Both wanting to get the job done to the fullest, to protect the public. It's a situation poised for honest misunderstandings, moments of stress and all that. I'll have the Information Office draft a statement and we'll clear the air."

He demonstrated the most unhappy and insincere smile this side of Oscar night, then turned and walked stiffly away.

"What the fuck was that about?" Harry whispered.

"You've got me. Let's get to work."

I quickly fanned through my phone call slips, nothing except two more calls from Roy McDermott with the FCLE, one with a brief and cryptic message: *The snook are calling.* I jammed the note in my jacket pocket and started issuing orders per the guidelines of the PSIT.

Within an hour we had turned the conference room into our situation room, sending undercover surveillance units to Nieves's home, an air-conditioning company van almost out front and a van marked CITY OF MOBILE WATER DEPARTMENT at the end of the block. A cop disguised as a meter reader had looked in the garage window, saw no vehicle.

"We're not getting anything," Rich Patten radioed. "No vehicle, no phone activity. No sounds from inside. We put a major-league lens on the electric meter. The power's holding exactly constant, no TV being turned on and off, room lights changing. The house seems empty."

I said, "Unit B?" The supposed Water Company crew at the end of Nieves's block, three cops in disguise climbing in and out of an open manhole.

"No action. White car went by before, but a Hyundai. If the target passes we're ready to block the street."

"SWAT?" I said. The special weapons and tactics van was a half-mile distant and parked behind a church, as close as they could get without standing out like an ostrich in the Kentucky Derby.

"Engine running, pulses calm. We're ready to take this bad boy down, Carson."

"The house is one big trap," I said to all concerned. "Let's hope he's home soon."

"Or a BOLO gets him," Harry said. A BOLO was a Be On the Look Out alert. All law-enforcement agencies in the vicinity had been sent Nieves's name and license photo, appended with the warning *Dangerous and likely armed, approach with extreme caution*. Translation: *If you stop him and he twitches, shoot the bastard*.

I nodded. "We'll go public if we don't find him in a bit," I said. "Send the info everywhere."

"Any info on the sister?"

I shook my head, *nada*. We were trying to track down Nieves's sister, but there was no listing with the phone company. She probably had a cell. Szekely had implied the woman was a homeowner so we'd sent a guy to City Hall's property records. We'd tried Szekely to check what else she might know, but the doc was flying to her Atlanta lecture.

I stood to shake the tension from my legs and saw Tom Mason scanning the murder books. Harry and I walked over.

"Sounds like you've tracked this monster to his lair, fellas," Tom said, pleased. "Helluva day."

I lowered my voice. "Uh, Tom, that thing with Baggs. . . 'High ideals and emotions' and all that shit. What the hell's going on?"

Tom tipped back his Stetson and stared. "You mean you don't know? You weren't in on it?"

"In on what?"

"The academy video, Carson . . . where you supposedly

did everything but challenge psychopaths to a killing match? It reappeared on YouTube late this morning. Not just on YouTube, but Yahoo, Flickr, Photobucket and a dozen other places. Even a site in Chinese. I heard that anonymous callers – male and female – told media outlets about the reappearance. People are seeing it."

"And realizing. . ."

Tom nodded. "There's no real threat: It's just you being you. Baggs has been buried in calls from reporters wondering how a few innocuous statements got translated into a death challenge. The Chief's been doing the political cha-cha ever since."

After a moment of perplexity I recalled Wendy's angry words. *We can rebuild the video*, she had said, *put it back up. Say the word.* I hadn't, but evidently someone had said it for me. I suddenly had a potent respect for social media.

"Where do I go from here?" I asked Tom, wiser in the ways of departmental politics.

"You and the Chief will make nice for the media," he said.

"You mean we'll stand before a bank of microphones, confess our misunderstandings like two wayward children, then face the cameras with phoney smiles and insincere handshakes?"

"Yep," he said. "Pretty much."

Gregory hadn't gone directly to Ema's. He'd gotten within a block and realized he hadn't brought powder with him.

It was necessary, his new fuel. He detoured to the whore's house for another five bags. That gave him eight bags of clarity. He'd had sex with the robot, too, but that only took a couple minutes.

He pulled into Ema's drive and parked. The sun was high and Gregory felt individual photons tickling his skin. He popped the truck latch, exited, and walked to the rear of the Avalon. He paused to stretch a kink from his spine, then bent and reached into the storage area for the cat trap.

He tucked it under an arm and closed the lid. The kitten mewed softly inside the wire mesh. Gregory caught the cats, Ema took them to the animal shelter, just as her friend had suggested. It was the one area where he and Ema had made something intelligent and efficient function between them.

He knocked her door but got no response. Rang the bell, nothing. He put his ear to the door and heard the television.

". . . *today's episode of* True-life Crime *presents a made-for-TV adaptation of the bestselling story, 'I Married a. . .'*"

Cops and cooking and shopping. Ema and her damn programs. He pulled out his key and let himself inside.

". . . *next week we'll be presenting another true-crime adaptation for fans of. . .*"

"Ema?" he called.

No sign of her in the living room, though several

magazines were on the coffee table, opened to various ads.

"Ema? Are you here?"

Still carrying the trap, Gregory went to the dining room. Not there. Kitchen. No Ema. He heard what sounded like a muted scream and froze.

What the hell was that? Something on the television?

". . . *don't forget to watch the best information team on the coast, award-winning news and weather from. . .*"

The television echoing through the house, Gregory tiptoed to the bathroom, an inch of light between door and frame. He nudged the door with his elbow and it swung soundlessly open. . .

51

"WHAT ARE YOU DOING?" Gregory screamed, staring at the cat in Ema's hands, black with white paws, its belly slit wide. The animal's mouth opened and a hideous gurgling squeal came out.

Dragna Negrescu dropped the cat into the sink. Her hand scrabbled to her bodice and pulled the shining pendant from between her breasts. "*Mănâncă mamaliga dvs, Grigor!*" Negrescu stepped to Gregory with the pendant held high. "*Poţi să-l miros?*"

Eat your mamaliga, Grigor. Can you smell it?

"WHAT are. . ." Gregory's voice stopped. Only his lips moved.

"Grigor," Negrescu said. "*Mirosul mamaliga.*"

Smell the mamaliga.

The smell of the dish filled Gregory's mind. The cat trap fell from limp fingers and opened, the kitten dashing away. He stared past the woman, past the wall, past the house. All he could do was stare.

Negrescu calmly studied Gregory as she washed blood from her hands, seeing dilated pupils and recalling his fast and sometimes incoherent speech at their last meal. Some kind of drug, probably inevitable. She sighed: this part of her journey was ending.

Last year she'd realized money would become an issue: live well and burn through the inheritance in a few years, or keep the money in stable investments supplemented with mindless labor, or. . .

Get more money.

"Come into the living room, Grigor," Negrescu said, drying her hands on a towel. "It's time we talked seriously. It's been too long."

Walking as mechanically as a robot, Gregory followed Negrescu into her pink-hued living room. She sat on the white frilly couch and patted the space beside her. Gregory sat. Dragna Negrescu smiled at Grigor with a beatific face found in a *Cooking Light* article: *How to Make Heavenly Pie Crusts*. She reached behind her neck and unbuttoned the pendant.

"*Ce este lumina, Grigor?*" she said, the orb of light rolling between her fingers. "What is the light?"

"Uh. . ."

"*Cred, Grigor. Ce este lumina?* Think . . . what is the light?"

"*Esti lumina, Ema.* You are the light. My light."

"Good boy. You've been in my house, haven't you? Ema's house. Go ahead, Grigor, talk."

"*Da, Ema,*" he said, staring straight ahead. "I was looking for your records. Your money."

Negrescu leaned against Gregory and stroked a strand of hair from his forehead. "What a good boy you are, Grigor. Such fine and useful instincts. What happened next?"

He paused, his mind ticking through events like a clock. "I killed Harriet Ralway. Her filthy, lying daughter said terrible things to me."

"You're going to kill Ema next, Gregory? Is that the plan?"

Gregory frowned. "When it's time."

Negrescu smiled. "You'll not kill Ema yet, Grigor. You have unfinished business with the police. Remember how they humiliated you with everyone watching? Made the *rahat* pour down your legs? Laughed as they stole your manhood?"

Gregory's eyes stared through Ema, through the wall behind her, through the walls of the house. "The police laughed, Ema. Everyone laughed at me."

"What happened next?"

"The big policeman pulled a stick. He w-waved it at me and, uh. . ."

"Look in your head, Grigor. What happened next?"

Gregory's eyes tightened in anger. "He hit me with the stick. He insulted me."

"Good. What happened next?"

"They . . . um, he, uh, I don't remem—"

Negrescu's hand lashed out and slapped Gregory's face, sounding like a gunshot. "We've been through this a hundred times, Grigor. I put it in your mind: Look at it and get angry. What happened next?"

"People called me a freak," Gregory hissed through clenched teeth. "A pervert. Shit boy. The police threw me to the ground. They insulted me."

"They told you to go home and learn how to use a toilet, didn't they?" Dragna Negrescu said. "Just like all those years ago. When you'd poop yourself when you ate too much on special nights."

"Yes."

"Their insults made you angry enough to kill, didn't they? To regain your honor."

"Yes. *Yes!*"

"It's been such fun, Grigor, seeing my . . . our work on the television, in the papers. We can keep going. Would you like that?"

Gregory slitted his eyes and made a buzzing sound with his lips. Negrescu stared at him, then stood. She put her hands on her hips and studied herself in the mirror, pleased with its report. She returned to Gregory and slipped her fingers through his hair, leaning until her teeth were at his ear.

"Do you know who I am, Grigor?" she whispered. "Can you see beneath my mask?"

"Ema."

"Ema? Not Dragna Negrescu, the records clerk from so long ago . . . the woman who rode you across the sea and into her dream?"

"You're Ema," Gregory said. "My Ema."

Negrescu licked Gregory's ear, her whisper growing husky. "There never was an Ema, my sweet little project. I made her from a few pieces of paper. Popescu showed me how to present her to you."

"Popescu," Gregory repeated. It was a word he thought he should know, but it seemed far away, on the other side of a towering rock wall. Ema planted a kiss on Gregory's head and the pendant flashed once again, followed by a few words in Romanian.

52

"I'm getting scared this guy is on a mission," Harry said, looking at his watch. There'd been no sign of Nieves. I considered the man's prowess and combined it with our feeling that he was falling apart.

"Let's go public, bro. BOLO on every form of media we can find. Contact every reporter within three hundred miles. Say he's wanted in conjunction with the recent killings. That'll get attention."

Gregory stood from the couch. He walked to the mirror and straightened his collar, patted down his hair. It had gotten mussed.

"I really have to be going, Ema," he snapped. "I have much to do." His face was sore on the left side, probably from all the faces he'd been making for his sister. His head felt odd and strangely disconnected, like pieces of dreams were floating through his skull. He wasn't even quite sure why he'd come to his sister's house. Or why her face kept flashing pieces of another face, scary but somehow familiar. All he really knew was something in the back of his mind told him to leave her house.

"Breakfast tomorrow?" Ema said, rising. "I'd love to hear about your volunteer program."

Gregory grimaced. He wanted to wash his hands but Ema's bathroom was a misery, all that light, the smells. It was like an operating room in there. "Maybe next week," he said. "I'll call you."

Ema brushed a speck of lint from his shoulder. "You never call, dear. I'll call you."

Gregory numbly endured another hug and left, closing the front door behind him, the trap in his hand. Within a few steps heard the television resume its former level . . . *nothing beats the great taste of Swanson Family Dinners. Be sure to pick up . . . We interrupt this program to bring you a special update. . .*

Gregory was backing down the drive when the door opened, Ema waving a handkerchief. "Yoo-hoo! Gregory!"

He cursed to himself, jammed on the brakes, rolled down the window.

"What is it now, Ema?"

"Can I see you for a moment, dear?"

We found out where Nieves's sister lived, but in a very bad way. The call came to 911 and we were at the house in minutes, siren blasting, engine pushed to its limits.

406

Cops swarmed the place. The sister, Ema Nieves, was on the couch, a frayed bundle of tears and terror. Nieves was on the floor in the hall, a 380 caliber bullet just to the left of his heart. His hand was clutching a boning knife, a wicked instrument. The front of his shirt was a river of scarlet. He was on his back and staring at the ceiling.

I took the poor woman's hand and moved her from the living room to the kitchen, helping her into a chair. I debated whether or not to question her at this sensitive time; a hospital might have been best, tranquilizers. But I needed to hear what had happened.

"Can you talk, Ms Nieves?" I asked.

Her eyes were closed tight. Tears had washed make-up down her cheeks. "I-I'll try."

"Can you tell me what happened?"

"H-hh-he . . . I couldn't. . ."

"It's over, ma'am," I consoled her, taking her hand in mine. "You're safe and that's a very good thing. Can you explain what happened?"

"G-Gregory tried to kill me," she sobbed, shaking her head. "H-he's my b-b-brother and he, he. . ."

Harry had brought a glass of water. Ms Nieves drank and it seemed to help her get steady. She wiped her eyes, handed the glass back, whispered, "Thank you."

"Take your time, Ms Nieves," I consoled. "I understand that it's tough."

Ema Nieves took a deep breath. She paused and closed her eyes as if looking for something inside her, strength perhaps.

"G-Gregory came by without calling. It was strange because he always calls. I was in the bathroom and heard a terrible banging on the front door. It scared me so I tiptoed into the living room. The next thing I knew he pushed through into the house. H-he had crazy eyes, like I've never seen before. He said I'd betrayed him, that he was going to cut my throat. He had a knife."

"Did he say why he wanted to kill you?"

She looked at me, hands shaking, her face a mask of confusion. "H-he kept accusing me of being a spy for the police. I didn't know what he was talking about. It was so crazy. He started to come toward me, waving the knife, getting louder."

I looked at Harry. Paranoia. Part of Gregory Nieves's dissolution, I figured.

"Has your brother been acting strange lately?" I asked quietly.

She stared. "How did you know?"

"You were with him when he tripped a waiter some days back?"

Another *how-did-you-know?* look. "H-he told me the waiter somehow had it in for him. It was terribly strange and embarrassing."

I looked toward Nieves's sprawled and lifeless body and saw the dark revolver on the floor a dozen feet from his body. A photographer was crouched above the gun, flashing off shots.

"That's your gun, Ms Nieves . . . Ema?"

She glanced at the weapon, head snapping away as though the image was too ugly to bear. "I l-live alone, and it made sense. I b-bought it this spring. Took lessons. I wanted to make sure I was doing everything right. Wh-when I heard the pounding on the door I . . . I took the gun into the living room and I, and I—"

Her wall of courage fell apart and she collapsed into my arms, crying as if everything in her life had dissolved into dust.

"I know it doesn't sound like it, Ms Nieves," I whispered, gently patting her shaking back. "But you're a very lucky woman."

53

Two weeks passed. It was a Saturday and the recruits had graduated in the afternoon. It had been a splendid sunlit ceremony, with flags and gunshot salutes and an eloquent speech about tradition. A pity the speech had come from Baggs, who wrote little of it and understood less. Our dual *mea culpa* media moment was one week past. There'd been a news blitz for a couple days, then a guy in Orange Beach got bit by a shark and everyone forgot about cop stuff.

I had a small party at my place. Harry was among the crowd, of course, with Sally Hargreaves. Director of Forensics Wayne Hembree attended with his wife. Rein Earley was there, taking bows for a fine and funny speech about her days at the academy. A patrol officer for a year now, Rein was Harry's niece, though few knew it. Doc Kavanaugh floated in, as wizardy as always. I'd invited Clair, not really expecting her to attend, but she arrived with a date, a fortyish cardiologist who was so good looking I figured he had to be gay or have issues or both.

Wendy was there, naturally. I hadn't seen much of her the last few days, what with cramming for the exams. She aced everything, by the way. I wish I could have invited the entire recruit class as thanks for rebuilding the video and its second life. But I'd offered some gratitude last week by taking everyone to a dinner I'd be paying down for months.

I was leaning against the rail and sipping a Sazerac. I turned my cell phone off, since everyone I wanted to talk to was at my house. Dropping it back into the pocket of my jacket, I felt a piece of paper. It was the message Roy McDermott had left on my office phone, *The snook are calling*.

I'd paid it no heed at the time, too much going on. But now it called up a conversation from a year ago, Roy and I flyfishing for snook at the Ding Darling Nature Preserve on Florida's Sanibel Island, the outflowing tide pulling the elusive, aerodynamic sportfishes though the brushy passes as the setting sun turned the twilight air to gold. A light breeze rattled the leaves of the palmettos. The early stars were winking down.

"My idea of heaven, Roy," I'd said, unwinding a cast, the water warm and lapping at the hem of my cutoffs.

"Close enough for me," Roy said, a dozen feet to my side and tying on a new fly. Then, after a long pause,

"You ever think of changing jobs, Carson? A lot of places could use someone like you, give you a leadership role. They treating you right at the MPD?"

I'd launched a cast across the shimmering water. "They're treating me fine, Roy."

"Things are changing at the FCLE," he'd said, quietly, almost as if talking to himself. He looked up. "If I ended up with some control over hiring, Carson, you wouldn't be against my giving you a call, would you?"

Three foot of fish rocketed from the water ahead of me, my fly in its mouth and my rod bending near in half. "Got a better idea, Roy," I'd laughed, following the fish out into the channel as line sizzled from my reel. "Have the snook give me a call."

I was mulling over the incident when Wendy walked up and leaned beside me. "Howdy, stranger," she said. She was wearing a sleeveless white blouse and very brief pink skirt. Her hair floated in the warm breeze and she looked so very young.

I tucked away my recollections for the moment and pretended to shoo her away.

"Sorry, lady, real cops aren't allowed to talk to newbies."

"That so? Maybe I'll go talk to the guy Dr Peltier brought. Yum."

"Jesus," I muttered. Wendy leaned close and gave me a peck on my cheek. "How goes the Nieves investigation?"

"New twists and turns every day. We found an animal trap in Nieves's truck and cocaine in the glove box.

Both explain a lot. But the big find was on his mantel: a vase filled with pennies. Each coin had a name taped to the back – people who Nieves thought insulted him is the presumption. He probably shook out a penny, then went into stalking mode."

"My God. How many pennies?"

"Forty-three."

"Talk about thin-skinned. Were you a penny?"

"Oddly enough, no cops were. Five names were people in the EEOSA. Others we may never identify."

Harry and Sally walked up, Sally shaking Wendy's hand. "Congratulations, graduate. Carson says you played a part in figuring out the Nieves motive."

"Oh no. It was just a game in class, a hypothetical."

"You started me thinking about pain having meaning beyond its infliction," I said. "It helped make the connection in the Square."

Wendy frowned. "But weren't you already thinking along those lines, Carson? 'A murder is too good a thing to waste?' Part of your hypothetical?"

"I, uh. . ."

"Of course he was," Harry said, slapping my back. "Trouble is, the poor boy's too dumb to realize how smart he is." It got a laugh, and provided a distraction, as Harry knew it would. Sally noticed her wine was getting low and went to refill, Wendy following. Harry watched them weave through the crowd to the kitchen.

"Lawd, Carson . . . how did we both end up with ladies that put us to shame?"

"I'm afraid Wendy's too young for me, Harry," I lamented. "May–December or whatever."

Harry laughed so loud it echoed off the house next door, like laughing twice. "For chrissakes, Carson. You can't even tell time. It's March–June or thereabouts."

"I'm still over ten years older than her."

"You happy? She happy?"

I nodded.

"Then let's change the subject, because it's ridiculous. You met with Ema Nieves this morning, right? How's she doing?"

I'd promised Ema I'd check on her every few days and stopped by earlier. "Ema's had time to think, Harry. Things are getting clearer."

"How so?"

"She mentioned something from the Ceauşescu days called the Departmentul Securitari Statului, one of the largest secret-police organizations in the Eastern Bloc. The DSS had officers at the orphanage and Ema suspects her brother was molested by them. They wore blue uniforms."

"Jesus. The Blue Tribe. But Nieves's only police contact here was with Austin and Mailey, and Austin did everything to help the guy."

"We'll never know what Nieves was seeing in his head. Or how it got there."

"But Ema's doing better, I hope?"

"She's quit her job, too torn up to work, but it seems she's the sole beneficiary of Nieves's will."

Harry raised an eyebrow. "Sole beneficiary?"

I nodded. "Gets it all."

He took a sip of his drink, both of us watching a light far out on the water, a freighter, I figured, halfway from hither and crossing to yon.

"I know Gregory Nieves got destroyed in childhood, Carson, but his money will do more good with a person like Ema. I sense a strength in there. She's a survivor."

"Ema might even wring some good from the horror," I said. "She's considering writing a book about how she missed warning signs of her brother's illness, hoping to keep it from happening to others. An agent already contacted her."

"*My Brother the Killer*?" Harry mused. "Those true-life things can go big, Cars. Bestseller list. Oprah. A movie. Has Ema told Doc Szekely yet?"

I nodded. "Ema called Szekely as soon as a book came to mind. Ema wants the Doc to make a few contributions from the psychological side."

"What does the Doc think of the idea?"

I glanced up at the moon, moving toward full and wearing a hopeful face – at least, that was how it appeared to me. After all the horror and uncertainty of this case it was finally good to have something positive to say.

"Szekely thinks writing a book is exactly what Ema needs," I said. "A project to keep her occupied."

I heard my phone ring in the kitchen, watched through the window as Wendy answered. She listened for a moment, raised a quizzical eyebrow, then put her palm over the receiver and called to me through the screen.

"It's some guy who says his name is Mr Snook, Carson. You want to take it?"

Wait if you wish, read on if you dare . . .

THE DEATH BOX

An exclusive preview of
J.A. Kerley's new Carson Ryder thriller

COMING IN DECEMBER 2013

1

The stench of rotting flesh filled the box like black fog. Death surrounded Amili Zelaya, the floor a patchwork of clothing bearing the decomposing bodies of seventeen human beings. Amili was alive, barely, staring into the shadowed dark of a shipping container the size of a semitrailer. Besides the reek of death, there was bone-melting heat and graveyard silence save for waves breaking against a hull far below.

You're lucky, the smiling man in Honduras had said before closing the door, *ten days and you'll be in Los Estados Unitos, the United States, think of that*. Amili had thought of it, grinning at Lucia Belen in the last flash of sunlight before the box slammed shut. They'd crouched in the dark thinking their luck was boundless: they were going to America.

"Lucia," Amili rasped. "Please don't leave me now."

Lucia's hand lay motionless in Amili's fingers. Then, for the span of a second, the fingers twitched. "Fight for life, Lucia," Amili whispered, her parched tongue so swollen it barely moved in her mouth. Lucia was from Amili's village. They'd grown up together – born in the same week eighteen years ago – ragged but happy. Only when fragments of the outside world intruded did they realize the desperate poverty strangling everyone in the village.

"Fight for life," Amili repeated. But her hand was the first to fall away and she drifted into unconsciousness. Sometime later Amili's mind registered new sounds and sensations. The deep notes of ship horns. The roar and rattle of machinery.

Was that the calling of gulls? The metal box trembled and Amili struggled to lift her head. Something had changed.

"The ship has stopped, Lucia," Amili rasped, holes from popped rivets allowing ample light to outline the inside of the module, one of thousands on the deck of the container ship bound for Miami, Florida. The illegal human cargo had been repeatedly instructed to stay motionless and quiet through the journey.

If you reveal yourselves you will be thrown in a gringo prison, raped, beaten . . . men, women, children, it makes no difference. Never make a sound, comprende?

Eventually they'd feel the ship stop and the box would be offloaded and driven to a hidden location where they'd receive papers, work assignments, places to live. They had only to perform six months of employment – housekeeping, yard work, light factory labor – to relieve the debt of their travel. After that, they owned their lives. A dream beyond belief.

"It must be Miami, Lucia," Amili said. "Stay with me."

But their drinking water had leaked away early in the voyage, a split opening in the side of the huge plastic drum, water washing across the floor of the container, pouring out through the seams. No one worried much about the loss, fearing only that escaping liquid would attract attention and they'd be put in chains to await prison. The ship had been traveling through fierce storms, rainwater dripping into the module from above like a dozen mountain springs. Water was everywhere.

This had been many days back. Before the ship had lumbered from the storms into searing summer heat. The rusty water in the bottom of the module was swiftly consumed. For days they ached for water, the inside of the container like an oven. Teresa Maldone prayed until her voice burned away. Pablo Entero drank from the urine pail. Maria Poblana banged on the walls of the box until wrestled to the floor.

She was the first to die.

Amili Zelaya had initially claimed a sitting area by a small hole in the container, hoping to peek out and watch for America. But an older and larger woman named Postan Rendoza had bullied Amili away, cursing and slapping her to a far corner by the toilet bucket.

But the much-traveled module was slightly lower in Amili's square meter of squatting room. Rainwater had pooled in the depressed corner, dampening the underside of Amili's ragged yellow dress.

When the heat came, Amili's secret oasis held water even as others tongued the metal floor for the remaining rain. When no one was looking Amili slipped the hem of her dress to her mouth and squeezed life over her tongue: brown, rusty water sullied by sloshings from the toilet bucket, but enough to keep her insides from shriveling.

Postan Rendoza's bullying had spared Amili's life. And the life of Lucia, with whom Amili had shared her hidden water.

Rendoza had been the eighth to die.

Three days ago, the hidden cache had disappeared. By then, four were left alive, and by yesterday it was only Amili and Lucia. Amili felt guilt that she had watched the others perish from lack of water. But she had made her decision early, when she saw past tomorrow and tomorrow that water would be a life-and-death problem. Had she shared there would be no one alive in the steaming container: there was barely enough for one, much less two.

It was a hard secret and a terrible one to keep through screams and moans and prayers, but Amili had stuck to her decision. Decisions were her job: every morning before leaving for the coffee plantation Amili's mother would gather five wide-eyed and barefoot children into the main room of their mud-brick home, point at Amili and say, "Amili is the oldest and the one who makes the good decisions."

A good decision, Amili knew, was for tomorrow, not today. When the foreign dentistas came, it was Amili who cajoled her terrified siblings into getting their teeth fixed and learning how to care for them, so their mouths did not become empty holes. When the drunken, lizard-eyed Federale gave thirteen-year-old Pablo forty pesetas to walk into the woods with him, Amili had followed to see the Federale showing Pablo his man thing. Though the man had official power it had been Amili's decision to throw a big stone at him, the blood pouring from his face as he chased Amili down and beat her until she could not stand.

But he'd been revealed in the village and could never return.

Decisions, Amili learned, must be made from the head and not the heart. The heart dealt with the moment. A decision had to be made for tomorrow and the tomorrow after that, all the way to the horizon. It could seem harsh, but decisions made from a soft heart often went wrong. One always had to look at what decisions did for the tomorrows.

Her hardest decision had come one month ago, when the smiling man drove into the village in a car as bright as silver, scattering dust and chickens. His belly was big and heavy and when he held it in his hands and shook it, he told of how much food there was in America. "*Everywhere you look,*" he told the astonished faces, "*there is food.*" The smiling mouth told shining tales about how much money could be made in Los Estados Unitos, how one brave person could lift a family from the dirt. He had spoken directly to Amili, holding her hands and looking into her eyes.

"*You have been learning English, Amili Zelaya. You speak it well. Why?*"

"*I suppose I am good in school, Señor Tolandoro.*"

"I've heard. But there's more, I think. Perhaps you yearn for another future, no?"

"I have thought that . . . maybe in a few years. When my family can—"

"Do it today, Amili. Start the flow of munificence to your family. Or do they not need money?"

Amili was frightened of the US, of its distance and strange customs. The heart fighting the head, she knew, the heart wanting the known quantity of the village community, aching for the closeness of her loved ones.

But her head saw the tomorrows and tomorrows and knew the only escape from barren lives came with money. Amili's sister Pari was old enough to care for the children. Thinking how their lives would change when money started to arrive from America, Amili swallowed hard and told the smiling man she would make the trip.

"I work six months to pay off the travel?"

"You'll still have much to send home, sweet Amili."

"How will I send money home if I am paying a debt?"

"You can live with others just like you. To save money."

"What if I am unhappy there?"

"Say the word and you'll come back to your village."

"How many times does that happen?"

"I've never seen anyone return."

Amili startled to a tremendous banging from above. After a distant scream of machines and the rattle of cables the container began to lift. The metal box seemed to sway in the wind and then drop. Another fierce slam from below as the module jolted violently to a standstill. Amili realized the container had been moved to a truck.

"Hang on, Lucia. Soon we'll be safe and we can—"
Amili held her tongue as she heard dockworkers speaking
English outside.

"Is this the one, Joleo?"

*"Lock it down fast. We've got two minutes before
Customs comes by this section."*

"What if the man inside is wrong?"

"He's never wrong, Ivy. Move it!"

Amili felt motion and heard the grinding of gears. She
drifted into unconsciousness again, awakened by a shiver
in the container. The movement had stopped.

"Lucia?"

Amili patted for her friend's hand, squeezed it. The squeeze
returned, even weaker now, almost imperceptible. "Hang
on, Lucia. Soon we'll have the aqua. And our freedom."

Amili heard voices from outside, gringo voices.

*"I hate this part, opening the shit-stinking containers.
They ought to make the monkeys not eat for a couple
days before they get packed up."*

*"Come on, Ivy. How about you work instead of
complaining?"*

*"I smell it from fifty feet away. Get ready to herd them
to the boat."*

Light poured into the box, so bright it stole Amili's
vision. She squeezed her eyes shut.

*"Okay, monkeys, welcome to the fuckin' U S of— Jesus
. . . The smell . . . I think I'm gonna puke. Come here,
Joleo . . . something's bad wrong."*

*"I smelled that in Iraq. It's death. Call Orzibel. Tell
him the shipment got spoiled. And ask what to do."*

Amili tried to move her head from the floor but it weighed a thousand kilos. She put her effort into moving her hand, lifting . . .

"*I saw one move. Back in the corner. Go get it.*"

"*It stinks to hell in there, Joleo. And I ain't gonna walk over all those—*"

"*Pull your shirt over your nose. Get it, dammit.*"

Amili felt hands pull her to her feet. She tried to turn back to Lucia.

"Wait," Amili mumbled. "*Mi amiga Lucia está vive.*"

"*What's she saying?*"

"*Who cares? Get her out of there, pour water in her mouth and call Orzibel.*"

"*Orzibel's crazy. He'll gut us.*"

"*Christ, Ivy, it ain't our fault. We just grab 'em off the dock.*"

"*What will he do, you think? Orzibel?*"

"*Orzibel will fucking call the big boss, Ivy . . . what do you think he's gonna do?*"

"*Whoever's in charge better deal with this fast, is what I think.*"

Amili felt herself thrown atop someone's shoulder. She grabbed at the body below, trying to make the man turn back and see that Lucia was still breathing. The effort was too much and the corners of the box began to spin like a top and Amili collapsed toward an enveloping darkness. Just before her senses spun away, ten final words registered in Amili's fading mind.

"*Oh shit, Joleo, my feet just sunk into a body.*"

2

One year later

It seemed like my world had flipped over. Standing on the deck of my previous home on Alabama's Dauphin Island, the dawn sun rose from the left. My new digs on Florida's Upper Matecumbe Key faced north, the sun rising from the opposite direction. It would take some getting used to.

On Dauphin Island the morning sun lit a rippled green sea broken only by faint outlines of gas rigs on the horizon. Here I looked out on three acres of half-moon cove ringed with white sand, the turquoise water punctuated by sandy hummocks and small, flat islands coated with greenery. Like most water surrounding the Keys, it was shallow. I could walk out a hundred yards before it reached my belly.

Which seemed a pleasant way to greet the morning. I set my coffee cup on the deck rail and took the steps to the ground, walking two dozen feet of slatted boardwalk to the shoreline. There were no other houses near and if there had been I wouldn't have seen them, the land around my rented home a subtropical explosion of wide-frond palms strung with vines, gnarly trees dense with leaves and all interspersed with towering stands of bamboo. It resembled a miniature Eden, complete with lime trees, lemons, mangoes and Barbados cherries. After a rain, the moist and scented air seemed like an intoxicant.

At water's edge I kicked off my moccasins and stepped into the Gulf, bathtub-warm in August. The sand felt delicious against my soles, conforming to my steps, familiar and assuring. I seemed to smell cigar smoke and scanned the dawn-brightening shoreline, spying only two cakewalking herons pecking for baitfish. Neither was puffing a cigar. I put my hands in the pockets of my cargo shorts and splashed through knee-deep water toward the reeded point marking one horn of the tiny crescent cove, revisiting the conversation that had led me so swiftly and surprisingly to Florida.

"Hello, Carson? This is Roy McDermott. Last time we talked, I mentioned changes in the Florida Center for Law Enforcement. We're creating a team of consulting specialists."

"Good for you, Roy."

"Why I'm calling, Carson . . . We want you on the team."

"I don't have a speciality, Roy. I'm just a standard-issue detective."

"Really? How about that PSIT team you started . . . specializing in psychopaths and sociopaths and general melt-downs? And all them freaky goddamn cases you guys solved?"

I smelled cigar smoke again. Looking to my right I saw a black man walking toward the shore with a stogie in his lips, five-seven or thereabouts, slender, his face ovoid, with a strong, straight nose beneath heavy eyebrows. His mouth was wide, garnished with a pencil mustache, and suggested how Tupac Shakur would have looked in his mid-sixties, though I doubt Shakur would have gone for a pink guayabera shirt and lime-green shorts. A crisp straw fedora with bright red band floated on the man's head and languid eyes studied me as if I were a novel form of waterfowl.

"You the one just moved in that yonder house?" he asked.

"Guilty as charged."

"The realtor tell you two people got killed in there? That the place was owned by a drug dealer, a Nicaraguan with metal teeth?"

The law allowed the confiscation of property employed in criminal enterprises and the place had indeed been the site of two killings, rivals to the drug dealer who had owned the house. The dealer went to prison and the house almost went on the market, but the FCLE was advised to hold it in anticipation of rising home values.

And it wouldn't hurt for time to lapse between the killings and the showings. When I told Roy I was thinking of looking at places in or near the Keys, he'd said, *"Gotta great place you can crib while you're looking, bud. Just don't get too used to it."*

I nodded at my impromptu morning companion. "I heard about the murders. Didn't hear about the teeth."

"Like goddamn fangs. Heard one had a diamond set in it, but I never got close enough to check. Saw him twice at the Indigo Lounge. He come in, I left out. You buyin' the place from the guv'mint? Nasty history, but the house ain't bad – kinda small for the neighborhood – but a good, big chunk of land. As wild as it was when Poncy Deleon showed up."

The house itself – on ten-foot pilings to protect against storm surges – wasn't overwhelming: single story, three bedrooms. But it had broad skylights and a vaulted ceiling in the main room, so it was bright and open. Outside features included decks on two sides, plus another small deck on the roof. Mr Cigar was right about the land: four untamed acres, like the house was in a tropical park. Plus the property abutted a wildlife sanctuary, eighty swampy acres of flora gone amok. I figured the dealer had picked the place for the wild buffer zone, privacy for all sorts of bad things.

"Afraid I'm just renting," I said. "It's too pricy for me."

A raised eyebrow. "Kinda work you do, mister?"

"In two weeks I start work for the Florida Center for

Law Enforcement. I came from Mobile, where I was a cop, a homicide detective."

A moment of reflection behind the cigar. "So I guess we both made a living from dead bodies."

"Pardon me?"

"I used to own funeral parlors in Atlanta, started with one, ended up with six. Retired here last year when my wife passed away."

"I'm sorry."

"Why? I like it here."

"I mean about your wife. Was she ill?"

"Healthy as a damn horse. But she was twenny-five years younger'n me an' only died cuz one a her boyfriends shot her."

I didn't know what to say to that so I walked his way, splashing up to shore with my hand outstretched. "Guess we'll be neighbors, then. At least for a while. Name's Carson Ryder."

His palm was mortician-soft but his grip was hard. "Dubois B. Burnside."

"The B for Burghardt?" I asked, a shot in the dark. William Edward Burghardt Du Bois was an American civil-rights leader, author, educator and about a dozen other things who lived from the late 1800s to the sixties. The intellectual influence of W.E.B. Du Bois was, and still is, felt widely.

"That would be right," he said, giving me a closer look.

"You live close by, Mr Burnside?"

He nodded at a line of black mangroves. "Other side of the trees. Daybreak used to find me heading to the mortuary to get working. Now I head out here and watch the water birds." He took another draw, letting blue smoke dribble from pursed lips. "I like this better."

"Dubois!" bayed a woman's voice from a distance, sending a half-dozen ravens fleeing from a nearby tree. "Du-bwaah! Where you at?"

"Not your wife, I take it?" I said.

"Duuuuuuuu-bwah!"

My neighbor winced, shook his head, pulled low the brim of the hat and started to turn away. "Stop by for a drink some night, Mister Ryder. We can talk about dead bodies. I may even have one you can look at."

I splashed away, the sun now above the trees and sending shadows of my temporary home out into the water to guide me ashore. I slipped wet feet into my moccasins and jogged the boardwalk to the porch, moving faster when I heard the phone ringing from inside the house, immediately followed by my cell phone chirping from the deck.

I got to the cell first, the ID showing my call was from Roy. I checked my watch, not quite 6.30.

"Morning, Roy. You're up early."

"Looks like we got a regular Sunshine State welcome for you, Carson. I'm looking at the weirdest damn thing I ever saw. Scariest, too. I know you don't officially get on the clock for a couple weeks, but I'm pretty sure this can't wait."

"What is it you're looking at, Roy?"

"No one truly knows. Procurement gave you a decent car, I expect?"

"I signed some papers. Haven't seen a car."

A sigh. "I'm gonna kick some bureaucratic ass. Whatever you're driving, how about you pretend it's the Batmobile and kick on the afterburners. Come help me make sense of what I'm seeing."

I hurled myself through the shower and pulled on a pair of khakis and a blue oxford shirt, stepping into desert boots and tossing on a blue blazer. My accessorizing was minimal, the Smith & Wesson Airweight in a clip-on holster. On my way out I grabbed a couple Clif Bars for sustenance and headed down the stairs.

The elevated house was its own carport, room for a half-dozen vehicles underneath. My ancient gray pickup looked lonely on all that concrete. I'd bought it years ago, second-hand, the previous owner a science-fiction fan who'd had Darth Vader air-brushed on the hood. After a bit too much bourbon one night, I'd taken a roller and a can of marine-grade paint and painted everything a sedate, if patchy, gray.

The grounds hadn't been groomed since the dope dealer had ownership, overgrown brush and palmetto fronds grazing the doors as I snaked down the long crushed-shell drive to the electronic gate, eight feet of white steel grate between brick stanchions shaded by towering palms. I panicked until remembering I could open the gate with my phone and dialed the number provided by the realtor.

Phoning a gate, I thought. Welcome to the Third Millennium.

I aimed the truck toward the mainland, an hour away, cruised through Key Largo and across the big bridge to the mainland. My destination was nearby, a bit shy of Homestead. Roy had said to turn right at a sign saying FUTURE SITE OF PLANTATION POINT, A NEW ADVENTURE IN SHOPPING and head a quarter mile down a gravel road.

"You can't miss the place," he'd added. "It's the only circus tent in miles."

3

It wasn't a circus tent in the distance, but it was side-show size, bright white against scrubby land scarred by heavy equipment, three Cat 'dozers and a grader sitting idle beside a house-sized pile of uprooted trees. Plastic-ribboned stakes marked future roads and foundations as the early stages of a construction project.

A Florida Highway Patrol cruiser was slanted across the road, a slab-shouldered trooper leaning on the trunk with arms crossed and black aviators tracking my approach. He snapped from the car like elastic, a hand up in the universal symbol for Halt.

I rolled down my window with driver's license in hand. "I'm Carson Ryder, here at the request of Captain Roy McDermott."

The eyes measured the gap between a top dog in the FCLE and a guy driving a battered pickup. He checked a clipboard and hid his surprise at finding my name.

"Cap'n McDermott's in the tent, Mr Ryder. Please park behind it."

I nodded thanks and pulled past. It felt strange that my only identification was a driver's license. I'd had my MPD gold for a decade, flashed it hundreds of times. I'd twice handed it in when suspended, twice had it returned. I'd once been holding it in my left hand while my right hand shot a man dead; his gamble, his loss. It felt strange and foreign to not produce my Mobile shield.

You made the right decision, my head said. My heart still wasn't sure.

I pulled away from the concrete road and angled five hundred feet down a slender dirt road scraped through the brush, stopping behind the tent, one of those rental jobs used for weddings and whatnot, maybe sixty feet long and forty wide. I was happy to see a portable AC unit pumping air inside. On the far side of the tent, beside a tall mound of freshly dug dirt, were a half-dozen official-looking vehicles including a large black step van which I figured belonged to the Medical Examiner or Forensics department.

On the other side of the van I saw three men and a woman clustered in conversation. Cops. Don't ask how I knew, but I always did. A dozen feet away a younger guy was sitting atop a car hood looking bored. I wasn't sure about him.

The entrance was a plastic door with a handmade sign

yelling ADMITTANCE BY CLEARED PERSONNEL ONLY!!! the ONLY underscored twice. Though I hadn't been cleared – whatever that meant – I'd been called, so I pressed through the door.

It was cool inside and smelled of damp earth, the reason obvious. Centering the tented space was a pit about twenty feet by twenty. Above the pit, at the far end of the tent at ground level, were several folding tables. A woman in a lab coat was labeling bags atop two of the tables. Another table held a small microscope and centrifuge. I'd seen this before, an on-site forensics processing center.

I returned my attention to the pit, which resembled the excavation for an in-ground swimming pool. Centering the hole was an eight-foot-tall column with two lab-jacketed workers ticking on its surface with hammers. I estimated the column's diameter at five feet and watched as a chipped-off shard was dropped into an evidence bag by a lab coat. When the lab coat stepped away, a photographer jumped in. The scene reminded me of a movie where scientists examine a mysterious object from the heavens. Shortly thereafter, of course, the object begins to glow and hum and everyone gets zapped by death beams.

"You there!" a voice yelled. "You're not supposed to be in here."

I snapped from my alien fantasy to see a woman striding toward me, her eyes a human version of death beams. Her black hair was tucked beneath a blue ballcap.

Her open white lab coat whisked as she homed in like an angry missile.

"Where's your ID?" she said, pointing at a naked space on my chest where I assumed an identification should reside. "You can't be here without an—"

"Yo, Morningstar!" a male voice cut in. "Don't kill him, he's on our side."

I looked up and saw Roy McDermott step from the far side of the column. The woman's thumb jerked at me.

"Him? This?"

"He's the new guy I told you about, Ryder."

The woman I now knew as Morningstar turned the death rays on Roy. "I'm in charge of scene, Roy. I want everyone to have a site ID."

Roy patted dust from his hands as he approached, a grin on his huge round face and the ever-present cowlick rising from the crown of semi-tamed haybright hair. He called to mind an insane Jack O'Lantern.

"I'll have someone make him a temporary tag, Vivian. You folks bring any crayons?"

Morningstar's eyes narrowed. "Condescension fits you, Roy. It's juvenile."

Roy climbed the steps from the pit and affected apologetic sincerity. "I forgot his clearance, Vivian. I'm sorry. All we have time for now is introductions. Carson, this is Vivian Morningstar, our local pathologist and—"

"I'm the Chief Forensic Examiner for the Southern Region, Roy."

"Carson, this is the Examining Chief Region of the

– shit, whatever. And this, Vivian, is Carson Ryder. We're still figuring out his title."

Morningstar and I brushed fingertips in an approximation of a handshake, though it was more like the gesture of two boxers. Roy took my arm and swung me toward the pit. We stepped down on hastily constructed stairs, the wood creaking beneath us.

"Now to get serious," Roy said. "Damndest thing I've seen in twenty years in the biz."

Three techs stepped aside as we walked to the object, stopping two paces distant. Seemingly made of concrete, it resembled a carved column from a temple in ancient Egypt, its surface jagged and pitted with hollows, as though the sculptor had been called away before completion.

"More light," Roy said.

The techs had been working with focused illumination. One of them widened the lighting, bringing the entire object into hard-edged relief.

A woman began screaming.

I didn't hear the scream, I saw it. Pressing from the concrete was a woman's face, eyes wide and mouth open in an expression of ultimate horror. She was swimming toward me, face breaking the surface of the concrete, one gray and lithic hand above, the other below, as if frozen in the act of stroking. The scenic was so graphic and lifelike that I gasped and felt my knees loosen.

Roy stepped toward me and I held my hand up, *I'm fine*, it lied. I caught my breath, saw ripples of concrete-encrusted fabric, and within its folds a rock-hard foot. I moved to the side and saw another gray face peering from the concrete, the eyes replaced with sand and cement, bone peeking through shredded skin that appeared to have petrified on the cheeks. One temple was missing.

My hand rose unbidden to the shattered face.

"Don't think of touching it," Morningstar said.

My hand went to my pocket. I circled the frieze of despair: two more heads staring from the stone, surrounding them a jumble of broken body parts, hands, knees, shoulders. Broken bones stood out like studs.

My hands ached to touch the column, as if that might help me to understand whatever had happened. But I thrust them deeper into my pockets and finished my circle, ending up at the screaming woman, her dead face still alive in her terror.

"Fill me in," I told Roy. "Everything."